AMITY

ALSO BY NATHAN HARRIS

The Sweetness of Water

AMITY

NATHAN HARRIS

LITTLE, BROWN AND COMPANY

New York Boston London

The characters and events in this book are fictitious. Any similarity to real persons, living or dead, is coincidental and not intended by the author.

Copyright © 2025 by Nathan Harris

Hachette Book Group supports the right to free expression and the value of copyright. The purpose of copyright is to encourage writers and artists to produce the creative works that enrich our culture.

The scanning, uploading, and distribution of this book without permission is a theft of the author's intellectual property. If you would like permission to use material from the book (other than for review purposes), please contact permissions@hbgusa.com. Thank you for your support of the author's rights.

Little, Brown and Company
Hachette Book Group
1290 Avenue of the Americas, New York, NY 10104
littlebrown.com

First Edition: November 2025

Little, Brown and Company is a division of Hachette Book Group, Inc. The Little, Brown name and logo are trademarks of Hachette Book Group, Inc.

The publisher is not responsible for websites (or their content) that are not owned by the publisher.

The Hachette Speakers Bureau provides a wide range of authors for speaking events. To find out more, go to hachettespeakersbureau.com or email hachettespeakers@hbgusa.com.

Little, Brown and Company books may be purchased in bulk for business, educational, or promotional use. For information, please contact your local bookseller or the Hachette Book Group Special Markets Department at special.markets@hbgusa.com.

Book interior design by Marie Mundaca

ISBN 9780316456241
Library of Congress Control Number: 2025937822

Printing 1, 2025

LSC-C

Printed in the United States of America

AMITY

I

NEW ORLEANS — 1866

I had few pleasures to call my own. There was the peace found in the attic where I was made to board, the transporting comfort of the books in Mrs. Harper's library, the deliciousness of the sweet bread I purchased with my allowance from the bakery down the road each Sunday of rest. But all of it paled in comparison to the joy brought upon me by Oliver, the terrier I considered my own and the most intelligent, loyal companion one could ask for.

Oliver belonged to Mrs. Harper's daughter, Florence, but I was his chief custodian, and in all ways that mattered he was mine. Florence kept him tethered to the shed in our backyard and each morning I would greet him with his bowl of food (my own creation that involved beetroot, leftover biscuits from the night previous, and a healthy portion of vegetables, all of which went toward preparing meals that rivaled my own). He would be waiting, the tuft of hair that fell from his snout almost imperceptibly, in its own way, breaking apart at the mouth as he seemed to smile upon my arrival. He had auburn hair with white spots all about, short yet curly, and paws that always sought out one's own hands, or one's chest, as though he wished to offer a shake hello. He came up to my calf and was as happy in one's arms as he was walking on the ground. His strength was impressive as well. The pole that kept him fastened would quiver as he leapt in excitement, which I could not get him to quit doing even with excessive instruction.

As I greeted him today, our neighbor, Mr. Claiborne, in his own backyard, was already spying on his gardener, demanding a standard of perfection that might never be met. I offered Mr. Claiborne a wave that was not returned before setting the bowl down.

This moment with Oliver provided me a buoy, a bit of encouragement to meet the errands that would soon require my attention — cleaning the home entire, preparing supper for Mrs. Harper and Florence, doting on Mrs. Harper as she lay infirm on the couch due to whatever malady she had decided to manifest.

It was not of my choosing, the course of the day. I had my freedom now that the war had come to a close, but as a servant to Mrs. Harper I was still shackled to her in all ways that counted. Which she made known by her incessant need for my help. And so it was that this occasion with Oliver was cut short, for I heard my name, already being called from inside the house.

"Coleman, Coleman, please," Mrs. Harper bellowed. Even Mr. Claiborne and the gardener shifted at the noise. Already I had prepared her and Florence their breakfast and cleaned up in their wake, and so I was disappointed to learn she required my attention without having had even the smallest chance of a break before the afternoon got underway. But it was no use to complain even to myself. I rose up at the call, dusting dirt from my trousers, and by the time I reentered the kitchen I could already see the dulled glimmer of the gasolier lit up in the parlor through the narrow hallway before me. The floor beneath me clattered as I walked and Mrs. Harper heard as much. She always did.

"Put the kettle on," she said, and I followed her instructions. The house was ancient, having belonged to Mrs. Harper's own father and his father before. Large transom windows banked against the full side of the dining room and they cast such a harsh light into the hallway that one could watch dust pirouette in the air as though it were a coordinated show. In the entryway, family portraits hung above the double-wide stairs, men of such identical appearance that I was hardly certain Mrs. Harper herself could discern her kinship to each of them.

There she was, on her chaise, so limp as to suggest she might slip off and plant herself on the ground and carry on moaning. The fireplace at the other end of the room had not been lit since winter, and on the mantel above it sat the garniture that Mrs. Harper had instructed me to pack before fleeing Baton Rouge two years ago. The antiques there — a bronze statue of three black Moors, a silver-handle dagger — were gifts from Mr. Harper to his wife, and Mrs. Harper would eye them affectionately upon approaching the fireplace, usually under the pretext of cleaning them, when in reality it appeared, to me, that she thought of them as a last connection to the man, and that to make contact with them was to feel herself in his presence once more.

"Mrs. Harper, how do I find you?"

"You tell me, Coleman."

"You appear as healthy as always, ma'am. Positively radiant."

"Oh!" She put a hand to her heart, let it drop off the ledge of the couch, fingers splayed, before placing it back on the bulge of her stomach. Although she was bedridden, her episodes did not preclude a sense of adventure concerning where it was she actually took rest. Occasionally one would find her in a guest-room bed upstairs, or perhaps slumped over the kitchen counter after retrieving a glass of water (and having glimpsed me coming by, to give rescue).

She'd shuttered the blinds; better to exaggerate the glow of the gasolier, a maudlin yellow that amplified the direness of her circumstance. Theatrics, but this was the way of Mrs. Harper, and had such effects not been coordinated, I would have thought her *actually* unwell.

"Florence has snuck out to the park with that underwit again," Mrs. Harper said.

"Hugh," I said.

"*Hugh*. To be so selfish as to leave me here alone all day. Motivated by nothing but her adoration toward a boy who does not even have the intelligence to recognize her displays of affection."

"She will be back soon. She knows not to miss supper."

"That's *hours* from now. I'm not an idiot, Coleman. I know you're attempting to pacify me. But when you must resort to lies...it's not just a failure of your position, but an offense as well."

I apologized, knowing that doing so accomplished little. Her attachment to Florence had become uncommonly strong when Mr. Harper abandoned the home for Mexico, upon a trip to survey the land there, only to never return. This was the rift that led to all others, for the women had no one else to turn to. Now Florence was of marrying age, desperate to leave home, and what resulted between the two ladies was something of an unfortunate equation: The sum of her mother's desire for the daughter resulted in the daughter's *equally* strong desire to be apart from the mother. The hostile emotions of each individual only increased, and so neither could stand the current circumstance — which resulted in a rising anger, a hatred aimed at one another, an escalating dispute I did my best to avoid.

Mrs. Harper's finger tapped against her breast in rhythm to a tune I did not know and her makeup gave off an unusually pallid color under the light. Other than Florence, no one knew her as I did. I had been hers and Mr. Harper's until the age of nineteen, freed with nothing to my name and nowhere to go, and so I had stayed in her care, as her servant yet with the same duties as those that had come before the war. I was taken from my mother when I was only a boy. This woman was all I had now, and I was quite aware that in times like these, when the friction of her empty life was too much to bear, when her bones and organs jostled and rattled with the torment of her husband's abandonment, the terror of her daughter's pending adulthood, the death of her parents whose house she now occupied, she would find some way to use me: to put me toward some task that might ease the weight that crushed her so.

The kettle, finally, was screaming.

"My shoes are with the cobbler," she said. "I'd like you to return them to me. As soon as possible."

"A lovely idea," I said, speaking over the kettle, as though the house was not currently under assault.

"Bring Florence as well. She knows the man's work and she has the courage to tell him if the quality is unsatisfactory. You do not have the nerve, Coleman. This we both know."

I steadied myself, as for reasons not yet described, Florence despised me more than she despised her own mother. But I was in no position to protest. There was only one other proposal I wished granted. One I always made when leaving the home: "Might I bring Oliver?" I asked.

Mrs. Harper's hand limply rose up and fluttered about, as though to dismiss me, or to dismiss the very notion that anything mattered at all. I would get her tea ready. Then I would fetch Oliver from his place beside the shed.

The air was damp and listless and the heat was something to wade through, thick as molasses. Our street was a quiet one, and although we were only nominally outside the Garden District it had the same regal air (yet it still managed to give Mrs. Harper fits that she was somehow relegated to outside the bounds of the city's aristocracy). At this hour one would commonly find the neighborhood empty save for a group of women out for a stroll amongst themselves, or perhaps a nursemaid with a carriage, and so I found it odd to bear witness, at that very moment, to the man across the street staring squarely in my direction. He was seated on the headrest of the park bench there, his feet where one might typically sit. Oliver was in the crook of my right arm. Even he gave the start of a bark.

"Oliver," I muttered.

The man's gaze was scrupulous. He was perhaps double my age, his bald head flagrantly hatless, as if to make a statement. He was smoking a cigarette, and I could see the joints of his jaw stabbing against his cheeks with each pull; if such an act might be menacing, then it was so. I knew individuals like this — the sort of man commonly spied in back alleys at dusk, or the last customer at a taproom that even the bartender shies from. I had learned many times over that they were best given a nod and ignored altogether, which was exactly the route I chose on this occasion, offering him even a smile as I turned, took to the street, and went on my way.

Vaguely unsettling, perhaps strange, and yet such a sight still did not come close to disturbing me. For where I was walking toward this man would fit right in, and perhaps he had simply found himself a place to rest the wrong street over. Indeed, the beauty of New Orleans proper was found in its colorful variety of humans — the loons and cons, the beggars and peddlers. I perceived them like a splash of wine in a stew, the mole on a beautiful woman, those little gifts that draw one into what can only be described as a quotidian reverie. An often droll world, for a moment revealing its contrasts, its irregularities, and suddenly becoming very much alive. I witnessed a gentleman on Felicity Street with a fresh-pressed satin waistcoat that seemed brilliant in the sun, his cane clacking, not a bead of dew on his head, his fashion impeccable. And beyond him were a gang I recognized from this block, painters on break, their clothes smattered in a medley of hues, each man laughing so hard they nearly dropped the sandwiches they held.

"Coleman, how you farin'?" one of them said as I passed.

"Rude to ask after the man before his dog," the second said.

"Happy as a bug, he is," said the first, putting a hand to Oliver's head as we passed.

I gave them a nod, a hello, knowing all too well they would give over the exact same words when I walked by next, the ritual of our passing one another. Across the road from me just then a fruit vendor eyed his produce with the same attention I gave a good book in Mrs. Harper's library, and a pack of boys harassed a man with a custard cart, begging him to serve them for free. You could hardly hear yourself between the clopping of horseshoes and the shouts from passersby and the boy with the newspapers and the beggar bugler who elicited jeers each day for his crass noises and inability whatsoever to bugle at all (although I knew for a fact that the owner of Aster's always gave him some soup come sundown, a well-deserved show of pity).

Already I was nearing Coliseum Square. The heat was now sweltering, my handkerchief sodden with use. But I had already spotted Florence. I let Oliver to the ground, and although he spotted her as well, I might mention that he stayed right by my side as we approached.

The fountain behind her sparkled in the sun, its froth white as ivory, like feathers bursting forth from Florence's very being as though she might grow wings.

"What on earth are you doing here?" She looked to Oliver, to me, then back at Hugh, who had just stood up to approach me himself.

"Your mother sent me to fetch you."

"I do not wish to be fetched."

"Ah, but the task is already accomplished."

Her features were strikingly youthful. Plump cheeks gave way to sharp angled brows (consider the child whose toy has been taken), and her red hair fell down the sides and front of her face like elegant colonnades. She was also quite stout, and if I could offer her a compliment, I would reference the considerable presence she had in every room she entered, the great shadow that her personality cast, a vivacity that worked like an enchantment on others that most women would fail to derive on their best nights. She could also cut a man down with only a look, a few quick words. Something I mention only to note that her eyes in that very moment were nothing more than narrow slits of contempt. I could feel myself withering before her, and perhaps my body might have failed altogether had Hugh not drawn near, forcing Florence to act with some semblance of ardor regarding this sudden encounter.

"Please give us a moment," Florence said, permitting him to first pet Oliver.

"He is a splendid little thing," Hugh said. "I do wish I had brought Mona now, had I known."

"I thought the heat might be too much for little Oliver, I don't know what Coleman was thinking," Florence told him, which was an outrageous claim, for Oliver fared perfectly fine in the heat, and it was, after all, her choice to keep him outside tethered next to the shed when she had all the opportunity in the world to allow him indoors. These lies were only part of the greater tactic of her keeping the dog in the first: some idea that Hugh's dog and Oliver — both of fine pedigree — might breed a litter, thus acting in Florence's mind as some symbolism to represent her and Hugh's future union.

"I will not be going," she said.

"Mrs. Harper will not be happy. You do not want her in a mood come supper."

"My mother will be in a mood regardless of what I do, as you know. I wish I could heal whatever ails her, yet I can't, and fetching her shoes will change nothing. Besides, Coleman, you are the one who will deal with it. I will be *here*. With Hugh. I imagine you wish you could do the same yourself."

"Stay *here*? With Hugh?" The man was now pointing and laughing at a fellow in face paint with an accordion strapped to his chest who was chasing pigeons around the park. "I think you're mistaken."

"Perhaps not with Hugh," she said with a sigh. "But if he is away out of that home, away from my mother and her nonsense..." Her lower lip jutted out, her chin raised in defiance, and I could not help, in that moment, but see the stubborn girl I had appreciated so much in a former life.

That early period together, when I first came to the family, was somewhat difficult to recall. What I know well is that I was given to Mrs. Harper upon her marriage as a gift from her father, sold alongside my sister June, and I was immediately put to use, for Mr. Harper's holdings were clearly more limited than he must have let on to Mrs. Harper's family, and he was barely able to eke out an existence that justified the lavishness of his spending. I was frequently loaned out to whomever in town needed assistance, whether that be in the field, before the blacksmith's anvil, or at the seat of a carriage delivering goods upon the orders of some local agent. I never knew what one day would bring in relation to the next, and

Mr. Harper was so beaten down from scant business due to the war that his mood was always one of irritation.

If there was any reprieve, it was my freedom at night when June and I could relax in our own quarters, our beds beside one another in the basement, as hidden there as we were intended to be. Cobwebs cloaked themselves over splintered chairs and abandoned toys from Florence's youth. Trunks of Mr. Harper's equipment were scattered about and often we would open them and assign his instruments magical properties, such as they might give us the ability to transport elsewhere, or become invisible — easier, then, to find ourselves away from our current predicament.

However dark and dank that basement might have been, it always had the feeling of being *ours*, that all formalities could be dropped to the floor like manacles; we could breathe freely; we could, in other words, simply be brother and sister. Yet it was around midnight, when the world went quiet, when we would often hear a creak upon the staircase, see the start of nightgown flow over the steps and would find, before us, Florence herself, having been unable to sleep and privy to our whispered chatter. She would assure us her parents could not hear, but that in her fright of being alone in the house she wished to join us for a time.

Well, the home was hers. She was welcome to go wherever she pleased. The two girls would share stories — or gossip — Florence from what she'd experienced at school, and June from whomever the guests of the home had been that day. I would watch them from my bed, and a strange sight I found it to be, the two giggling endlessly, hidden by the shadows and with so much darkness about that one would not strain to think them sisters.

Back then I would venture that the three of us would remain close for some time, and yet the silliness of such thinking would be only too clear in hindsight. For Mr. Harper acted as a corrosive element I had not considered, an actor who would soon unbind us from one another, reduce our affection to hatred. It was not that he disliked our relationships, or even had negative aims (although surely he found them imprudent). It was simply that he liked my sister more than his own daughter.

June would stand beside Mr. Harper as he had his afternoon tea, telling her of news related to the war, to his profession; June would make him laugh with a little aside that ridiculed passersby on the lane before the home; June could sense when he required a bit of whiskey before bed to calm his nerves. His daughter mirrored his parvenue of a wife, a woman beneath him not in station but rather in intellect, someone easily affected and prone to childlike ideas. For this, Florence was shunted.

What if that was all? Perhaps Florence might have learned to cast aside the envy that seemed to be suppressed only by her outbursts and insults, her ever-increasing appetite, a collection of maladies that seemed to anger and horrify her father even further. She might even learn to forgive the man. Yet if one is to follow along of what came next, a more concentrated outline of the man's own demons, it becomes clear how the family could not recover from his actions.

Mr. Harper, a deputy surveyor, found his work dwindling, his debt ever growing. Who was to authorize government assignments when the government has no money nor has even been rightly determined at all? A man of models and numbers, bearings and distances, these things had now been robbed from him, and one could discern in the bruised pouches cradling his eyes, the tremors that caused newspapers to flicker in his hand as he read, the silence that grew to consume him whole, that the life he knew was vanishing before him. Perhaps it was a result of his own pain, his own failures, that caused some share of insanity to pervade his decision-making. Perhaps he was only recognizing that his life in Baton Rouge had come to an end and was best forgotten. The war was coming to a close when his job had been terminated altogether as the Confederate government faltered toward its slow but certain collapse. A day would arise in early spring when a fellow landowner would knock on the door and ask after him.

The conversations that followed were held in private, over the course of a number of weeks, yet June relayed all of the information to me as she heard it herself. There was a group of men, all of them in fear of retribution from the Union, who were jettisoning for Mexico, to build a life that accorded with their beliefs and to seek great fortune while doing so. The country was in a state of flux, the Mexicans under the rule of a monarchy imposed by the French. A rebellion was rising up in opposition, and control changed hands constantly among the factions. In the void, a persecuted people from the United States might find freedom. Be left alone to live the way they wished to. Crops grew at a miracle pace, and such fertile land needed to be divided and mapped for all who risked the journey. Railroads needed building, and facilities for storage might be required as well. Word had reached them that the French might pay for such skills. Didn't he have some tutelage as an engineer? Might that not be handy? All of which could lead to so much work that a man like Wyatt Harper might never have another day of idleness again. Money could be sent home to his family until the job was completed. And somewhere in the strange workings of his own mind, in a final show of his bizarre infatuation, Mr. Harper decided not only to go, but also that he would take June as a servant in his temporary home on the frontier. The rest of us would depart for New Orleans to Mrs. Harper's childhood home, for Mr. Harper's estate in Baton Rouge would be sold to finance this journey — the money given over to the pool of funds the captain was steadily procuring.

I recall the occasion of my sister teaching me how to properly set a table, informing me of when winter curtains must come down for summer ones, how to dust the nooks and corners of the home, her cheeks wet with tears as she mocked my failures lovingly. I remember the packing of her chest, stealing, as though I did not notice, the cap I had only recently outgrown; the moment when we left for New Orleans, Mrs. Harper in tears as I drove, looking back to face those sobs and seeing her daughter stunned silent by her mother's grief, her father's rejection, the loss of her childhood home that she might well never see again.

So it is that Florence's petulance to me felt like less a hatred directed at my own person than a hatred aimed at the world that had spurned her. I was a witness, a knowing party, the servant who knew her deepest secrets. I'd learned in my role to accommodate her pain even as I housed my own.

Indeed, if anything I envied her. To expose one's anger was a privilege. One I often, in private, longed for myself.

Here she was before me in the park; the sun casting her aglow like a diamond spun under the gaze of a jeweler's loupe. Oliver had returned to my side, sniffing the grass, looking up at me with searching eyes. Hugh lingered behind Florence like her very shadow.

"If you insist," I said, "I will go retrieve the shoes alone."

With this, Florence looked upon me with the pity of the victor.

"Get me on the way back," she said. "I'll join you for the walk home."

I patted my side for Oliver to follow, and left to collect Mrs. Harper's shoes.

The sun loomed overhead like a penny spat clean. As we neared home, the silence between Florence and me was so deafening that you could hear Mrs. Harper's shoes click together in their box with every step, as though a fourth party walked amongst us.

Florence's skin glistened under the heat, her cheeks blotched, matching the shade of her hair. The gate to the home was shut and I placed a hand to open it before Florence stopped me.

"A moment. Please," she said.

One could look past the brick steps leading to the front door, see the opened curtains behind the window shutters, and know without question that Mrs. Harper had already witnessed our arrival. She was probably off now, scurrying to freshen up before greeting us with a moan, clutched to the railing of the stairs, begging for assistance.

Florence glanced at the house just as I had, but as the seconds passed our gazes averted to the ground, then met, as though in the silence had been ushered forth an apology, a salve to cleanse the tension born in the park.

"Why do you do it?" she asked under her breath. "Why do you stay here, caring for her? Putting up with it all. You're *free,* Coleman. You do know that. She would let you go."

It brought to mind the only instance when my sister had asked me to abandon the family with her. It was a week before she'd departed with Mr. Harper, when we were packing his goods, alone once more in the basement. Her hand fell upon my wrist, and her words were quiet, deliberate, spoken in a manner of seriousness we did not often share. *We could go,* she'd said. *Start anew. Away from them. You know that, don't you?* I'd stood there, Mr. Harper's toolbox in hand, and my arms shook not from the press of its weight but from the idea of leaving the family forever, the ever-dwindling security of my position, the little semblance of routine which I craved more than anything else.

"Mr. Harper says he will send for us shortly," I'd told her sheepishly. "There is no harm in waiting. Freedom will find us all the same there, won't it?"

Her hand, then, falling from my wrist in defeat...

June never mentioned such a notion again and even when I broached the matter myself, some days later, more open to exploring the possibility than I'd been at first, there was no encouragement from her to take action. For I believe she knew, better than anyone else, the cowardice that lay at my core. My fear of the unknown. The answer to Florence's question was now clear, in that way. I needed only to look toward the vista before me: that home, that street, Oliver waiting in the backyard for his next meal or his next walk. It was all I had, and it was all I knew, no different from my previous life in Baton Rouge. I could not say this. No matter how close we had grown in a different life, Florence was still my employer. I was still her mother's help.

"You and your mother are fine women," I said. "She treats me well. And it's my honor to return the favor."

Florence laughed, her head swiveling in disbelief. For the first time that day, her tone was kind. "Hand me the shoes, Coleman. Let's tell her I went along to get them. How does that sound?"

"Thank you," I said, certain not to betray my relief. "It is appreciated."

"Yes, I'm sure it is," she said. Then, repeating herself: "I'm sure it is."

She gazed into the box with a look of approval before nodding for me to go forth. I picked up Oliver when he lingered at the gate. He was trying to lick my face as we entered the home, and for a moment I was so focused on this point that I failed to recognize the silence of the place, the strangeness of Mrs. Harper's eventual greeting, curt enough to be unusual: "In here," she said, beckoning us from the parlor.

By the time I entered, Florence had put the shoes down on the console table and appeared to be transfixed, or at least confused. Mrs. Harper was seated on the sofa. Across from her was the man I had spotted outside on the bench, now sipping sherry from the finest set of glassware in the home. His face was rutted at the forehead, pockmarked at the cheeks, his pate polished to a glimmer. The tint of wine lined his lips like a violation, and the way he eyed us upon our entrance, as though we might pose a threat, was so lacking in manners that I immediately grasped upon a darkness within him that diffused like a blooming shadow.

I had not even enough time to inspect the peculiarities of the circumstance before Mrs. Harper pointed at a paper in her hand, waving it like a clue, or relic, something long sought and finally received. Her smile, so full and wide, was as strange as the man's disposition. Mrs. Harper displayed many emotions, but happiness was not often amongst them.

"Florence," Mrs. Harper said, "your father has written. He asks that we join him in Mexico. That we hurry to meet him, no less."

The room was stunned into silence before Florence's shrieks, and Mrs. Harper's tears of joy, brought along a mood of celebration. I looked to Mrs. Harper herself as if further answers might be provided, but the two were so caught up in the moment that I appeared to be invisible to them.

"Mrs. Harper," I said, sensing something amiss, and yet she only shooshed me with a quick stare, her head resting on her daughter's shoulder. That was the moment Oliver slipped from my hands. I watched him mosey over to the man in the corner, this man who had said nothing, this man who had apparently delivered such unexpected news as to upend the entire household. He extended his hand to Oliver, and the dog licked it greedily, which felt like a betrayal I could not square; the man was now staring at me, just as he had been outside. There was a glint in his eye, and I was prepared to ask after his name, his position, had he not taken the opportunity to raise his glass in my direction.

"A refill," he said.

"Do as he says," Mrs. Harper instructed. I nodded cheerily. Then followed her instruction.

2

I hauled Mrs. Harper's trunk in one hand, my own valise atop it, and in my other I carried Oliver and made sure to place him down when he began to kick at my side, as if to tell me there was business that needed tending to.

First there was the porter who passed us, taking off his cap to say hello to the dog and holding up the family he was assisting.

"This here is Oliver," I announced, "and I speak on his behalf when I say it is a pleasure to make your acquaintance." The man laughed, which was common, as most everyone took joy from such a silly statement, which might explain why I employed it so often.

Next there was the gaggle of women who yelled at the sight of an animal so sweet and all reached down to put a hand to him. I told them of his fine pedigree, of how he brought happiness to all of New Orleans, and so long did they linger that they nearly missed the departure of their ship.

The third introduction was a small child in a bright blue hat whose father was signing papers for what appeared to be cargo received. "This here is Oliver —" I said, before I was cut off. A hand was on my shoulder. A voice in my ear.

"*Enough with the dog.*"

With this I took Oliver from the child, who watched us off solemnly. I returned back to the side of Florence and Mrs. Harper, and yet still did not deign to apologize to the man beside me who had, with little authority, taken control of the Harper family only one week before and set us off on this voyage.

His name was Amos Turlow. As we now knew, he had been sent by Mr. Harper to fetch his family and deliver them to Mexico. He did look right for the job. The man was large enough that he appeared capable of surviving within the deep intestines of the most unforgiving of deserts; his body, I figured, capable of feasting on its own muscle and fat for months on end. The fabric of his shirt, stretched so tight beneath his vest, seemed to utter groans when he made sudden movements, and I often thought his sleeves might tear off entirely if given a tug.

Neither Florence nor Mrs. Harper questioned the man's dark disposition, his uncivilized air (returning to the family home at odd hours reeking of tobacco and alcohol, spitting phlegm into his endless stream of handkerchiefs that I was later made to wash), all that made me wary of him. One night, while bringing hot water to Mrs. Harper for a bath, I asked her quite plainly as to whether or not she truly trusted herself and her daughter in the hands of such an individual.

"God no," she said with a chortle. "I would entrust my daughter to the care of a catamount before that man. But it is Turlow who Wyatt has delivered to me. And if it is Turlow who will take me back to my husband…"

In private, I will admit that my trepidation was mixed with an equal dose of optimism. For if one were to actually locate Mr. Harper, it might imply that June was with him, and the possibility of laying eyes on her once more, to reclaim our relationship as ours, well who would not make a deal with the devil himself for such a guarantee? Eventually, I felt only lucky to be invited on the expedition at all. What followed, as the days ticked by, was a feeling I hardly could recall experiencing before, a burning at my chest, a warmth I could not measure. I believe that had been a feeling of hope. Hope of the good that might befall me if our trip was successful.

A breeze struck the port and carried with it the rank smell of fish.

One could witness men beside great bundles of goods — kegs of grains with their tops peeled off for inspection, vats of sugar and lard, furs loaded so high on pallets as to appear like the shedding of a monster slain. Prices were being argued over with increasing fervor, voices rising into one garble of unceasing noise, and by the time we arrived at the steamer my senses were so overwhelmed I hardly had my wits about me.

Our steamboat was awe-inspiring, sleekly carved, painted red and white with its name across its midsection: *The Jubilee*. The captain stood before it on the dock, hands in the pockets of his frock coat, and when Turlow approached, the two of them warmly greeted one another and immediately entered into conversation as though they were old acquaintances.

"Are you afraid, Coleman?" Florence was beside me, both of us staring at a number of horses being led up the gangplank.

"Not in the slightest," I told her, although my response did little to remove the grin from her face.

"Perhaps you should stick a toe in the water. You will see it's nothing to be feared. Truly. Give it a go."

I know why she had made the comment. It was nearly lore amongst our neighbors back in Baton Rouge, and oddly enough the origins of the story pertained to my grooming habits, of all things. As a younger man, no older than sixteen, I had begun to pay close attention to my hair. I discovered that with the steady work of a comb, a spritz of water, and a dollop of raw egg stirred, I could part it in a style similar to Mr. Harper himself. Although I did it in the name of fashion, I also thought this would gain my master's favor, yet it took but one afternoon of Mr. Harper drinking with his friends to learn how wrong I'd been.

The men were gathered under an oak tree before a small pond in town, a park where the finer folks of Baton Rouge would collect on Saturdays, waving to one another, mingling at their leisure. By noon they were well-intoxicated and began to compliment my hair as a rib, telling Mr. Harper that he and I must be brothers, how similar our style was. Though I tried to hide in the shadows of the tree, hoping their jeers might quit if I made myself invisible, they only continued as the day progressed.

Mr. Harper was not laughing. He began to tap his glass against the table, whiskey sputtering to the ground.

"Coleman, why don't we see how similar that hair of yours is to mine without the sorcery you've wrought with your comb. Go over to that pond. Pour some water on your head. Give it a shake."

The laughing ceased then. They told him to let the matter go, and yet Mr. Harper would not relent. "It was not a request," he said, finally looking upon me. "I am telling you to do it. Now."

Wetting my hair was not enough, and he wished, then, to see me enter the water to my chest, against the pleas of all others present, and the humiliation, the great dread that racked my being as I found out the pond was quite deep, too deep for a man who could not swim, is difficult to express to someone who has never been forced into such a precarious position. Never did I forget the clinking sound of his glass against the table as he barked at me, asking for a refill before I'd regained my breath, before my feet had landed on solid ground. I did not deign to part my hair like that again in his presence, and still the greater consequence was that I had been afraid of even the shallowest bodies of water ever since — something I had unfortunately told Florence in confidence the day after, not ever thinking it might be used against me years later. Yet the girl now exulted in the embarrassment of others. Anything to conceal her own pain.

"The only feeling I have is one of excitement," I told her. "Seven days on the open water with you? Heaven itself could not offer an equal pleasure."

Florence's smirk did not waver, and I felt within it her admiration of my sarcasm, the look of a child who has met a play partner willing to participate in a quarrel merely for the sake of a quarrel.

"I wish I could say the same," she said, "but knowing you will be in steerage, while I will be first class — well, Coleman, we will hardly see each other at all. A sad thing."

"Sad indeed," I told her.

Suddenly here was Mrs. Harper squeezing between us, words streaming from her mouth as though she had been in dialogue for hours without anyone knowing the wiser.

"Have you seen the menu, Coleman? Sardines on toast, fresh bass, ice cream and wafers for dessert. Do not get me started on the activities they are planning for us. Apparently on the final night there is to be a ball, and they said they would be delighted if I were to help plan it. I believe that's something of an accomplishment, as many of the guests on board have traveled on far more illustrious ships than *The Jubilee*, and this being my first expedition, I believe they must see something special in my demeanor to afford me this opportunity…"

"The luggage," Turlow yelled out from beside the captain, which was a relief, as I'd listened to Mrs. Harper parrot this same speech all week, and the thought of hearing it once more was almost too much to bear.

I handed Oliver over to Mrs. Harper, who was still prattling on, and began to carry the luggage onboard, gaining a new vantage point of the other steamboats belching smoke from their stacks like factories laid out at sea, the port workers scurrying about like aimless schools of fish seeking refuge from the greater mass of industry. I did not look at the water overboard, the endless floor of blue that merged with the endless horizon of sky, as I could already feel my throat run dry at the distinct knowledge, now, that I would be stuck aboard this vessel, with nowhere to escape, for a week's time.

I did not know what might befall me. What might come even when we made it to land. What I knew — perhaps the only thing I knew — was that my heart still burnt like a flame at the prospect of who I might find at the other side of the sea. That if there were any chance I could reunite with my sister, the one person who would make me whole, there was not a single body of water I would not traverse to see her. Better to grin and bear it. To stifle the fear of the unknown that racked me to my core — just as I had when June had been taken from me in the first.

As we awaited our departure, one could feel the listlessness of the boat's occupants, the buzz of anticipation brewing, and when it came, it met every expectation I had conjured in my imagination. The ground trembled as though an earthquake had split the world in two and the fissure was right beneath my feet; then followed the deep bellow of the horn, and all the passengers, as though given a cue, began to wave at those on the port. There were tears of joy, of sadness, the waving of handkerchiefs, the children on men's shoulders hoping for one last glance of this gigantic vessel that, as though harnessing magic, would be present one moment and have vanished in the next. The flag soon went up in glorious fashion and the steamer was signalized down the harbor; off, certainly, for what was to be an experience the likes of which I had never known.

I was allowed access to the upper deck to tend to Mrs. Harper and Florence, although their room came with the accommodation of a cabin girl who made my duties somewhat obsolete. I would climb the stairs occasionally only to find them happy amongst the other women, planning the activities of the day or socializing over a game of whist, and with a shooing off by Mrs. Harper or a nasty look from Florence, happily ensconced amongst the younger gentlemen aboard the boat, I would return to the lower deck. The steerage cabin was more or less inhospitable. The hot-water spigot was broken, the straw beds so close together as to bring me up against the back of another man, the ground littered with spoons and dishpans collecting flies and maggots.

Each morning I would return there, tin bowl in hand, to await the arrival of the cook's help, the ration of slop he would provide (which I would share with Oliver). But once breakfast was served, I would return to my own makeshift quarters in the open air near the stern. I'd made a small bundle of clothes into a bed beside the livestock and some bales of crop that an officer would come by to surveil every few hours (as though I had plans to steal away a pallet of cotton and hop into the ocean, riding the load to the nearest town to sell it for profit). How quickly one gets used to watching men and women alike squat before the taffrails, relieving themselves even in mid-conversation with another. Vomiting was equally acceptable in this manner, and in such a way I had the pleasure of witnessing all varieties of excretion at all hours of the day.

The weather at night was downright frigid, and I held Oliver close to my chest, my teeth chattering upon his head, jealous of the easy sleep that came over him in the nest that was my own body. Although I was mostly ignored, there was a boy who would occasionally appear from the bowels of the boat, and although I was quite vigilant about my surroundings, aware of thieves and undesirables, I failed to detect his every approach. It was near-dawn on the third night at sea when he appeared before me and lingered there like a ghost. Great streaks of coal maculated his face like war paint. His hands were equally sullied. The whites of his eyes stood out like piercing moons struck against a pitch-black night. I had the sense that he was not from New Orleans, but perhaps a child of Mexico, stuck on this vessel indefinitely, and although I could not be sure he spoke English, I could tell, as with most children, that the allure of a kind dog was enough to pull him out of his shell and draw him near me.

"What is your name?" I asked.

When there was no response, only his blinking, I pulled Oliver from his bed, the dog unfurling with a stretch of the limbs, shaking its head against the steady breeze of the night.

"This here is Oliver," I told him, "and I speak on his behalf when I say it is a pleasure to make your acquaintance."

Did the boy understand? Who could say? But he giggled as Oliver sniffed the coal on his palm, and when he ran his hand along Oliver's mane, the smallest smile struck his face. Even I nearly laughed in response to the sudden change in his disposition. I started off then, telling the boy that this very instant served to demonstrate how the bond between humans and animals was so virtuous as to possibly be divine — a common language between species that needed no *shared* language at all. No one species made a better companion than another, whether it be horses (a coincidence that one just defecated beside me), or parrots, or cats. All could be an exemplar of loyalty, and to care for them was to encourage one's own compassion, and thus bonds with animals made us better humans, and better humans made the world a better place to exist.

The boy was bleary-eyed, his mouth agape, and his gaze had begun to drift. I had been told by Florence many times, and was wholly aware, of how my ramblings came off to others, but this felt extreme, and it took my turning to find Amos Turlow before me. He was holding a bowl, steam dissipating from its reach, like a veil of fog before the man's face.

Turlow nodded his head, and the boy receded once more to whatever hidden hatch he'd crawled out of.

"You look like a vagrant down there," he said. "Come and stand with me. I've brought you some soup."

I pulled myself up, not sure if it was the chill of the night or the gumbo that sent a shiver down my spine. The smell of the onion was mouthwatering, the hunks of fatty ham like sweet candy melting on my tongue. I could not have asked for a better blessing and it took some acting to conceal my happiness. Still, I managed.

"I wonder," I said, "why you'd wish to bring me this meal instead of socializing upstairs. It sounds lively."

Above us one could hear a fiddle played in time to stomping feet, followed by peals of laughter, a song ending and another beginning. Turlow sniffed in displeasure and wiped the wet from his nose with the back of his hand. "I'd sooner go two rounds in the sheets with a cactus than spend another evening with those idiots. I don't say that lightly."

"A rather rude comment to make. I for one would love the opportunity to — "

"Stop right there," he interrupted. "Why do you talk like that? I must know."

"Like what?"

"Like you're *learnèd*. I'd wager you could not stand an examination in a single subject beyond tending to those two women up in first class. And yet you talk like some teacher."

I recoiled, pulling the bowl from my mouth to my breast as though it might be used as a shield.

"Mr. Turlow, I assure you I *am* quite well-read. Mrs. Harper allowed me to use her library at my leisure since we arrived in New Orleans."

This was only a partial truth. I believed myself to be more learned than most, actually. For when Florence had been tutored at home in Baton Rouge I had, at every opportunity, permitted myself to tasks about the house that might keep me in range to hear them. When she advanced to learning in the schoolhouse, I made sure to offer my services in escorting her there, keeping station close by throughout those sessions when I was not needed back at the house; absorbing, in effect, the same lessons she did. And when her workbooks were discarded, Florence finding them too difficult, not worthy of her time, it was I who made them my own, devouring each word between their covers. Thus began my journey with the written word, a journey that never ceased. I was not just learnèd but intelligent, and yet I do not believe such a thing was believable to Amos Turlow. He looked at me with great skepticism, even hatred.

"So you have read a book or two. And did those books teach you how to act as well? I'll tell you I've met some uppity Negroes, but none who put on such a ridiculous performance. Spent too much time with those folks up at that party and not enough with your own kind, if you ask me."

This man had made me feel naked before him. Perhaps there were parts of myself that I concealed, as anyone might, but in the elevation of my behavior I only strove to be a better version of a former individual I wished desperately to forget: a child that did not even have the privilege of knowing his parents; a boy who knew only of toil; a grown man so scared of his own freedom that he clung tightly to the chains that kept him in bondage. What was once a mere conversation had turned into an attempt to turn my insides out, a show of cruelty, the sort of engagement I wanted no part of.

"Every man tries to hide the parts of himself he finds shameful," I said softly. "Why you might wish to discuss such a thing, I cannot say.

If you'd like me to stand here and bear it, I will do that out of respect to Mrs. Harper. But I'd prefer not to."

At this, his face softened ever so slightly. His hand shot up in protest, and he started again in a tone I can only imagine he found to be one of warmth.

"This has nothing to do with Mrs. Harper. Allow me to rephrase my—"

"It really is fine."

"I insist. What I was getting to, in *kinder* words, is that we are much different, and yet, in reality, beneath this act of yours, I don't think we're much different at all—"

"Now that is a baffling comment. I don't believe I've met a man whose nature and doctrines were more different than my own—"

His hand slammed down upon the handrail with a roar that frightened even Oliver to attention.

"Might I *finish*? Is it within your ability to stay quiet for even a moment's time? No wonder the only creature who pays you mind is that dog!"

A wreath of silence descended over us, as chilly as the air itself, but just as quickly as it settled, Turlow collected his words and spoke again.

"I'll have you know that my brother and I grew up in a sorry little hut next to a sorry little gulch near a town you've never heard of. Mom dead, father left us, grew up with our aunt and uncle. I cannot recall that man saying more than a few sentences to us, and he looked to be shocked still by a past life even I could not imagine. He would leave at odd hours, return still without a word, and it was known he was to be left alone. We did the woman's bidding, which amounted to petty thievery, stealing vegetables from nearby farms, sending us into town each Sunday so we could beg outside the local church for that dime families had withheld when the plate got passed. We were tools of that woman, my brother and me. Had nothing to call our own except one another."

Turlow's voice had the deep vibrations of a trombone played in close quarters, a noise that swelled and shook the ground beneath one's feet like the very waves of the sea. The story he told was a stunning one, describing his slow maturation as his aunt's myrmidon, her orders becoming more and more destructive, and one could sense the humanity of two young men being diminished to nothing by this woman who cared little for them beyond their use to her. He was quite exercised by it all, his face ripening in color by the mood of the conversation.

"Yet on our last morning in their home, my uncle pulled us up from our mats upon the ground with a vicious tug and instructed us to wait outside. It was as cold as this night. I remember that well. He spoke at length, and there was something chilling to how measured his words were, how comfortable he appeared in that last gasp of darkness before the sun revealed itself. He told us we were men now. That we would all now work in tandem. He told us of a fellow who had wronged him, who had withheld money he was owed."

The boys followed their uncle to where the gulch widened into a stream, where the dense woods were like the lid upon a bowl, holding in the mist of the morning so tightly that they could hardly see their own feet before them. Near the stream was a man with his fishing rod, a man no older than their uncle, a man so occupied with the labor before him that he did not even turn at their arrival. The way their uncle led them, the angle in which they arrived through the tree line, made Turlow certain that his uncle had planned this from a previous venture. That this was a setup from the first.

He told me of the man turning at the sound of them at his back. That at once the mist seemed to dissipate entirely, that they could witness the orbs of the man's eyes go from a speck of wonder to wide lakes of panic.

"There was a strangeness to it that clouded over my fear," Turlow said. "The odd sight of my uncle's knife, for I did not know he possessed such a weapon. Or the swiftness of his movement, the brutality in which he thrusted the thing to the hilt, for he was a man who moved at a snail's pace. And I wondered, watching the fisherman fall before the stream — watching my uncle slice him at the side, and fill his body with stones like a filleted fish, and toss him into the water like a thing disposed of — if this was what my uncle had been conserving his energy for all those days. For mornings like this one. Mornings he slipped out to make others his victims and plunder them for what little they had.

"I could not tell you what pained me more: the awful look of that body, or the feeling of betrayal that my brother and I had been bred for this moment. Trained in lesser acts of indecency to be ready for this greater one. Somehow this was the breach I could not overcome."

Before casting him to the water, his uncle had taken the man's fishing rod, a few coins from his pocket, even the fish he had managed to catch.

"He told us there were a raft of men who owed him money. That he had been wronged at every turn in his life. And that he was only getting what he was owed, piece by piece, man by man. It did not matter if one, in particular, was a stranger."

He said he left that night. That he took the man's knife with him as well.

"As though that might stop him in the future. Never truly trusted another soul other than my brother. Never saw the world the same way."

Turlow pulled a cigarette from his vest pocket, lit a match, took a pull, and his visage — that cragged surface of scars and shaving knicks, ember-red blemishes and cratered pockmarks — seemed hollowed out, phenomenally weary, as though the pain of the story had been borne from the plume of smoke that had entered his lungs and was now lost to the sea.

"And I see in you a man who's been hurt in his own right," he said. "Your suspicion of all that goes on around you. You're an attendant. Just like me. Watching over Mrs. Harper, that girl of hers, even suspicious of those folks in steerage. Beneath this act of refinement, beneath whatever behavior you've leeched from those books, you're a survivor as well, looking for what's right around the corner so you may be one step ahead. Isn't that right? I bet you've noticed quite a bit about me no less."

I thought for a moment before leveling my response.

"I have noticed some things," I muttered. "You spend more time beneath the ship than in first class. And as you said, you appear to find the passengers not to your liking, and prefer the company of the crew."

"Mm. And that is very true. Consider the captain of this vessel. A decent human if ever there was one. Commanded a war-boat for his country, invested most of his savings in this very ship, and due to a gambling debt is on the verge of forfeiting hull and engine to a businessman back in New Orleans who cares nothing of this vessel at all. The captain pays enough on insurance to keep him penniless, and whatever profit he gains goes back to some rich bastard who I am sure is sipping cognac as we speak while getting his pecker warbled like a flute by a ten-dollar whore. Where is the fairness there?"

"Well, I am sure no one *forced* the captain to enter the gaming houses—"

"Or those boys like the one you just saw, trapped in that boiler room, working around the clock like galley slaves? What God forced that lot upon them?"

I asked, politely, what it was he was getting to, and Turlow flicked his cigarette into the darkness of the night, the faintest rumors of smoke still trailing from his mouth.

"My point is that I was once as lost as all these outcasts we speak of. Yet I did not let it break me. No. I transcended my misfortune. I realized I must not be just an attendant, such as you, but also an *actor*. I do not make my money gutting men, but helping them. And just as I will help Mr. Harper. That is my only goal. And so I ask that you believe as much."

I was both skeptical and puzzled. Why on earth did my trust mean anything to him? As though he could read such signals upon my countenance, he continued with something of a reasoning aimed at my concerns.

"I know you find me crass," he said. "I care not one bit. What matters — perhaps the *only* thing that matters — is that you recognize my reputation is earned. That to trust me is to assure you safe passage not only to Mexico, but back into the hands of the only person that matters in your life. That sister of yours."

A faint mist of water, flung up by the constant churnings of the paddle wheel, hit me with a spray so fine that it caused me to flinch. The bowl in my hand quivered and broth sloshed onto my feet; Oliver scurried to smell the residue. I don't know why I did, but I reached down and placed the bowl there, letting him have the last of it while I gathered my wits about me. Rarely was I speechless, yet Turlow had rendered me so, and it was with great mercy that Turlow deigned to keep talking, for I think I would have stood in silence the rest of the night.

"Read this," Turlow said as I rose back up. "My instructions. Given to me by Mr. Harper himself. The same letter given to Mrs. Harper."

The edges were rubbed smooth from wear, the ink smeared where Mrs. Harper's tears had fallen.

"My sister," was all I could utter. "What has Mr. Harper done? Is she in danger? Mr. Turlow —"

"All I know is in the letter," he said, waving it about so recklessly I feared it might fall from his grip and land in the ocean. I could tell my urge to read it wafted off me like a scent. I could hardly contain my desire any better than Turlow could detect my desperation. He brought it to his chest and spoke once more.

"One promise," Turlow said. A small, imperceptible whine escaped my throat. My sight fell to the endless darkness of the sea, back to Turlow, back to the letter. "You cannot speak on the letter's content with Mrs. Harper. When she read it that first time, it was only delusion that brought her to find anything to celebrate contained within these pages. She is not in her right mind, and I do not wish for her to disrupt our travels by some mention of the truth. No. What we discuss tonight is best left to a confidence we share."

"Fine," I said, shamefully quick no less. "I will do as you say."

"And say nothing to the girl, either. Mrs. Harper refuses to share the truth with her, and I want no trouble between those two."

"I understand. I do. Just — please."

Now I had it in my grasp, and already I was shocked to see the familiarity of the writing. More so, I could *hear* Mr. Harper in every word. I was prepared for him to materialize at my back, barking instructions on what was expected of me for the coming day. I could hardly stand still.

...discovered land that holds promise... Untold numbers of crops could be born here, cotton not excluded... I can promise $1,000, 200 acres, and a stock in the bounty of whatever might be found in the mine itself... Dire help is needed in return... an unrelated cause dear to my heart...

I readied myself to hear of Mr. Harper's request for his family to be retrieved, yet following his introduction there was nothing of the sort.

Nothing at all. Hardly a word of Mrs. Harper. Not a word of Florence. The words, then, came at a faster clip, and so dizzied was I by their revelations that I hardly absorbed them beyond the naked directive they contained.

"*A young Negro woman, my dearest confidante, has absconded from our shared home... in the thrall of savages... converted to their cause by way of her very ignorance... I believe that only one man might entice her back to my dwelling. I will need you to locate her brother, a former slave that was in my keep...*"

I'd grown used to trying moments — learned to stymie the fear born from the shadows of the basement that frightened me as a child; never to flinch from the hand that might strike after a job poorly done; to stubbornly, and steadfastly, keep my focus locked upon my duties and nothing else, if only to keep at bay the trouble that gnawed at my soul. Yet I was not prepared for this. My bearings escaped me. The wind could have toppled me with a gust. I wished only to return to the deck of the boat, to pull my wool blanket over my body, bring Oliver to my chest to keep him safe, and let the moment pass.

"Do you understand now?" Turlow asked.

"I see," I said, my voice catching. "I understand."

Mr. Harper was not interested in reuniting with his family. What he wanted was my sister, who had somehow been taken. And what that required was something to entice her back into his grasp.

It was not his family Mr. Harper sought. It was me.

June:
Part One, Mexico, 1864

She could testify to the fact. That in those first few days, traveling on unmarked roads cloaked in dust and creekside banks enveloped in gnats, she could feel the forfeiture of a previous life give way to a new one. It had begun that very first morning they'd left Baton Rouge, the summer of 1864, when her master — former master soon, for he'd promised her freedom in Mexico — told her she should quit calling him master at all. Mr. Harper then, she said. He'd placed his hand upon the small of her back, bunching up her dress, a ball of fabric held to steady his nerves, to tamp down his childlike fear. No, he said. Not Mr. Harper. I'm Wyatt to you now.

He had the power to snatch her soul, reduce her spirit to nothing, and he and his family had done it many times through the years, each one counted, none to be forgotten. The first when she realized, as a young girl, that Mrs. Harper would be the only mother she had (her own pawned off to another family; and no mother at that was Mrs. Harper but rather another master to obey); the next when it occurred to her just how endless her responsibilities would be. That she, in fact, would act as Coleman's mother; that any chance of her own youth would be transferred to him without her even giving permission to the sale. The third when Wyatt had done that unnameable thing (let it go unsaid, for now, because some memories are best laid to rest). The fourth upon seeing her brother off on that carriage to New Orleans, his pain and angst laid bare as she realized that all those mornings of his she'd protected — mornings she did his tasks so he could sleep a while longer, thumb through another page of his books, practice his speaking in the mirror like some actor, like some new person cobbled together from scratch — meant nothing. Absolutely nothing. If she could be stolen from him so quickly, if their shared world could be altered so drastically by the sudden whim of Wyatt Harper, then wasn't their bond an illusion altogether? How silly of her not to see it coming when they'd done the same before, robbing them from their mother so suddenly that June could barely say farewell. She had been no more than twelve, Coleman two years younger.

Still stunned, she hardly said a word those first few days through the Louisiana countryside. The men, to June, were lost in some form of bereavement, impersonating cowboys when they had been born in feather beds and raised to wear suits, drink liquor, and lounge about their palatial estates like royalty — their idleness the very symbol of their lauded stations. Now, having passed through Houston — a city that seemed only a greater representation of Baton Rouge, the church spires slightly taller, the buildings with more floors yet less grandeur and less character — they stopped at every opportunity to trade tobacco with passing merchants when they had endless tins stashed in their wagon's sideboard; purchased hides from Indians which they planned to use as rugs to line the floors of Mexican dwellings they'd yet to build; made fires before the sun had yielded to the chill of the dark, just so the performance might be seen in the light, the slaves made to stand and watch, given instruction, like children, on how to pack the logs properly, when most knew better than those men standing before them.

Sixteen wagons in all, eighty people, beds crammed with Negroes stooped and bowed so as to fit more precious cargo, and she had heard the leader of their caravan, an Alfred Highsmith, tell them with a swell of resentment that they had ancestors on those ships that did just the same with less room, didn't complain one bit, so he best not hear a word on the subject. Said they should feel free to sing some of their songs if they like, as he rather liked them, really; missed hearing them as he went about his fields and his house.

But there would be no songs.

They had already crossed into Texas, a half day's ride past Fredericksburg, before she could truly bear witness to her surroundings with a clear eye; before she could extinguish, for just one moment, the impression of her brother, that burgeoning shadow that had settled in her mind and refused to budge from her memory. But in that second, stepping down from the wagon and witnessing the unfamiliarity of the desert, its very endlessness, something ripped bare within her like the husk of a corn stripped clean with a single tug. *This* was her new life. These sad and pitiful people thrown together, shadowed by the enormity of this desertscape, a place she recognized to be safe for no man or woman. Not even safe to wander through. Yet she would be made to do just that because these men had decided to be stupid for no reason at all, like men were wont to do. They were scared by the threat of defeat in that endless war: by the threat of their livelihood being altered in even the slightest fashion. Better to run to the desert and jeopardize their livelihood than risk the possibility of humiliation, of those bands of Negroes and delicate white men from the North rushing into their towns like demons from hell, raping their women, pillaging their homes. Inventions of the mind had forced them to such madness. It was almost enough to make her laugh, had she not felt the actual threat of that scorching heat upon her neck, that ball in her throat from thirst. Elements that were far too real. She thought it not a joke to die in a ditch with your lips cracked so dry it hurt to cry out for help — your heart shriveled up so small without any water in your veins that it can't even pump. That's what would happen, too. She might've been safe inside Mr. Harper's home, but how many men in the fields had she known to fall in just such a way?

They were eight days on. The ground was red as a clay backroad and yet had none of the forgiveness. A man amongst them, gaunt, lanky, with a journal forever being pulled from his pocket, held some claim to the art of botany and would continuously share his insights of plants he could identify without even a guidebook. It was an endless number of cacti and brush that June tried to keep track of, yet even she eventually thought it tiresome, a parrot gawking just to hear its own voice. (When Highsmith told the man to quit, it did seem for the best.) After this there was hardly any talking at all as they traveled; no noise of any animals save the distressed whispers of the brush left in their wake. And there certainly was not the sight of a single human other than the inhabitants of those sixteen wagons.

So, she said it. Said the words, because she'd held them inside the entire journey and she grasped that Wyatt — out here far from society, from any sense of order — could not punish her as he once might have. No, he needed her now. She could speak her mind like any man or woman present without fear of much repercussion.

"Right foolish," she said to the Negro beside her, spooling out bedding for Wyatt. "Every white man here has gone mad. They don't even know it yet."

The woman did not care to respond, but there was a particular expression she offered June as she smoothed the bedroll out. A lilting of her head to the side. A flattening of her lips and a rolling of her eyes. Like she knew. *Of course she knew.* As though June was the foolish one for taking this long to realize how great a blunder this whole expedition was.

A call from a white man from a different wagon fell over the desert, asking them to huddle up. The man stood with one leg bent up on the spoke of a wagon wheel. He was pug-faced and red and his shirt was tarnished yellow from sweat. Beside him the oxen and horses drank greedily from what was little more than a puddle.

"We have been called," he said. A collective glance spread amongst the black folk in the caravan like a shared groan; for they knew an artless preacher from his very cadence, the imitated theatrics from so many others before him, and in hindsight who else but such a man would demand their attention after such a trying day? "There will be records made of what we accomplish in the coming weeks," he said. "We have been chosen. Let no doubts inform you otherwise. Let no trial suspend your perseverance..." Spittle ran down his lips to his chin. He waved his hat about and held it to his chest and finally threw it on the ground when the scene called for such a display. He spoke of a river ahead, how God's pleasure would shine down like the sun, splitting through the clouds, cutting through the water and allowing safe passage. All of them would be reborn, cleansed, as though they'd waded through the River Jordan itself.

The whites clapped, even a few of the Negroes, and June and the servant woman now behaved in lockstep: their arms folded up against their chests, eyeing one another with a shared exhaustion regarding this exhibition, this afflicted man's attempt to unify a people who had no business outside of Louisiana, let alone in this desert. Only when she found Wyatt staring at her with some show of disapproval did June clap as well. The preacher grinned proudly, bowed and picked up his hat, and encouraged everyone present to speak to him further, in private, about his visions of the glory that awaited them all.

He would be dead by the time they reached Mexico, cleaved nearly in two by a Mexican soldier; forgotten quickly, and never spoken of again.

At first, Wyatt zealously kept June to himself. During the day she was not to speak to the other travelers, certainly not the men, and at night they slept beside each other under the stars, both of them swaddled in quilts. He would stare at her. What that gaze contained was difficult to express. A despondency, but beneath it an ever-churning lechery. It was at its core a manifestation of his possession over her: to gaze upon her without scruple, without even flinching, if only because she was his and this was his way of proving as much. He'd inch so close that his grime-ridden hair, a red not unlike the ground they lay on, would drape over her wrist like a curtain. If she looked over to him — she tried not to, yet in time there was the unwanted magnetism of someone so close, and as when confronted by a predator, one must brave the threat — she could see the smooth vaulted bank of his skull threaded with bulging veins that pounded in tempo with the fever of his passion; could note the worrisome blister pulsing at the corner of his mouth; smell the rankness of his breath, not from any food or drink but from something foul that rested at his core.

That night, after the preacher's speech, lying there beneath the stars, he took the step to rub a knuckle against her cheek, sharp as a razor after days clutching and unclutching reins, fixing faulty yokes and garnering splinters from sideboards that had begun to slip from the wagon's body. He then whispered in her ear with an alarming softness that had a calm that seemed born of a budding insanity: "Do you recognize how lucky you are?" The chance of riches, he said. The beauty of the wild laid out before her like a fantasy come true. Didn't she *love* the adventure of it all? "It *is* dangerous," he went on. "And that frightens you. That's why I didn't bring Coleman. I knew it would only worry you more, and it is the last thing I wish to do to someone I care so much for. Really, I was doing you a favor, June. I certainly could've used the extra hand. You could thank me. You should. Thank me. For all of this. For sparing him as I spared my own wife and daughter."

On occasion she had failed to reply to such statements. It was after he had humiliated Coleman, forcing him to enter the pond that day in Baton Rouge, that she had taken it upon herself to *ignore* him, an act so egregious it went unaddressed by the household. The days passed with her feeding her master, cleaning his clothes, laughing at Mrs. Harper's jokes when he would not and yet nary a word passed between her and Wyatt. He had broken their agreement, one that went unspoken but was well understood: She would never say no to him. She would wake early, sleep barely, and do all that was asked of her with a smile, the load of work that would cause a band of same-aged help in another home to drop dead from tired bones and crushed spirits, if only Wyatt might keep his evil from burdening her brother. Let the boy toil under the thumb of another man each day, loan him out as you please, but she begged him with her eyes, her body, whatever it might be, to keep the boy's mind from being poisoned by wickedness and cruelty, to allow his capacious soul, that strange innocence, to remain in the world untainted. Why he hadn't that day at the pond she could not say, but finding her brother in the basement, shivering cold, unable to change himself from the fear that rattled him, curled at the foot of his bed like a boy half his age — she wouldn't stand for it. She'd die before it happened again.

So she protested not with a single act but by her very reticence. If Wyatt asked her to darn his socks, she would begin only when Mrs. Harper echoed his words from across the dining-room table and made sure to avoid him when bringing them to his bedroom.

When he called her to his study, eager to pace about, inform her of his newest invention of little utility or complain about his treatment from a colleague, she would dutifully stand and listen but provide none of the sympathy he sought. No words of encouragement. No touch upon the forearm in support. At the first opportunity she would excuse herself, whether due to a sudden illness or a pressing matter with the upkeep of the home she could not be kept from. He would stand still, then, a finger upon the rim of his cup, silent before assenting to her departure.

She avoided him outright when she could, but it was her company he craved. Her very presence fueled him, soothed him, provided a calm when the world was a rocking and unsteady place. They shared a silent fellowship that was its own language that betrayed their stations and hinted at something more. It meant nothing to her. It gave Mr. Harper life.

Her withdrawal brought a pallor over the home as if the shades were permanently drawn; it stiffened visitors' backs; spread like a disease. June could apprehend Mrs. Harper pleading with her by the very means in which she fanned herself anxiously on the porch like she might be signaling a call for help. Or there was Florence, eating ravenously, her fork scratching her plate like a cat taking to a post; chewing with her mouth open, screaming at her parents, all just to layer sound over the anxiety that ran through the hallways and slipped under closed doors. It was three days in when night fell and Mrs. Harper and her daughter turned in early that Wyatt called June to the washroom. He beckoned her by name and when she entered, the room was drowning in the soft glow of candles. He could not fully submerge himself in the tub, for it was fit for a person half his size, and his legs poked out the end like an oversize child, pendant on a footstool he kept for this express purpose.

He tapped the copper tub with a hand.

"Sit."

There was only a moment's hesitation. He did not look in her direction. For a time it was as silent as it had been for those painful few days, until a smile flowered over his face and he rolled his shoulders.

"I don't know what got into me at the pond," he said. "Too much booze I suppose."

"Aw, now, don't you worry about that," she said. "You ain't done nothing wrong. You just a playful old man, ain't you?"

He liked this. Wyatt never did wrong; wrongs were done unto Wyatt. Her place was to assure him that he was on the right side of every transaction, every argument, every encounter in the small history that was his unremarkable life. *I don't know what got into me.* Those few words he'd uttered would be his apology and his absolution. She knew what the cost would be to hear them.

"My shoulders," he whispered.

He turned slightly and the rust-brown water rippled and fell upon her toes. The heat stuck her blouse to her chest, brought moisture to her neck, and she recognized the awful sensation that she was somehow underwater alongside the man, suffocating with no air to reach her lungs. The walls were closing in, the lilies drawn there wilting and peeling under the wetness of the room. The wooden casing of the bathtub, sodden and worn from years of wear, yielded easily to her elbow, sagging ever so slightly as she began to massage the sinew, rub the knots, the man moaning, touching himself, his toes curling on the other end of the tub.

His face, first in pain at her touch, thawed itself into something obscene — his eyes fluttering, his lips pried open and his teeth laid bare. His chest rose. The water quaked and she wished to be anywhere but there: took herself down to the basement under the covers during those treasured moments when she was left to her own thoughts, listening to the patter of mice, the snores of her brother, away from this nightmare. And what a failure of imagination, what an embarrassment, that that cold dank place might be her only reprieve.

He rose up and shivered like a dog. He turned to face her. One more spell of silence. Lurching over her, dripping water on her shoulders.

"June," he said, as though he were waking from a deep reverie. "Where is my towel? Don't you see I'm shivering?"

Lying there beside their wagon, lost in the wilderness, she felt that inkling of the power that had coursed through her earlier in the day. The old life was gone. Wyatt's study, his seat at the head of the dinner table, the comfort of his couch and his evening baths. What lay before them was something neither of them could possibly weigh. A mystery that made everyone equal. And still, still, she knew it was not yet time to claim her independence. Even if it had grown clear that soon she would be free — as though it were a message flashed out from the abyss that stretched between the stars, made known to all who were present — she also knew it was imperative to bide her time until the perfect opportunity announced itself.

She could bear anything. Certainly more than someone as pathetic as Wyatt Harper: a man who would abandon his family, everything he knew, for a project so outrageous as this one. He was a *child*. She could vanquish a child. His life had been a celebration, hers an occasion to mourn. She would make it her goal to switch their roles for good.

"Thank you," she finally said to Wyatt, turning to face him for long enough to make the words sound sincere. "You've done me a favor, I think.

Wouldn't never see the likes of this place without your courage to take us. And it is a fine adventure. Sure enough."

Her praise was the ultimate gift. His voice was low after that; leaden with fatigue.

"I'm going to give you everything you've ever wanted," he muttered to her in return, his eyes shutting slowly, the relief of this enough to slow her heart, to ease her, slowly, toward sleep herself.

They encountered great cascades of nothingness and when an occurrence ruptured from the blank of their surroundings it was almost always unwanted: torrents of dust that picked up in the wind and nearly buried them, waking to a stampede of ants that had marched their way toward a jar of preserves in numbers so vast that the women would shriek and check their bodies for bites hours after, lamenting the awful desolate place they had been forced to travel through. The heat would simmer and stoke to the point of cruelty and they would all wonder what god had been so needlessly provoked. Yet when it finally began to cool, the sky often took to a magnificent red hue that brought a wondrous spray of gold to the desert floor, epic striations of color that slashed through the few clouds present and left even the preacher amongst them speechless.

After the wagons were corralled at night, the men in charge drank and the wives who were present would form their own circle a few feet beyond them, but soon the two began to merge if only for lack of a reason not to. By June's estimation, their chatter showed a startling lack of curiosity. Harkening to memories of yesteryear — parties thrown and marriages that had been arranged — or what might come in the future for their family members left behind. It all carried with it the odd quality that they were not leaving their home permanently but were perhaps undertaking some circuitous route back there and would soon return to a place entirely unchanged from the one they knew upon their departure.

After one evening just like this one, while the white folk were in such a conversation huddled around a fire, June found herself alone. She was crouched in the back of the wagon, tallying supplies as she did each night, when she realized just how fruitless a task this was. Realized, more importantly, that Wyatt would not even ask after the results, for he hadn't the night before, or the night before that one. So she made what felt at the time to be a radical decision: stood up, in naked sight, climbed from the wagon, and moseyed over to the help resting under the night's sky as one.

These were men and women with a few idle children of their own, most in the same tattered linen shirts and breeches that had assuredly been their only uniform all last season. Many, she'd learned, had once been owned or still were, in name. A few had their freedom. The women sat with their legs to their chests, chins to knees, their petticoats scattered about the ground and pooled together like they'd been knitted as one blanket. The men, what few of them there were, simply lay flat beside the women with their hats over their heads, lost in that single moment of comfort.

"Finally found your way over," a woman said, looking up at her. "I'm Nancy. I know you're June."

June said nothing.

"I had a baby talk more than this woman," Nancy said, "and she could hardly say *momma*." Nancy was younger than June, and June wondered, as they snickered, where that baby even was.

"He doesn't let me do much," June finally said. "Or say much. He doesn't even know I'm over here."

The children had stopped playing. The silence buried her thoughts and she could not find any more words to say, anything to bring herself into the fold with these strangers she had ignored so long and now urgently wished to belong to. It felt as though serving Wyatt had stunted her ability to speak to anyone else at all. She thought of Coleman, who would have marched up to them the very first day of the journey, extending a hello to each person, landing on a compliment for everyone who came off cold and a fact or curiosity to provoke the more diffident individuals into conversation. What she would do to trade his talents for hers in this moment!

There was a hand at her back; a soft touch that slowly crept up to her arm, casually, in the way a mother coaxes a child to relax. It was the woman she'd spoken to when they'd made it to the desert that first night, preparing the beddings. She said her name was Celia. Her lips were taut, serious, and the skin beneath her eyes was so dark it took on the color of a bruise. But her actions belied her countenance. In hand, a cup of water.

"Some honey in there," the woman said. "Sit. Drink something."

June was hesitant but Celia had the answer to her nerves, grabbing hold of her wrists, staring into her with an indescribable knowingness, a deep sense of reassurance.

"That man's so soused you'll have to wake him yourself if y'all are gonna keep up with the pack come sunup," Celia said. "Now sit. We ain't gon' let nothing happen to you."

With that she fell to the desert floor amongst them and drank, the honeyed water coating her tongue, her throat, a taste so pleasing she wondered what made her worthy of the gift.

Two days on they reached a building with whitewashed walls that was little more than dilapidated stonework, the paint now stripped by the wind and heat to the color of ash. Men, some in uniform, some not, milled about it and made no effort to welcome them.

The wagons came to a halt. June didn't know if it might be the liquor from the night before but Wyatt's features now gestured toward some inward frailty, a fracturing of his spirit. The pustules on his lips became more pronounced and his gaze was often focused on some vague point of termination in the distance that was impossible to gain on. He would whisper commands or suggestions to the other men in the caravan in a tone only she could make out, as though his designs deserved to be heard by her but weren't qualified enough to pass the scrutiny of the others. He drank their reserves of water far too quickly and when they paused for rest many eyed him with caution.

But this outpost was apparently an indicator of good news, as Wyatt's bulging lips widened into a clownish, quivering smile, and he leaned out from the wagon canvas and looked at the leader of the group, howling in delight.

"Ye of little faith," Highsmith said in response to his celebratory wails.

"I believe it now!" Wyatt hollered. June nearly recoiled at the man's vigor when he fixed his gaze on her, still smiling — desperate, it seemed, for the same reaction he had, though she had no idea where they were.

He told her it was an abandoned military fort; that travelers collected here to trade and find safety in numbers from the Indians. There would be others with supplies, and more importantly — this was the most important matter, by far — it indicated they were only a day away from the river they sought, from that point that would confirm their passage to Mexico.

A firebed kindled up ahead before a hole-ridden U.S. Army tent. A white man, pink-headed with a coned beard, wearily walked over from it and invited Wyatt and Highsmith and the other leaders to break bread with him and his party of ten and proposed they purchase some logs he'd cut to aid in crossing the river. As was the case for the past few days, Wyatt left June with no instructions, mostly, she imagined, because the general act played between them — that there was anything much to do in the first place — had concluded some time ago.

June watched him off. She soon located Nancy and Celia amongst the rest of the caravan. Nancy, seated in the back, had her legs hanging off the end of the wagon and behind her Celia, comb in hand, was working Nancy's hair. The intimacy of the act was somewhat captivating. June had never had a woman dress her hair since she'd been grown, certainly never with a gentle hand, a hand so assured as to bring an ease over the entire afternoon. She wanted next. They were discussing who should prepare supper that night and when June arrived they asked who did the cooking back in Baton Rouge and for a stretch of time she'd forgotten this previous existence, those other lives she'd lived, and she had to pause to recollect.

A single memory: shelling a mountainous plate of shrimp, one by one, only for Mrs. Harper to burst into the kitchen, in one of her moods, informing her that she was too sick for the night's party to go on. All that work for nothing!

"You looking to run that fire tonight?" Celia asked. "Those boys are getting sick of beans and ham. You can see what we got stored back there. Cobble something together."

"No," June said, quicker than she meant to. Perhaps she could've said more, but what more was there? She didn't feel up to the task. It seemed, amongst her own, this should be enough.

Celia tugged with great effort and Nancy's hair expanded, wavered, dragged as thin and drawn as the strings of a harp.

"Can't blame you there," said Celia. "Can't blame you one bit."

A glint of sunlight blinded her momentarily. There were hills here, small hills, but hills, and coming down the nearest one was a sight that June could not entirely square. A black man draped in fantastical plumage was saddled upon a horse. His clothes were the fur of animals yet dyed purple, and a silver gorget hung about his neck in three tiers — the shining object that had captured the reflection of the sun. For so long she had seen so little and this sudden fluctuation, this blossoming amongst the barren landscape, struck her as momentous. A turban was swathed upon his head like a curled-up cat, and his body swayed back and forth on his mount with a flow that brought to mind a baby rocking in its cradle. She immediately thought him to be magnificent, royalty, but of course he couldn't be royalty, so she kept on guessing what this man was while she gaped at him. A trail of Indians came in his wake, following the man toward the fort. Following him toward June.

For a moment she thought this to be the Indian raid the white men dreaded so greatly, yet these people came toward them so lazily that it was clear to all they meant no harm. It was as though they were in a trance, saying nothing to one another, looking only ahead. She knew they were not to be spoken to. That these were serious individuals who knew this place in a way that she did not and Wyatt did not, and that Wyatt would have no allowance for her to engage with anyone who might lay claim to such an authority.

Which was why that interaction only an hour later was so surprising. She was watering the oxen when the man appeared before her, still on his mount. He removed his turban to reveal a head of patted-down woolly hair. He had an odd crouch to his back from riding, June imagined, a sort of weariness, or comfort, the difference she could not tell. He was looking not at her but at the sun, falling between two of those little hills up ahead, descending for the night.

He spoke then, words soft as a cushion.

"They say the first drop of blood ever to grace the earth fell from the sun. How the first man was made."

A finger in the air, tracing a fall, a drop, as though the blood had been pricked right before them. She didn't believe it, of course, but she was curious. And though she feared Wyatt, she feared him less every day, and so she mounted the courage to gather her voice and raise it up.

"Who'd teach you such a thing?" she asked.

"My father before he passed on. His father told him before that, I imagine."

"It is a pretty thought," June said. *Careful with your words. Make them perfect, now, like a table arranged just right.*

"I got a few of those," he said.

"Pretty thoughts?" She faced him up, hands on her hips, and she could see the whiskers on his face twitch, as though he were holding back some delightful comment he couldn't bear to keep in any longer. "Well go on, then. Ain't much pretty out here. Like to at least picture something nice."

He was about to begin, but his jaw clenched, and in her mind's eye the table she'd arranged — the glassware, saucers, silverware too — all fell to the ground in a mess. Something gone wrong. But then he beamed.

"This place is many things," he told her. "Ugly ain't one of them. You just need to be familiar. It takes some time. The proper eye. Like that, there."

He pointed again, this time to a tumbleweed scurrying into the distance, doubling over itself without pause. "You know what that is?"

Strange, because she *did*. The thought struck her like a jolt, a prick of delight; of all the things the botanist had educated the group on, this was perhaps the only thing she remembered.

"We got a man in our group," she told him. "He said it grows up with some water, green and healthy. Dead one minute, alive the next."

A Resurrection Plant. There were many sorts like it.

"The Rose of Jericho is what I've heard it called," the man said. "I like that name mighty fine."

The rose of what? Her mind was scattered, working too hard to keep up with his words. She had so many questions. *How did he know those Indians? Did he lead them? Might he bring her onto the back of his horse, keep her at his side for the rest of his days?*

She straightened out these thoughts; returned to the moment.

"It's pretty, too. I'm telling you. Lots of beauty out here."

She'd let him go on all day.

"What you plan on doing over there?"

"Over where?"

"In Mexico."

"Bide my time," she said quietly. "I got my brother coming this way after we pave the path. And then when he makes it... I ain't really thought past that point. But we'll be free then. We'll make our way as we please. Do as we wish."

"You don't have to wait for your brother to do as you wish."

"Maybe. Ain't really as simple as you say. Got to keep that man with me happy. I don't have no one else down here."

This he wouldn't abide by. He uncoiled himself from that slouch upon his horse, was now inches taller, and she thought it a privilege to be allowed the sight, the beauty of a man like this in a position so impressive. Never in Baton Rouge. Never in her life. It was her turn to stare.

"You'll see," he said. "Free is free over there. More simple than you can ever imagine. You won't *need* no one else."

A call, deep and guttural, something wrought from the part of a throat she had no access to, and June turned to find the Indians facing them, nodding, and with the slightest click of the boot the man's horse was signaled in their direction. She didn't want him to go, but didn't know what to say to keep the man beside her. The question that followed was random, forced, entirely harmless but embarrassing only by the way she asked it; the desperation palpable in the scritch of her voice.

"Tell me one last time," she said. "That plant. What's its name? I've already forgotten."

His gorget tinkled like an ornament as the horse set to a canter. He didn't even look back.

"I'd rather you remember my name," he said. "Isaac."

She repeated it once out loud. Before she could offer her own, he was gone.

A day later, the desert split in two and the river they spoke of so fervently gushed forth from its main. June could not believe the noise — the sound of the water rushing like an interminable collision. At one point she covered her ears, which Wyatt found amusing. She said it looked dangerous, best avoided.

"It wouldn't be an adventure without the hazards!" he yelled, all while looking forward to the wagons ahead — looking for guidance himself. Those Indians along with Isaac had offered to guide them over. Said they'd be risking their own lives if they didn't have an expert hand at their side. But Highsmith had scoffed, right alongside Wyatt. And now the whole pack was on its own.

They disembarked where the channel narrowed and Highsmith called the men together, white and black, all hands being needed for the cause. A sense of unease rose above the sounds of the river. Hats were in hands, attention on Highsmith, and it was all June could do to stand and watch alongside Celia in silence, languishing under the heat, the stress of the ordeal. The men were ready for this. The logs were hauled up from the rear wagons, where they'd been tied off like sleds. The men used rope to tie the logs together into rafts and reinforced it with vines and roots pulled from the ground.

Wyatt walked toward her, hammer in hand, grimacing with excitement. "Highsmith says it's shallow enough here. We'll get the equipment over first, then the pack animals." *Good omens*, they said, *fortunate turns of fate*.

June knew better. For days, weeks, they had made prognostications of great magnitude and yet nothing that had transpired spoke to anything except great hardship soon to fall upon them all. That was what life was, her own a demonstration. Perhaps even *hardship* was an incorrect term to apply in this instance, as it was simply a consequence of living. For when it appeared things might get no worse, that was when your brother might be snatched from you; when you would be thrust into the wild where the sun dried you to dust; when you'd suddenly be forced to fend for yourself amongst strangers, predators, heathens, and deluded preachers.

And that preacher. Still sermonizing every day, even now as the last loads of cargo crossed the river. Only when his voice pierced the calm of the afternoon, speaking not of his savior but of rash injustices, did she turn to witness the two horsemen who had suddenly appeared in their midst. Mexican soldiers, those rebels they had heard so much of, well-mounted, sabers at their side and starred caps upon their head. The yellow buttons down the blue of their tunics appeared like an embedded trail of gold and June mistook the mud upon their pants at first to be some design.

The preacher was intimidated by them not in the slightest. He spoke with them as fervently as he ever had before while the others waited on.

Sandy, a Negro who had his papers and was free to travel as he pleased (not that it mattered here and now), scuddled over that way to listen in. He returned bright-faced with concern and June didn't even need the man to explain what he'd seen. It was all right before them to witness themselves: the odd imbalance between the preacher's hand waving, his spitting and screaming, and the equanimity of the soldiers — clear suggestions that this would spell some significant misfortune for the preacher and a minor inconvenience for the men with swords and rifles.

"Someone needs to save him from himself," June whispered of the preacher.

"I don't think those two men got a word of English between them," Celia said. "Preacher man is yelling at a wall."

"They speak it broken, but they speak it fine," Sandy told them. "Mexicans said there were outlaws this way across the border. That everyone in the party could get over safely with their help, but it would cost. That preacher man ain't paying a dime. Says they're outlaws themselves, no different from the Indians. Says this ain't even their side of the river, but the Mexicans don't seem to see this side no different from that one. Sure enough."

She listened. The preacher cursed the Mexicans, cursed their god, assailed them as corrupt, and June thought it strange, so strange, that a man could get so drunk on the courage offered by his own savior that he might miss the clues sent by that same creator — a creator telling him, quite clearly, that he was in the presence of a grave threat. Or perhaps that was the idea: to face such an enemy head-on and feel protected. Such a notion seemed to be a rather silly one, and so it was June, sensing the tension in the air, who began to step back from the confrontation before it ruptured into something tangible.

Celia followed her, repeating, over and over, that this was a problem for the white men, not her, not little old Celia. She was right, June knew. And she also knew it would not go as they imagined in their schoolboy dreams. The white men would save no lives, would vanquish no heathens, would become no heroes. Indeed, the entire series of interactions that followed was rather foreseeable, however grisly.

June watched from the riverbank beside their now-empty wagon. Wyatt and Highsmith and the other white men came to the preacher's aid, guns drawn. From what she would learn later, the Mexicans demanded only the goods of one wagon. The preacher's wagon would do. And they would supervise their crossing and let them on their way. Yet the men of the caravan would have none of it.

Dust rose like dew after a short-lived storm. None of them had seen the soldiers hidden in the dense cluster of chaparral beside a ditch on the trail, all of them rising as one. Stricken with shock, not a single white man shouldered his rifle when those soldiers rose up. A few soldiers grabbed the preacher by the collar; the white men did nothing as the preacher wallowed, shedding tears, his bluster given over to pleas in equal measure.

Highsmith screamed, pointing and trembling, demanding the preacher's return. Wyatt did the same — his voice high, pathetic. June ached for him to quit; wished, desperately, against her passionate desire to be rid of him, that he would not go so far as to embarrass himself before getting killed.

The heat was like a gauze; it was difficult to breathe, and she could not pull her eyes away as the botanist, the smallest amongst the men, finally went to aim his pistol and just as quickly crumpled to the ground. Time seemed to slow as June witnessed his death — saw the blood upon his shirt, his wound like a water pump given one weak draw, a small breath let free before a full flow that drenched his entire chest and face. The men scattered, more falling as they ran to their mounts and wagons, yet the Mexicans on horseback had moved not at all, like the subjects of an unfinished portrait. Frozen there. She would remember that sight the rest of her life.

Wyatt's hand seized her shoulder. He practically threw her into the wagon as he screamed at the oxen, shaking the reins with fear. The animals took off into the water and the sky was colorless, all white nothing, until June realized it was the tent of the wagon she was now staring at. Her gaze drifted to Wyatt, that bug-eyed old man panting like a dog.

Heartless place. Heartless! They cut that preacher's face in two, Wyatt was wailing, grabbing at her, but she peeled back, refused his touch. *Did you see?* he said. *My God. Oh, my God.* She knew he would not be the same after this. Knew, with a sick happiness, that *nothing* would be the same. That for the first time in her life, the coming changes might fall in her favor.

"Are they coming for us?" Wyatt asked. "Look, dammit. Do something for once. So worthless as to fail to glance behind your own ass. I said to *look.*"

So simple a command, but one she would not follow. She'd witnessed enough. Had seen the complacency of the soldiers in the wake of the botanist's murder alongside the preacher's and knew they were not coming. There was a simple tax to pay for entry into their country and it had been paid, and they were now waiting for whoever came next down that trail. Instead she took in the gorgeousness of the river, the ease in which the oxen drove through it, the white froth upon the blue-black water, a new life only a few feet from her grasp, and she smiled, yes, she smiled, leaning forward, taking in the true form of the beautiful sky above them — the sun splitting the clouds, shining bright upon them. And yes, June did indeed feel cleansed. Perhaps even reborn. As though they'd waded through the River Jordan itself.

3

Mrs. Harper turned from her vanity mirror, powder jar in hand. "What has gotten into you, Coleman? I've asked a question."

I apologized and stood stiff at attention.

"I wish to know if the dog will behave in the ballroom," she said. "I've promised them all a performance, but a false move will make a fool of me."

Mrs. Harper swiveled back once more. Her dress was honeybee yellow, a hoop skirt that was exaggeratedly robust. (I had never seen her wear one, and it appeared, at certain angles, as though she were seated in an upturned soup bowl.) She had had her attendant fetch me some time ago, eager to put on a show in the ballroom for the final night before we made it to land come morning. A woman would be crowned Queen of the Jubilee, and Mrs. Harper was eager to beat out the others. It was to be her finest achievement, and I heard all about her journey toward this success, from the near-flirtatious banter with the various gentlemen on board as a means to sway their votes, to the impeccable grace she had shown whilst waltzing, and even her selection of orchestral music which had been played at her recommendation to laudatory applause. Tonight was to be the capstone of her efforts, a talent show before the dance, and I was to be there with Oliver to put on a performance, a display of his many tricks.

It mattered not that Oliver was no circus animal, and *knew* no tricks. He would, apparently, learn as we went along.

Oliver was asleep on the bed, which would have usually been an unwelcome scene to Mrs. Harper but rankled her not in the slightest at this moment, as though she was aware of the rest he needed for the coming performance.

Entering the room I had spied the young cabin girl who had fetched me. She'd taken her position outside the door, hands at her back, her apron a small white bank upon her blue blouse that I figured she used to warm her hands. The night's cold, I knew well, was biting. I had half a mind to propose inviting her in before Mrs. Harper had already beckoned me toward her.

"The pearls," she said, waving her finger at the jewel box tucked within her trunk. What should have been a harmless directive only spoke to how Amos Turlow's letter had cast a pall over the entire trip. Mr. Harper had given him clear instructions, and Turlow had explained the particulars to me: that I was the only subject he wished to have transported to Mexico, with all the material goods Mrs. Harper might possess. It was, Turlow told me, Mrs. Harper's interpretation that the letter was simply wrong, that by no means was I to go alone; her husband had simply omitted an important note that she herself had gathered in the empty margins of the page. Indeed, she and Florence would be joining the trip. Were very much desired by Mr. Harper, no less. The family would be reunited, and not another word on the matter would be said. If this was agreeable to Turlow, she would be more than happy to bring every jewel, every diamond, that she had stored away. And so here we were, all of us along with those jewels, and although she was clamoring to put them on, to wear them with her usual pride, she knew quite well they would be sold out from under her in due time. And the woman cared not a whit.

Indeed, there was a childlike sense of joy, and wonder, to that look upon her face. If someone was to ask me to describe Mrs. Harper, I would not reference her naive perspective on seemingly all topics, or even the selfishness that informed her every action. I would rather speak to her uncommon perseverance, of maintained confidence, that colored her personality in the face of almost incessant heartache. She was a woman who claimed the world while her world collapsed around her, and it would be inhuman not to grant her that scrap of a compliment in the face of the betrayal she'd now been subjected to.

"I very much hope you win tonight," I said, looking at her necklace sparkle in the mirror. And I meant it. I very much did. "If only Mr. Harper could see you now. So much we have weathered in his absence."

My voice was low, and tender, and my question that followed, I suppose, only meant to reassure myself that she possibly was not as delusional as I feared, knowing what would come when she reunited with her husband in the coming days — the disappointment that I was certain would follow.

"Does the past ever worry you regarding what might come? It could be so different, after all these years."

She raised her chin, looking over her own features, the beaked nose, the sagged pouch of her neck, before grinning once again. "Such a strange query," she said. With this she placed her hand on my own, tapping it ever so slightly. "It is the sort of love you will never know, and I imagine that is why you ask, for it mystifies you. And yet some things can't be explained. Best not to ask at all. To know your place, if you will. So often you do, Coleman. Which is why I excuse the blunder."

A creak of the door, a cold burst of ocean air, and before I could apologize for misspeaking, Florence had entered the room. The smell of her perfume fell over the cabin — prominent notes of roses, always, as strong as a blow to the face — and her eyes already were on her mother.

"Wearing the pearls, I see," Florence said.

"I look my best in them, no?" Mrs. Harper said.

"Yes. I only thought I had half a mind to wear them myself."

"Any other night I would say nothing of it, but I really want to put my best self on display. What of the amethyst? Purple suits you..."

As their voices carried on, back and forth, I moved from my chair to the bed, marveling at the softness of the top sheet, letting Oliver come to my lap and rest there. I believe I had discovered exactly what he had when he'd settled on this location to rest. I then imagined what life would be like had we taken this trip alone, had we been afforded this cabin ourselves. We could invite the cabin girl inside, allow her a seat while we all were given an opportunity to simply appreciate the warmth, the cocoon of comfort found here. She could go to her quarters early to rest. Not a peep of noise would be heard throughout the night but perhaps the rolling whoosh of the sea, the only marker of time passing that one might need. After dinner I would bring some dessert back from the dining room for a midnight snack, half for Oliver, half for myself, before both of us dozed off with our stomachs full.

At some point, while I had once more resigned myself to a dream, the women had begun discussing Mrs. Harper's plan with Oliver. Florence was polite but not without criticism, saying that it might be taken as a bit of a cheap trick, not worthy of Mrs. Harper's class, while Mrs. Harper herself offered that the passengers had all been eager for the show, and I realized that this whole plan had been conceived by Mrs. Harper as a means to procure the title of Queen of the Jubilee.

"And Mother," Florence asked, "not to be rude, but how is it even your talent if the *dog* is putting on the act?"

"The dog is my property. If Coleman has taught it these tricks then they are my own, in effect. At least that's how I see it."

"I'm not sure others would agree."

"Why are you so resistant to this idea, Florence?"

"I only want you to win."

"And I believe the dog is the critical piece. The people will rally behind a dog in possession of incredible feats."

"If he will even accomplish the feats. Under pressure, with the gaze of the ballroom upon him, I worry if he'll be able to harness his full abilities to — "

"He is only a *dog*," I said, the room suddenly so chilly as to bring the proceedings to a halt. "He cannot do flips, or somersaults, and I do not know wherever you got such an idea, Mrs. Harper. He is certainly intelligent, I grant you that, but even Oliver has his limits."

I sighed; simply sighed.

Florence looked upon me with muted exasperation. The fashionable strings atop the shoulders of her dress flowed like small replications of her hair, small tassels clumped in a row, as motionless as she was now.

"Who asked *you*?" she said.

"You are lucky I let you bring the dog, Coleman," Mrs. Harper added on.

Perhaps it was the letter Turlow had shown me. Perhaps an accumulation of anguish that I could no longer let pass. But I felt something rising within me. I felt the need to counter their words. To respond to this, too. Yet before I could, just as I meant to, the door opened, the help poking her head in and cutting through the tension that had overtaken us.

"The party has begun," she said.

Florence straightened her dress, surveyed her tassels. Mrs. Harper checked herself in the vanity mirror once more.

"The dog," she said to me.

It felt as though I had not uttered a single word at all in the animal's defense.

"Oliver. Come," I said.

There was a tang in the air from the herbs and lemon ladled upon the plated snapper, the heady scents of pear borne from the champagne; the sour odor of mildew emanating from those who were dancing, perfume and cologne failing both the women and the men. The talent show had yet to begin but already the tables had been cleared, the front of the ballroom stripped bare, and couples had moved in for a square dance before the festivities began in earnest.

Mrs. Harper was showing Oliver off to a table of older gentlemen in tails, and I was against the wall, beside the servers, five Negroes in a row, platters in hand, towels draped over their arms. An odd sight, me beside them, as though we were waiting to be selected for a dance. A joke I made to the nearest attendant, who did not deign to look in my direction. Bumpers of champagne sat in circles upon his platter, and I figured, considering my nerves, that it couldn't hurt to ask the server if I might have —

"*Now, you know better,*" he whispered.

I pulled my hand back. I was some strange, unwanted occupant here: too low for the help, certainly too low for the guests in attendance, and so it was that I had no place at all. I nearly wished to recede into the wall, to pass into the nonphysical and materialize somewhere far away from this boat where I might find myself amongst similar company, whomever that might be.

I heard a loud cackle and looked to see Florence stooped over in laughter before a young man, both seated beside one another. He was exceptionally handsome, and I found it equally depressing to witness the efforts Florence put toward impressing such men while failing to see, time and time again, that they had absolutely no romantic inkling regarding her whatsoever. Beyond Hugh, I had never seen her encounter more than the most hesitant suitors — something she refused to acknowledge, let alone respond to. How she tried with her garrulous laugh, her wit, her charm, to foster some level of attraction. When it came time to ask a lady for a dance, these men would soon turn to another girl in the shadows, the one with cavernous dimples and a lake for a sternum; the girls who blushed at a single word of conversation. No pearl necklace nor amethyst would alter this reality.

The song was slowing to an end, and I was filled with nerves with what was to come, the ridiculous embarrassment that was to find me when I went onstage with Mrs. Harper. The smells of the room, so many of us cloistered as one, almost matched that of the farm animals at the stern of the ship. I turned, going straight for the door, ending up on the skylight deck, a view of the ocean's infinity before me.

The moon cast an astonishing glimmer upon the sea, a slick film of silver like a trail across the water, thinning and widening as the reflection marched on; one could walk upon it, I imagined, and end up on a different planet altogether. I welcomed the chill of the night, the purity of the air, and I let the elements wash over me, my mind at rest for once.

It was not to last.

Shipmen were hurrying about, first walking, then sprinting. Two hastened into the ballroom in a fit of urgency. I turned to watch their progress when I heard someone at my back.

"Coleman." A rough voice, steady but intentioned. "I've been searching for you."

I looked to find Turlow checking his timepiece, peering about me, as though I had hidden something from view.

"Where is the dog?"

"Oliver?" I nodded inside. "He is readying for the talent show. Shouldn't you be in attendance?"

"I told you how I feel about those people."

Turlow had yet to look me in the eye, and I had no interest in dealing with whatever matter he might now confront me with. Had his revelations not caused me grief enough?

"I believe your letter has thrown me," I said. "There is a version of myself that would be elated to be in that ballroom, and yet in my current state there's nowhere I'd like to be less. I can only think of my sister, of her predicament."

"There will be time for that. But there are more pressing concerns as of right now."

"I am like... I am like a book that has undergone extensive revisions. That's it. As though a new edition has been given over to the public that is almost nothing like the original, the author deciding to change all of the particulars of his characters, his plot. I can hardly recognize myself at times."

"Coleman, you are not listening to me."

"I consider my love for my sister and I realize that it is not only the bond we shared through our time alone that endears me to her. It is not just the love she showed me. Putting my own welfare before her own after she had spent hours serving the Harpers. Stealing me food when she knew I had gone hungry. Not that I had said a word of being so. She always just knew. No. It was all of that, but not *just* that."

"You must listen —"

"No, I'm speaking. And really, Mr. Turlow, you are making my point. The reason I long for her, I believe, above all others, is that she *listened to me*. That I felt that I was seen. She is the only individual, I believe, that treated me as a real person. Above all else that is the hallmark of a life well-lived. To be acknowledged. To be heard, and listened to. To have that again. What I would do."

At this I noticed the captain of the boat walk by us at a rapid clip beside an officer holding semaphore flags; the captain nodded at Turlow before hurrying on. Looking up at the pilot room, above the ballroom, one could see the two officers had exited so quickly that the door was still ajar. In the distance but growing ever-present, a faint ray of light, a blinking eye tearing through the darkness.

Turlow appeared to have not heard a word I'd uttered. His timepiece was in his hand, as was so often the case. He looked over the taffrail in great consternation.

"We promised to trust in one another, and now you must honor that commitment, Coleman."

"What exactly *is* it?" I asked — for there it landed. That familiar feeling of orders being prepared, laid at my feet, an urgent issue that I would now be forced to resolve.

"I need to tell you that there is a fire in the boiler room," he said. "We believe the boat might sink."

This was not what I'd expected.

"The boat?"

"Is sinking. Yes."

For the first time since I had met the man, I noticed his voice register some greater emotion than outright indifference — some element of impatience, what might be considered a small marker of actual unease. Turlow's vest was wrinkled at the chest. His hands were unsteady. For a dash of time, he appeared *human*. Those below us in steerage were first murmuring loudly, then screaming. One could detect, however faintly, that acrid smell of smoke slowly taking to the air.

Passengers began to stream from the ballroom. Turlow put his sweat-soaked hand upon my wrist and gave me directions.

"Follow my every move," he said. "Stop for no one."

4

Shrieks now rose from the ballroom, from the deck beneath us, and the ship was soon consumed in chaos. A great mass of bodies exited the ballroom doors. Turlow was telling me of rescue boats, our signals for assistance having been received — that light I had seen in the distance the greater vessel itself — and yet I had slipped from his grasp before he could finish another sentence.

I was overtaken by panic and it became clear, as my mind organized its priorities, what I must do next.

"Oliver," I said.

I pulled away from Turlow.

"Coleman, no — "

I went against the strong current of those exiting the ballroom, calling Oliver's name, calmly, under the impression a soothing voice might somehow rise above the furor.

Deckhands directed everyone present to head downstairs, to remain calm as the fire was extinguished. One man hit me square in the chest and fell to the ground, feet stampeding upon him until, weathering the impact of the endless collisions, I reached down to help him up. Glass shattered. Instruments wailed before crashing upon the ground.

There, at my front, tears streaming down her face, was Mrs. Harper; Florence at her side, holding her hobbled mother's shoulder, guiding her to the exit with a stern grimace of determination. Perhaps at times I had thought Florence's resolve to be an act, some way to conceal her pain, some hidden weakness, and yet this changed my thinking, watching how alert she was, how forceful, in leading her mother through the fray. I tried to harness her strength myself.

"Where are you going?" Mrs. Harper asked me.

I could only tell her to follow the others; that I would be by their side in a moment's time.

I was preparing to get on my knees, to peer under tables, when the server who had withheld the champagne from me grabbed my shoulder. He directed me toward the exit, off to the side, where Oliver had hidden himself away from the panicking masses. He was hamstrung, frightened, more like a cat than the courageous dog I knew so well. He tried to step forward, only to pull back in hesitation, repeating the steps with the same result, so scared he did not hear my calls or turn to see that I had come to his rescue.

By the time I had him in hand, the ballroom was almost empty, and there was a strange standing of calm. I had not seen a single piece of evidence of the rumored fire that had caused such pandemonium except those faint whiffs of smoke.

I left the ballroom. To my left the mass of tuxedos and gowns were fighting to gain exit to the stairs leading to the lower deck. To my right, against the pleas of various deckhands, a select few were fighting to gain access to their cabins. It was down that way that I saw the slightest sparkle of that honeybee dress, the powder blue beside her, and I knew well that Mrs. Harper would not be denied the opportunity to get her possessions at all costs. I thought to call out, to beckon them back, but I knew my words would go unheard, just as before; as it had always been. It felt like a dreadful mistake they'd made, but I could only watch them turn and wind down the bend of the ship, disappearing from view. A certain shame ran through me, but I was forced to tamp it down, to focus on my own survival, which was very much in question.

"Turlow?!" I called out instead. "Has anyone seen Amos Turlow?"

"I know Turlow," a deckhand said, a man no older than myself, his face sheeted in perspiration. "He went down to the rescue boats. You'd be wise to do the same."

The deckhands squeezed past me, heading toward the stairs themselves, calling for the others to make way. About twenty yards ahead, a man was lugging two trunks from his room, his wife screaming at his side. There were great blossoms of a foul scent, a putrid bitterness that had pried itself into my esophagus like a threat. The smoke was soon all around us. I could feel Oliver's heartbeat against the palm of my hand.

There was then a *click* underneath my feet, so slight yet so reverberant that it could have been either a scurrying cockroach or an earthquake, some undefined clamor that lasted barely for a moment's time. Only when it happened again did I feel any sense of terror. I thought I heard Oliver whimper, like an echo that coursed from his body into my own.

"Get one end," the man with the trunk said, giving commands over to his wife. "For the love of God, grab the back and move — "

It was in this instant that he disappeared. A blast so loud shattered any remaining calm in the night. A wall of flames ate the ground where the man had once been and devoured him whole. His wife, now stuck behind the lashing flames, called out desperately into the open maw leading down into what I gathered to be the boiler room.

Flames began to spread. I could only think of Mrs. Harper and Florence, still in their cabin without knowing what they would find when they returned this way.

There then was a steady cleaving, the sound of grinding metal, followed by the slightest pitch to the boat's disposition. I turned on my heels. Screams shot up from the bottom deck and men and women and children began to jump into the abyss with the plopping noise of stones cast into a pond. Gazing over the taffrail, one could see the two lifeboats of *The Jubilee* already being lowered amongst the mayhem, wobbling under the weight of their new passengers, filled to the brim with those lucky enough to have claimed a seat. It grew clear that those who were on the stairs, begging for access, would not find room aboard. No, they would find their end either in the ocean or stuck on this vessel. A choice I'd have to make myself.

To my back were bodies clamoring upon one another, to my front a great wall of spitfire. In my life I had been abused in all manner of ways, yet nothing compared to the sensation of pure molten heat — the deck slowly shuddering, splintering, as it devoured the walkway before me. Further explosions from the other side of the ship wailed on like great moans cast down by the gods.

"Florence?" My voice was a whimper, no different from when I called for my sister after a nightmare, when I wanted nothing more than for her to hold my head against her chest and sing a lullaby, stroke her hand through the part in my hair as I imagined a mother might. Anything but the darkness. "Mrs. Harper? Someone. Please."

I turned to the taffrail and looked at Oliver, wondering, for the first time, if he might survive the fall. His eyes were saucers, welled up with his trust in me, his innocence. My throat was so dry the words were nothing more than a peep. "I am sorry. I'm so sorry, Oliver."

I could not jump myself. The fear of the water, the fear of the height. But for Oliver...

That was when a man bellowed so loud the noise tore itself free from the endless screams of the other passengers. I clutched Oliver to my breast and turned to find Amos Turlow gaining ground before me. He snaked his way through the crowded gang at the stairs, demanding that they move aside, his shoulders wide as an ape's as he bowled ever on. There was an energy to men like this, a pulsation of their person, their need to survive, to accomplish a task, somehow so great that they seem to transcend the typical makeup of the rest of humanity. For that second in time, there was not a person I was happier to see before me. He extended his forearm, slick with sweat already,

"If you let go of my arm," he said, "I'll have you gagged and bound before we set foot in Mexico and will not cut you free until my job is finished."

I clamped my hand down upon his arm. We hurried forth as a wave beneath our feet, rippling the wood, caused those before us to slip, to fall, the boat seizing under its wounds. Turlow gripped the staircase railing, guiding us onward by sheer force. The heat followed us relentlessly. He nearly had me by the neck as we descended the stairs, stepping over others as I pleaded with him to slow down, to consider the interests of the less fortunate. He threw one body backward. He grabbed collars, shoved backsides.

I held onto Oliver so tightly that I know, in that second, he feared me as much as he feared what was transpiring, yet I could not let him fall from my hands. The steerage deck was chaos, each step a gallery of horrors. With a squint I could eye a woman covered in grime cowering beside a child whimpering for his mother. Two men fought to gain purchase on a life belt as they both attempted to pull it over their own bodies, neither having any success due to the other. A corpse on the ground was of an improbably dark hue, arms charred crisps, its thighs creased with embers like a burnt log just extinguished. I coughed incessantly, covering Oliver's eyes as though this might save him from whatever befell us, yet Turlow's composure was everlasting.

At that moment we were at the rear end of the ship, exactly where I had slept the previous nights beside the livestock. The horse, my companion for so many nights, was absolutely terrified, neighing, drawing upon its rear legs, its bared teeth lumined against the starlit sky.

"We've missed the lowering of the boats. We must reach the bow now," Turlow said.

"All that way?" I said. "It's not possible. There are too many bodies. Even you cannot get us through."

Turlow cracked his neck with his palm as though it were the affirmation of a decision. He then turned back toward the horse's pen—unclasped it with one quick motion. A matchbox appeared from his vest. He opened the gate and eased the animal out with a coo, a tone I had never heard escape his mouth. When the horse calmed, for one single moment, the match was lit; he put it to the beast's tail and I watched it grow, lost first to confusion, then madness. The animal thrashed about in place, bucking with bellows of terror. Turlow delivered a kick to its backside, whereupon a magnitude of hysteria descended upon the deck that topped all that had come before.

The tail of the horse, like a lantern brandished against the night, whipped and bobbed as the poor creature stampeded down the railway. An iron wall would not have stopped it. Bodies of men and women were trampled, others jumped into the water before the chance of collision took place. Fragments of crushed human littered the floor and walls of the boat and I was speechless, numb to the violence, as Turlow had us follow in the animal's wake of destruction.

A path had been cleared. He shoved me this way and that, screamed invective and commands, and soon the madness was at our rear, and before us nothing more. We were at the bow of the ship.

Peering over, one could finally spot the endless sea, that terrible expression of infinitude. Bodies, writhing or limp, littered the water, and it was all I could do to avert my gaze, to try not to gawk as I thought of myself meeting such a demise. There was a momentous shuddering. My feet glided. I realized, for perhaps the first time, that the ship was sinking right before us, taking on a lean that it might never recover from, slowly shuttling us to the water without our needing to do anything at all but wait.

"This is it, then," I said. "Turlow. I do not know you well. You do scare me. But I wish to thank you—"

Turlow placed two fingers in his mouth and let out a high-pitched whistle. Seconds later, another repeated back to us from the water.

"There he is. That is our rescue boat. That is the captain."

The relief in his voice was almost jarring. Turlow took what might have been his first breath since he retrieved me.

"I saw the lifeboats," I protested. "There was no room—"

"They'll make room. Now I need you to jump," he said.

I stuttered. The fear was so resolute I felt myself to be a stone there, some figurehead built into the bow to warn coming ships of our passing.

"I...I do not know how to swim."

My gaze fell on him pathetically, as a boy might eye his disappointed father. Turlow leaned down, his breath hot, his height somehow double my own.

"Take my hand. Dip over the rail. I will drop you in calmly. Twelve feet at most. *Twelve feet.* Your legs will bear the impact. You might be sore, but you'll survive."

"And Oliver?" I asked.

"Hand him over. I'll jump next. I will cradle him like a loaf of bread and we will all glide to that boat there. This is nothing. Trust me, now."

He held my shoulders. He forced my posture straight. He tilted my head up, so high that I could see not the ocean, but only the smoke that swirled before us, polluting the perfect night sky, a pall over the stars and the moon. He took Oliver from my hands.

"You will be just fine," I told the dog, which I thought to be an errant lie. Really, I was certain our doom had been sealed. I would be witness to his death. The very cause, perhaps.

I took Turlow's hand and hopped over, crying out as I was struck by the utter airlessness between myself and the ocean floor. I was suspended there for a brief pause then Turlow, without warning, let go of my hand.

The water flooded my nose, my throat, and I was plunged into a coldness I could hardly fathom. I opened my eyes to a looming nothingness, as though death had already found me. I was absolutely stunned, the chill a vibration that held my body in place, unwavering in its grip. I willed something deep within myself, some last sliver of energy, of courage, and swam to the surface. There, amidst the carnage, lay in focus a sight that countered the terror of the sinking ship, filling me with what little relief I might claim from the night: Turlow on his back, slowly and gracefully swimming toward the rescue boat, with Oliver paddling beside him. The little dog had his head thrust skyward, struggling to make way yet managing all the same.

I mimicked Oliver. Yes, I began to paddle in the manner he did, one hand slapping the water in front of the other, following Turlow all along, amazed by my ability. It was not swimming, precisely, but I refuse to let any sense of modesty suppress my satisfaction with the attempt I made, my great success in getting myself to safety. A hand reached down for my own, hauling me into the boat and placing me on a seat beside a deckhand as drenched as I was.

As Turlow toppled in himself — Oliver in hand — the result of the night, my safety being secured, dawned on me like a miracle. Horrors continued around me — I turned back to see the smokestack lowing, whining, toppling into the upper deck with a howl; the endless pleas of passengers grew distant but still layered themselves over the quiet of the night in recurrent waves, awful echoes we all wished would cease; one man attempted to board the boat only to be prodded with an oar by the captain, who said there was no more space to give — and yet, with all this taking place, I could only tremble with the joy of my own survival. I felt embarrassed yet ecstatic, and when Turlow handed Oliver to me I put my face to his own, shivering along with the dog as I petted him anxiously, warming him, warming my hands, both of us seeking solace in the other.

With a few deep breaths, I finally surveyed my surroundings. It occurred to me that the boat was filled, almost exclusively, with those who serviced *The Jubilee*: the captain and his second-in-command; a number of officers; the coal shovelers now had oars and were hard at work rowing with shipmates; even those young men who had served in the ballroom. My gaze wandered down the side of the boat to find Mrs. Harper's servant girl doubled over, consoling another, rubbing a hand that lay in her lap.

Only when she leant back did I see the blue dress, the red hair, the plump face and severe eyes. I had never been more relieved to see her.

"Florence!" I cried out. "My God!"

A lurching quiet crept over the vessel. Whatever had defined their conversations — the bravado of young men having survived, those last whimpers of excitement that coursed through them all — I had punctured it with one declaration of my spontaneous happiness. I went to stand, but before I could, Florence did so herself, patiently finding her balance, marching down the boat in my direction.

"I'm so glad you're safe," I said. "Tell me what happened. I must know. I thought... well I was so sure that... and what of Muriel? Did your mother survive?"

Her dress was so wet that it hung limp about her like a wilted flower. Her hair dripped upon my lap, her teeth were chattering, as were my own, and neither of us seemed able to speak. She sank to her knees, as there was no space to sit. She put her head on my thigh, beside Oliver, and wept.

The eeriness of the silence surrounding us, the great racking of her cries, was a scene that took the boat hostage. I could not recall the last time she had let me see her in such a state. Not since we were children. We should not have been touching, and everyone present knew this, but there was no means to stop her. So I simply held her head. I let her grieve.

"Mother is dead," she said, over and over, no matter how many times I pleaded with her to recognize that I understood. That it would be okay. "She went in to get her belongings and she did not return. I barely made it myself. I had to leave her. I had no choice. You must believe me, Coleman. Tell me you believe me."

For the first time in a long time, I had no words to express myself. I had witnessed catastrophe on the human scale before but never with such an exaggerated magnitude, never stripped so bare to its raw form. I glanced at Turlow, could see that he was now whispering in conversation with the captain, worry on the brows of both men.

I peered down the row of survivors, all of them staring at us, and soon landed on the boy from the boiler room, who was sitting right before Turlow. He was eyeing me without even a trace of expression. His gaze went from Florence to me and back again. There was no malice, no warmth, but almost an acknowledgment of a fact previously unknown made clear — that this was one, just one, glimpse of the great universe of horrors that had rendered him mute. I wanted to find a modicum of relief, yet it was as though he was telling me this was just the beginning. That there would be more to come.

And then my eyes went to where he had propped up his legs. Beneath his seat, jutting out from the stem of the boat ever so barely, was an object so familiar that I felt my chest cave in, my heart race, my entire body fall prey to a pressure I could not dispel. I'd carried that very trunk onto *The Jubilee*.

"Florence, tell me, did you manage to retrieve any of your mother's luggage?" I whispered.

"Not a thing. The room was in total disarray from the boat jostling about. I could not make sense of what was where, and told my mother as much. To leave it all, for there was no way to take anything in such a state of chaos. But she wouldn't listen."

I went quiet, and so the boat plunged into total stillness once more, having made it so far from *The Jubilee* that we could no longer hear its howling, the capsized behemoth already a mark in the distance, a spasm of red-glow flickering at our backs. All that came to our ears now was the lapping of the oars.

And there was Turlow, perched upon the lip of the boat, staring at me just as the boy had. His face had within it an element captured from my memory, something familiar that I had somehow displaced. It took me a spell, and then came to me in a flood: the same expression I recognized from Mr. Harper after he'd delivered a beating, or following a drunken spat, when the anger dissipated and the liquor wore off; when the fog retreated from the shores of his mind and the world settled about him. He would sit there, expressionless, and look not at you but *beneath* you, his features soft like a child recovered from a tantrum. Before me was a man reckoning with a truth he did not wish to face.

Florence's eyes fell on the trunk then. "How—" she began, and yet at the sight, even Florence could find no further words to spare.

June:
Part Two, Mexico, 1864

Alfred Highsmith had led them to an outpost of civilization that sat at the floor of an enormous range of mountains, the Sierra Madres, that according to Wyatt cut through the States and split Mexico right down the middle as well; for all June knew, it carried on in all its brawn elsewhere, reaching on toward the end of the world. There was endless work to be done to ensure their own survival, namely the pitching of tents, the preparation of food for those first few nights, an establishment of a perimeter to keep watch, and yet before it all, the bodies of those whose lives had been taken would need to be buried.

Shovels were produced and passed about to each able person, and already they were digging graves for the dead. The botanist was amongst them, as was the preacher, alongside the others who had fallen victim to the soldiers' attack or succumbed to their injuries in the two days that had passed since then.

June was given no voice in the matter, nor even a shovel to be of assistance. Wyatt, rather, returned to her with a command from Highsmith himself. She was to join another fellow, Newton, alongside Celia, to retrieve water from the lake.

"Just up the way," Wyatt said, his voice unusually reserved under the circumstances, the sound of dirt being shoveled at his back like the sound of shallow breaths emerging from the earth itself. "Do not dawdle, now. And follow his every instruction."

Newton Baynard had a large wagon, but its cover had been whipped to shreds by a dust storm. The man himself was smaller than even she was, prone to outbursts after long stretches of silence, and she was struck by their detail, his incisive commentary on his father who had guffawed at the thought of this journey; his wife who failed to show her gratitude toward him, and a son who spoke out of turn at the most displeasing of times. (He had an enormous volume of commentary on the cost of equipment that his father had failed to bargain down to a fair price.) But then Baynard would go quiet again, his thoughts bubbling to another boil, and June would nod at Celia after a long stretch — guessing, in something of a game, when he would erupt once more with another remark to pacify his wounded soul.

But for all his odd habits, one important asset of Baynard's was that he'd been to this place before, had taken the journey, and knew the way to this lake. And sometimes when June nodded to Celia behind the man's back, sensing another tirade aimed at God knew what, he would rather offer a courteous nod, and mumble a few words, instructing them on how close they were, as evidenced by the thick stand of shrubs that had suddenly appeared, the loam of the desert floor growing a shade darker, yes, and finally the sight itself of the tarn before them shimmering bright, rippled by the occasional gust of wind that seemed to carry down the mountainside.

"The barrels," he said, thinking nothing of the sight, and wishing to waste no time. "Let's get them filled. The people are thirsty. To say nothing of the oxen."

They took to the cause with a surprising verve. There was, if anything, a bit of tranquility to their task, the water rising to June's knees as she entered it, cold but then warm; the process of watching the barrel slowly fill up and grow heavy; tamping down the lid and then rolling it back to the wagon. Each did their part with no complaints, just quiet occasionally pierced by Baynard's groaned protestations of his life that, once spoken, brought him peace once more.

June took her time with the barrels, tipping each one slowly toward the water as though to move too quickly might spell ruin — send the thing floating off. Slowly she would step further along, water reaching her ankles, her thighs, until the barrel was full, and she would turn back, pulling it along with the same straps that had fastened it to the wagon.

There was something sublime in the barrel gulping at the water, replenished as it were, and it made June feel whole herself, however crazy that sounded. And it was this feeling which she ached after: that redemptive sensation that even with so much spilled from her soul it might be refreshed with only the steady hand of a greater power. (Any power, to be certain, for her own was weak, and yet she'd managed to come this far, to survive this long; reach this lake and do this task by her own hand to serve the others who were thirsty, sick, impoverished. Undeserving people, many of them, but she would attend to them all the same.)

So much she wished to have returned to her person, salvaged parts long lost to her, forgotten fragments of memories and feelings that she might fold back into her being if she had the capacity to do so. Some things she felt fortunate to recall at all.

Coleman, she learned in time, had almost no memory of their mother to speak of, almost as if the past was a place beyond his reach, or one he did not wish to frequent and had consequently forgotten; the pain of that time too much to hold on to. But June remembered her well, even though that woman, Charity, did not treat her like a daughter but more like her own help, perhaps knowing, from the beginning, that they would not long be twined.

Promised elsewhere were the words their mother used. *You promised to another* were some more. She kept that promise, too, even as June prayed each night, each morning, long into adulthood, for a different one, one of comfort, safety, an assurance that all would be well. What she would give for the past to be swept up as an illusion, something rectifiable, mended like a garment in need of fixing and made right again!

Even then she could recollect her mother nursing Coleman, sitting on a step of what must have been a cabin, their home; her hair parted down the middle with two small curls like arched fingers bowing down the center of her head toward her little brother. Her mother's head concentrated on her infant son with what June took for love; only for the woman to poke her head up in frustration at the boy's refusal to latch on — complaining to whoever might hear that he was going to disrupt the whole damn run of her day if he kept causing a fuss.

Coleman would be fussy for the rest of his days, June thought, smiling at her reflection in the water of the lake. But Charity would never know as much, and what June could recall of her, beyond that one window on the past, was dispersed in bits and pieces, torn away by her own memory's stubborn refusal to recollect all that had been lost to time. Grabbing at the woman's dress, yes, she recalled that. The woman's gaze on her when she returned from their master's home, pointing at her as she played with the boys, being instructed to return back inside, where they would sit, quietly, her mother's eyes closing as June peppered her with questions, wishes, demands. June would often wonder what went on in that big house where her mother spent her days. But now she knew. For she would relive it herself, only a few years on...

Memories, questions, the endless chatter in the back of her mind that kept her connected to the past. It frightened June to think of what she might be losing now — memories of her brother, those small portions of the past that kept her spirit fed, that seemed, every day, to grow more distant in the past.

A whistle dragged June from her thoughts, and she turned to see Celia, her eyes filled with an odd light. She was whistling a tune as she filled her own barrel, lost, it seemed to June, in a world far from the one she inhabited herself. The barrel was long full. June seized one end, letting it float, reveal itself as they got nearer to shore, growing heavier before she picked it up and started to carry it with both hands.

Baynard was standing before his wagon, a few barrels already filled and lashed to its side. His hands were on his hips and the legs of his pants dripped water into a puddle that collected around him.

"They'll all take this for granted," he said, more at her than to her. "Folks always *expect* water, for it is a necessity, but we will know better. The toil it took."

June only told him it was little work for what was gained.

"You say all that now," Baynard muttered. "But this ain't hardly enough for the oxen. We'll be back in an hour. Two more trips today, I'd suppose. Let's see how you're faring by the time the sun goes down."

On their final visit to the lake, two days on, Newton had lost all will for careless chatter. He had sunk into his fatigue and June was made so uncomfortable by his silence that she nearly started to speak about the oxen's health, Baynard's unbuilt water pump, anything just to fill the void between them. Celia had been called to a burial for a woman who'd passed with a fever that would not break for anything less than death itself.

"Should we get a third?" June had asked, fending off the sun with the back of her hand as they loaded barrels into the wagon.

But Baynard seemed not to care for the idea, appeared to think they'd established a skill that another might take some time to pick up on, as though it required anything but a willingness to get wet and lift a hunk of wood. June, as always, dismissed her own opinion and remained quiet.

It was after they'd filled the barrels one last time and already started their journey home that the wagon hissed and snapped, the carriage nearly collapsing on its side, and Baynard immediately began to swear to the high heavens as the horses halted and the evening seemed much darker and the desert much vaster than June had ever considered it before that very moment.

He jumped from his seat and inspected the wagon, but June knew, already, just as well as he did, what had most certainly occurred.

"It's the front wheel," Baynard said. "I don't even see what we struck. For all I know it was no more than a damn pebble."

Suddenly the wagon felt much like a coffin. A heavy weight born from the shadows encroached upon June on all sides, some unseen force of evil, one that wished to see her sent from the wagon altogether and wanted only to watch her run toward the horizon where the endless maw of the wild might go right on ahead and devour her whole.

A memory, one she wished to discard, came to mind then. She and Coleman were on the cusp of being gifted away. Their mother was more absent than ever, and they would wait for her arrival at night, sleeping in their only bed beside one another, eyes on the window, and when finally she returned home, Charity would have them get on the floor, beside one another, with no bed, no cover, only each other for warmth. There was something undefinably wrong with the woman, in her distance, her chilled demeanor, the wish to ignore her and Coleman altogether; the ache, June assumed, of knowing they would soon be gone.

And on quiet Sundays at rest, when Charity remained home, any knock on the door, any unknown movement outside, would cause her to command that they go lie under the bed, shielding them from any unwanted contact with the world, the other slaves with their requests, asking for aid in such causes she wanted nothing to do with, or occasionally a demand from the big house (which she would close the door to receive). Never did their mother offer an explanation for why they needed to hide other than that there was a lurking danger, one that might pounce upon them, that they were not to meet. So June and Coleman would hold hands, and the unsayable — whatever loitered outside the front door — lay in the chasm between them and their mother. This approaching specter would be the agent that would separate them all forever, June was sure. And it felt as though their hiding might confuse the monster, real or not, that would at some moment grab them by their shirt collars, force them into a wagon, and send them to their new homes.

That was when June would feel the suffocation of that small, dank space. The cold floor sending shivers down her spine and the splintered wood of the bed's frame catching her hair. Coleman's jagged breathing as his own fear took over and really she could not judge him for dislodging these memories from his mind forever, and she envied him for having the capacity to do so at all.

Instead she was left with those moments of utter terror, the sight of her mother's bare feet as she wandered toward the door; then, the door swinging open to reveal a cold world gauzed in a morning mist that seemed to beckon her and her brother to a great beyond she wished, more than anything, never to encounter. The pulsing of her heart in those brief periods was no different from how she felt in the wagon and it was why, what could have been a few minutes later, or many hours later, that the sight of a pair of horses approaching before Baynard's oxen felt like a fever dream, some awful engagement with the same men who had, inevitably, come to pry her and Coleman from their mother and deliver them into the hands of Wyatt Harper.

"Mr. Baynard," she said. "There's some horses coming down the way."

"Horses?"

He had not spoken in some time, and she realized that whatever had made the man pleasant enough company would make him unhelpful in this coming encounter: for Newton Baynard was entirely harmless. Whoever might approach on a horse, like this, out here, would think him not only a nonthreat, but someone to quickly dispatch. Not that she was any better. She would be sent from this earth faster than he was.

Which was what she prepared for as the two horses slowed, as fate cast its sights upon her. Yet it would be her great lot that she'd be ruled worthy of reprieve. It was, of all people, that Negro she had met before; Isaac, who now appeared before her as though assembled from the shadows alongside another man on his own horse, both of them slowing down at the sight of the broken-down wagon, heads cocked at the sorry look of the oxen and perhaps even June herself. Isaac no longer wore his turban, and that tussock of hair of his stood high on his head. He'd replaced his strange raiment for those of a cowboy — a blue denim shirt and white suspenders and riding gloves that trailed down to his forearms.

Her heart leapt from her chest as she heard Mr. Baynard at her back, digging within the chuck box for what she knew was his shotgun, but already as he closed the box had the two men pulled pistols from their holsters, pointing them at Baynard before the poor man could even get his loaded.

"Slow down there," Isaac said. "No need to point no guns. We're all friends out here. Ain't that right?"

He was looking not at Baynard but June, and in the proceeding silence she thought to answer, to tell him *Yes, of course they were friends, certainly not enemies,* but by then Baynard had swallowed his fear, aimed his shotgun at the ground, and nodded solemnly in agreement with Isaac.

"If you say so," he said. "I reckon we are."

"That's good," Isaac said. "I'm Isaac," he told Mr. Baynard. "This here is my cousin Titus."

"Hiya," Titus said.

It appeared Baynard had no recollection of Isaac, or did not mention any, but he was happy to relay his troubles with the wagon, the broken spoke, and Isaac listened as he ran his hand along the rim of his hat, nodding along to the story while his cousin remained silent.

Isaac gave a shrill whistle of sympathy. "Bum wheel's the last thing you want to have out here," he said.

"Well what of you two?" June said, her own voice surprising her. "What brings y'all out here at this hour?"

Isaac grinned. Titus only averted his eyes to the ground.

"We ain't far from where we stay at," he said. "We just had some business out here and saw a little show of life in the distance. Found you two. I'd say you're lucky we did."

"So y'all know how to fix a wagon spoke, then?"

"I didn't say that much," Isaac told her. "But we can at least get you back to your people."

For the first time, Titus's eyes were alight—surprised, or perhaps confused, by Isaac's show of goodwill. The man was weary, June realized. They must have been nearly home, and now, for all they'd done today, whatever show of energy went into that business of theirs was about to be made that much more arduous by an added leg. She could not help wondering if Isaac was paying her the favor, or Baynard, or if he'd volunteer it to any harmless wanderer he might have found out in these parts.

"If you can get me back, I can return with the tools to have this fixed and be on my way. It isn't far, we've camped down—"

"We know where y'all have camped down. Right south of here, no?"

Another pregnant pause, and lost within it June sensed from Mr. Baynard a chill of discomfort—that these men knew more than they might ever let on; were one with their environs in a way he, and the others who had settled here, might never fathom.

"What I mean," Isaac said, "is we saw y'all on the other side of the river. You told us where you'd be set up. It's no big mystery, is it?"

This was enough for Baynard, who was now leaning on his shotgun, his other hand on the side of the wagon, and he seemed more than pleased with this development, as it seemed clear to all present that no better terms would be provided and these men, at the very least, could bring them home.

Baynard shifted, standing at attention, held up by a new thought, a plan, that he seemed keen on sharing.

"Why don't we do this: One of you stay here with the girl, guard the supplies, and I will go back with the other and fetch us some help. It won't be long, I figure. An hour at most, and we'll make haste."

Already June was moving to embark back upon the wagon, to wait this out with the oxen, whomever might stay back beside her, Isaac or his cousin, but she felt herself freeze when a single word shot out from Isaac's mouth.

"No," he said, and with a bluntness that struck June with a shock. Never in her life would she have come back with so curt a reply to a man in charge, even Baynard, and she wondered for a moment what he might do with being so quickly rebuffed before realizing they were at the whims of Isaac, in this man's own domain, and Baynard would have to take whatever reply was on offer.

"No?" Baynard said, curious as to how to proceed.

"The girl," Isaac said. "I don't think it right to leave her out here. How's 'bout I take her back. You stand pat with Titus, here. Y'all will manage on your own for a time."

To his credit, Baynard did not take this harshly, nor was he flummoxed. He merely set his shotgun down in the chuck box, stared up ahead and nodded politely, although June knew what dark, angry thoughts lay behind those pinched brows of his, the long trail of complaints that would float off from Baynard's mind like smoke from a chimney, an endless tirade on the disrespect showed him not just by the world but by all its inhabitants, even those as low as he thought this stranger on a horse. And yet that was for him to keep to himself now, perhaps to hand off to his wife when he returned home, or relay to the other men who would roll their eyes, dismiss old Baynard, the doddering codger who never, by his own estimation, got his due.

June felt for Baynard, not just this day, but on the many trips they would take over the next six months to the lake, for this would be her duty for a time, and she'd learn to reconcile with that fact, and be thankful it was he, and no one worse, that she was forced to spend that time with; but she was *grateful* for a man like Isaac, and savored the benefaction he'd allowed her by saving her from this broken-down wagon and the endless hours she'd spent on it. She could brave the lake another day — but it was time for this one to be over.

"Go on, then," Baynard muttered to her, but she did not need his assurance. Without giving him another look she went in Isaac's direction, approaching his horse awkwardly, unsure how to manage so large a beast, one that had no familiarity with her, was liable to shy and buck from her faster than she could take a step backward.

A lovely creature, that horse: coat black as the night but with white spots that gleamed in the dark like puddles of bright radiance. The mare's eyes were on June aslant, and it breathed slowly, as though it knew a ride was upon her, and best to preserve her energy for what lay ahead.

"You won't start her," Isaac said. "She's a calm girl."

She thought Isaac might get down, help her up, but he only furnished her a hand, sheathed in a buckskin glove, and she eyed it suspiciously, knowing this would not be enough to get her even halfway up to him. But she did not see Titus behind her back.

"Ready?" said Titus, but already he had a hand on each of her hips and she felt a rush, as she got out a quiet *Yes* in agreement, as her own hand fell into Isaac's, and as her foot found purchase on a stirrup. With the work of all three of them she was, suddenly, stationed at Isaac's back.

"You said you know the way, right?"

"Well enough," he said.

It felt as though Isaac took it as a provocation, for in hardly a moment, with a tip of his hat toward his cousin, they blazed a trail through the countryside with such speed that June could hardly catch her breath. At first she felt terror and gripped so hard on Isaac's vest that her fingernails nearly pierced the hide. But he gave her hand a steadfast pat with his own, as if to reassure her, and then they were off at an even faster pace.

The horse's clopping gallop was an endless barrage in her ear; the jostling nearly bucked her off her seat; the wind sent her cheeks aflutter. But after a time, when they slowed ever so slightly, she began to deduce the small pleasures of the ride. She felt untouchable, soaring above the flat eternal forever that was the desert — and the mysteries of the place no longer terrified her but rather left her in awe.

They treaded in obedience to no laws, no rules or instructions of another, and never had she felt so free as she did holding that man's haunches, upon the back of that horse, barreling toward the campground fires that stood in jagged relief against the darkness blanketing the night's sky. *What if we just kept on?* June thought. *Beyond the fires themselves, plunged back into darkness, awaiting whatever lies next on the journey until daylight returns and the world regains its order?*

It did not sound like a bad plan to June, but by the time the thought had passed they were already coming to a halt, the reins tight in Isaac's hand, the people of the camp — those men and women all too familiar to June — standing at attention at the approaching stranger.

"Apologies for the pace," Isaac said. "But I must say I'm not too comfortable leaving them out there all by their lonesome. At this hour, vulnerable like that…"

"It wasn't safe?" June asked.

"Not enough to leave you there."

She could do nothing but smile at this, her head mere inches from the man's back, hands still on his sides.

"I told you I'd see you again," he said, recalling that first meeting of theirs, one that felt so long ago. "And here I am. Just as promised."

"I don't know if this counts, though," she said. "Saving me and all is nice, but it don't make up for a proper conversation."

"Well, we might have to table that until we find a moment of peace and quiet out here."

She could only laugh to herself.

"When," she asked, "might there ever be peace and quiet in a place like this?"

But there was no time for Isaac to reply, and whatever lightness had been kindled between them peeled away into the wind as they readied to meet the others.

Already they were yelling imprecations as they dismounted, Isaac calling them down to a settled but still brewing fervor. Wyatt and Highsmith stepped forward, Wyatt putting a hand on June's shoulder as though to protect her from further harm. Highsmith, meanwhile, stepped up to Isaac, and with the same authority he had showed Newton Baynard, Isaac explained to them the situation and the steps he'd taken to rectify it.

"Have you been harmed?" Wyatt asked her.

She dusted off her dress, and by doing so removed Wyatt's hand from her shoulder.

"I'm just fine," she said. "Worried about Mr. Baynard, is all."

"We'll get Newton taken care of," Highsmith said. "Thank you…" Highsmith eyed Isaac up and down, considering, for a moment, if he should continue to pursue a compliment paid to an individual so foreign to himself. Finally he settled on "...my good man."

"It's no trouble at all. Now once you get a party readied, I will bring you right back to Mr. Baynard. But best we make haste."

June's eyes landed on Isaac's, and with nothing more than a glance, she felt a surfacing, within her chest, of that same sense of excitement she'd felt holding on to his waist; and all at once she recognized that this man, still staring back at her, must have felt something thrilling himself, whether or not it was from the ride or perhaps her presence, and either way, this agreement they shared — one that had been unsaid but entirely felt — roused her into speaking. She felt, with unabated certainty, that their time together should not end. Was equally certain he felt the same way.

Already they were collecting their equipment, harnessing the horses.

Her eyes were still on Isaac's, though, that feeling between them still a blossomed, ever-present thing, and she could understand why Wyatt stepped between them; wrung her wrist with his hand, squeezing till her hand was numb as he led her back to their tent.

"You rest," he instructed her. "Leave that to the others. Mr. Baynard will be just fine."

For a moment, seeing the tent before them, the darkness of its insides, she felt a pang of loss — a trampling over her heart. But she knew, somewhere in that loss, that something special had been gained. That feeling on the back of that horse. A feeling, she was certain, she'd relive once more, no matter the cost; and a memory, unlike so many others, she would strive not to forget.

5

It did not take long for the bodies to wash ashore. The scene reminded me of wartime in Baton Rouge. I recalled those early mornings when quiet usually reigned and I would hear a faint wail at first, like that of an injured mule, carrying toward town. Once I was chopping wood in the front yard just so, and June came out to listen as the noise drew closer — it grew in depth, in tone, developing into that of those injured men, all of them having wandered from battle toward safety. Soon they were upon us, beaten and battered, hobbling down the lane, headed for the field hospital with looks of anguish, knowing there was so little to hope for there. Their bodies, alive but less than whole, were reduced to no more than their torment. In time it would be an endless stream of them. Homes taken over by the injured, the diseased, the moans a steady thing, a song suspended, drawn out, long into the night. It became our duty to listen, to watch, to endure; to witness.

As it was for me, now. I could only watch on, and soon all I could think about was what had transpired since the previous night. Immediately upon landing in Mexico, Florence had assaulted Amos Turlow with a viciousness I had never seen lashed upon a man in all my years. She accused him of having stolen her mother's possessions, letting the woman die, and failing her father who had hired him in the first place. Turlow, with his usual deficit of any emotion at all, claimed that she was understandably feeble after such a harrowing experience. He then gave her Mrs. Harper's trunk without a second thought. It was his alibi, really, that he took the trunk only when he'd gone to fetch Mrs. Harper himself and found nothing but her possessions. He thought it the kindest thing to do. Not noting that the other passengers' trunks had been stowed away in the rescue boats as well, five in all, goods I'd seen the captain and his men squirrel away into town without a second thought. All of them stolen; all but Mrs. Harper's. Florence would not allow it.

"I'm going to look for my mother," Florence had told me when we made it to land. There was a familiar anger to her, one I knew well when she was overtaken by a certain darkness, and there, shivering with grief, it was all too understandable. "I want you here. Eyes on that trunk. Do not let that man even put a hand on it, do you understand? It's all we have."

"Of course," I told her, although I was as frazzled by the preceding events as anyone, and assented only to relieve her of a bit of anxiety. Nonetheless, there I was, seated upon the trunk with Oliver at my side. From my perch, the town of Bagdad appeared to be surprisingly colorful. The streets were as wide as anyone might find in New Orleans. Stores were filled even at this early hour and I assumed that such a place of trade, positioned on the coast, had lured many to it in the very manner that had drawn Mr. Harper to Mexico himself.

I could spy Florence a good fifty feet down the way, holding her skirt up from the sand and rocks, still searching for any sign of her mother. Turlow was speaking with the captain once more, who seemed to be in great distress, French soldiers circling about them both. No one watched over me. I was beholden to not a single soul. And for the first time in a long time, I felt the urge to do my own bidding, if only so I might find distraction from the terrible night that had come to pass. I could not be still like when I'd seen those injured men in Baton Rouge. No. I felt the need to shake free from the torment.

"Oliver," I said. "Why don't we go into town? Just for a moment."

My desires were manifold. I wished to reach my sister, but I did not want to do so with the aid of Turlow, who I knew to be deceitful, if not also involved in Mrs. Harper's death. I would also need to reckon with Florence. However corrosive an element she might be, there was not a possibility I would let her wander the Mexican shores alone, abandoned by the only acquaintance she had following the loss of her mother. Still, I was done sitting idly by heeding her endless instructions, and the draw of a small walk, for my own comfort, felt rather earned. I beckoned Oliver and let him into my arms. I stood up from the trunk; and then I simply left.

I had no change of clothes, smelled like a farm animal, and drew glances from nearly every man and woman who passed me. A gang of mongrel dogs scampered by, yapping at Oliver, but I paid them no mind, and had Oliver do the same. A bespectacled man in fine clothing glared down at me from his balcony — and those balconies were endless, all of them crammed with lounging men speaking loudly in a language I knew not a word of, and as if upon hearing them, and sensing the need to communicate, to find my place in this alien world, I began to yell myself at the people around me.

"English?" I exclaimed to no one in particular. "English? Might any of you speak English?"

A woman shawled in black, her face seamed and leathered by wear, grimaced at my every word as she passed; a young boy pointed me out to his mother as some curiosity before she forced his finger down in a display of politeness. Each storefront was shaded by a white canopy, and before the stores were more vendors, sitting on the ground, many of them under their own forms of shade — what looked like oversize paint easels, tripods holding a wooden plank that guarded the individual underneath it from the looming sun. I could see what was being sold but not the person, and I had the sense that no one in my vicinity recognized anything before them except some strange jester with his dog, both best ignored.

There was one name I knew that might help me. A man Turlow had mentioned as a guide, a man privy to the desert, who went by the name of

William Free; Turlow had told the captain while we were docking that this was the individual who would be guiding us through the desert. He was a former scout in many wars, a man who had mastered almost every language spoken in this part of the world and was skilled in every weapon he might have need to handle. It sounded like a man who might help me, if only I could get before him and share my piece. So it was that I called that man's name too, asking if anyone knew the way to him.

"William!" I called to all who might listen. "Does anyone know the way to a William Free?"

This felt to be a useless undertaking until a voice landed on me, slipped under the growing burbles of the vendors and their customers; it was in English, a single word, one so familiar to me that it brought me back to America, back to Louisiana, a comfort and a curse all the same.

"Boy," the man said.

Then, the following: "A long way from home, aren't you?"

He was in a chair before a white-stone building, an iron gate keeping its insides a mystery. A white man. His features were flat, eyes wide set like those of a fish.

"I'd say the same of you, sir," I said, giving a nod of my head, "as we both look a bit out of place."

He squinted, his eyelids as pale as the wall behind him. "You came in on that boat," he said, both question and statement. I informed him that I had. That I was hoping, perhaps, to be pointed in a particular direction if possible.

"What direction would that be?"

"I need to know the way north. I believe my sister to be kept near the border, and I must find her, as we've been separated for a number of years. Perhaps you know the fellow I mentioned. William Free?"

"Dangerous up at the border," was all this man said in return.

"I have been attracting danger since I set foot out of Louisiana," I told him, "so I am willing to take on the risk."

"No dangers like these." His features were suddenly bright. "See, you got the Indians. Each tribe its own kind of savage. They'll gut you, sharpen your teeth for arrowheads, and use your scalp to line the soles of their moccasins. You got the Mexican soldiers, some of them in cahoots with the Indians, some not, but they'll put chains on you like any well-bred white man might have back wherever you came from."

His voice now neared a whisper.

"Do not even mention the French. Juaristas still fighting them out of these parts. I've seen a few of those men more savage than any Indian, believe me."

"I know many Frenchmen," I said, "having lived in New Orleans, and I assure you they're very civil people."

"These aren't American Frenchmen. These ones are from *France*."

I informed him that as far as I knew, many of the French I'd encountered in Louisiana were originally from France themselves, and yet the fact seemed only to sow more suspicion. He sat back in his chair and crossed his arms. I had, apparently, offended him.

"If you can't grasp the difference between a Frenchman and a Frenchman, then I imagine you won't be offended when I say I don't see the difference between a well-dressed, sharp-tongued servant boy and a nigger born in a mud hut out in Africa. All's the same to a man like you, isn't it?"

How smug he appeared when offering a point. I was used to quieting myself in the face of such ignorance, but this man's reasoning was so outrageous that I found it impossible to leave things be. Yet as I readied to respond I heard a familiar sound: the voice of Florence Harper, growing louder. It immediately put the conversation to rest.

"To steal my mother's possessions!" she was saying. "To load them into your boat moments before she returned to her cabin to fetch them! To allow her to *die*!"

How peculiar it was to see her here, muddied but still bright in her blue evening wear, pale cheeks swollen with grief, as though the tears she'd shed all morning had been absorbed and collected there.

At my chest, a hand fell upon Oliver's chin, rough, calloused, but rather gentle: the hand of Amos Turlow. He stepped up to the walkway, readied a cigarette.

"You two have met."

"You know this man?" I asked.

"My brother Cyrus," Amos said, jabbing his cigarette in the man's direction before setting it between his lips.

"Look at you, Coleman, standing there, lost in thought as always," Florence said. "Why on *earth* did you wander off?"

"I was seeking help."

"So you find the criminal's *brother*?"

"Take this trunk," Amos said to Cyrus. He then pried open the gate before the door, the darkness within as foreboding as the darkness of the ocean the previous night.

"Both of you," he said, nodding to us. "In."

I put a hand before Florence and stepped back, and when Cyrus moved forward, I placed my foot upon the trunk itself.

"To think we would follow you," I said.

"I'll remind you that Mr. Harper has made me your guardian," Amos said. "It would be wise to follow his command."

Cyrus, his rattish eyes dim with hate, bristled at my disobedience. But I'd already caught sight of his deference to his brother; the way his back went stiff with excitement when Amos had arrived, the sudden contentedness that flicked upon the corners of his lips at the sight of him. I figured Amos the older of the two. Cyrus would do nothing without his permission. I would make my stand here.

"What has doing that earned us other than my mother's death?" Florence asked.

"On this point, I must agree with Florence," I said before addressing Amos once more. "We deserve the truth from you."

I could see that Cyrus, having watched on as the town descended into bedlam, had similar questions himself.

Amos, after another pull of his cigarette, finally acquiesced.

"Alright. Here you are. The captain took a stray comment of mine regarding this trunk and your mother's jewels, and sent one of his heathens from the boiler room to take what he might get away with while that party was on. It's a petty grift. The man has done it before, and I've heard rumors of as much, but he had no business running such a racket on a client of mine. Yet he did it, and in doing so left the boilers unattended for a time. You know what happened next..."

He paused, and in the silence I could still, in my mind, hear the horrific sounds of the ship capsizing.

"That's all it takes. One mistake. I doubt he'll even pay for it, as it will be a bribe paid and forgotten, but even if the state produces charges, it has nothing to do with me, as you seem to think. Now this is all becoming a bit outrageous. You wish to find your sister, and I have been paid to help Florence find her father..."

His eyes locked on mine, the two of us now tangled in a lie, one at Florence's gain.

"I only wished to retrieve the trunk for the good of Mr. Harper and for his wife and daughter, in the face of that captain's treachery. I thought I'd find both women. One of two is not so unsatisfactory."

Florence could not help herself. She burst into another of her proclamations: "*Unsatisfactory*. That was my mother! She deserves justice, and I believe you were working that scheme with that captain — "

"We are done with this now," Amos said, his voice suddenly trenchant. "You are nothing more but a grieving, miserable woman who wishes to blame those around her for an unforeseen tragedy. Accusing me of crimes I had no part in."

He took another drag of his cigarette, appearing to think the matter through, then offering a shrug.

"But who am I to stop you from declaring them? I say you make your feelings known to the whole town — the whole world, no less. Go tell the Watchman what I've done. The French give him great leeway in solving matters around these parts. He's only across the way."

Turlow pointed to what appeared to be a drunk man with a pistol at his waist, stumbling across the street like a candle flame steadying itself against the force of the wind.

"A worthless roustabout he is!" Amos said, yelling loud enough to capture the man's attention, to humiliate him before the entire street corner. "Good at nothing but putting his lips to a cup of swill." A milliner passed us, towing a pile of hats on a cart, clipping Florence before carrying on.

"A roustabout, yes!" Cyrus said, piling onto his brother's words, as brothers will do. "Watchman, please help us!" he screamed, teasing *me* now. "Arrest us. Show them the way to William Free! *Direcciones!*"

"This is *Mexico*," Amos said, his eyes darting to Florence. "A place you know nothing of. And I have just offered you a cool spot indoors where you might relax for a time before we depart to find what little family you have left. Take the invitation or go off and do as you please. Better yet, wait here for that captain's trial, one that might never take place, and be the first to testify to whatever conspiracies you are privy to. Far be it from me to protest. Take the dog, too, if he'll allow it," Amos said, nodding at me. "God knows I no longer want it in my presence."

I thought Florence might burst into tears, as she was prone to do. Yet she moored her emotions. She looked upon me, searching for some support which I could not offer her. No… I could only take my foot off the trunk and watch Cyrus pick it up himself.

"It's *my* dog, not his," she said under her breath. "I need no permission to take him anywhere."

"Whatever does it matter!" Amos said. "You two and the goddamn dog. I swear, it never ends."

Ignoring this, Florence went on, her voice firm now, with what little courage she had left to summon.

"I'd like for you to let me keep my possessions alongside me. If I am to go in there. The dog, and Coleman. And my mother's trunk. That is all I ask."

He gave her what appeared to be a yawn of agreement. I tried to study what was before us, the hallway into an unknown dwelling, but the blackness was all that gazed back upon us. As if pulled by a draft, we followed the men inside.

The back entry to Amos Turlow's home was open, and from what light crept in one could catch glimpses of the parlor, hides of animals lining the walls and carpeting the floor, an oak table, a crude map of Mexico tacked against the wall.

By then we were upstairs, and darkness once more spread about the place, so much so that I could not even make out the railing of which I gripped onto.

"Right in here," Turlow said, and Florence and I found ourselves ushered into a dank space that smelled of a sickroom. The heat here had somehow pinched the air and held it still. I'd been sweating—now I was drenched. A candle was lit, and before us was a bedroom with almost no trappings: a mattress with a single sheet, a chamber pot in one corner; in the other, a naked oak desk, a single chair.

"Is this a prison cell?" Florence asked.

"It's temporary," Turlow said. "We will be gone by sunup. Believe me, I want this over as quickly as you."

"My father did not pay for me to be in a prison. I can be allowed to roam the city as I please. To have a properly made bed."

"He didn't pay *that* much," Turlow murmured. "I have some business regarding that captain of *The Jubilee* to take care of. They requested my testimony. My brother will watch over you and bring up some food. Please. Simply be quiet and wait out the night. You need not look further for safety than the four walls you find here."

Turlow exited the room with his brother and slammed the door; a creak rang out from behind it, followed by a shudder; a click. Florence went for the knob, to find, as we both suspected, that something had been put in place to keep us confined.

"We must remain calm," I said.

"Remain *calm*?" Florence said.

So she went on, assailing me with threats and accusations once again, and I steered my thinking to Oliver, who was, as always, calm in my hands, his smallness textured by the tinkling bell of his breaths, quick and endless, in tune with my heart. In the dark we felt more as one than ever, and only when he leapt from my hands, barking so as to participate in the tidal wave of energy caused by Florence's outburst, did I deign to stand up for myself.

"*That is enough,*" I hissed, to her great surprise, as evidenced by her sudden silence. "We gain nothing from dissecting the past, or airing grievances against one another. Whatever you have lost, I have lost many times over, and look at me, still standing, still alive, having put it all behind me. Just as you must do as well. There is no other option. So please, I beg of you, to quit your griping. Just this once."

There was banging on the door, which Oliver addressed with another bark before a voice called for us to quit our screaming. I knew it belonged to Cyrus.

"He's guarding us," I said softly. "We are prisoners here, just as you said. It's perhaps best we just wait. This is no worse than the basement in Baton Rouge, or the attic in New Orleans. I've lived with less. Think of Oliver. He lives beside a shed. In comparison, here we are kings."

"We are not animals, Coleman."

The room was quiet, absolutely dark, and only by the noise of her dress dragging could I tell that Florence had gone over to sit at the desk. I myself sat on Mrs. Harper's trunk, asking Florence if she would heed my advice, but no words came from her corner. This lasted an inordinate amount of time; the door opened only for Cyrus to pass us coffee, some bread, and a few strips of bacon. He bit off food from his own plate as the door shuttered once again, muttering some complaint of his brother celebrating at the bar while he was kept here with us misfits, and that he was as unhappy as we were, such it was that we should quit our whispered bickering.

The candle had nearly extinguished itself before Florence spoke again.

"I won't go with him," she said, her voice so low now even I could hardly hear her. "If I am to find my father, I will not do it at Turlow's gain. This I swear to. I don't care if I die in the process."

I had taken to lying down, my shirt unbuttoned halfway to allow myself to cool off, Oliver upon my chest. I raised my head, startled by her voice, and finally sat up against the trunk.

"Then what?" I asked, knowing, already, that in some random space of time that had passed without my noticing, any remaining chance for peace along the rest of our journey had vanished. Not a single person I had met in my life could sustain a conviction quite like Florence Harper — and now, I knew, she had one. I was well aware that I'd thought the very same thing only hours before, but faced with the reality of attempting an insurrection, I retraced the route I'd taken to such an audacious position and decided to dismiss my final conclusion altogether.

"I must say, in all these hours I have not thought up a single plan against them. In all honesty I am a bit frightened by the Turlows... I don't wish to associate with them either, but do we have another option?"

The skin upon her face, once as smooth and fragile as porcelain, had been pummeled by exposure into a vast webbing of red splotches, her freckles pronounced under the glow of the candle. The look on her face only emphasized her anger.

"I know exactly what we shall do. First, open the trunk and avert your eyes."

When I showed confusion, she only stood up.

"My mother's clothes are perhaps the only ones I have access to. I am covered in grime and salt from the ocean. If we are to escape, I'd like to be fresh for the occasion."

I protested, told her the plan was a poor one, that we would get ourselves killed, but again, Florence was not in the mood to negotiate. Which is how I ended up holding a chamber pot (which we had both taken turns to help fill), hiding beside the still-locked door to the bedroom. Florence had changed into a summer dress, and had then retrieved the silver-handed dagger from her trunk, one of the artifacts we were to take to her father. It was dulled — but she was certain it would do for the job she had in mind.

I felt Oliver's fur against my ankles, standing guard beside me, ready to pounce, just as I was, and yet a question still remained.

"You are sure of this?"

The candle emitted a coarse black smoke and was about to collapse upon itself like a foundering tower. We had only a brief period of light left to us.

"What will you say?" Until that moment, the thought hadn't crossed my mind. "How are you so sure he'll come?"

"You won't be happy with what we must do. I understand as much. But we must recognize that no white man, whether he be in Mexico, the United States, or anywhere else in this world, might ever resist the call of a woman being sullied by a Negro. Even if only for show."

"Florence, you mustn't."

"Yet you know I *must*. This might be the only ploy at our disposal."

I stood down, realizing, however much it pained me, that in this instance she was right. "Go on, then."

She took a deep breath, cleared her throat, and gave me the slightest nod to acknowledge the beginning of her performance.

"Mr. Turlow!" she bellowed. "He is assaulting me! I cannot get the monster off of me! I am begging you to help!"

The door unlatched almost as quick as Florence had spoken.

I held my breath, stepped back, then executed the plan as Florence had drawn it up: emptying the contents of the pot upon the man's head. He gave a terrible groan, twirled about like a madman, reaching out for his assaulter, yet Florence was already on him.

I wanted to hide but could not help witnessing, right before me, visible with only the light from the hallway's window, Florence lean down and plunge her father's dagger into the man's foot, so deep, so true, that it stood upright in the wood.

He issued a blistering scream, an outpouring of pain, the man cursing us as he reached out once more to grab me.

"Now!" Florence said, and with that I came to, grabbing one of Miss Harper's socks placed at my side, twisting it taut in my hands, forcing it into Cyrus's mouth, muffling his shrieks. With this I pinned him down, spattered in urine myself, tackling him, his leg arched at an odd angle from the dagger keeping it still. Florence, using the sheet from the bed, now tied his arms at his back. I came to her side and reinforced the knot so as to insure its integrity, just as Cyrus managed to spit the sock from his mouth.

"What in God's name," Cyrus began, at which point Florence slapped him quiet. Each word he spoke next was calm — measured by his defeat. "You do know he will kill you both, right?" With this he cried more tears, slobbering onto my sleeve. "He'll kill *me*." Florence stuffed the sock back into his mouth. This time so far to insure it would not come back out.

I grabbed Oliver, not needing to even call his name, for I had not lost track of him since the boat's capsizing. I handed him to Florence and then hoisted up the trunk. At the door, the calm breeze from the hallway was immensely gratifying after hours spent in confinement. We bounded down the stairwell, careful with every step to keep the trunk steady. The window to the parlor was open, and carried the sounds of the city's vitality, occasional jeers and voices caught in argument, broken bottles and distant laughter. I paused for one more moment, taking in the noise, the fresh air that circulated here, the sense of opportunity —

"Focus, Coleman! You must come, now!" Florence calling me to attention. But there was one last thing I knew would be of assistance to us. That map upon the wall, with all of Turlow's notes written there. I unpinned it, rolled it up, and slipped it under the crook of my arm. I found Florence at the back door, frozen in profile, nodding in anticipation; even Oliver was sniffing the air, as if having located some nascent discovery.

I walked into the alleyway behind the home and almost ran headfirst into the horse that was tied off there. The alleyway was wide, the rear of the neighboring homes cobbled stones with no windows, their doors shut. The ground was burnished by a soft trickle of light that migrated from the main road that we could, at that point, not quite see.

I felt along the spokes of the wheel the downward curve of the chuck box, ran my hand upon the coarse cloth start of the canopy. "Well," I said. "It will do, won't it?"

Such a risk — the daring attempt of such an escape — would have been absolutely out of the question to the Coleman who had lived in Baton Rouge. And had I known then what I knew in Bagdad, I would have left with my sister when she'd asked me to. But here I had no other option than to carry on with Florence's plan. My cowardice, if given in to, would only lead us back to the Turlows'. And after our actions with Cyrus, I feared Amos Turlow more than ever before.

"Climb in the back," I urged her.

The wagon dipped as I felt her weight against the bed, and I pulled the horses from the water trough. Harnessing those two felt as familiar as when I'd driven Mr. Harper's horses back home. It was, I told myself, like any other leisurely drive. The light chill of the evening was bracing now. The alleyway was one long grip of mud, populated only by some chicken coops and lean-tos, and the two horses glided forward at a slow trot, worried not by the lack of space, following my commands at the reins with a relieving obeyance.

We turned off onto the main road with my still having a tight grip on the reins, keeping the horses at a patient speed; shards of light were thrown upon us from the windows of the shops and homes still frequented at such an hour. The shaggy dogs that had lunged for Oliver suddenly walked before the horses, fed by a man tossing bread at their feet, each following him for their piece, and perhaps they were his, loved as much as I loved Oliver, and I thought of how little I knew of this place, and who was I to have judged those animals as strays?

I looked back at Florence, holding Oliver like an idol of protection. The fear ricocheted across her features, detailed by those fragments of light that had snuck into the bed of the wagon. Her brows stiffened when my eyes landed upon her own. Her lip stiff. Only when I faced back toward the road did I see why she had hardened her gaze. Before us, now, was the Watchman we'd seen earlier. His lantern flickered, burnt red, and the shadows of the light spawned and spread in a mass upon his feet. The man was inspecting what must have been a suspicious sight, and I could feel my insides clench at the thought that he might find us in the wrong — or, worse, report us to some higher authority. And who knew what might come of that response?

"We are just taking our leave," I said, my own voice faltering. "Don't mind us."

He placed his lantern up beside his head, craning his neck, catching sight of Florence before looking at me again.

"Please," I said.

In the span of a blink, a breath, he examined the wagon once more. He then said a single name. "Turlow." He shifted, peered back down the road, each way, and back at us. And in the calm of his demeanor, the slack of his shoulders, some resignation, perhaps — even an understanding of some sort. Then he spat, a loud, propulsive wad of saliva, which carried with it all he might mean it to.

A second name, then: "*Señor Free.*"

I leaned forward, nodding *yes* with some excitement at his recollection of William Free's name, his twisting of Amos Turlow's jeers into something of a favor, a show of unity with our cause. With only a point, a gesture down the left hand of the road, did the Watchman relay his directions. The lantern fell back to his side.

"That way, then," I said. "And how far, if you do not mind saying?"

I do not know if he understood me. But his arm, already arched, aimed high, even higher, as though William might be found amongst the stars, and with that he cantered off with the speed of a slug, each step labored as he disappeared into the night.

I repeated the name to myself, as though to evoke the word, as the Watchman had, would promise us our deliverance. *William.* I doubted it as I led the horses that way. Doubted it with each trot, as I remained awake, through the night, traveling to a man I had never met, on horses I had never led, all in search of our safety; in search of a guide.

6

I drove by intuition, the occasional consultation with Turlow's map, stopping the wagon only at the sight of a root doctor foraging beside a bush, a rough-hewn gentleman with a bag upon his breast who, when given the name William Free, provided the point of a finger in what I took to be the same direction the Watchman offered previously, and so I commanded the horses to carry on just as they'd been doing the entire night that came before.

The rising sun shimmered in the distance. A peep, followed by a groan, let me know that Florence had woken, and just as soon Oliver yawned with a yip, and both were then at the lip of the wagon beside myself, staring off into the same nothingness that had faced me for countless hours. What I would have done for even a moment of rest! But I said nothing of it.

"You do not possibly know where we are," Florence said, her breath hot on my neck as she sidled up next to me.

"I have a general aim, and have stayed true to it."

She did not ask me to elaborate but retreated to the back of the wagon, delivering herself to the shade. I could glance Oliver going to her, giving a sniff of his nose, and then returning to me; repeating this routine over and over.

"Quit," she said to the dog.

Yet he did it again.

"I said *quit*," she repeated.

"Do you think it might be the smell?" I asked. "I believe it might have been wiser to have changed clothes *after* dousing that man with urine."

"And you smell better than I do, Coleman?" she asked. "Is that it?"

From the corner of my eye I could see her lift her dress to her nose, wince, and finally, for the first time since the night of her mother's death, give the start of a smile.

"Look at us," she said, her laugh filling the wagon. "Reeking of urine. Lost in Mexico. We have really done it now, haven't we?"

I've frequently surmised that emotions collect in less of a spectrum than a continuum — bending to the point of creating a circle, and so it is that grief can connect in the distance with humor, which is the only way to explain how I found myself laughing alongside Florence, both of us near delirium at the oddness of our predicament.

"Will we perish out here, Coleman?" she asked.

"Of course not. Not immediately, at least. I believe we have the right path in mind to assure us at least a few more days."

"We have no food. No water."

"People have survived in this desert for many generations. I'm sure we'll find the means to do so as well."

"We are *not* those people. Let us be honest with one another. And the horses won't make it much longer themselves."

"Perhaps," I said, failing to locate a rebuttal. "Who could really say?"

"What I would do with some buttered toast! Perhaps one slice with just a drizzle of honey. Oh, how wonderful that sounds!"

"I cannot promise that much. But I can assure we will make it farther than here without losing our lives."

Already, at this morning hour, I was learning that the sun had a talent for slipping through the thin sheet of the wagon's bonnet rather easily — its powers scorching, more so as I felt the ongoing effects of dehydration. Florence was right. We would not make it long at this rate.

"Do you recall," Florence said with the start of another laugh, "when my mother wished to paint the interior of the Baton Rouge home gold? Father gave her permission to do so, as long as she kept him free from having any role in it. She spent days meeting with painters, looking at hues, telling us of every development. Then when the day came, those gruff men pouring in with their brushes and cans, smelling like poison... Well, she trembled like a child. Could not bear the idea of such a dramatic change to her home, even though she craved the thrill of something new. *Anything* new. And then we were forced to flee Baton Rouge, and it was almost a favor put upon her, I believe. To be free of the monotony. I sensed that when my father wrote as well. When we boarded the ship. *Anything* to break free from the tedium of her life."

There was no more laughter. Florence had, I noticed, opened her mother's trunk. She pulled from it Mrs. Harper's shoes; the same ones I had fetched some days before.

"That was the look she had before she died. That look before the painters. That same look she had in the carriage as we left town. That gasping, quaking fear of the unknown. I pity her. God, do I pity that woman."

I peered back to find Florence staring at those shoes, a look of resolve, of concentration, fading from her face, before she dropped them back into the trunk with a thud.

"She would be proud of you," I said, but Florence would let me go no further.

"There's no need for such words. But thank you. Perhaps you're right. I like to hope as much."

I turned back to the road, and finally, only at that point, was there a gleam in the distance. I cannot express the powers of a shining light, a minor oddity after the doldrums that came to be endless miles of shrubs and coarse sand. A chime, was what it was, fluttering at the smallest passing of a gust in the air, attached to a roof, attached to a home, and I could not believe my eyes when I recognized, finally, that we had arrived at some sort of estate.

"Is this it?" Florence asked excitedly. "Have we made it?"

There was a single dwelling, made of what appeared to be mud and wood with a roof thatched with leaves. It had an open entryway with no door, and there were no windows. The horses slowed without my needing to command them to do so, the sight enough, apparently, to indicate our arrival.

There was no sign of any life. I told Florence as much. "Perhaps," I said, "William Free is inside. He might even be happy to meet us. I can't imagine he receives many visitors."

I did not tell her that it was just as likely that we might simply meet our demise in a few moments' time, for who really knew what this hut held in store for us, but considering our recent misfortune I felt that a note of optimism was the only tonic appropriate for the occasion.

Oliver was pacing at my side, his panting faster and faster, eager to disembark. After so long driving, I felt the same as he did, perhaps without such enthusiasm. What I needed was *rest*. Whatever might be offered at this home was better than holding those reins any longer.

"You can stay behind if you'd like," I told Florence. But she was already out of the wagon before the words reached her. I followed along, taking Oliver with me.

"Is anyone in there?" Florence called out.

I followed her to the door, thinking, maybe, that I should stop her there — that we should reassess things before we entered. But already she was walking inside, still calling out for William, ready to meet whoever or whatever might be found inside.

The flooring of the home was nothing more than dirt and some twigs that had fallen from the thatched roof. Casts of a single set of feet, grooved into it, tracked in every direction one might glance. Boards covered the walls and poles lined the ceiling, their points meeting at the center of the roof to form an apex. There was little more than a board for a bed and pottery lined up against the walls in ascending sizes and shapes: jugs, bowls, platters, I could go on. A single table sat in the center of the place. Upon it, there were only a few papers in a mess, as well as a compass. A fine compass, no less. Silver, spat-clean to the point that I might see my own reflection. Etched into the back was all I needed to know we were in the right home, at least.

"*Free*," I said to Florence. "This compass has his name on it."

Florence ran her hand upon the wall, dirt falling to the ground. An earthy scent wafted through the air.

"So we are in the right place," she said. "All of this bodes well for us."

"How in the world have you reached that conclusion?" I asked.

"We at least know he resides here. And just look at his wares! How many expeditions must this man have been a part of to collect such things!"

"Maybe," I said. "Or these things speak to a barbarity of the sort we cannot even imagine. For all we know he stole that name, this compass. We must remain careful."

"Barbarity? You let your imagination outrun you on occasion, Coleman. I do say."

Florence had discovered a water jug beside a pile of hides, and already she was putting her lips to it, the water flowing as she downed it. She wiped her mouth and handed it over.

"Is it safe?" I asked.

"Oh, just have some water," she said.

So I had my own fill — then cupped my hand, poured some into it, and went to the floor so Oliver might have some as well.

"Don't give it *all* to him," Florence said.

"He's hardly had any!"

"Well, who knows when we will get more — "

This, for better or for worse, was when we heard a loud clanging reverberate within the hut; a shadow fell over us. Even Oliver stopped lapping at the water in my hand. I got up quickly, rubbing my hands dry on my pant leg.

"Who might you be?" a voice asked.

There was a man at the entrance of the home. He was short, gaunt in face, with raven-black hair that fell on both sides of it, concealing his expression. Beside him he had dropped a trap box—within it a lifeless animal, what looked to be a fox.

"My name is Coleman," I said to him. "That is Florence. This here is Oliver." I pointed at Oliver, as though in need of someone to place blame upon, as though it were the dog that led us to invade this man's private quarters.

"We mean you no harm," Florence said.

He chuckled at this, although he did not smile. Slowly but confidently, he glided forward—took the pitcher of water from the table and had a sip himself.

"I can see that much. And now I know your names. What I'm still wondering, really, is why you are in my home."

I stammered for a moment, still nervous, eyeing the blood upon the man's pants, the flecks of mud upon his face. You'd think he'd just come off a battlefield.

"We are in search of my father," Florence told him, before launching into our story, William not moving one muscle—hardly even breathing, by my eyes—as he listened on about the shipwreck, the Turlows, the fact that we knew he was in league with them, but might—just might—wish to aid us in their absence.

"So I understand," he said, "you've just left the Turlows and come here? To me? Having escaped as prisoners?"

Florence was a bit pallid, as though to speak of her mother's death, our arduous journey, had caused her great exhaustion. So I did my best to assist her.

"That is exactly right," I said. "We have every aim to go north to Texas, still. But we do not trust those brothers. And yet we have nowhere else to turn but to you."

"I had a deal with the Turlows. Some fine goods, a portion of land—"

"What if you could have all the land," Florence said. "And treasure, no less. Now. I will give you all the fine goods in our possession that we've brought from home..."

"Florence," I said, for this was not something we'd discussed, but on she went, firm with every word she spoke.

"...My mother's trunk contains her fine jewelry, a few antiques of my father's that he instructed us to bring, all of it worth a good amount of money along with our gold, our silver. And we are going to see him, shortly. My father. The man who has sent for us in the first place. He will be happy to give you all that was promised to the Turlows. This is all we can offer, but it is more than the Turlows can, and I trust to it you'll take an offer that pays you more than ever promised by those two."

William waved her off, bristling at this.

"I need a moment to think. That is all."

He sat, then in one quick fall his short hands lay across the table.

We all remained silent at his request. A golden film fell over the dwelling, streaming forth from the sun outside, illuminating the man before us. He was rather boyish, really. Not a trace of stubble on his face, his eyes a darkish brown, but lively — darting as he contemplated us and considered his circumstances.

With this he stood up suddenly, and I feared he might strike me, hurt Florence, but instead he retrieved a small bowl of earthenware from the other side of the room, filled it with water from the jug upon the table, and put the bowl upon the ground for Oliver before sitting back down.

"I don't know the brothers well," William said. "They came to see me some time ago regarding your group. The journey north, to aid in finding your father. You seem to think they were involved with that boat sinking, which I don't know a thing about, but it isn't a stink I want associated with my name. Then again, who knows if you're telling me the truth..."

Florence had regained, at least for a time, the energy she had on the beach: frenzied and determined, her words coming quickly.

"What you know, if nothing else, is that we are the ones here with a deal to offer you," Florence said. "I could go on regarding the Turlows, but why waste time?"

"You talk like you got this all figured out, ha?" William said, his voice raised, enough to cause even Oliver to pay him mind. "And what if you don't? What if I go ahead and loot that wagon of yours? Leave you here to deal with the Turlows when they come calling."

"And what of the land?" I interjected. "You'll have none of it. Unless, I suppose, you jail us just like those brothers did and force our passage north. But I know that's not an option for you."

"Really?" William said. He showed the start of a smile. "And why is that?"

"I don't believe a man who would show kindness to a lowly dog, as you have done, would treat guests in such a way. And I don't believe you to be disgraceful like those brothers. You were a scout in the military, from what I hear. A man of morals, and one with his duty. I'd surmise you'd rather help us than see us die, especially if it is to your gain. But tell me, William. Tell me if I am wrong. If so, do as you will with us. For we are at your mercy."

William crossed his hands at his chest, staring at me with great concentration. With his index finger and thumb he pinched his nose, then closed his eyes, opened them again, and gave a sigh.

"Show me," he said. "Whatever you've brought in that wagon. Leave it with me, my portion, and I will escort you north to Nacimiento. I will claim that land myself."

"And that is all we ask," Florence said, relief in her voice.

Now William was standing again, muttering apprehensions to himself, for it appeared that as quickly as he'd come back from a journey, another was about to begin.

"You will not regret this decision," Florence was telling him as we headed back outside.

"Already I am beginning to. But as I said. I'll see what you have, and we will take inventory of what we might need. And then..."

"We will go?" I asked, picking up Oliver to follow William, our new guide.

William had one requirement before our departure: enough time for him to skin the fox he'd captured and prepare a meal, a process which left me overawed. There was great skill in the efficiency he showed opening the animal from anus to lip, discarding the organs, starting a fire, and putting the meat to it. You would think the routine was a daily one, but he told us it was rare to eat a fox, to be thankful for the chance and hope to not fall ill, really. (I did not wish to tell him I was so famished I would lick the juices that sputtered off the meat and had landed on the ground.)

While the fox was set to fire, we unloaded the trunk, following William's directions to bring it to the back of his home. It was there he had installed a water pump, beside it a chest-high pile of hay. "Help me," William said, so I did, grabbing large handfuls and pushing them to the side, Oliver circling us as we finished the task.

Revealed to us was a secret compartment. Rows of shaved poles, thatched like the ceiling of William's home, were laid across the ground, tied together with thickset leaves to create a board, a good ten feet in length, sturdy and of good construction. William gripped a pole on one side of the board, I took the other, and together we flipped the entire unit backward with a unified heave.

A darkness, compelled by the sun slipping beneath a cloud, rendered the pit black for a time. Then with one quick stroke the sun returned, a bright yellow ribbon casting light on it again. I had to squint to see what lay there: great mounds of valuables. Trinkets of gold, half-moons of silver, sea pearls, and a carved green pendant resembling a human eye that I personally found to be sinister. All of this was hidden away there.

"Well," I said to William. "Here I was thinking you were a pauper. Sure enough you are a wealthy man."

He nimbly jumped into the pit and had me hand over the trunk. "I'm nothing of the sort," he said. "Not yet at least."

"My eyes must deceive me, then."

"They don't."

"Then your ambition is far beyond that of most men," I said.

"It is a conversation for another time. Help me out, now."

"Wait," Florence said. She was antsy, watching over Oliver as I readied to help William from the pit. "Might I keep those clothes? My mother's shoes? Even the trunk? It is all worthless, those bits. It's purely sentimental. It would mean the world to me. Say no if you wish."

The man hardly gave it a second thought, a shrug really, before picking up the trunk, lugging it up with two hands, a quiet grunt, and sliding it back out of the hole and onto the ground. I could see the relief on Florence's face. Something saved. The memory of her mother somehow left intact, just by staying close with the few objects left to her.

"It's fine," William said. "But it'll be you hauling it around from now on."

"I'll bring it back to the wagon myself. I will watch over it every step this way forward."

Before I could offer my assistance, she had grabbed it with two hands and was lugging it off while William placed hay back upon the pit.

"I suppose we'll eat," he said to me, the smell of the hay now percolating, strong enough to bring me to sneeze. "Then we will be going."

"Stay close now," I told Oliver, sighing as I picked him up with a single swoop before heading to the firepit myself.

7

William and I spoke as he drove, two days having passed since our having met, the party moving at a smooth clip through the desert with intermissions only to rest. I had finally time to sleep and gather myself. If anything an air of easiness was on hand. William would be sullen, distant, for long periods, but it was when he pulled his pipe out from his pocket, taking a long suck as his eyes reddened and he wheezed in fits, that he became rather affable. These were opportunities I took advantage of. On this occasion I listened to him with rapt attention as he elaborated on his origins. "My mother was an Indian, Tickanwa-tic" he told me. "My father was a white man."

"Is that so?" I asked.

"He trapped for a time and then constructed a trading post. Beautiful home. Icehouse in the back. Sitting room inside beside a hearth where tribe leaders would come and discuss their transactions, smoke as they rested up before heading off once more. They would tell stories for all hours. I would serve them drink, replenish their pipes, but mostly listen. All I wanted was to listen."

On he went, telling me how he was learned at a fort in Arkansas at his father's request; his schooling kept him distant from the trading post, from his home, and so in fact, beyond their rare appearance at the post when he was a boy, he had never met his mother's people at all.

"But she told me all about them," William said. "When I paid visits, the stories poured out of her. Offerings from the past. There were dreadfully trying times and endless fights with neighboring rivals; the warriors deserted and started their own bands. Her own father was close to the chief, and was felled in battle. I would dream of my grandfather. Barefoot upon his horse, covered in buffalo robes, watching over me. I still see him now."

In time, William's father urged him to join the military, and in doing so he demonstrated a great facility with language and so became an interpreter, a scout. He showed me a few of the many tongues he spoke, and I was enraptured, each language flowing so naturally, sprung seemingly from the previous one but wholly different.

"What a talent. You must impress everyone you meet."

"At the very least I can speak with them. Which is my aim."

William had a face so rutted that it appeared as though it had been fed on by minnows. A sad man, one might gather on first blush, but he was nothing but pleasant company.

"Such an interesting composition," I said. "Well-educated with the presentation of a white man, the bona fides of an Indian, and such a bevy of talents and stories. It's captivating, William. All of it."

He frowned at this, although I could not figure as to how I'd possibly offended him.

"You are a strange man," he said.

"How astute you are!" Florence called up to us. She had been silent for some time, minding her distance, but apparently this needed to be said.

The spell of the moment was gone for a time. I had allowed myself the pleasure of going shoeless, and to feel a chasm of air between each toe — to let them breathe for a moment while my legs hung over the bed of the wagon — was of great relief when we'd had so few comforts since leaving Louisiana. I was meanwhile checking Oliver for fleas when I noticed William checking his compass from the perch beside me, and I decided to break the spell that kept us quiet.

"Where did you have it made?" I asked.

"It was my father's originally," he said. "He gave it to my mother when they first met, so she might remember him upon their first-time meeting. When I was of age, going off to enlist, she gave it to me. Said it would always lead me back to her. I believe she meant it would remind me of her. But sometimes it does act up, spinning wildly, at strange times no less. When I have fallen ill, or under some hardship. It is those days I wonder..."

Florence had perked up at his story. Her head was beside us now, extended from the wagon's rear.

"Is she alive?" she asked.

"She passed long ago."

"I'm so sorry," Florence said.

Silence possessed the wagon once again. Little was before us, but dustings of cacti littered the ground and there were the smallest pockets of pink or yellow flowers. The horses stuttered and grew cautious, the reins tight in William's hands, and before I could mention the fact, we had turned off the road, bound for some untold direction.

"Where might we be going?"

"I've tried to be polite," William said. "But you both smell *rotten*."

"Oh," I said. "There was an unfortunate incident in Bagdad. I meant to save you from the details."

"And you may, but I do think both of you are due a wash."

With each slew of the wagon, we came closer to a bluff. The heat was inflexible, unremittent, and wavered only when the horses were at a steady trot; as we slowed, then stopped, it settled and then built to something of a boil.

There was, I realized, a copse of trees below us; sprawling stretches of glittering orange and yellow leaves and dense thickets of greenery.

"There is a stream just north of here that has gone its own way from the Rio," William said. "Perhaps you make use of it."

The thought of any body of water appearing after so much of so little was hard to fathom. And yet the trees, the growing sounds of insects, appeared to speak otherwise. By habit I put Oliver to my breast, knowing, with experience in Baton Rouge, the odd threats that might lay waiting in a swamp.

We were privy to the sounds of critters scurrying before us, beyond us; the rustling of leaves and the gentle pitch, that quiet echo, of flowing water.

"I played in rivers like these as a child," William said. "Usually when my father was away. He preferred baths, and thought us insane for wishing to take to the water, but there are few things so refreshing. It will revitalize you. My mother insisted on as much, and on that fact she was right."

The ground went soft, from dirt to mud to sediment, and soon before us the trees broke open for a snatch of space where a small stream patiently eased its way through the desert.

Oliver, wriggling from my hands, jumped down and was the first of us to sprint right to it, his coat soaking wet in hardly a moment's time, and just as quickly he was back beside me, wagging violently about.

"He is as active as he was back in New Orleans. You'd think his life has changed not at all. What resolve he has! He could go around the world, see the horrors and wonders of a thousand lands, and find nothing but joy."

By this point Florence already had her feet in the water, her dress pulled up to her pale shins.

"I intend to feed and water the horses," William said, "if you two can make do on your own."

Florence caught William's attention before he had a chance to depart. "Are we safe here?" she asked.

William deliberated over her question, his finger hovering over his lips, before offering the only answer that seemed to present itself:

"You're as safe here as anywhere else."

"Yes," Florence said after considering his reply. "I suppose that will have to do."

With that, William left us. Silence once more crept over this small, strange slip of wilderness. Florence was staring at me again, a forever-unsettling occurrence.

"What is it now?" I asked.

"Could you turn away? While I bathe. However best I can with this dribble of water. I will do the same for you."

I consented, turning to face the trees before sitting down. In no time I had Oliver, wet as a fish, scampering up my back with his paws. I told him not to challenge a man who could not meet him eye to eye, and when he came around in front of me he got up on his hindquarters and delivered a hard stare as though this might be a more proper invitation to play.

"Florence is already in the water," I said. "Go pester her." As quick as I said it, he was gone, trampling about in parts unseen.

"I love that dog," I said.

"Yes, yes, I am well aware," Florence said. "No need to remind me."

I perceived a barbed edge beneath her words, and it was always a complaint of hers that somehow loving Oliver, and wishing to voice such an idea, was anathema to her more mature sensibilities, an annoyance best dismissed outright. I never found her comments worthy of even the slightest acknowledgment, since my tenderness toward the dog made all the sense in the world to me. For Oliver was a godsend in a time when I needed one more than most. How fortuitous for Miss Harper to have taken him in after we'd left Baton Rouge, where I'd been stripped of everything of value in my life (most importantly my sister, but one could also count the few others who treated me like family, from the tailor who'd been freed and would discuss his trade for hours for my own amusement while he took his breaks, to Mr. Virgil Sutton, a man who declared me the devil when drunk but when sober would walk with me back home after a day loaned out for labor and treat me like a son for as long as the bottle was kept from his mouth). I could only find it odd, even ironic, that Oliver had been purchased for Florence in reality, and it was Florence who considered any exhibit of tenderness toward the creature to be beneath her. But I did not need to argue with Florence. Any provocation, after all we'd been through, felt more and more unworthy of our time together.

"The water is cold but it is invigorating," Florence said.

"I'm glad to hear."

"It's not deep at all. You can just sit in it, lap it onto your skin."
"It does sound nice."
"I say as much only so you know you have nothing to fear."
"It did not look deep enough to cause any worry."

There was a kindheartedness to her attempt to assuage my fears of water, fears she knew well and would, in the past, have been so quick to tease me for. She appeared to recognize this fact herself.

"I am sorry for what I said before we embarked on our trip. Knowing how scared you were. You know how I can slip into a nasty mood. It does not take much."

"It was forgiven the moment it happened."

A hawk perched on a tree supervised us as though we had encroached on its territory, and soon it took off and reappeared upon a different tree beside the first, while still chastising me with its stare.

"You know, Coleman, we must stay light on our feet in the presence of this man," Florence said.

"William?" I said, with more than a little disbelief.

"Consider the facts. He knows Turlow to be after us...the desert to be dangerous...all of this nonsense about his mother and father he's shared. I do not buy it entirely. I do believe he aims to escort us to my father, but I am only saying it's wise to keep one eye open at night."

"I disagree. To me he seems a man of good morals. A favor was done in his name and now he intends to pay it back."

"Again. Your trust in him is born of nothing. He is not a proud hero sent to be our ward, Coleman. He's a mercenary."

"You simply cannot trust a single individual in this world, can you? Just because you have lost someone you care about does not mean others must lose hope in finding what they seek — and doing so in a proper fashion, without cunning. Carry on thinking however you wish, but do not try to corrupt me with such unkindness."

"If I am unkind, you are naive. Which perhaps is so evident it should go unsaid."

So quickly we vaulted from apologizing to fighting, even as I willed myself not to, and what a strange sight it must have been, two parties arguing without even a look in the other's direction, but so it was, and so we went on, me directing my vitriol at a hawk in the sky while responding in reality to Florence, and Florence, meanwhile, yelling at my backside.

"*What insights* you have from strolling about the parks in New Orleans," I said. "From holding court beside your father at the dinner table while I serve you your oysters and pudding. Bring you honey and toast each morning when you call my name."

Florence cackled so loudly that the hawk took flight. I could hear her slap the water with her hand; Oliver barked at the commotion.

"You *must* be joking. For no one, no one, has had a more charmed life than yours. A house servant of so delicate a makeup that he could hardly do more than pour champagne."

"How can you say such a thing? I had a hand in every trade there was to ply in Baton Rouge. Whatever job your father sent me off to complete, I got done."

"Under the tutelage of others. Do you not think we heard of how poor a job you did, Coleman? They would tell my father that you worked with the intensity of a woman. A woman carrying child, no less. I believe the blacksmith said that one. They asked if we could send June next time!"

"Do not involve June in this."

"I only speak of the facts. That you spent your days reading while others toiled. That my father was either drunk, or too mad, to properly discipline you. A shame it was, too, for you now have not a single skill with those soft hands, not a single means to help us out of this predicament or any other. And for you to tell me I am unschooled in the ways of the world! You'd be wise to trust me more than a half-breed Indian who knows you not at all. A man who cares nothing for you."

"And do *you* care, Florence?"

At this, finally, I turned. Florence flinched in shock, caught by surprise. Her shift was still on, but still her hands quickly clasped themselves over her breasts. I saw nothing improper. No, I only wished for her to see *me*. To recognize *my* person.

"Coleman," she snapped, but the voice that reached me was one of another time, a time before this place, this new life, and I had no need for it. I did not look away. My eyes remained fastened on hers.

Never had I seen her so flustered by my behavior. I could almost feel the beating of her heart from where I sat. Water dripped steadily from her hair and she wiped at her nose like a sick infant, thinking, perhaps, of what she might say next.

The silence was remarkable: A stone could have been heard as water worked to smooth its surface beneath the stream. It went on, ceaselessly, for some time.

"I do care," Florence finally muttered. "Unless we somehow — until we find this settlement. This is it. For both of us. We are all we have. So yes, Coleman. I care. Now will you turn away?"

The hawk had returned, chest puffed, its stare no less malicious, wondering, perhaps, why it was we had not vanished in its absence.

"Might I take my turn?" I said, my eyes once more on the ground before me.

The grime enmeshed upon my clothes had been built up for so long that each article clung to me as though melded to my body. To take off my pants, my shirt, was to feel suddenly free of a great burden.

"I'm out," Florence said. "You may go on ahead."

So I turned. I entered the runnel. The sun could not penetrate the chill of the water and it felt as if a spear of ice had been shot through me. I gripped the air with clenched fists, my teeth chattered, and from the fringe of gravel beside the water, Florence did her best to withhold her laughter. Oliver was in her lap, trying to break free and reach me, but it was for the best I be left to endure such a thing on my own without his disrupting me.

"I *did* tell you it was cold," Florence said.

"Not *this* cold!" I said through clenched teeth.

I began to thrash about, stomping my feet, yet soon my body had mitigated the temperature and I was, all at once, surprisingly comfortable. The water was almost pleasant. My body slackened. Then, without a thought, without even giving my body the instruction, I plunged into the stream, surrendering to the freezing water, the dire need to be cleansed absolutely. What followed was not the sensation that had found me when Mr. Harper had me so close to sinking at the lake on that fateful Sunday years ago, or even the creeping certainty of death that struck me when I dove into the ocean when the ship had capsized days ago; rather it was a resoundingly quiet calm: the thud of my own heartbeat filling my ears mingled with the weightlessness of a womb, the hatchling's egg. The quiet was resolute, the same which finds you between dreams, or in the small breath of time when noises so loud — a child's cry, gunshots in battle — are stamped out and the world is made still for an interlude that is somehow as piercing in volume as the noise that preceded it.

And in that small span of time, I was plunged into the past. In Baton Rouge, to be specific. Mr. Harper had installed me at the stables for reasons that were unclear. A winter evening, and the winter brought out the frenzy in Mr. Harper, the frigidness of his own soul.

I was shoveling hay, mindless work, and so it was only more memorable when my body lurched, as if a spirit had appeared, and I wheeled about to find Mr. Harper and his friend, Mr. King, entering the stables. Mr. King was a government employee just like Mr. Harper had been, a man similarly lacking in charm and intellect, and perhaps it was this commonality that forged their friendship.

"There he is," Mr. Harper said, his tongue slipping on his words. He did not smell of booze but it emanated off him like the fog of heat that escaped his breath. Mr. King's face was mottled red by the crisp evening air and he examined me from a distance with a fervor I could not explain.

I said nothing, for at the time I said little if not instructed to, a trait that was usually helpful but appeared, in this interaction, to be of little use. I was, all at once, on display before these men.

There is little to gain putting to words what came next. It is no different from those other embarrassments cast upon me by Mr. Harper, all of them best forgotten. But if I were to speak on that one occasion, I would mention that his words, those slippery things he could barely fish out from the sea of liquor he'd consumed, had the rare ability, without physical harm, to strip my spirit bare. To unlatch my soul from my being. And I believe it was his goal. For why else would a man speak to his slave about the slave's sister in such a lewd manner? Share regalements of her anatomy, tell his subject of his own sister's passion in the bedroom, of how it had been decided that such a woman's brother must have that same zeal, and if he does not, then there must be something wrong with that man himself. Something perverse, inhuman. Might he take his pants off? For Mr. King had placed the bet of a brandy on there being nothing there at all. How else to explain such a strange nigger, such a shy freak, when his sister is such a whore? This nigger: one that speaks to no women at all, and accomplishes so little to fill his master's purse? Perhaps such a slave was a woman himself.

Well, let's see. Undress, Coleman. Earn me my brandy.

I could feel the whole of the memory burst out from within me, and I wondered if others had suffered from a similar malady — stifling a piece of their past so far within themselves, tamped so densely that it takes flight from their chest, their very soul, with the force of a cannonball blasted from its barrel. What insufferable pain it was indeed, and I could nearly feel my blood, my very life source, jettisoned out of that blasted wound: every ounce, every drop, until I'd just run dry. That is how I felt, then. Emptied whole. The river filled with my insides.

I rose up from the water. Florence had let Oliver bound about freely, and already he was dashing toward me, lunging into the water with a steady bark, slowly disappearing as he worked his way in my direction to force me into playing with him once more. I could not help laughing. It was then, bolstered by the dog's good cheer, the security his presence brought me, that another memory came to mind, wholly separate from the first. Much better, I might add. One of my sister, when I was no more than eight years on. We were in the basement together, during one of those late hours. I would, before dawn, when the morning to come was too much to bear, sneak into my sister's bed to seek out refuge. I would pass my head beneath her arm, rest my body against hers, share in her heat, smell the scent of her sweat and lose myself in her hold. I cannot relate the great source of safety I found there. For a moment, before I unlatched myself, and we simply slept beside one another, I felt like I was protected. That nothing could go wrong. In a world where so often I felt tainted, corrupted by others, there was a restoration that occurred: that of my safety, of my ingenuousness. What a treat that was as a young boy! So pitiful, as a grown man, to wish for that feeling still.

I found Florence staring at me with the placidity of a toy doll, and immediately those flickers of history were snuffed out from the present. Surely she wondered where my mind was, although she said nothing, and I had the urge to say everything right then and there. To speak of what Turlow had told me regarding her father. To tell her further of all that her father had done to me, done to June. Perhaps, however impossible the chances, it might even *help* her. Allowing her to remain beholden to fantasy seemed wrong. But to reveal the truth would be indescribably hurtful.

Let it be known, however it might have appeared at times, with Mr. Harper being aloof, and often cold toward Florence, that he also loved his daughter, and she returned that love. *Special.* That is what he called Florence. Introducing her to others as his "special daughter," informing her that she must complete her schooling, for she was so apt, so perceptive, so special, yes, that with only a few years of learning she would surpass the intelligence of most grown men. He feared in private, June told me, that Florence's intelligence would hold her back from finding a husband. Men would be intimidated. And yet this tickled him. To spar with her verbally or take on her ire when she was at her worst seemed to be a means of their bonding. And always, at day's end, she would go to his study, kiss him on the forehead, and although he would hardly look up from his work, a hand of his would reach around her waist, a hug good night from a man who displayed almost no affection for others.

Florence never lost an opportunity to see to that hug, no matter her mood. She cherished her father. And I was certain the prospect of reuniting with him was a driving force in a world which had left her with little to live for. Who was to say that, simply because June had become the eye of Mr. Harper's affection — an obsession even — that he didn't still wish for his daughter to join him in Mexico? An afterthought is still a thought, and a single letter does not hold all the truths of one man's inner workings.

I could have said all of this and more. It seemed ridiculous, yes, but it struck me that by excavating the past, by reckoning with all that was on my mind then, I might earn the only opportunity to fashion the future I wished and that Florence deserved herself — one of happiness and innocence. Those things I craved so long ago, and still craved in that very instant, in the waters that had cleansed me. Yet I had no chance to do so. Florence spoke before I could voice a single word.

"They're here," she said.

"They…?" my voice wandered and then fell silent as I turned to find a legion of towering shadows reaching across the mire. Dust and dirt fell from the ledge above us. There was William on foot, and on both sides of him a Turlow brother.

Not all was accounted for, I realized, for the brothers appeared somewhat underwhelmed by the sight of us. I knew the transaction of power well — knew that if Turlow and his brother had discovered me, and had the chance of reclaiming us, they would be all but ready to cheer, as that is what men do when victory lights upon them. But a look of woe was cast about the face of Turlow. I could glean it in the knitting of his knuckles as one fist clasped the other; the sparkle of sand in the deep-lined crease of his brow, the moroseness of his gaze. Before me was a man under duress.

At this I heard some declaration in Spanish. Behind the three men appeared what can only be considered a platoon. Perhaps ten men in all. Mexicans on horseback, one lining up beside another, each in pressed blue tunics with holstered rifles at their sides. All eyes rested upon us. One of them whistled, then spoke quickly, and it was William who translated. Not that he needed to. It took little to understand the command.

"Come now," William said, despair in his voice. "We're to go with them. They've asked that you move quickly."

June:
Part Three, Mexico, 1865

A soothing voice in her ear, each word pronounced with love and beneath that love, the childlike whisper of a joke, a teasing tongue: *"Sis, you look like you've lost sight of the shore! Where are you? Wake up!"* June's breath caught as she roused herself, and those words of her brother's in her ear — that phrase of his, said whenever she'd woken from a nap so disoriented as to find herself lost in the world — were nothing more than an echo lost to the sweep of time and space between them.

Her thighs were raw from chafe and the floor of the jacal was so damp, and already so hot, that she could hardly bear the exertion it took to stand. She reached for the water jug, discovered it missing, and finally forced herself to her feet. It was impossible to describe the willed miracle of facing the desert each morning. One could do little through the day but notch the passing of time in the lazy movements of the sun, in the diminishment of a spot of shade as it passed overhead and finally disappeared altogether.

She stepped out and into a world of adobe huts and slipshod tents, stick homes with their roofs thatched with tarp and mud. All of their constructions built upon a forbidding, sunblasted labyrinth of shrubland.

A year had now passed since they'd left Baton Rouge and already she'd been repeatedly proven wrong about the wherewithal and industry of these men who she'd thought fools for coming to this place.

She recalled those first few nights after they'd arrived, the eagerness of the men in charge, their words filled with hope. They spoke of how the vast plain would bring them unfathomable wealth, and there was little talk of the meting out of land that Wyatt was so passionate to partake in (although he tried, time and time again, to redirect the conversation to his profession, his expertise). Rather June listened to what sounded like a tall tale, a whispered story of a mine, fraught with silver, that all of them would help tunnel. Wyatt, rejuvenated nonetheless by this development, was already asking her to retrieve his papers and his pencils, so as to map this place from where they were now. They'd rest their second day. And on the third, he'd make the journey and sketch out the mine and its range in full. The discovery, he told her, would beckon only more good men to Mexico. And soon it would be Wyatt's place to create, for all comers, an entire city from nothing. Land surrounding a rich vein of silver that he might divide and dole out himself.

Wyatt would undress for bed, still brooding with a frantic energy, ready to meet the day that would follow. "I will build us a house at some point," he said. "An estate, rather. There is clay here, and stone, and it will not take much to construct it. Others will envy the place. They'll want their own, just like ours."

That was not to be true, and for whatever it was worth, June would be the one who sourced the clay from the mountainside; June who had molded it for them alongside Sandy, and made sure it was to Wyatt's perfection. Now the jacal was nearly done, and she was more proud of it than she liked to put on; aware that, all along, she did it in place of having nothing to do at all — for Wyatt's gain, no less.

She walked on in the morning light, equally in need of some fresh air as she was for water. She heard a bleating ripped out over the camps, one of the goats up ahead in its pen, and the man milking the animal, Kirkland Mays, shook his head, as if embarrassed by his charge, before continuing on with his efforts.

It had been something of a sensation when Kirkland had disappeared with a few others and returned, days on, walking stick in hand, with a small pack of goats in tow. He would not say what he traded for them, but it was rumored to be almost half the goods he'd taken to Mexico, and still deemed worth it for the goats' milk, and later the younglings they birthed. Even Alfred Highsmith — the man who had led them this far and was the foremost advocate of any acts of enterprise — had embarrassed Kirkland for this newfound endeavor, only to laud the man for the value the goats brought to the camp as time passed.

Wyatt would not consent to such a quiet existence. Today, as with all days, he was cutting out paths to the mine, discussing excavation plans with Highsmith, the sort of work he would return to the camp to discuss in detail with her late into the night, one-sided conversations where her involvement was limited to rubbing his shoulders, nodding absently, wondering when he would cease talking and allow her to resume her daydreams of a better life.

He assumed a harrowing discipline that only exacerbated his mania, rising at the same early hour, speaking to himself incessantly, drinking copious amounts of coffee. June was to have his breakfast ready by the time he had dressed and his tools polished to an exacting degree by the end of each night. He would watch her as she took a rag to each link of his surveying chain, so best they shine to impress the other men, so they may know the quality of the tools, and thus the quality of the man, they had brought to the desert. Afterward, she would fall back to sleep, and when she woke again, alone, the preceding hours with him felt as distant as a dream.

The costs of the mine had been financed partially by the Mexican rebels who held claim to the territory, protecting them from Indians, aiding their work, for a large share of whatever silver deposits might be discovered.

"They are ever present," Wyatt had told her. "I find them to be valued investors, very knowledgeable of the land and willing to give us the freedom we need to work. Captain Diaz, their leader, is much attuned to whatever knowledge I might share with him, and trusts that I will not only help get the mine up and running but map his territory with great accuracy. I've told him in confidence that with free rein to canvass the land, with an aide or two, we might very well discover more mines to excavate. It only makes sense. He is in total approval. They commend my expertise, those Mexicans. More than I could say of my own government." (Strange, June thought, how quickly he could abandon his stance against the same men who had bribed them at the border, slaughtered his fellow travelers, only because they now offered him protection, a chance to make his fortune.) So he would go by candlelight each night, shoulders hunched as he looked over his drawings, his mutterings obsessive and increasingly bizarre before she put him to bed like a child, swaddling him in blankets and telling him his food would be prepared in the morning. She wished desperately to be gone from him, and the shame was incalculable, each morning, when his absence infused her with a loneliness she could not square. Wyatt was all she had. It had not been a choice.

"Were you looking for me, June?" a voice said.

By now she'd passed the goats' pen, was on the outskirts of the camp, where the sun crashed upon her like a rolling wave, an endless tide. She was busy staring at the hill of shrubs before her and it took a moment to register Celia beside her, her hair bespeckled under the sun. The woman's sudden appearance startled her some.

"I'd just been passing by," June said. "Was off looking for some water. No need to sneak up on me like that!"

Celia giggled in amusement. "No one's sneaking up on you, June. We ain't spoke in a few days, and considering there's only a few of us out here, that's a little bit of a feat. I just came to say hello."

When Celia and June had first arrived in this place of their own making, outside Nacimiento — those early days when they were tasked with retrieving water alongside Mr. Baynard and all manner of other tasks, back when there weren't more than a few moments each day to take a breath — they would confide in one another, exchanging jokes, mending the other's clothes, washing together when the mood struck. Small acts of gratitude, of love even, to maintain their sanity. They'd eventually discussed how they might get gone from Mexico: pick an hour, the darkest hour, the warmest night, steal what food they could, and make their way, following the path they'd seen the men take and strike out against whatever might come their way. They'd risk it all to make it to the closest *puebla* (she knew the word, kept it close to her tongue, practiced it when need be), and when they arrived they'd ask the way north; ask their way out of this mess they'd found themselves in.

Little did June know how comfortable Celia was with her former owners, a short man named Tolaver Bowles and his wife, two individuals who had been so clobbered silly by the withering elements of the desert that they let their former help do whatever she pleased. Celia took solace in Sandy, and they would disappear at night together, return in the other's embrace, and it was something of a betrayal, or a lesson in her own selfishness, that June heard that woman's laughs, credited them to that man, and took each one as a theft, stolen from their own bond. Celia stopped any talk about leaving soon after. Sandy had all the work he wanted in a day, enough food to live and the chance to build a home if that mine started producing. Why would a man with such good fortune choose to leave it for who knew what?

"I don't mean to be rude," June said. "Apologize if it came off that way. Sometimes I just wish to be alone."

Celia sighed, exasperated, but didn't budge from her spot.

"A year out and you're still angry. At what gain? We ain't getting out of here, you know. These are our lives now, way I see it, so there's no need to draw no ire from that point. Best get used to how things are and carry on, just like we did back home. I wish it was different."

June couldn't find the words she needed to reply. Oh, she felt them — in the tightness of her throat all the way down to the coiled, pounding pain that pulsed, day in and day out, at the bridges of her feet with every step she took. She *was* mad. Mad at Celia for her deference to Sandy, and to Tolaver Bowles. Mad at Wyatt for his reliance on her to feed and clothe him, to keep him sane in a world that had little sanity to go around and none for her; mad at her cowardly brother for not wishing to escape when they'd had the chance; mad about her endless string of misfortunes and the monument of hopelessness that were the mountains at her back and the barren desert before her; mad at all these Negroes who had surrendered to this place and the white men who still, somehow, through it all, appeared to thrive as they always had.

"I earned the right to be mad just like I've earned a right to be by myself, Celia. Why don't you respect that and leave me be?"

Celia, giving up, dropped her head and receded, ghostlike, back toward the camp.

"Just be careful out here," June heard her say at her back. "They're always warning us 'bout those Indians. You don't want no part in that. Stay in sight."

But June wasn't scared of any Indians. They'd all seem like decent folk when they'd come along to trade. In fact, as long as Isaac was with them she was wishing for their next arrival. Little did she know it would not be long until her wish was granted.

It had been two months on when June was preparing coffee on a quiet evening, anticipating Wyatt's return from the mines. All had been calm, as dull as most nights, when the ground suddenly shook as horses galloped into the camp. She heard voices crying out in a language she did not know. The surface of the coffee in her mug rippled as the raucousness proceeded. She walked out of the tent to find a band of Indians approaching, fewer than she'd expected, perhaps fifteen, young men, mostly shirtless, the reins of their horses festooned with bauble that clinked against the side of their horses with shrill chimes.

The men in camp ordered the women inside, but June was alone and had no interest in following these men's commands. So she came out to greet the scene before her — hungry for whatever bit of excitement, dangerous or not, might make the day a memorable one.

The men on horseback were in a spell of rage, screaming words she thought to be curses only by the way they rolled off their tongues. One of them, who she took to be the leader, was holding a bag that jostled in his hand. The men of the camp began to retreat, and there were calls to bring forth weapons, yet one voice rose above the others, and it was all she needed to inch forward through the crush of onlookers, ignoring the screams at her back for her to retreat.

A few white men did indeed step forward with guns. They might have shot, she figured, if it wasn't for Isaac. She thought she'd spotted him, thought she knew that voice. He was the first to tell the men of the camp to put down their arms. Maybe they would have balked if he were alone, but beside him were not just the Indians but four other black men, including Titus, rifles nestled on their mounts, ready for whatever might transpire.

"We have here a misunderstanding, is all," Isaac said, and with that he stood tall and told the camp dwellers why these young men had traveled all this way to this here settlement. They were in need of some answers. No fighting. Just some answers.

They were a small group whose people had traveled to Texas, been attacked by assailants who had gone into hiding in Mexico, and this bag of objects was all they had taken from the perpetrators.

"What they got in there is some evidence. They want to see if it matches up with any of the men present here. Just let them do as they wish, and I promise we'll be gone from here quickly."

A silence fell over them and the Indian looked at Isaac for a nod of approval before opening the bag to reveal a stovepipe boot, wide enough for the largest man's trousers to be tucked into — and, in an even stranger turn, a single yellowed tooth. An examination period followed, one where the white men present were so frozen by the oddity of this occasion that they allowed the Indians to measure their feet against the dimensions of the boot and to open their mouths to allow the men to see if there were any gaps that might snugly fit the tooth.

"This is outrageous," June heard Highsmith say, and Isaac apologized, telling him he knew as well as Highsmith did that this was a waste of their precious time, that these were not men of his kin, but youngsters who had come to his people's home as strangers; that he only wished to assist them on their journey. After this, Isaac said, they'd carry on, and go all the way down to the ends of Mexico if that is what it took to find the revenge they sought.

They were bony, underfed boys. June could not imagine them going any farther, nor what dangers might come their way. So she spoke up, out of some odd place of caring, and noticed she'd done so only after the fact.

"They're gonna get themselves killed. Best you put an end to this. Tell them to quit while they're still in one piece."

Isaac could offer her only a shrug in response.

"They're stubborn, but warriors still. You want to be the one to tell them they're wrong? I'll tell 'em for you. Say the word."

June shook her head resolutely.

"I just thought you looked to be in charge, is all. Figured you could set them on the right path if you wanted to."

"*No one* is in charge out here," he said. "They asked for help, and I like to help folks. Just like I helped you. No wrong in that, is there?"

And really, thought June, who was she to blame Isaac for not sending them back toward Texas? Why complicate something so simple as a favor?

"You know," he then said, a smile parting his lips, his whole demeanor changing up on her. "I remember that ride we had fondly. I was a little worried I scared you picking up speed like we did. I kept you in mind ever since then. Wondered how you were faring."

She'd thought about him as well, endlessly, with each passing day, to the point it felt like a big embarrassment, something kept to herself, and it was for that reason she couldn't quite muster a response. Indeed, the memory of their second encounter, coupled with this sudden confrontation, was enough to clutter her mind and make her stammer. It took a spell for June to catch herself, find her voice, and by then nothing would do except the bare truth she could not let him shirk from a second longer.

"I thought you'd come again," she said. "You knew right where I was and you ain't want to come again?"

Another smile as he ran his hand through his hair.

"I'm here, ain't I? It wasn't going to happen overnight."

"A night out here is an eternity," she said. "And you only come out here for these boys."

He was laughing now, his whole body roiling on that horse of his.

"What?" she asked. "What is so funny?"

"I just..." he managed to stifle his laughter and himself down. "We've gone and met twice now, and I never even caught your name. I've been worried sick thinking about coming back here 'cause I didn't want to get off on the wrong foot by having to ask what it was. Have you thinking I'd forgotten when you'd first told me. Lo and behold you're mad as all get-out already. Hell, I've lost the game without hardly playing."

This, well. This humored even her.

"June," she said. "My name is June. There's no harm in asking a girl her name. I don't think I ever got a chance to share it."

"Alright, then. Good day, June. I missed that smile of yours."

She hadn't even known she'd been smiling, hadn't seen her own face in so many months, and suddenly a glow, as effulgent as a lantern sparked to life in the bottom of a cave, lit up within her. This was all it took to forgive herself for so many nights contemplating this man she hardly knew, the sorry state of her wish, that pathetic wish, to see him again whilst knowing that day would never come. But it had. *He* had. She could hardly believe it, and did not know what to say next, stymied as she was by the sudden emergence of happiness, of hope — the sort of feelings she had not felt since she'd had a holiday in Baton Rouge, those rare windows of liveliness: dancing in the grips of a freedman one New Year's Day; the odd pang of pleasure when a boy she'd been told was no good had rushed upon her as a dare in the street and stolen a kiss that she'd realized, afterward, she'd wanted all along, if only to experience the sensation of another's lips upon her own.

The Indians had the attention of Highsmith and the other men, and although she spotted Nancy and Celia eyeing her and Isaac, she had no care in the world for what they thought. Paid them not even a second glance.

"Come over here," she whispered. "With me. While we got a chance."

Isaac nodded to his partners. Told them to keep things civil; that he had other business to attend to.

"Find us some peace and quiet," Isaac said.

Which was exactly what June had been thinking herself.

They walked alone in the short time they had together and the words flowed so quickly that she hardly had a chance to reflect when the encounter reached its close. He'd told her he'd been busy, so busy, as they had a good load of crops — beans, corn, alfalfa — all of it his own, land given to him for the warring he'd done on behalf of his Indian brethren, men he admired more than any other he'd met in his life.

"They treat you well," he said. "You answer the call when they put it out, like when they asked me to look after these boys for a day. See them off safely. But in return for your work, they're as loyal as they come."

He spoke of his story, telling her of how he'd gone from a small boy hunting vermin in the swamps of Florida to a man trusted to keep the borders of Mexico safe from slave-catchers, and how with it all he had made a life here, the sort of existence one might come to respect. His people, a good three hundred to start (more now), had been forced to leave their homes with nothing, the U.S. government hounding them the whole drive to Mexico, those slavers constantly at their backs. Isaac made it clear his people tried to avoid the wrath of any powers that be. The French emperor Maximilian was installed as a leader and was lenient to Isaac's people, and the Juaristas, fighting for independence, took no issue with their claim to the border territory either. Yet either faction could turn on them at any point. The country was unstable, a fickle thing, and no one had true control of this part of the desert where the Indians, the whites from the north, the Spanish and the French all passed through and claimed it their own — as though a declaration itself was all it took to bring law and order to the last place on earth that had either. What mattered to Isaac was that the Seminoles had made it so far in the face of so many threats. Created a life here. He was proud, was what it was. June could see it in his grin, right between his boyish dimples; in that twinkle born of some resonance charged from his person that seemed to clear shadows from the valley before them. The man was infectious, his love of riding his horse, Starlight, filling him with the same enthusiasm as the memory of racing up pine trees as a boy during a torrent of rain when the swamps rose up high. It fascinated a young woman from New Orleans with so little to show for her years.

"I'd like a slice of this life you're going on about," she'd said, and when he asked why she hadn't claimed it yet, like they'd spoke of at the fort that one day that felt to be a lifetime ago, she did not answer exactly, but rather volunteered her piece, telling him of New Orleans, of the Harpers, of her brother. Of that boy's ability to keep her alive just so she might have another soul to live for; told Isaac of the boy's love of riding down every rail he might find above a set of stairs; how he'd never had a bad word for a single man woman or child, even the bullies — especially the bullies, who loved to tease him from one side of town to the other. And then she laughed, cried, a mix of both at once, and the man eyed her like there was something strange but understandable in the words that fumbled out of her mouth.

"I'm still waiting for him here," she said. "Just as I told you before. I know it's silly, but the only way I see him again is if Mr. Harper sends for him. Which ain't gon' happen. But I don't have nothing but my faith in the promise right now. So I keep waiting. I just keep waiting."

"You don't got to say another word," Isaac said, and when he put her hand in his own, and said he'd be back soon, that they were not done speaking, she believed him with that same bit of faith she'd stored away for her brother.

And he did return. The first when he'd claimed to have lost some livestock, but then found her alone in Wyatt's tent and slipped a pressed flower into her hands. They'd chatted again like they'd never been apart and he told her more of his people, of his father who'd escaped to his own freedom in Florida, the esteem that man had conferred upon his sons;

about his mother, who was even stronger than his father; and his brother, who had his own farm up north. He told June where she could find him if she was ever in need:

"Right through the dip in the valley, and at the point where the brush is waist high, where you think it might just capture you in its clutch, and break right through, you'll see the mesquite trees with red bark, yellow thorns. Keep going." (When the days were long and she lost her spirit, those last words rung in her ears: *Keep going.*)

The next visit he'd come to trade with Highsmith and the other men, rolling up in a wagon with wheels so large, so high, they went up to a grown man's chest. Once he'd done his business he'd told her he'd brought her something special and behind one of those wagon wheels, with the men scattered, the two spiraled into a recklessness born from nothing but their shared infatuation with the other. He'd gripped her dress and pulled her close and only after their lips locked, when the smell of his tobacco was flush upon her nostrils, his knuckles knotted against her thighs as he leaned into her, their eyes locked upon one another...only then did she tell him she was ready. That she could not live on the prayers of her brother's arrival, or under Wyatt Harper's control. She would go to Isaac's land. She'd get a slice of that life she'd sought so long. Only once her proclamation had come to a close had she seen Kirkland Mays herding his goats to pasture right before them, staring at them entwined. A twitch struck the corner of his lip. His mouth hung so low that she could see right through it to the dangled jewel of flesh hanging at the start of his throat.

When Isaac's wagon set off June returned to Wyatt's tent as though she were heading off her own discipline. She sat on the stool beside his workbench and waited, and when he arrived late that night, she knew from the pain in his eyes, the way he held his hand to his heart as he drew near her, that he'd been told. It was a question, now, of what the punishment might be. How loud he might raise his voice; how heavy he'd lay the blow; how long he'd take to unbuckle his belt and take his piece of her.

But he did none of that. Rather he crawled down upon the floor, his head at her knees, like a spent schoolboy in need of his mother. Dust rose from his person in a bitter brume that clenched her throat and welled up her eyes; he put his head in the crook between her legs, his face flush against the cotton of her dress. He was quiet. Smelling the fabric, his breath heavy, his nostrils latched upon her as he ingested her scent, like drawing blood from an open wound.

"We're to pack up tonight and leave this place in the morning," he finally said, his voice excited and urgent. "The mines will be our new home, now. There's silver, June. And we've found it at last."

He was far too cordial all morning as they drove on, his voice optimistic, his hand often finding the small of her neck. It had been a week since Isaac's visit. The longest week in her whole life.

"I have already cordoned off the land for our next home. It might take a year and some help to make it livable, but we will manage together. We always have."

Next home, she thought. After so much work put into the first...

"Already had ourselves a nice little place," she said tentatively. "You weren't happy with that one?"

The shock of her comment made him guffaw.

"That primitive thing was a travesty. I should have never let you and that Negro put it together without my supervising it. This edition will outmatch it in every way."

It had been an hour by now. She could see the start of the mine in the distance, men the size of ants, horses the size of insects. And she could imagine the dusted-over clearing they'd come upon in short order littered with pickaxes and shovels and those men, miserable men, doing miserable work, bags of rock heavy upon their backs, falling from their teetering wheelbarrows, the soldiers watching on and witnessing all the exhausted labor from their mounts like the overseers they were. It would be a wretched sight, but no more wretched than anything else she'd seen the last two years. There was no new further point on the map that charted her anguish. With nothing else to give, she could only put her hand to her face, smooth the grief from her brow, her nose, her lips, and finally — finally — speak up.

"What if I don't wish to?" she asked. The words were quiet, but she made sure each one came out clear over the sound of the horses, the jostling thuds of the wagon's insides.

"Come again?" Wyatt said.

"If I do not wish to go. I am free, ain't I? What if I don't want to go to this mine of yours, Wyatt?"

The reins tightened. The tongue of the wagon faltered with a vicious creak and the horses' legs nearly buckled, so startled were they by Wyatt's command. His breathing was heavy. Like the night before, she thought he might strike her. Yet as on that occasion, he did not. Instead, he placed the reins in his lap, put one knee over the other, and nodded to the side of the road.

"Get out."

She was so bewildered as to be rendered speechless.

"Is that not what you want? Here you sit, like a whiny, petulant child, begging to be released from my care. Well, go. No one is stopping you."

"I don't have a thing to call my own —"

"Because everything you have is *mine*. I make sure you are fed, that you are shielded from danger. I saved you from a war and brought you to a place where you might find some semblance of freedom. And how do you treat me in return? Moping about for months on end bemoaning the sorry condition of your life."

Wyatt started to laugh, but stopped himself, finally turning to her, his face enameled with a day's worth of sweat, his neck collared in bug bites; his gelid eyes so cold they stunned her frozen still.

"Have you seen yourself lately? Reduced by your own wallowing into a decrepit hag. Loafing about the camp like a bum, consorting with God knows who. And I let you do as you please. Don't you see? I've *let* you have your freedom. But perhaps it was not enough to make you realize how desperately you need me at your side. Now *out*."

He made her choices clear, once again.

"Correct your behavior, or return to the camp. Either way, you will exit my wagon. Do you understand me?"

She understood. With less time than it took for her to disembark, she had already made her choice.

June followed the wagon to the mine, the rhythmic creaking of the wheels faint but always near, for Wyatt would not allow her to actually leave. Never that. He would routinely look back, keeping her in his sight, ready to turn and retrieve her, she was sure, if she showed any intention to head back to the camp. When she finally caught up to him, parked now, unloading the wagon, he had already moved on from his flash of anger. Quite quickly she was embraced once more by Wyatt; was being introduced to men she did not recognize, white men new to Mexico, soldiers who were being promised a helping hand — her hand — if ever they needed their uniforms washed, their horses brushed. The leader Wyatt had told her of, a Captain Diaz, was eager to make her acquaintance. He was squat but broad-shouldered, in finer clothes than any man in that rugged place, and although his English was limited, he nodded his head in vigorous appreciation of her arrival, a sudden brightening of his gruff exterior.

Up ahead of them, shabbily dressed children peppered with soot sifted through ore. An endless barrage of noise was born from men screaming directions, sharpening pickaxes, scrubbing their pots. *How long until he asked her to help those men as well?*

The sound of the mallet rung out as they assembled the tent, one more step in the endless consecution of procedures necessary to survive. The only thing different this time was her close eye on the supplies they brought in — noting what she would take with her when the time came to escape.

"June," Wyatt said that night, biscuit in hand, a tin cup of whiskey in the other, his shirtsleeves rolled up to his forearms. "I should tell you,

Captain Diaz has promised me more land for the work I'm accomplishing. Many acres. The man will make a fortune from this quarry, and if all goes well, I will be in line for a fair share. But there is much to do. The terrain is so rugged here, so vast, that they hardly have a grasp on their own domain. I can only imagine the other mines that will be discovered once I have an expedition together and I can get to properly canvassing this place."

Wyatt's brow furrowed as his thoughts overtook him.

"But I must keep Diaz happy, first and foremost. Only if *he* is taken care of will *we* be taken care of. Not just with security from the imperialists and the heathens, but with contracts for all that work to come, the riches they promise. He is fair, but I can see that he is out for himself..."

She was already on their blanket roll, hoping for, practically begging, the man to lie down and pass out. But now he was talking of the risks of his current venture, the prospects of the future, the trustworthiness of the very Mexicans he had just lauded. She watched on impatiently as he finally ate the last of his biscuit, drank the last of his whiskey, shut the flap of the tent.

Then he drew near her body. Forced his body against her own.

"Rest now," June said, closing her eyes as finally, with this suggestion, Wyatt nestled under the blanket beside her, his head upon her chest as he spoke.

"I aim to. I know I have talked you down to no more than a nub. But I just must say... I'm sorry about my behavior earlier. That was not right of me, but I plan to make things right. Listen, with this land I am being granted... Forget that home I spoke of building. What if there was another? Yes, a second. Your own space, June! To retire to when you wish. We can design it however you please. Right beside the one we share."

Always, always there was the teasing of a reward to coax her into obedience. It would mean nothing tomorrow when Wyatt was consumed, once again, by all the assignments that lay before him, those errands and jobs and duties of the desert that made him feel whole; that made him feel grown.

"A home in my name? Well, nothing would make me happier, Wyatt."

His hand was upon her breast, his head slipping down beneath her armpit as he slowly, but surely, let the whiskey swoon him to sleep. "There is more... I wish to name the mine after you. If they allow it. What would you think of that..."

Time grew slow, and she counted the seconds passing with each breath of wind that blew the flap of their tent open to let in the cold; with each fragment of whispered words overheard from a neighboring encampment.

"...June..." His eyes fluttered beneath their lids. June's heart beat so fast she feared it might rouse him. But then, like an answered prayer, he was snoring.

Soon he was muttering to himself in the throes of his dreams, and when it felt right, she shimmied from his grip, as careful as she could manage.

"You know how I get at night sometimes," she said, suggesting her need to relieve herself. The words were quiet enough not to wake him — loud enough to give her an excuse. She grabbed the satchel she'd placed beneath the bedroll. Found the jar of water she'd readied, beside their makeshift dresser. Then fetched the salt beef and hard bread she'd rolled up in her other blouse.

Wyatt had not stirred. For a spell she thought to take note of him one last time: that beard he'd spent so long teasing straight, that bulged rib cage rising from beneath his shirt; the wisps of red hair that fell in a tangle and covered his eyes. But she did not have the time to give such things further thought. She was gone from him already. Gone from this place. Once and for all. Ready, finally, to regain the life that had been stolen from her.

Each step outside the tent she took with great caution, as though any false move might cause Mr. Harper to tune into her absence, wake and come recapture her. Never had she felt such fear; yet never had she felt such elation. In a passing moment, without ceremony, the camp was a murmur of distant voices at her back; the few fires yet to be extinguished mere dots of color in that wide sweep of darkness she saw when turning to make sure she had not been followed.

From the beginning she had mapped out her own navigation in her mind's eye, knew the landmarks to follow (for Isaac had told her every instruction she'd required, and she had not forgotten a single word of them), but to be alone so completely in the desert made it only more evident as to why they'd traveled in a caravan. Why they made that original trek as a group. What was she thinking, out here all alone? With no protection. No means to stay safe. June thought of Isaac, though. Summoned the image of their first meeting before crossing into Mexico, and what his confidence inspired in her: a sense of hope. A sense that life could be different.

Who could say why, but she realized, of all the many things that might come to her from that short flash of time with Isaac, that he'd never again uttered the name of that tumbleweed they'd seen. And it seemed fitting, in that moment of terror and elation, that it would come back to her — so suddenly that she gasped. *The Rose of Jericho.* In the moment it felt as though her decision to flee Wyatt had unlatched the name from her memory, confirmed her decision, and offered the very courage she needed to truly, finally, find freedom.

The Rose of Jericho.

Let it represent all she might find in the new life Isaac had in store for her. The new life that would replace this one. That dried-out bush of a thing restored to something majestic. Yes, the Rose of Jericho would mark her new beginning.

She would be reborn.

8

We'd been abducted, forced into a covered wagon before the chance arose to even ask why. Oliver was on my lap, Florence to my side, William Free on the other, with two soldiers guarding us from behind the driver's seat, guns upon their laps. One of the two was no more than a child, and slept soundly with a whinnying snore, and there was no looming feeling of danger from him or his partner, who was on the threshold of sleep himself. The only real threat in the wagon took root across from us, for that was where the Turlow brothers sat. For a frantic few minutes they had argued with William, demanding their share of Mrs. Harper's jewelry, berating him for the betrayal of guiding us on whilst they'd been left behind, all of which he brushed off with hardly an excuse to his name, other than the one that mattered: that they would have done the same thing had they not needed his help to find Mr. Harper. Cyrus certainly had no answer for this, being somewhat stupid, so he was now simply staring at us with a malevolent air, caught up in his rage.

"There is no need to stare at us with such ire," I said to Cyrus.

The man was seething.

"Lucky you got these soldiers here or else I'd come snuff you out right where you sit. I mean that. After all the trouble you've caused."

"That *we* caused?" Florence said. "The irony to such a comment."

"You shut your mouth," Cyrus said, "or I will make you, girl. Just watch."

"I'll do no such thing. I've met men with less wit and more ill-intent than you've ever possessed a day in your life — "

"That is enough!" Amos said, his tone pitched just so as not to rouse the soldiers.

He put a hand to his brother's shoulder, quieting him, before turning to us.

"Allow me a question, while I have the chance. Did you really believe you might successfully sneak out of Bagdad, steal my wagon, and make it this far without us finding you? And you wish to speak of others as dolts. Such a senseless decision. With just the result you should have expected."

"It was a risk we were willing to take," Florence said. "Stealing my mother's trunk, locking us up in that room. We had no choice but to escape."

I thought it wise to back her up. "Besides, Amos, it would appear you are detained right alongside us, so I do not believe you fared any better. At least in your absence we found William, who I believe has our interest at heart."

Amos then removed his hat and took the opportunity to scratch his scalp, flakes of sand and dirt floating onto the wagon floor. Then, with a stare as incandescent as ever, he finally gave an answer.

"William here helped you not one bit. Really, you have no idea what is in store for us," he said. "We are being taken to the Birdcage."

William's back immediately went erect. He turned to the half-asleep soldier and tried to exchange a few words in Spanish — only for the man to swat him off with the back of his hand, silencing him.

"The Birdcage?" William asked Amos. "You're sure of this?"

Amos put his hat back on, nodded to William.

"It is not as ominous as it sounds," William said under his breath — attempting, it seemed, to reassure himself more than anyone else. "Nothing more than a garrison for their army. Like any other."

"Lies," Turlow said. "I'd venture most would rather cross the Rio during a hurricane than pay a visit to the Birdcage. Any captives the Mexicans have, they're brought there. Tortured. Killed."

"All rumors," William said. "You've not been there yourself."

"And I suppose you have?"

"That does not answer our question as to *why* we are being taken there," Florence said.

There was another piercing gaze from Amos; another sigh of exasperation.

"The Juaristas have been after Cyrus and me for some time now. All it took was that boat crash for them to catch wind that I'd come back to town. No idea *why* they're so keen to have us locked up, though; I been trying to figure out why for some time myself, and I'd say I'm due an answer."

This made William snicker, suppress what looked to be his disdain, and finally, after so long remaining quiet, he felt compelled to speak.

"You know right well why," he said. "You've run as a smuggler for years. Firearms, booze, but mostly bodies. Kidnapping women and children onto those boats, putting them up for sale when they got across the border into Mexico. All for a few pieces of silver or gold."

"Ridiculous," Turlow countered. "I am merely a guide. How might you claim to be any different than myself?"

"I require a *willing* client. But I expect after this I might be out of the business of transporting anyone for some time."

"What is this?" Florence asked William. "Who else has he done this to?"

"All sorts," William said plainly. "The man transported slaves before the war, but that work dried up, of course. I hear nowadays he has answered the call of some of the Frenchmen down here who prefer their women from the States. Fair-skinned. The younger the better. Isn't that right, Turlow?"

"I knew all along," Florence said. "A depraved criminal, and a poor one at that. And to pull us into your mess — "

"As though you'd fare better without my help! A couple of misfits. Children, really. Without passports. Without a means to find safety. And certainly not in Nacimiento. This is better than the alternative, I tell you that much."

One of the soldiers beside us leaned forward on his haunches, gave a single verbal command with a note of anger, before sitting back once again.

"He wants us to be quiet," William said. "I must say I wish for the same."

"Yes, silence," Amos said. "A fine idea."

William, to his credit, let the conversation die, and no more was said from either side of the aisle. I thought I dozed off for a moment, but could not be sure. A water bladder was passed beyond me, and when it brushed my chest I roused, and found the soldiers chatting to one another, talking over us. The younger one gazed upon Oliver with some curiosity, eyed me with suspicion, before turning his attention back to the road.

Florence put her hand on my shoulder and leaned into my ear. "Coleman, where do you think my mother's trunk is?"

"It is in the wagon train somewhere, I'm sure."

"They sent us into this wagon before I saw them even attend to mine. It is not even my clothes. But my mother's shoes…it sounds ridiculous, but it is all I have left of her."

Florence gripped my forearm so hard I thought she might break the skin. Her fingers trembled — trembled, I'm sure, with the weight of her worry; with the endless hardships of our journey; with the mere specter of all that might come next. I could only attempt to allay her fears.

"They would not dispose of the wagon or your trunk," I said. "Everything will be fine. Imagine this as any other ride in New Orleans. We are bounding up Canal Street. Two cabinetmakers are lugging a dresser on each end, dashing by us as we ask them to make way. Children are playing tag and discarding their caps in a pile as the heat grows heavy. And yes, your mother is waiting for us to return, panicked by your absence as ever."

Her grip on my shoulder went slack.

"I can picture it," Florence said, and although I did not know she'd closed her eyes, I watched her now open them. "And yet I still want those shoes."

I took notice of two girls up ahead, frolicking hand in hand, skirts dappled gold by the sun. They looked at the coming caravan with a smile, a wave—one I returned—before resuming their stride. On both sides of the road, farmers labored under the heat, tilling land with bundles on their backs, faces hidden under straw hats.

"A pleasant day they're having," I told her. "Perhaps that is what's in store for our own."

Florence, with narrowed eyes, appeared dubious.

Amos, who had been peering past the soldiers, gave his brother a nod and informed us that he could see the garrison in the distance.

There on the side of the road were shoots of grapevines stretched farther than the eye could see; the other side was one of lush greenery. Children played in a small artery of water that appeared man-made, a furrow that the wagon train avoided by use of a wooden bridge. All of it paled against the site before us. The estate up ahead was more like a village. Small residences bleached white, pure stone with open windows, jutted from the ground like enormous dice. There were many stables; soldiers played cards in front of their barracks; an aged woman polished a soldier's boot, her feet on a churn stool.

And there in the center of it all was a sight of some magnificence: a church like none I had ever seen, its plaster the color of clouds. Its archway was wide enough to fit an elephant. The most curious feature was at the top of the building. The dome that capped the church had been damaged, and so much stone had been removed that it was something of an illusion—an exposed skeleton of a spire, so fragile I was not sure how it might withstand even a gust of wind. How long until the whole thing collapsed? Yet its structure appeared to be sound, and in the wide gaps of space between the sinews of the remaining construction, the way it led up in the fashion of a cone, one could see how such a building might, very well, call to mind a birdcage.

The caravan came to a halt. The soldiers hopped out without a word. A horse in our pack snorted so violently that it shook the wagon bed. Oliver began to bark at the commotion, and I found Florence's voice in my ear again, breath sour from the heat, the salted sweat on her skin close enough to smell.

"Do you ever wish," she said, her gaze on the Birdcage, "that you could just disappear? How I ache for that now! To just be gone from this place."

"Disappear," I said, pondering the idea. I had no answer at first, for with the driver's seat empty, I could spy the entire desert before us, the perfect model for a landscape artist's eye, colors of such hue, small hills of such rolling, supple beauty that I could envision them already rendered upon an oil canvas, framed in gilded gold, a masterwork fit to be acquired by a family of great prominence. Only after another moment captivated by the sight did my attention turn back to Florence. I thought of the memories I'd invoked in the water some hours ago, moments when I'd wished to be invisible only to be suddenly seen, and yet in so much of my life I'd wished to be seen but never was, even by the likes of Florence, and so the subtleties of my answer to her question seemed so shaded as to only sow confusion. Thinking it best to withhold an honest answer, I once more took it as my duty to reassure her.

"Perhaps, in my darkest moments, but I see only light around us here. It's beautiful, isn't it? Maybe we offer these people a confident posture. Remain clearheaded. Don't you think so?"

Her eyes had narrowed once again. "I don't imagine we have much choice in the matter, do we?"

She had a point, but I did not have time to say as much. A soldier's hand was upon my shoulder.

In a row we were led past the Birdcage, beyond it, and on this narrow path more small adobe buildings, just like the ones we'd seen previously, and yet, for a time, they showed no signs of activity. It was only when a soldier stopped, looking at the heel of his boot for some debris, did I peer down myself and recognize a glimmer on the soil. A substance thick enough to draw the glint of the sun — the color of the waxed stamp Mr. Harper had often used to seal his envelopes. But it was not wax. Blood, rather: a trail of it leading up to the doors of the place, snaking, hidden, amidst the patches of grass that spotted the ground.

It seemed my duty to say nothing. To remain calm. But this was for naught, as soon there were soldiers approaching us from ahead, one only a shirtless youth, no more than sixteen years of age, pushing an overflowing wheelbarrow, his head bandaged with his shirt, accompanied by an older gentleman in full regalia. A swarm of flies danced amongst them, the boy waving them away without success.

"Good god," said Florence. "That smell."

One could not look away as they drew beside us, and there was no way to ignore the contents of their barrow, a memory I surely would never forget. Two bodies. White men — French soldiers, I figured. Their loose appendages hanging out the side, limp enough to brush against the grass. Mouths agape, teeth missing, splinters of hair upon their blood-crusted chins and their torsos upon one another, some last act of disgrace, to be piled together this way, carried to God knew where.

Florence retched beside me, and I struggled not to do the same. One of our captors turned to us, spoke briefly, and said nothing more, his attention turned back to the road before us.

When I asked what he'd told us, William paused, unsure how to answer, before doing so regardless.

"He said..." His voice was strained before he could finish. "He said they will feed them to the scavengers. That as with us, there will be nothing left of them by nightfall."

An hour had passed since we'd been detained. We were kept in the confines of an animal pen far beyond the church, where little noise from the villa reached us. Our group had company in the likes of a single docile hog that looked ready for slaughter. On more than one occasion a child's giggle could be heard, an eye would appear through a wooden plank, and quickly vanish as the laughter faded back toward the town square. There was a tank of water we were told to drink from, but the hog was sleeping there, and no one dared to challenge its claim on its territory or wished to sample the sullied water it reigned over.

Florence was leaned up against the wall of the pen, her dress as dirty now as it had been before we'd entered the stream only a few hours ago, and I handed her Oliver just so I could rub my eyes to stay alert, for the pen, with its darkness alone, was something of a respite from another day spent traveling.

"Do not nod off on me now," Florence said, petting Oliver behind the ears to keep him calm. "What of carrying on? Besides, you had the whole drive to rest."

"How was I to rest with the stench of those soldiers wafting over me and that ugly Turlow brother staring daggers in my direction the whole journey?"

"He is looking at us now, you know."

"Don't say such things."

"Look."

"Florence, please."

"I looked," she hissed, "so you must."

My curiosity betrayed me, so I did take a quick glance, and sure enough Cyrus Turlow was eyeing us like a hawk. Something was off about the man, an eccentricity of his skull, the way the eyes ventured too close together, and I feared he suffered from some malady that might be associated with that of an idiot. I quickly pointed at the pig to remove any idea I might have been studying Cyrus and turned back to speak with Florence.

"The pig, yes," Florence said, playing along.

"Indeed."

"You worried about something?" Cyrus offered.

"No," I said. "Not at all."

"You don't think I *see* you staring? Amos, they're planning something. I'm telling you."

I began to respond, telling him I meant nothing of it, but his brother was quick to once more demand my silence.

"So I am not even permitted the opportunity to defend myself," I said. "Perhaps you should address your brother's qualms, as he is the one that voiced them."

"Do not play the oaf. You are always listening, always forming some pithy reply that no one wishes to hear but that you must voice no less."

"If I am listening, it is only to aid our goal to be free of this place, a mission we share. Now on the matter of pithy replies —"

"You both will be quiet," Amos demanded. "I cannot think when you begin pelting me with words as you do."

At this I happily shut my mouth. My shoes, already ragged, were sinking into the mud. The smell was one of excrement, coupled with heavy wafts of hay. I could not help turning from the hog's direction just as the door to the pen creaked open and a small man — a fragile, bespectacled man — greeted us with a nod hello. He dared not step into the mud. But he stood at the entrance, his face lost to the darkness of the pit while the sunlight at his back detailed the hairs of wool that stood on end of his military jacket. He had no epaulets, no insignias. A soldier of unknown rank that we had not yet seen before.

He said only: "*Hola*."

William rushed forth toward the light and attempted Spanish with the man but was waved off before he could begin.

"English. English is fine." He put a finger to his own chest. "I am Ignacio." He told us, then, that the General was expecting us for supper.

"Supper?" William asked in surprise.

Ignacio repeated himself. "Supper."

"Thank him for us," I said, "We are hungry, and that is very kind."

I was closest to the door, and when we eyed one another, I noticed his faintly drawn mustache, feminine lips, large almond eyes framed by his glasses that had little anger to them. I feared most soldiers; not this one. I was reminded of the men I would eye about the *Tribune* back in New Orleans, well-read individuals of great esteem who placed *Dr.* before their name although some had not even the credential; men who gave bracing speeches and wrote columns filled with words I did not know and could not quite follow. In other words, the sort of fellow I admired. When his eyes rolled from one of us to the next, eventually landing on mine, I did not know what he might possibly want. What might lead such a man to address me. I thought for a moment he had gleaned something from my spirit, as I had from his.

I could not have been more wrong.

"The General has a wish," he said. "The dog. He would like to gift his daughter the dog."

His hands were already upturned before me, and when I hesitated—his lips pursed, his eyebrows raised—he spoke as though I'd missed a social cue of some embarrassment.

"So you will give it to me."

It was as though Oliver had understood the man's words. He cowered behind my ankles, and I could feel the familiar contours of his slight frame lean into me, as though begging for safety. I could have told Ignacio off. I could have fought the man. I could have sowed panic, opened the door, snatched Oliver and sprinted into the fields to face the mountains, beginning my own adventure — one with an ending more unknown than this very one I've detailed. I could have done so many things, yet I did none of them.

I merely stood there in silence as Ignacio picked Oliver up and left the pen without another word. I will never forget that image of Oliver, held at the chest, his legs wading against the air, looking back at me with pleading eyes. The door closed in his wake. Darkness fell over us as it had before, and I found myself lost in the shadows, ignoring the Turlows' jeers, the hog's grunts, and even Florence's words of consolation, as I searched helplessly for a morsel of resolve, the smallest figment of hope, that might get me out of this place.

The church known as the Birdcage had no pews, no pulpit, and only one cross — so large, and placed so high upon the apse before us, that its removal appeared to be a feat beyond possibility. We'd been told it had been stripped bare during battles ancient and numerous, the last of which had been won recently by a Mexican front that had outmaneuvered the opposition at every turn. The space was now the General's: a courtroom, then, to host his guests.

A banquet table intersected the crossing before the altar. Soldiers took up most seats, their uniforms reduced to their undershirts, a few with napkins tucked into their collars. At the head of the table sat General Chavez himself, older than the others, hair black and slicked; a small flap of skin, knotted at the arch of his lip, disrupted the natural order of his smile. But this was no impediment to his charisma, nor did it make him shy in the slightest. With each bite of food, each waving of his fork for a refill of wine, he grinned with eager satisfaction and displayed great color of personality, and when he spoke the other men laughed, and so the air of the feast — beyond my own melancholy — took on a festive complexion.

The women, including Florence, were seated on chairs against the walls of the church, eating the same food they'd served the soldiers and retrieving more of it when the General made the request; they seemed by all accounts content and spoke to one another freely as they dined with their plates upon their laps and children at their sides.

I was seated at the edge of the table, as far from Chavez as possible. Not a complaint could be made of the food itself. The current of heat that fused the rice and red beans, the braised goat and peppers was as violent as sniffing salts — as delicious as it was hot.

Shackles had been placed upon the Turlows upon entering the Birdcage, for as Ignacio explained, they were well-known criminals by the General's estimation: extorting farmers for protection, selling land they had no claim to, quick to anger and rumored to kill, not to mention liable for the sinking of *The Jubilee*, an act which had cemented the bounty on their heads. Hardened criminals masked as enterprisers, and now, finally, found out and arrested. They were not to be given food, and it was some joke, I gathered, that they'd been forced to sit beside us and watch us dine while they ate nothing at all.

I would not have said a word the entire dinner had I had my way, as I was occupied by my thoughts pertaining to Oliver: where he might have been held, and in what circumstance he'd found himself. I'd conditioned myself to hide my feelings; show no anger; to subsume any complaints harbored in my heart. Mr. Harper would have had it no other way. And yet I struggled to do just that as a sense of agitation overtook me, threatening to erupt at a moment's notice. This would have been easier had I been left to stew silently; but the man who had taken Oliver, Ignacio — now seated at the far end of the table beside the General — made this impossible.

He demanded my attention with a wave.

"The General wishes to know if you have been mistreated," Ignacio said.

The clamor of silverware and miscellaneous chatter was reduced to a mere trace of noise — then to nothing.

"He knows how often your kind have been…" Ignacio located the word after a spell. "*Exploited*. By men such as the Turlows."

He looked to Chavez for approval, but received no expression in return, only a few more muffled words that Ignacio then delivered as well.

"These two being worse than most. What is the word the General is using…"

"*Scum*," William said, offering his own translation from beside me. "The word is *scum*."

I wiped my lips clean with my napkin. I let my eyes go bright.

"I'm just happy to be alive, really. And to be enjoying such a meal, no less."

Ignacio did not look to Chavez as he translated, and with a nod from the General, the room was soon atwitter again. A girl, no more than six years old, approached Chavez, and he put her upon his thigh. She wore a marvelous white dress and had sparkling brown hair held in a tight ponytail. Chavez bounced the girl up and down as he ate, and I figured, with a percolating anger I still could not entirely suppress, that this was the girl who had been gifted Oliver. It must have been. The General tickled her nose, gave her food from his own spoon, and the others watched her with what I almost took to be fear. Yes, somehow I was mad at this child, this apparently precious child, but I collected myself. I peered about the table, from the soldiers to William to Florence (now against the wall, eating quietly amongst country women she did not know or understand) and finally to the Turlows, jaws jutted, staring once again in my direction. I smiled politely. I ate as though each bite was a gift.

It was Amos Turlow who took up the occasion to speak his mind.

"If no one will defend my brother and I," he said, loud enough for all to hear, "then I will. We are not *scum*. We have done nothing wrong. I believe there has been a misunderstanding, to put it simply."

"A *misunderstanding*?" Ignacio said. "Transporting the vulnerable into our country? Bribing French soldiers, circumventing our power so you may make a profit? You claim none of this to be true?"

Amos winced, shook his head in disbelief. "Absolutely. It is all a lie."

"Our soldiers' eyes deceive them, then. Those storehouses they have come across in your wake, abandoned but littered with the soiled clothes of women and children. The testimony of citizens who have seen you deliver what you consider *property* to the Frenchmen who have tried to take over our country. What of the brave, honest workingmen who have faced your wrath and paid with injury when they tried to confront you?"

To this, Amos had nothing to say at all.

"Hear this," Ignacio said. "President Juárez imagines a country free from such flagrant acts of criminality, and in line with that, the General wishes to make an example of you for the people of Bagdad and for the territory of Tamaulipas. And so you sit in shackles, as you deserve. It is only the beginning."

Women from the seats behind us were laughing. It did not seem related to Chavez's declaration, yet it felt so. Amos was quick to speak over them, although he stammered at first, shaken by what he had heard, while still eager to say his piece.

"None of this is true. I deserve a chance to defend myself. This is no trial."

"Might I?" Florence said from the back wall to the man's great dismay. "Coleman and I were stored away in a house of his in Bagdad. I would imagine we were not the first placed in that room with the door locked behind us."

"She never ceases!" Cyrus said.

"She is a vile girl," Amos followed with. "It's her who should be in cuffs."

"And yet I am free," Florence said, her voice rising, "while those chains seem to weigh heavily on you."

A burst of shouting followed from multiple parties before the General gave orders — slowly, calmly — to Ignacio.

Ignacio gestured to Amos and Cyrus.

"He wishes to hear no more from either of you."

The General pointed at the two of them, slumped beside one another, and shook his head. Ignacio followed this with a few choice words:

"He is not impressed by what he has seen of the notorious Turlows. He is… what is the word?"

"*Underwhelmed*," William offered.

"Yes, *underwhelmed*. By the stupid one mostly. So he may go."

Cyrus looked to his brother, pained and confused:

"Where am I going?" he asked.

A great gust of wind circled down from the open ceiling above us and washed away the warmth of the evening in a single bitter gust. General Chavez, a hand on Ignacio's shoulder, whispered a single declaration, and with that command a soldier rose from the center of the table and grabbed Cyrus by the lapels.

"Get your hands off me," Cyrus pleaded, but to no avail.

"This does not have to go this way," Amos said, his brother howling while being ushered outside.

"He said not to speak," Ignacio ordered Amos. "I tell you to listen to the General, now."

For a spell I glimpsed Florence, who seemed rather amused to take in the spectacle of this dinner — particularly the treatment of Cyrus — as entertainment with her food.

"He'll kill you if you speak again," William said to Amos. "He would be pleased for you to find out if he means it."

The General's daughter watched us all with amusement. Her leg swung like the pendulum of a long-clock. A bright red barrette laid down her hair and it gleamed, beautifully, in a room that was otherwise drab. She took a bite of chicken, and when the rice fell upon her lap, she said only "*Papa*," at which point the General snapped his fingers at a woman against the wall. She was quick to rise with a napkin, quick to brush the rice from the child's lap.

"*Llévala*," the General said. With this the child kissed the General's cheek, rose up, and made a dash for the door, the woman able only to trail behind, calling for the girl to slow down. Words that went unheeded, it appeared.

Upon her exit, the General shifted his attention to William, seemingly intrigued by his contributions to the conversation that had been unprompted, and until then unremarked. He pointed his fork at the man.

"The Indian speaks out of turn himself. Your tribe," Ignacio said. "The General wishes to know your tribe."

William stalled, picking at the food on his plate. A cockroach skittered upon the ground out of sight.

"You're held in high regard, are you not?" Ignacio asked. "For what reason would the General not be aware of you?"

"Perhaps so. I did not grow up amongst my tribe. My father was a white man—"

"Your mother's tribe, then."

"They are called the Tickanwa-tic."

"Ah. *Tonkawa*," Ignacio said to the General.

There was some hidden poignancy to this revelation that I did not gather, for every soldier at the table latched his gaze onto William. Whispers rose to a din amongst even the women, who had long been silent along the walls of the church.

"The General knows them well," Ignacio said. "They are heathens, right? Eating others?"

The General bared his teeth, clicked them together, lips wet with spittle, and the very noise caused the other soldiers to shudder, to look away.

"He wishes," Ignacio said, "to know if he is wrong. If the rumors are untrue."

William wished not to say anything at all. His own fork was unsteady in his hand, and he placed it down and stared at the General with a sympathetic eye — the same expression, in our short time together, of kindness and sympathy that had drawn me to trust him.

What followed was a passionate address, William explaining to all of us how his mother's people — proud warriors alongside innocent women and children — had been brought to their knees by the white man, his aims and unquenchable desire for power and land. He spoke of strong bonds with neighboring tribes that had been ruined by greed, violent divisions. The Mexican government was not spared, either. It was all rather stirring, and I must say I had not a bite of food, a sip of water, while William carried on.

"You may laugh, and spread rumors, but the truth is that my mother's people are not to blame for whatever calamity and barbarity you assign them. I'd look elsewhere, maybe even in your own heart, to see where such impulses stem from."

He finished with little more than a shrug, as if the words had been spoken while under possession of another, more spirited man, a being that had now passed through him, dissipated into the warmth of the night.

Once more, in a long string of occurrences in my life, I found myself speaking when surely no one wished for me to. I could feel the heat of every individual's stare fall upon me.

"William saved my traveling partner from a madman. As a point of integrity alone, he's attempted to reunite her with her father, and me with my sister. To create some association with him and others, based only on his background, feels unjustified."

Ignacio relayed my words quickly and with no inflection. There was a twitch upon the General's perpetual smile as he considered my statement. He gave a reply. A soldier stood up, one different from the man who had taken Cyrus minutes before. He came to my side, put a hand to my shoulder.

"Let him be," Florence said. "He speaks out of turn but means nothing of it."

But the man ignored her words, and it was Ignacio who spoke once again.

"He does not want him taken anywhere. He just wants him seated closer."

"*Sí*," the General said. "*Me cae bien.*"

"He likes him," Ignacio said, gesturing toward me.

The General issued a thunderous clap, twirled his finger in the air, energized by the food, the cigarettes, who knows what. "*Es hora para el postre.*"

Suddenly, two of the younger women stood up and departed, returning moments later with a suds-spotted pail — prepared to clear the table. Ignacio told us, then, in the mode of a declaration, that it was now time for dessert.

A high-pitched wail emanated from outside the church. No one batted an eye. Many of the soldiers had departed. The table was sparse. Candles had been lit and still the sparkled jewelry of starlight braided the skies above us, visible through the open ceiling. I was now four chairs down from the General, Amos now alone at the far side of the table, and Florence still against the wall behind him. What appeared to be bread pudding was served for dessert, although I was offered none and was left to observe the soldiers eating their own portions.

The General did not eat. He did not smoke more cigarettes. Rather, he twisted a ring on his finger as the joy he'd had during dinner seemed suddenly robbed from his countenance. He rubbed his temples, grimaced, looked up, and the light from the stars above struck his skin with a glittering magnificence that lay in contrast to his now-stark demeanor. Then, as he'd done so many times before, he spoke to Ignacio, who put his spoon down and did not pick it up again.

"The General wants answers," Ignacio said to me. He asked after Florence, the Turlows, why those two sought us and why we were found at the river with William.

"We are searching for my father," Florence said from her perch against the wall, although the General did not deign to privilege her with his attention.

"You should listen to her," I said, "as it's true. But there are other reasons as well."

I was hoping my tone to be a reasonable one amidst the tension of the night. I reiterated our aims: Florence's father's wish to reunite with his family; my own wish to reunite with my sister; the freedom we might all find in leaving the United States. The General's hands were clasped beside his plate. Only when I spoke of the mine, the land promised to Amos, did Turlow himself grow quarrelsome.

"I said," Amos exclaimed, "not to speak of the mine or that land!"

His cuffed hands pounded upon the table. Flies had been buzzing about the remains of food, and they now scattered at the noise.

But I was not afraid. It was he who was in cuffs, not me.

"And why not?" I asked him. "This man asked for the truth, so I gave it to him. I care not of that mine — or of you particularly, Mr. Turlow. Cunning has gotten me nowhere in life. And I am no liar."

"Think for yourself, Coleman!" Amos said. "For once! William wants that land, just as I do — just as Chavez will. No one has any care for you, or this girl, or your dog, or anything but their own gain. Are you so stupid as to think otherwise?"

Only upon this final question did Chavez snap — a literal snap of his fingers — at which point the nearest soldier slapped Amos with an open hand upon the cheek, his chains clanking as he recoiled from the blow. Then Ignacio spoke again, a short-whispered conversation with Chavez.

William tapped my leg to gain my attention.

"He is saying the mine intrigues him. Yes...the General wishes to know more. He is *pleased*."

"Free me," Turlow said to the General, desperation threading his every word. "I will lead you to the mine myself, and I will give you half of the land promised to me. Only I know the way. William's estimation is a vague guess. The servant and the girl have no brains between them."

"And *you* do, Turlow?" Florence asked. "Although I must say you're better off than your brother, a man so oafish I found myself thinking the pig in our housing quarters appeared more intelligent in comparison."

"One more word," Turlow said, his chains rattling as he tried to shift his body to face her. "Ask yourself why you are even here. Why you're needed at all."

"Turlow," I said under my breath, pleading with my gaze for him to say no more. Florence heard this, of course, and I could practically sense her confusion, of a conversation in the past that involved her but had taken place in her absence. (I knew how such occurrences angered her: causing endless rows with her mother, with her fiancé Hugh, with her father, that would last all night. Gossip concerning her, but without her participation, was absolutely sacrilege. But this was no time to explain. No time to caress the truth into a form that might please her, in any way.)

The General was still conversing with his men. William listened but said no more, and finally the remaining soldiers rose up as Chavez did so himself. Chavez dropped his napkin upon the table, loosened a cuff of his shirt, then the other, and spoke in my direction once more.

"The General," Ignacio said to me, "would like you to speak with him outside."

"*Him?*" Amos said. "But why?"

Not a single eye in the room was not on me. There is no word for the buzz of energy that coalesced in that moment. In the dark quality that emanated from the General, the anger of Turlow, and the sheer dizziness created by the church itself, its walls lurching upward toward the stars, its puzzling elegance that terminated in the endlessness of the sky above us all. Nothing was normal here. I was at a loss for words.

"You must join him," William said. "Say you will join him."

"I — " I began. "Yes, I will go wherever I am wanted."

The General looked satisfied. It was Ignacio who spoke next, his gaze going from me to Turlow.

"You," he said to Turlow. "You are no longer needed here."

At this final statement, I looked up to see the General making ready to leave. Turlow was then pulled to his feet by the collar, a soldier forcing him toward the front door of the chapel. He howled, pleaded, but his protests, like his brother's before, were soon so distant as to be unheard. By the time I turned my attention back to the table, Ignacio himself was preparing to leave. It was a different soldier who beckoned me to stand.

I glanced at Florence — for support, a show of faith, or any expression at all. We had not been separated since we'd ventured into the interior of Mexico. It felt, to me, like one more rupture in a long line of them. To be without the assured, defiant presence of Oliver, or alongside the tempestuous distraction that I found in Florence, created the sensation of being detached from the two ballasts that kept me stable. But I did not see the same worry in her eyes. Her brows were knitted in concern, but she smiled. A placid smile, strange, resigned but at peace.

"Keep your head, Coleman."

This was all Florence had to say, and even if she was performing, pretending to be calm for my sake, I took great gratitude in the offering.

9

The glow of the stars tracked across the sky and illuminated the evening. We were now in the courtyard situated behind the church, although whatever had grown there had long been stamped down to no more than dirt and dust, and the only sight at the end of this patch of earth was an outhouse and a bench beneath a withered tree. Immediately before us were a table, a set of chairs, where I presumed the soldiers might lounge on warm evenings such as this one.

"Sit," Ignacio said.

"A beautiful night," I said, heeding his direction.

He glumly raised his chin in agreement.

"Although there have been demanding and even frightening moments in my travels, I must say I've found one reward to be the beauty of your country."

I went on then, regaling him with the account of my trip, the shipwreck, the days spent battling dehydration and the sun, fearing Turlow's return, but Ignacio gave me only a cursory glance and I garnered that my words were doing little to gain his trust.

"I wonder," I said, "if I am still in danger? Of what is to come next?"

Ignacio tapped ash from the cigarette in his hand — put it back to his lips. He appeared exhausted by the evening, by his duties, and for a spell he said nothing at all, detached from the conversation. Perhaps he simply needed a moment of silence. I did not give him one, but I paused for a brief spell.

"Well!" I said finally, putting my hands into the air when no answer was provided. "Maybe both of us are ignorant of what the future holds. But please let me know if you learn any more that might be of interest. I am nothing if not patient, and curious, as to why we are kept here. If we may leave…" I gathered that Ignacio had picked up on my nervousness, and maybe this was why he finally decided to speak, either out of pity or the fear that I might engage him with another winded digression.

"He finds you curious. And you speak more than the others. Perhaps he thinks you are more willing to give him information. But I do not know."

"He should not expect much from me. I'm something of an impostor."

"What do you mean?"

"I mean I have experienced very few things and know less than most. And what little I've gleaned has been learned from books. From accounts not my own."

"Really?" Ignacio sat forward in his chair, caught by this one word — *books* — more than any other. "What is it you read?"

The answer was complicated. It still felt like a secret to share when I wished to, for, in my previous life, almost no one had asked or bothered to care what I did in private. Florence and her mother knew that I was often in the attic, amongst the books kept there, but any reading was presumed to be instructional in nature, for these were the works Mrs. Harper had always permitted: manuals on the keeping of a home and maintaining proper etiquette. But there were other works. Compendiums regarding Mr. Harper's employment, for one. I read them early on, back in Baton Rouge, if only to practice the skill…but they were tedious. No, what I came to prefer was in fact the literature. Novels! Any and all I might discover. I shared all of this with Ignacio.

"I could say more, if this interests you," I offered, then: "If you wished to hear."

I did not wait for him to reply.

"Begin with the classics," I said. "Have you any poetry here in Mexico?"

Ignacio did not answer this either, only raised an eyebrow, but I did not take this as any reason not to expound on my beliefs. I told him that even our home had some poetry, romantic and lush, the work of Blake and Shelley, and some fantastical adventure tales, stories of trappers on the prairie like Natty Bumppo, or stories of devilish rogues and the women they tempt in the vein of Charlotte Temple.

I would have been remiss not to mention those narratives to Ignacio that resonated so closely with my own experience. Works that once had been viewed as contraband, which I acquired after the war with my own pittance; memoirs that depicted bravery of such a degree that I questioned their veracity when I first laid eyes on them.

"Barber, and Roper, Douglass and Brown and Wheatley," I said. "Many more. So many more. I found their stories to be as courageous as any narrative recounting the passing through of difficult seas by explorers, or those pertaining to the gallantry of soldiers at war. I do believe that. These narratives of individuals seeking freedom, I have read a few of them, and only in utter secrecy while outside the Harpers' home, but they brought me hope during occasions of great despair. With time, I'd like to read every single one. And between us, well..."

Here I leaned in myself, making sure to whisper, for even in Mexico, far from home, it still felt like a secret I was about to dispatch that might land me in trouble:

"...I would like to write my *own* story one day. If I live to do so. If I ever might learn to brandish a pen as those heroes did. That is my wish."

He looked at me uneasily before staring off once more at the stars.

"Well, I can dream, Ignacio," I said. "Afford me that much."

He pulled at his pant leg, crossed his legs: what might be called a gesture of approval.

"Whatever you say, my friend."

"And yours?" I asked. "What do you dream of?"

"Me?"

He seemed honestly surprised by my interest. Still he hesitated, but finally did answer.

"Well... I only wish to return home. Across the river."

"Really?"

"*Del Río. Tejas.* I had fifty acres to my name."

"That is very impressive, Ignacio. And I might add, I had no idea you were from the States. I misspoke earlier."

He frowned at me with disappointment, as though this one comment had imperiled whatever trust we had built.

"To you they are the States. To us..."

I stopped him there with a show of my palm.

"Certainly. I understand."

A melancholy silence fell over the garden, before Ignacio appeared to gather himself.

"Why do you not go home?" I asked. "It sounds like they'd cheer your return."

"*Go?*" Now there was the start of a smile upon his face — a droll smile, but a smile nonetheless. "He would not allow it right now. The General is... a powerful man. We do as he commands. Or what his daughter commands so often."

I could tell this rankled him.

"She is the only one who has his ear."

"That *is* interesting," I said, for in my short time here I had gleaned that the child, bouncing upon his hip, demanding food for her plate, gifts from her father, to be something of the princess of this castle, this kingdom. The proof of that point was information I was happy to store away. But I said nothing of it then.

"But you wish you could leave, no?"

The smile disappeared. He told me of the General's son, an honored soldier himself who had died fighting the Americans. That he was the General's source of pride — and since his death the man had become only more brutal. Cared for nothing but power. Power above all else. To keep his soldiers here, doing his bidding, under the banner of his country, was perhaps the greatest source of his power. That is what I gathered, at least.

"I know these sorts of men," I muttered. "Any perceived deficit masked by their ruthlessness. A sorry state to be in, and yet so common."

Ignacio nodded spiritedly, as though I had said the words he'd wished to say himself.

"His wife can be of help, but she does not come to the villa often. The General's parents are ill. She tends to them. Returns when the chance arises. When he calls for her. Many wish they could come and go as they please. Only she has such freedom."

"So you are left to dream of home, if it is even your home anymore. Left to dream of what might be."

The night was still brilliant, and bright. Shadows unfolded beneath the tree at the far end of the garden and extended nearly to our feet.

Without my realizing it, the General had arrived, standing beside Ignacio. We had been lost to our own thoughts — but no longer.

He ordered Ignacio to stand with no more than a tap upon the man's shoulder, then took the vacant seat himself. Stared at me. I did not have it in me to stare back. I looked upon my tattered shoes with not a dash of the confidence I tried to project.

The General uttered a few words, and Ignacio, lurking from behind, translated for him. "It is time, he says, for you two to speak."

From the moment the General had arrived, one could sense a sudden shift in the atmosphere: a heaviness in the air. Something foreboding. His features were almost entirely hidden to me, but I could discern, as though grafted by the dark itself, a snarl upon his face, a physical accounting of whatever suspicion he carried with him as he sat down.

The General mumbled something to his back, and Ignacio leaned in to listen before disappearing once more into the shadows.

"He was occupied with the Turlows," he said. "But that is over with."

A woman appeared with a cask of wine and a number of goblets upon a tray. Placed the tray on the table before excusing herself.

Ignacio said, "You may drink."

So I took a glass, sipping whenever General Chavez cared to. There was a slight tremor affecting my hands — would you not be afraid? — and I could see General Chavez catch sight of this. For a time he drank in silence, but when finally he spoke, the words spilled out of him, fanged with a venom issued from the deep wells in which he brought out each consonant, each vowel.

Ignacio translated for him, telling me of the General's plight, the troubles brought amongst his people by all sorts: the French, men like Amos Turlow, or even worse, the American soldiers who skittered about the borderlands, eager for them to give up territory that was rightfully Mexico's to begin with.

"Even his supposed allies...he speaks of the soldier in charge of Nacimiento and those mines where you wish to go. Corrupt, now. A soldier he once trusted who now hardly returns news of what transpires in that portion of his district. War has made him dishonest, untrustworthy."

"A pity," I said.

"And how many lives have been lost due to such turmoil? How many husbands felled for no reason at all? Indians, too, like your friend. What is his name..."

"William," I said, my eyes shifting between the General and Ignacio, knowing not toward whom to direct my speech, wanting not to disrespect either.

"*Sí*," the General said, going on.

"The General would have liked to negotiate with them. But they refuse, so they are humbled instead," Ignacio told me. "Put in their place. We live in safety here now. Although outside of this villa..."

The General whirred his finger around in a circle as he sipped his wine, shaking his head.

"The General works to make the borders as safe as his home is. It is an endless battle."

"War," I said, taking another sip of wine. "It is troublesome."
"More than troublesome..."
I'd pause here to say that the diatribe that followed went on for some time, so long that I had begun to lose interest in Ignacio's translations, an endless volley of statements I had in fact heard so often in my own country, lamenting the death of young men (and the righteousness of whichever army the speaker preferred). General Chavez once more made a pivot toward the nature and freedoms of natives of the land that tracked in many ways with the treatment of the Negro in America, for it appeared to me that both parties — made to suffer at the hands of men in want of resources and power — were thought of as no more than pawns, even as the General wished to speak of them as though they were equals, as though he had sympathy for their plight. I gathered that he might bother to care for the Indians who roamed these lands — how would I really know? — and surely had a curiosity regarding me as a black man, but beyond that he seemed chiefly concerned with the independence of *his* people, which of course is understandable, for who does not look after their own first?

I tell you, such chatter was common at my expense — Mr. Harper extolling to me on a stroll of how necessary it was for the white man to protect the lesser species; inebriated revelers at one social event or another expressing to me, in a moment of confidence, that they felt such sorrow for the Negro race as the loss of the war would lead to nothing more than entire destitution for my people, as the system my kin knew would be gone, and we, of course, were nothing without it — and yet even if they were wrong, my greater grievance was that I was forced to endure it time after time, as though I was a man with no interests beyond the trials of my people; of my people's place in the world. Yes, my every decision pertained to it, for one might be hung from a street lamp or taken for a whipping if it was forgotten, but in moments like this, was it so wrong to be worried not of the plight of the oppressed as a whole but rather the survival of my own person? Perhaps I simply wished to know the whereabouts of my dog; or where my trusted new associate in this journey, William, and my charge, Florence, were currently being detained. On this beautiful night, in a land I did not know, beside this General, I simply did not care to hear how I might sympathize with his mission to vanquish enemies and save his country.

"Are you paying attention?" Ignacio asked. The words struck me like a pinprick.

"Why, yes!" I shouted, far too loudly, betraying how far I'd strayed from the conversation. "Of course I am."

"Then tell the General what you think," he said. "He is curious. If you, too, think that you have the same aim to stop the insurgency of the white man, and how we might resist them. As your people did."

One might blame the wine, or the endless activity of my imagination, but I could not come up with a single response to such a question. Was he not the general for a reason, to strategize against his enemies? And how was I to give voice to the howling inferno of pain, and grief, and resistance, that informed my people's insurrections, many of which foundered before they'd begun? None of which I had been involved in. I knew nothing of what he sought to learn.

"Ignacio," I said. "Please tell him...tell the General I cannot help him in the way he seeks. Tell him I know nothing of war, or resistance, or fighting at all. Perhaps I might educate him on how to cleanse varnished furniture versus that which is unvarnished. Or the proper order in which to lay utensils upon the dinner table. I am well versed in cleaning a commode and calculating sums, if help is needed on either of those fronts, although I imagine it is not. But all of this he speaks of is not my area of expertise, and I am as ignorant to it as I am of astronomy, or arithmetic, or reading Greek. If there is anything else I might help him with, if it might aid my cause no less, I would be happy to do it. That I wish only to see myself removed from this place alongside Florence, and perhaps with her possessions, as she requested they be returned to her."

Ignacio blinked once, his hand clutching the head of the chair behind the General. Was the man offended? Was he about to order my death? It was then that something remarkable took place, for I heard a pitter-patter, followed by a fit of laughter, and who was to enter the garden but the

General's daughter, chasing Oliver, his tongue loose in his mouth, feet bounding with every step, as he outran the child. He had not seen me yet. I was not to be abated from my line of answers, from this conversation that, for all I knew, might decide my fate.

I felt, of all things, *at ease*. My shoulders fell. My heart had slowed. I had said my piece. There was no more to do but to listen to Ignacio repeat my words, or some form of them, and watch the General take to his wine, nod eagerly, and stare at Oliver, who upon turning, had finally spotted me.

My hand, by habit alone, clapped against my thigh to gain his attention. What a pleasure I got in seeing him turn my way — baring his teeth in what I could only call a smile, his tail shaking so violently as to wag his whole body into a tizzy — and gambol toward me without a second's hesitation. He looked no worse for wear from our time apart. His coat shimmered under the moonlight. Soon his paws were upon my legs, and he was yapping wildly, the child standing back in some disbelief, as though the very bond I shared with this animal I had given care to for so long was a shock. Then he was off again, chasing around the garden, rolling in dirt, making a general mess as the girl attempted to give chase.

Ignacio coughed, and I returned my attention to him and the General.

"You cannot help the General, can you?" said Ignacio. "Or even provide conversation."

"That is not the case whatsoever!" I said. "I just do not have any authority to speak to such matters. Of war and strategy. Of rebellion and our common suffering. Surely you can make him understand."

But I had been weighed on the scales; I had been found wanting. The General muttered to himself, shook his head with disappointment. His words were sharp, cutting, and he did not find it worthwhile to look at me while he said them.

"You are a simple servant," Ignacio said. "He sees that now."

There was a huff from the General. His daughter was at his side now, watching me — watching Oliver by my side with envious eyes.

"He found your words filled with heart at the dinner table. But not now."

At this the General stood to depart. My mind was a jumble, but it was, of all things, Florence's words that came to me. A finger to her temple. *Keep your head, Coleman.* I oriented myself to the situation at hand, categorized what needed to be done to reemerge in this exchange not as worthless, but as a *resource*. So I took a risk: I told him I was not done speaking. That there was one thing in which I could help him. One thing I could think of that appealed to his most cherished love. One which involved the person most important to him.

"General Chavez, you do know that this dog is quite rowdy. God forbid he might endanger your daughter, even by accident. You know... I could show her how to make him obey a few commands. She deserves an animal that is not prone to acting out. I'm sure you would agree. But it will take a lesson or two. Allow me to help her."

Ignacio translated, speaking to both father and daughter, as they both listened patiently. The General made no expression at all while Ignacio relayed my offer. But after the statement had been said, the girl turned. Grinned. Apparently amenable to this idea, if not downright enthused by it. *"Papa, me gustar a mucho."*

The General's eyebrows rose at his daughter's sudden display of happiness. Seeing as much, he gave me a shrug of approval — a gesture, one that possibly saved me from a much more dire evening.

"Puedes quedarte. Tengo asuntos mas graves que atender."

There was an air of surprise in Igancio's voice.

"You are to stay here with her," he said equably.

The General muttered a few more words, flicking his hand in the air to dismiss this conversation.

"He says... to instruct her as is necessary. I believe that is right?"

He considered his own words. His eyes tracked onto his superior, as though for some show of confirmation — but General Chavez had already stood up. He'd headed toward the door to the church, leaving the three of us alone there to follow his orders.

"Yes," Ignacio said. "Instruct the girl. Make the dog obey her... or else you will face your own punishment."

The girl was beside me now, smiling ear to ear — excited, I imagine, for our lesson to begin.

I had harnessed my resolve so far enough as to stay close to Oliver, but at the cost of having to entertain Anna, an unruly child who almost matched Oliver's energy. I treated her no different from an adult, instructing her with kindness but terseness, which she took with a sense of comedy if anything, and one got the feeling, from her willingness to participate and her gaiety regarding the lesson, that I was entertaining her greatly; that such fun might be a rare occurrence out here where the children had so little to occupy themselves.

"Tell her, Ignacio, that a dog must be fed at least once each morning, and if it pleases the owner, and the dog has behaved, once more in the evening. That a dog like Oliver requires an excessive amount of exercise, or he will be so rambunctious at night as to keep the whole house awake."

At some point she had threaded her red barrette into Oliver's fur, right at the neck, and it looked as he ran as though a large bug had latched onto him and would not let go.

We played a little fetch, me throwing a stick to Anna, her catching it, throwing it back to me, allowing Oliver to run between us.

"Eventually you must always let him have his reward. It is cruel to do otherwise."

And as I handed Oliver the stick, noticing the displeasure on her face at the end of the game, I assured her there was much more to learn.

"So much more. Have you ever owned a dog, Anna?" I asked.

She shook her head no.

Anna wore a white dress, the collar tight at her neck, sprouts of yellow flowing down the side like sunflowers, and it was a joy, I must admit, to see how much fun she was having. Still, my questions usually met with silence, just as this one did. Her hands were clasped behind her back. She fidgeted in the manner children do so often when questioned by an adult.

I decided to sit on the grass — to meet her where she was. I told her to sit beside me, to pet Oliver as he chewed his stick. She smiled her gap-toothed smile, agreeable to the idea.

"Well," I said, glancing this way and that, speaking in a near-whisper. "You should have seen Oliver as a pup. A baby."

"*Un cachorro*," Anna said.

"Yes!" I said. "There is nothing as delightful as a puppy. And the bond you build with him, the time spent in those early days, creating a friendship. It is a unique experience. But a secret remains…"

Another wail let out, no different from those I had heard inside the church. Ungodly moans, with different inflections. So I perched up on my thigh, for a moment, gave Ignacio my full attention, and asked what it was we were hearing, fearing that I'd gathered what they were already.

Ignacio's eyes went to the girl, then back to me.

"Coyotes," he said curtly.

But it was difficult to move as the moans carried on, ringing in my ear, layered upon one another and matched, in at least my imagination, to more bodies that appeared to me just like the ones I'd seen in that wheelbarrow.

A hand was tugging on my shirt. Anna's hand. "*¿Cuál es el secreto?*"

"The secret," Ignacio said. "She wishes to know the secret you speak of."

"The secret," I said, my voice wavering (but my performance, by my estimation, as excellent as it had been at the beginning of my speech), "is that a dog like Oliver, one of good stock, binds himself to a single individual. All his life. To take him from his owner would be like, well, taking you from your father. Can you imagine?"

Ignacio paused, put a single finger to his chin. Then, with a note of skepticism: "I know what you are doing."

"Tell her," I said. "What might you care, Ignacio? You have orders to assist me, do you not? Tell her the words as I said them."

The grass rustled; a ribbon of moonlight spilled over the man. He spoke to Anna quietly, calmly. He never took his eyes off me, as though I was to see this as a favor — a gift.

Anna pulled her hand from Oliver's coat immediately.

She pointed to the dog. Pointed at me. *"El perro no es mío!"*

"You're saying the dog is not hers."

I parried this comment.

"How *could* he be?! A friend, yes, as I am to you as well, but Oliver has never been in your care, Anna."

I allowed my gaze to go upward, as though lost in thought, and then I feigned excitement, as though I had just landed on an idea that would satisfy her, a solution to the problem at hand.

"What we must do," I whispered, once again, nodding toward Anna, "is have your father find you a *puppy* worthy of your love. One that is yours and yours alone. That's what a child like you deserves. Only the best. Isn't that so?"

Anna was silent, lost in contemplation. A wisp of hair fell upon her forehead, and she placed it back upon the crest of her hairline, patting it into place. I did not know if she had been convinced by my speech — if Ignacio had lent my words the credential, and honesty, I wished to convey all the while. The voices of the tortured men continued to ring out. The night was still at this hour one of magnificent beauty. It never grew easier to reconcile, how beauty and horror might commingle in a single moment; to see a cityscape washed clean with the mist of the previous night's rainfall, the streets bathed in the warmth of the morning sun, only for it all to be swept away, polluted by gunfire and the cries of soldiers as they met their end in the very moments that followed. And here I witnessed children playing amongst the spirits of dead soldiers, old women darning clothes while men tortured others only a few miles away. I had seen so much violence, so much death, that in that span of time, before that young girl, I had nothing but love in my heart, the hope that she would be spared such sights; that perhaps in the grandness of the universe, where all is called into balance, I had seen enough horrors for both of us. For a moment, I considered giving up. Handing Oliver over to the child. Perhaps, in a way, she deserved his love, his attention, more than even I did. For I was already lost. And she had so much life ahead of her.

But I am no perfect man. So I muted the voices of those tortured men that rung out in my ear. I put myself first. I did, as always, what was necessary to keep my spirit intact.

"Let us call the General," I said to Ignacio, pulling Oliver to my side. "We can set him right, can't we? Let him know he should gift his most precious daughter not a mangy old dog who belongs to another. But a puppy. Her own. Can we do that now, Ignacio?"

You would have thought Anna could understand me, for she looked between Oliver and me back at Ignacio with generous eyes, the eyes of the child she was, and without waiting for him to answer, she started calling out *Papa, Papa,* as though the man might materialize with that single address. When he did not appear, she jumped to her feet, bounded off, and I stood up and gathered myself, wiping the dust from my backside, standing beside Ignacio as we waited, patiently, for the girl to return with her father.

"*El idiota,*" he said to himself. Then, to me: "This nonsense with the dog. You will get yourself killed."

"Perhaps. Perhaps not. We need only a moment to find out."

I could hear the bodies, the steady drumming of boots, the rising chorus of men caught in serious conversation; a lantern appeared in the doorway leading to the porch, a hand upon it, a body following behind. Who was it but William himself! There was an unreadable expression upon his face, a graveness, perhaps even a sureness, and he gave me a knowing nod before coming to the porch, standing above myself and Ignacio. Others followed, soldiers from the dinner table, their clothes damp and their foreheads beaded with sweat; and finally there was the General and his daughter. Behind those two the others formed a line, as though reporting for duty, and I was down in the garden — as though I was the one with their pending orders, and they need do nothing but await my word. I could not help feeling once more stifled by the fear of the General's retribution, if only for taking him from his business. He had parchment rolled up in one hand; the fingers of his daughter in the other. There was a cutting asperity to his tone, and I could feel his frustration without knowing the words he spoke.

"He wishes to know why you've upset her," Ignacio said. Grumbling from the soldiers, the General whistling to quiet them down, lest he miss my response. "Why she has spurned her gift."

There was no time to hesitate. I had only my tongue to convince this man that I deserved my dog, and perhaps even my freedom. And only one opportunity. Best to use it.

"Tell the General," I began, "I have found his hospitality to be gracious. His daughter to be charming and bright."

This seemed to go over well. The General put a hand to his hip, leaned into my momentary silence, and Ignacio urged me to go on, informing me that the man was growing impatient. There was something in that moment — that sensation of all eyes being upon me. Of having the General's undivided attention. I could tell by only his focus, his rapt attention on the scene I'd created, that he was attending to my every word.

"But Anna is intelligent enough to know that she deserves the best, the finest. This dog is a mutt, like those you might find wandering the desert. It is not fit for such a refined young lady. You yourself saw it running amok."

There were murmurs, now. Even Ignacio spied me with another look of uncertainty.

"I'll only add that this animal is of great significance to me, even if it is fit for the wild. I have spent many of my years with him. And although I've lost much in life, and have grown used to doing so, I would hate to lose this dog on top of so much else. Surely you understand."

Ignacio sputtered, quit his translations outright. He turned to me.

"You should not say that."

"But I said it."

"You will only make him angry."

"He will respect my honesty."

Ignacio did not have to do the translating anyway. A familiar voice peeped up from the line of men at the General's rear; it was William, of course; William who translated my words when Ignacio would not. The man gesticulated delicately, his cadence soft, and I could sense his talent, then, to convey my meaning as I wished it to be shared, and I knew, knew quite well, that regardless of the General's reply, I had indeed said my piece. I trusted William entirely, in the same way I believe he'd come to trust me.

The soldiers shared glances of ambivalence. One man started to chuckle until another man poked him with an elbow. Anna patted her father's pant leg, speaking in a high-pitched tone, commanding him as her father commanded his own soldiers.

The buzz of crickets rung in my ears and punctured the short moment of quiet amongst us. I found myself at a crossroads, awaiting the verdict on what would be my fate.

I did not need to wait long. Anna walked down to me. She smiled at me, pointed at Oliver.

"*Quédate con él. Él es tuyo. Papa me conseguirá mi propio.*"

"What did she say?" I asked Ignacio.

"She said... that the dog is yours," Ignacio told me, exasperated by the exchange.

Anna gave me a cheerful pat upon the pant leg just as she had done her father, before walking back toward him.

I expected the General to shout. To impress his will over me. But he did nothing of the sort. He coolly fluttered his hand in my direction, turned back toward his soldiers.

"He says you can have your dog. He only thought the child would want the gift. It means nothing to him. Nor do you... beyond your use at the mine."

My use at the mine.

The soldiers were abuzz, taking orders, passing them along, saluting as they marched back into the church.

William was leant over the railing of the porch. He captured my attention and beckoned me over.

"We're to leave soon," he said.

"We are?" I asked, exasperated.

"For the mines. He wants to see to it that his underling, Captain Diaz, is not siphoning from the government what is rightfully the people's. That any Americans involved have no control whatsoever. That includes Mr. Harper."

"Mr. Harper?" I asked, for it felt strange to hear the name in this context.

"Yes. And I have told him that Mr. Harper asked for *you* in his letter to Amos Turlow. Turlow has confessed his role in all of this. And I have backed up his story. The General is happy to send you along. The deal to him seems reasonable if it leads to a peaceful resolution. All of what was promised to Turlow will be the General's. Perhaps more, if his men can manage it."

Though stunned, I managed a reply.

"And everyone is aware that Mr. Harper has sought me out?" I asked. "Even Florence?"

"She was present, yes." William's voice was quiet with exhaustion, and I could tell that whatever trial I had faced here was perhaps less taxing than the negotiations he had had with the General in private.

"We will all retire tonight to where we were held before," William said, readying to leave.

"But tomorrow we will go?" I asked once more, in need of his reassurance.

"Just as I said. In the morning. Yes. Before the sun has a chance to rise."

June:
Part Four, Mexico, 1865

There, before June, buried under a cover of dirt, was the carcass of an ox, convulsing, having overcome its own death by some means she could not fathom. It would rise to face her, she imagined — gore her in two.

But she had made a promise to herself: To fear nothing on this journey to escape Wyatt Harper. Joy, she figured, might more likely be found in death than lying beside that man another night. *Do not stop here,* she told herself. And soon, step-by-step, she was right before that fallen ox — found the dead animal's eyes pecked out by scavengers, its body writhing not from its own doing, but due to the teeming mass of carrion beetles feasting on what little remained of the animal. Nature at work, no more no less. Nothing at all to fear. If anything, a signal that she should carry on. That her bravery had been rewarded.

Night had turned to day. Awake by now, she had no idea if Wyatt would be after her. How he might weigh the loss of her presence against the siren call of the mine, the work ahead of him, the prize of his silver. It did not matter in reality, for he was at her back with every step, the din of his voice, asking after his coffee, requesting a kiss on the lips, on his chest, lower, lower...

Unceasing, his needs. The past called after her relentlessly. It crept upon her with the intensity of the now-rising heat.

All their voices. Coleman's, calling for her from his bed, asking if the sounds in the night that scared him were something more than the usual rodents that roamed the dark, the usual creaks of the floorboards; or there was the voice of Florence asking her to come out and play, knowing not that she was in the process of patching up the child's clothes from the last time they'd been out to do the same. Mrs. Harper was asking for her tea, the whining treble of her tone no different from the pitch of the boiling water that June had already put on. They swirled and materialized in echoes that might only be born in a place as quiet as this one, some empty void detached from humanity, where spirits spawned and nightmares came to be true. As she passed abandoned brush shelters, whispers leaked out from those strange collections of twigs and mud, haunted homes long given back over to nature, still inhabited by the voices of those who once dwelt there.

Someone save me, she thought, her will to carry on reduced to nothing. But there was only June to answer the very plea she'd issued.

Save yourself.

The desert was endless. She'd done just as Isaac had said, hewing to the dip in the valley, hugging the mountainside, never stopping to break, for she knew if she stopped she might not go on, and whoever followed this same path might come upon her as she'd come upon that ox. Her flesh picked apart by vultures, roiling under the bite of a thousand beetles. Worth not even a grave, that girl.

It was when she was certain she could not go on — when her feet cried out with every step, the heat like a hammer on her neck — that she noticed the red bark upon the trees before her. The yellow thorns, but not even thorns. A more welcoming display. Bulbous boils, like cotton, but far more beautiful, radiant under the piercing gaze of the sun. *Mesquite trees.* The same sort Isaac had told her to look for.

At this moment it was not her voice, or a voice from her past, that found her, but one from her future. Yes, Isaac's voice. Telling her himself to go on. That he was waiting beyond those trees, just as he'd promised. It was as though she could see him there, beckoning her with a single finger, big gallon hat upon his head, white teeth beaming from his cheeky grin.

With that, she took another step. Then another. Each came easier to her. More of a march, or even a dance; less of a nuisance. Knowing, now, that she was on the right track.

The young woman stopped June in her tracks. Her skin was the color of cinnamon, hair fine as silk, wearing a marvelous red dress and beads in endless rows that snaked around her neck. A colorful head wrap shielded her from the sun, and at a certain angle, June could hardly make out her face at all, as it was lost to the shade. For the first time, June wondered what she must look like herself: two days traveling in the desert with hardly any water at all. Her hair a puff of tangled wool; her skin so wicked of moisture that it cracked if she even attempted to smile. A wild thing. Who was to be wary of who?

"I'm June," she said. "Searching for a man. Tall fellow." She put a hand up to the sky. "Isaac. He told me to come this way. I'm not looking for trouble. Maybe some water, a bit of food. But no trouble. And I'll go without the food and water if need be."

The woman placed a hand upon her side, cocked her head, as though another moment was required to assess the sight before her.

She coaxed June forward with a nod of her head, friendly-like. So when she turned and started off — legs veiled by that dress, the steps so brisk she appeared to be floating — June simply followed at a distance.

She did not even notice the horse behind her, a man on the saddle following her so lackadaisically he seemed unattuned to her presence. She stiffened in fear at the sight of him, but soon he was at her side, in front of her, wandering off from the minor imposition that had gotten in his way.

"Does this place got a name?" she called out to the horseman, the woman, both of them now leading her, although the feeling remained that they were on their own journey that had nothing to do with her at all.

"Where am I...?"

Cautious words. For June thought — no, prayed — she already had the answer. It was her final hope that she was right where she'd meant to turn up.

She could hear the squawk of a chicken, one man calling out to another, and piece by piece, a vision of the place before her became clear as day.

Small dwellings were propped up beside one another, wooden posts pockmarked with sod and dirt and clay holding up a vast webbing of thatch for a ceiling. Others were no different from a log cabin, some interconnected by a roof, others hugging one another with a small cooking station in between.

No more tents, she thought. No more of that endless clamor of hammers and nails, the arguments of Highsmith and Harper about what should go where as they constructed their empire. This place, she thought, looked right lived in.

But where were the people? The woman before her had disappeared by the time June had caught her bearings. The man on the horse had taken off. She met only silence, and in her time, she'd learned that the slightest demonstration of peace often preceded an awesome show of bloodshed. What she wanted was a sign of familiarity, a calming presence. What she wanted was Isaac.

She flinched when she heard something monstrous, a loud bellow, but told herself to keep calm. It was only a laugh — a deep belly laugh at that.

A man was before her with a beard to rival any she'd seen in all her years, his face slashed with divots worn in by time. He was holding a bottle of hooch in hand, pointing at her from a rocking chair on his porch. The way he was stuck to that chair, the smooth repetition as he bounced to and fro, informed her that this was a well-practiced pose, repeated over many years.

"I'd say you're lost," he said to her, "but I'd be wrong. Not close enough to anywhere on this earth that might cast you off and land you here by chance."

"I believe I might be right where I wish to be, sir," she said. "I'm looking for someone. His name is Isaac."

"Isaac?" He slowed the chair to a stop without even putting his feet to the ground. He could control that chair with his mind, so in tune with it he was, she thought.

"Well, I can show you to Isaac. Damn near raised the fool... Isaac! Boy!"

The street was as wide as many in the towns she'd passed on her journey through Texas, but there were no white folks here. No Mexicans, either. Black girls in checkered dresses ran alongside boys in long pants, lost in a spell of fun the likes of which she'd never been privileged to have at such an age. She could see, now, how far this little town went on; caught glimpses of the rows of corn, the plentiful number of individuals milling about their day in the distance.

She believed this was the place she was meant to find, but still could not believe the sight that soon found its way before her. The old man paused at the entrance of an open barn, right near what one might call the center of the town. A group of men were huddled around, of all things, a single cow. Inspecting it like some puzzle that required great concentration to solve.

"Isaac," the man called out. "Got someone here asking for you."

The crowd parted, a booming voice issuing from within.

"Luther, if you're trying to pull one over on me again, you're 'bout to earn my ire for the last time..."

Isaac's head popped up from somewhere beneath the cow, his eyes squinting in her direction along with those of everyone else present. He was, if anything, surprised.

"Who's that girl you got with you?" another man called out.

"You don't worry about that," Isaac said. He pulled his gloves off, gave the cow a pat on its haunches before, finally, walking in her direction. It felt already to June like some moment of celebration. How agonized she had been for days — but her mere success in coming this far now filled her with a pride that nearly made her bawl. He was dressed down here in nothing more than a loose shirt and brown pants, but he had his pendants on, shining under the sun, nearly blinding her, and his shirt, dewed with sweat, exposed the contour of his chest, gave preview to his body.

The old drunk's hot breath was on her back. The other men were snickering. But in the next moment, as Isaac put a hand upon her chin, she heard not a peep. There was, it felt to her, no one else but her and Isaac in the world in that single moment. She wanted it to last forever.

"June," he said.

"Isaac," she said.

"Let's get you cleaned up, why don't we? Ain't doing nothing out here but arguing about who might own this damn cow who wandered this way. Nothing as interesting as you appearing out of nowhere."

She'd faced damnation, been unfurled into a world unknown and reconstituted by the desert's power, its mysteries, its obstacles, into something whole. That's how she felt, for the first time since she'd been free. *Whole.* It took only his hand upon her chin to make that feeling certain.

Her voice was no more than a hush when she said yes.

"I figure I could use a wash."

His hand dropped to her side and found her own. He whisked her away while the other men gaped, heads askew — wondering, she figured, about this strange woman who had found her way to their little corner of the world they'd made their own.

A few checkered calico dresses had been dropped off by other women of the settlement. She left the ones that were too small outside the door to Isaac's, as he had told her to, and they were gone the next time she looked there. She asked who she should thank for such a demonstration of charity.

"Just the sisters," Isaac said, as though this were a well-known party

June should already be familiar with. "They're always ready to assist a newcomer like yourself. Especially after a journey like the one you had to reach us."

He was sitting on a stool, watching her rise from the blanket she'd wrapped herself in to sleep.

"I wish to thank them," she said.

"I think you'll have all the time in the world to do that. Once you get your feet back under you."

It must have been many hours of rest she'd taken, for it was day again. Yesterday, upon rising, she'd rinsed herself with a pail of cold water behind Isaac's house, scared not a whit of who might see her, for the water was a balm better than any salve or oil. When she'd returned through the back he was looking away, shaving down a piece of wood, and only nodded to the blankets on the floor, telling her to rest, that he would bring her some food in time. She was asleep before she'd taken a bite, although she was hungry as all get-out.

Now, sitting up, having finally gotten herself dressed, she could take in the place she hoped to call home. Colorful carpets littered the sawed-wood boards of the flooring. In two corners stood large vases made of clay. Trunks lined the far wall, all of them closed, each their own mystery. A small fireplace was opposite her, though the thought of its warmth was enough to nearly make her wretch. (But essential, she figured, when on cold nights even the heat of another body might not be enough.)

"So you came," he said. "Left that man behind?"

"Yes."

"And how'd you manage? I love a good story."

She told it in detail, Isaac sitting silent all along. She could not tell if he was impressed by her risk to come here or found her nutty, but it hardly mattered to her now. She was here, and really, it was her own questions she wanted answered. And she had so many of them.

Isaac sat on that stool, a red handkerchief in hand. He dabbed at his forehead as he answered before slipping both hands back into his pockets, his foot tapping lightly in a flow with his words.

"I'd like to know who that old drunk is," she asked first, not knowing why. "He said he'd practically raised you."

"*Old drunk*, ha! No. That's just Luther. The one who led us here years ago. Was something like our leader," Isaac said. "Well, still is. He's been brought down by time... But you have to respect a man who delivered his people this far with so little."

Isaac had a way of lingering on his words, lazy-like, consonants whittled down like that piece of wood he was shaving in his hands.

"And the Indians you ride with?" she asked. "I saw one coming up beside me when I entered this town. What of them? They friendly?"

His smile flickered but did not disappear. "Mhm. We work together. But we ain't one. They mind their business and we mind ours. We're a farming people. They ain't. We quarrel a bit. They think we're using too much water, accuse us of stealing this and that. It's always been that way. But it don't matter. We ride together when we need to."

"The government...?" she asked.

"Or the Juaristas. Only one reason we have this land," he said. "Because we do what either party needs done. Keep crops growing aplenty to feed them if they're in need. Protect the land, too. Keep it safe. Deal with more than a handful of slave-catchers, but there's also Apache that get up to some mischief. And in return, if we keep things peaceful, they all let us be. There is nothing better than that, I tell you. I wake when I wish, sleep when I wish, go where I please, and do work — real work — only when they come and ask me to. But it ain't often. When it does, though, I do be gone — days at a time."

He leaned over near her. Put the piece of wood in his lap.

"You okay with that, June?"

She sensed a proposal in his words: a tacit agreement of what was expected of her in this place. A maintenance of his made world while he was gone from it. To hold his ground steady. She knew that agreeing would oblige her to his desires, his needs. She also knew it would give her the chance to make a life of her own here, unbidden by another. What might she do in private, on a bright morning with no one knocking her about to make the coffee, prepare the laundry, visit the water wagon for a trip to the river? What might she truly do with a moment's reprieve?

"I imagine I'll be so busy with my own affairs I won't mind. Besides, I hardly know you, Isaac. You can do what you please. I can't miss a stranger much."

"A stranger you went through the desert to find," he said.

She smiled at him. "Don't make you no less of a stranger."

"Not for long, though."

Isaac bolted up with some hidden reserve of excitement.

"Wait until I show you around these parts. Old Luther done peeked his head in more times than I can count waiting to get a proper meeting in. And Starlight needs a brushing, you could join me in that. And my cousins are here too, you know, they ain't had a chance to say hi..."

He appeared ready for any number of things that might have her interest, might fold her closer into this place, into his life, yet it would all have to wait. He'd have to have a little patience.

"Before all that, though," she said. "The food?"

Already he was dashing over to the fireplace, grabbing a bowl from a small table he'd placed beside it. She almost laughed at the way he lumbered about, his limbs heavy and long, like they might go and knock something over without the man noticing one bit.

"Just a little cornmeal left," he said. "It won't be like you're used to, but it's good. You'll see. Few scraps of pork on the side, but I ate most of that while you was asleep. Couldn't help myself—"

She shushed him, not with a command, but with the speed in which she grabbed the bowl from his hand. There was no waiting on this, no being prim and proper. Her hunger was overwhelming.

"I can get more, if you need it. It's nothing to go ask the sisters."

June swallowed, her eyes almost tearful from the juice that trickled out of the pork — that sensation, lost to her for so long, of a decent-tasting bite of meat. She'd grown used to so much less. *Hunger*. She had the thought it was not something she'd have to worry about again.

"No," she told him. "This will do just fine."

They called this place Amity, and there was far more of it to take in than June had first imagined. Isaac led her down the road, grabbing her around the waist and pointing at whomever he wished to introduce her to: a shy man who said no words, too busy he was tidying the fetlocks of his horse; a young woman half June's age who startled her with a wave, eager for her to return for a meal later that day. This was Isaac's cousin's wife, and she seemed nice enough for June to take her up on that offer of supper. Old Luther came around again, hugging her so close she lost her sense of sight as her eyes nestled into his beard. Still, there were more of them, he said. Many in the cornfields.

"How many can there be?"

"Plenty. It's a town all its own, ain't it? Out here in the middle of nowhere. Who would have thought."

Not June, to say the least.

On the townsfolk came. Quite a few were simply in their chairs before their cabins, playing cards or sweeping, hanging clothes, and it was not lost on June that these people went through their day with an air of ease, a dignity in their answering to no one, that she'd only dreamed of. If only she'd known this place was real. If only she'd come sooner. She could have brought Coleman. Pictured him right there, minding his own business, left alone with his wild thoughts — thoughts too smart for her, the ones he could work out only in private, pacing endlessly as he did when he believed no one was watching, which pleased him so. The regrets she had in leaving him... but it was no time for regret.

"You see the fields?"

He snapped her from her reverie with those few words.

"How could I miss them?" she asked, peering out behind the houses. Long green stalks mixed with hints of yellow just turning out where the husks made themselves seen. Not in rows. Not like anything she'd seen back home. More wild-like. The plants growing as they pleased, but healthy all the same.

But it was the sight beyond the plants that truly caught her eye. More lodges — *jacals* is what they called them — similar to Isaac's home, smoke rising from them as they passed by. She spotted a woman nursing her child at her waist whilst knitting an object she could not make out. But she could swear it was the Indian woman she'd seen when entering Amity. A man was beside her as well; June was certain they were looking right at her. But the distance made it seem unlikely; the mere sight of it was unworldly. Far enough to feel distant, close enough to be the mirror image of this very camp; the couple an eerie replication of her and Isaac.

"Like I said," Isaac told her. "They're only right across the way. We watch out for them. They do the same for us." She noticed a halting nature to his tone, something unsure about the words that could not be resolved by the time they'd left his mouth.

More questions cropped up in her mind, but they were quieted when she found his hand clasping her own, and only with his touch did her mind settle; her thoughts sharpening toward nothing more than an image, in her mind, of the two of them together here, amongst all this living. Embedded in a community the likes of which she'd never fathomed.

"There's still more to see," Isaac said under his breath.

"I'm gathering there always will be with you."

His hand fell from hers, and she ached to find it once more, but the man was talking of his horse now.

"She'll be clamoring to say hello. This way," he said, pointing her back toward the stables. They walked together side by side, arriving to the smell of fresh hay, a doorway mapped with a constellation of flies.

Starlight approached them as they walked in. Her mane was better brushed than June had managed on her own hair, and she smelled fresh from a bath. If this man tended to his horse this well, June wondered, then how might he treat his woman? A thought she stored away for later.

His hand was extended to her again.

"Oh, my, Isaac…?" June scoffed a bit. "I don't know. After last time…"

"You ain't like that last ride?"

"I did, very much so, but we was going mighty fast. I'm not sure I have it in me to try again right now."

Solemn Isaac was, hearing this, as though there were no greater sadness in the world than a woman losing trust in a horse she had the privilege to ride.

He put her hand in his — slowly placed it upon Starlight, letting her feel the horse's rib cage, its chest expanding with every breath. The horse was beautiful, with a dark pinto coat and black splotches that shimmered with ridges like so many leaves.

"Some people think I named her *Starlight* for those white spots on her. I can't blame them…"

Starlight was calm, unnervingly calm, moving not a step while June came closer to her.

"…But that's not it. It's the peace you find when you ride her at night, under the stars, when she's gliding through the dark, not a soul in sight. She's even calmer in the dark. Don't you remember? Not just the pace, but the peace?"

She nodded, remembering that night they shared upon Starlight, the happiness between them, the intimacy of the quiet night and the calm that had welled up within her.

"Go on and dare yourself to try again. See for yourself. No better time than now to just get up and go; if I've discovered anything, it's that. Trust me. At least try to."

He put her hand back upon Starlight. He was getting her mounted on the horse before she could protest. (Not that she would have protested now, after his little speech, which she less believed than found rather kind — moving, in its way.)

"I have something in mind to show you," he said. "Wait and see. You ain't going to regret this night, that much I promise."

But she hadn't regretted a moment since she'd arrived in Amity. Riding into the night once again with a man like this seemed not a risk, but one more step in this new life of hers, one that was happier and more daring than she ever imagined she'd have the chance to experience.

They rode quietly toward a signal in the dark, what June first took to be the glint of eyes — a pack of wolves, maybe — but turned out to be nothing of the sort at all. Her vision corrected itself as they drew near, and Isaac finally told her what was there, all around them, peering back from the beyond.

Many years ago, he said, a group of travelers were laid siege to here. They'd been carrying loads of earthenware, glass, urns and vessels, precious cargo perhaps, and when the fighting ended, whoever had attacked this unfortunate band had also given them the honor of a proper burial. Isaac was of the opinion that whoever had initiated the assault had mistaken the group for another, and only some time after did they realize their mistake and try to do right by the dead. That cargo — all those vessels, broken to pieces — had not just been left scattered about. Rather the shards were fastened to posts, placed atop the burial mounds, some show of recognition to the gods on behalf of the dead; and still, even to this day, no one had removed them. Isaac wasn't sure most knew this place existed at all. It was, to him, something of a private domain, one he and a few others of his tribe took to tending, as though it had a holiness best kept secret — stored amongst themselves.

Some wagons simply lay empty while others were half subsumed by the desert, their wheels choked by sand, grass reaching through their beds. A single yoke was somehow disconnected, a lonesome thing that was hitched under a mound of soot, staring now toward the sky forevermore. She took a step beside the yoke, looked down to make note of it, and when she looked back up the moon had struck those posts with the slightest angle of light, all of them shimmering now in the dark, a silvered tapestry winking back at her.

Only when they'd walked a ways did June realize, looking around, that this abandoned caravan had been corralled together when they'd been attacked, and now she and Isaac were in the midst of the phantom wagons, the soft center, where the burials had been done and the posts installed.

"Over this way," Isaac said, lacing his hand in her own, guiding her forward.

"This here," he said. "This here is for my father." A mound like all the others, but one of special importance. He told her then of the man. That he was a runaway, had ended up in a fort in Florida, where the British had recruited freedmen to help their cause.

"They taught him how to march, use their guns, and he helped build that fort. When the British left off to go negotiate upriver, there was no one left to run the place. So he did that himself. Watched over the others, more freed folk who'd turned up, some Creeks, too, all living together. It was peaceful if you heard him tell it. They'd trade with whomever came their way, and they kept out of trouble, didn't want no trouble at all. But word got back to the law, and the law ain't having no band of free blacks keep a stronghold like that, what with weapons and livestock and all. So they came for a fight. My father helped make it a good one. Told me he lasted eight days in all. Then he fled, eventually settled down near what would come to be his people." He nodded. "My people."

"He sounds like a special kind of man," June said.

Isaac's eyes were on this makeshift grave, a series of pendants, laced as one, atop the ground.

"I had these made up just for him. Just like the ones he wore himself. He ain't make it to Mexico, if you're wondering. I just...well, I never got to see him again. He was sick near the end, and it wasn't right to put him up to a journey like the one he had in store. But I couldn't help feeling like he deserved a resting place. Maybe it's more for me than him, I s'pose."

She knew well of the urge, the need, to make space for those who were gone. When word got back to her, funneled down from Mrs. Harper's father, that her own mother had died, June could not make sense of her grief. If one could even call it that. It was anger at the woman's distance, a newfound understanding — born of her own aging — of her mother's courage in attempting to raise her and Coleman at all. Admiration for her bravery in never showing them her fear — which was constant, June was sure, because she'd faced the same trials herself in the years to come.

Nothing was left to June from her mother, but with the news she had gone outside for a moment, recessed by Mr. Harper to have some time to herself, and without a thought she had decided on a shaded place, beneath their sweet-gum tree; that this could act as the woman's grave; that if she needed to visit her, to tend to these feelings, it was here that transaction might take place. She never told a soul, not even Coleman, in fear it might taint that site or mar her connection to it. It was necessary for her to go on, no matter how ludicrous, to claim that place as her own; just as it was necessary for Isaac to claim this one. It felt right to share the story now, though, for she would never see the tree again, and her mother lived on only in her heart. Isaac deserved to be trusted with this piece of her soul, a confession that spoke to whatever tender part of her she had left in the world. And then, when she had finished, she offered Isaac a hand upon the shoulder, as he bowed toward his father, or the memory of his father, and joined him in the silence that held ownership over the night.

Isaac lit a candle, placed his hand like a saucer over its top, protecting it with a carefulness June found kind. He took her hand in his free hand. The night felt reserved for them, accommodating in its stillness, and they waded through the dark led only by that sole flame until they came upon one of the wagons on the far side of the circle. Its wood was not splintered but almost sanded over, soft as butter on its sides, and the canvas top was unmolested, so intact it might be used as a better blanket than June had had access to on the journey to Mexico.

There felt to be no rhyme or reason for Isaac leading her to this wagon in particular but she had no complaints, both of them sitting cross-legged, eye to eye, the candle on the ground at their feet, flitting toward one, then the other, as if grasping for touch.

He didn't say a word. It was as though there was a procedure in place for this ritual, one he did not care to share but was nonetheless adhering to. Once more she was prepared to encounter a sense of fear, so far out in the wild, but with Isaac it never came to pass. However shallow it might sound, it was what she valued so much from him in the time they'd spent together. The way in which he imposed himself upon his surroundings, upon space itself. His warmth, like the flame before them, spreading over wherever he might move. Well-fed he was — large, bounteous. His presence defined, to her, the meaning of *safety*, and in that chasm of security, of what was blossoming to be his love for her, she found solace.

She wondered, studying the lines of his broad face, what solace she brought him. Then she asked a question, puncturing the silence.

"What made you want me, Isaac?"

"Why ask a question like that? At a time like this?"

"Don't you think I ought to be curious? You got women back in Amity, don't you? There were others you saw right alongside me. But you ain't want them."

"No, that's true. I wanted you, June." He teased her, grinned, told her a pretty girl is a pretty girl, does it need more explanation than that? But she did not let the matter pass.

"Tell me."

Isaac smelled of tobacco and sweat and hay, all those scents emphasized by the intimacy of the wagon, the space between them that somehow seemed to shrink as they sat before one another in a trance brought on by the night, by this place. The candlelight strewed rolling shadows upon the canvas tent; living, frantic things.

His mouth opened, as if for a breath, then closed again. She could see his mind working, although not on what, which surprised her. So often was the case with men, that she could perceive, with only the mood, an energy of the room, what they might require of her, language providing only a means to explain what was already so clear. She could read an apology, an assuagement, words of comfort, or a false laugh on instinct alone. It was routine, really. But Isaac stumped her.

"I can't say I was sure you were more than just a pretty thing at the river, no," he said. "But when we seen you work those barrels in the water — with that white man, and that other girl — that was when I knew."

She recalled that day, with Celia and Mr. Baynard, the endless toiling, the water up to her chest, the soggy barrels heavy with their burden.

"When the wagon broke?" she asked, thinking of his rescue, their riding Starlight into the vast beyond of the desert.

"No," Isaac told her. "We were there on patrol, early morning saw you two, and I told Titus we ain't moving until they make it back to their camp. We were watching the whole time from our perch up there."

"You could have helped, then." This said with a note of humor.

"Didn't want to interrupt."

"And still you ain't answered my question."

"Your strength," he said, so quickly it brought her to attention. "Titus done made a bet with me. Gave you all an hour, at most, and when we heard that man exclaim there would be more trips to come, Titus said there's no way those girls manage. But I sat there for the longest time and I witnessed a woman with so much grit that even under the heat of the sun, under the weight of that barrel and the weight of whatever unholy mess laid across your heart, you ain't stop to take a breath. You outworked that man and that woman and you did it with something I guess is just pure grit, something deeper than grit, and I admired that, loved it no less, for the way you ended that day with the same dignity in which you started it. Had nothing to do with your labor, but the way in which you greeted and ended the task before you like it was nothing. And I don't even think you noticed how exhausted that man was, and I seen the way that other girl didn't make it back to work a second round or a third. I've never seen a woman work like you, June, or talk with the pluck you got, or move with your spirit. I figure I'm only half the person you are, but maybe I can be whole if I keep someone like you around. Call me selfish, then. Maybe that's what I am."

She could not quite land upon the proper words to reply. Isaac did not seem to require an answer at all. He had given her what she'd wanted and now he wished to move on, pass this over, and return to what it was he did here. That private act, or process, that he enacted in this place; an act, no less, that he had granted her access to. His eyes were downcast. His mind now elsewhere.

"What are we doing?" she asked, wishing not to interrupt, but also pawing toward the dark for a bit more guidance, the proper way to play the role that was expected of her. "What you want from me here, Isaac?"

"You don't have to do a thing," he told her plainly. "I certainly don't want nothing from you. I'm just thinking 'bout mine. Maybe you can think about yours. I like to have some time with them. Out here. But if you want to be silent — sit and do nothing more — well, no one here to stop you."

For a time again he spoke no more. His hands were in his lap and his head nodded ever so, as though he'd heard the start of a tune, and with another moment, hungry to return to normalcy, she found herself staring out of the canvas flaps, eyes on the farthest wagons at the other side of the circle, jutting out like boulders embedded in the valley, returned back to nature. And with that glimpsed thing she felt the crush of time upon her, so strong was the sensation, the fear, that she turned back to Isaac, who was now grumbling to himself, to whomever he was in contact with from a beyond she could not divine.

Once more she was lost to the moment, groping for a way forward, frightened, finally, by this night, by this bizarre practice, urging herself to run, but she located Isaac's words again, thought it best to trust him, to follow them wherever they might lead: *Think about yours.*

And so she was back in Baton Rouge; back with Coleman. How small he was as a boy, the bones of his spine visible whenever he walked before her, poking out from his back; his neck thin as a chicken's. Her love for him was so deep a thing that it took root at her core, stirring her at night, blossoming and expanding like it was feeding on her insides. When he returned, at the end of a long day, she would put her hand on the back of his head, twist the small curls there into little balls, the touch of him enough to quiet the demons that roamed about Harper's basement, lurking, encroaching ever closer as her spirit waned.

She recalled a day he had not returned home. Florence had been the first to come downstairs — as June was just about to get her apron on to serve dinner — and informed her of as much. The man who had retained him for the afternoon, Mr. Harper's old acquaintance, had actually just arrived to join them for the meal, and Coleman had not come in tow. Curious, the man said, for he had actually sent the boy home early.

June did not pause before taking the apron back off. Usually at this time her legs had begun to buckle from the day's effort, her eyelids falling against her wishes, but now she felt a great gathering of her energy reserves, a hidden pool she could dip into only when warranted by a problem such as this one.

Ready now, she turned toward Florence, who did not seem entirely pleased to be involved in this herself.

"Should I go get him?" June asked.

"I think that would be best."

June provided her a smile, followed her up the stairs and found Mr. Harper and his friend on the porch smoking. Mr. Harper looked disappointed, even pained by this unusual occurrence, and was eager to have it resolved as quickly as possible.

"Please fetch him," he said, aiming his cigar down the road, sending her in that direction, and she knew very well what might result if she did not return quickly enough.

She well knew where he was. There was a bridge leading toward town, where he would go and loiter with any spare time away from home, absorbing the sight of the passing carts and travelers, his curiosity sated, it seemed, by being able to witness the goings-on of this one small quarter of the city.

It had rained recently, and within a puddle before a tall oak June had witnessed her own reflection. The exhaustion in her face — how old she looked in contrast to her age! An anger boiled within her.

She first spotted a mess near the bridge: bottles, a row of fishing rods with their lines jumbled as one, tools as well, all sorts of what could either be refuse or possessions.

And there was Coleman with another boy — Heath, she believed his name to be — who belonged to Mr. Dobbs, an esteemed physician fond of the same elixirs he gave his patients.

Coleman was regaling the young man with some story about his jaunt downtown once, where he had seen the press where the *Gazette* was printed, had asked about the machine, which was really like some gargantuan loom, very complex, and the boy simply nodded along as Coleman, and it was mostly Coleman's doing, carefully picked up the detritus, carefully organizing the items into piles that reflected their sort. The other boy was telling him he'd never seen such a thing, found it hard to believe it existed. Would look for it himself when and if the opportunity arose, for what a sight it must be.

When Coleman saw her approach, he appeared totally flummoxed by her appearance. He excused himself, but the boy seemed unfazed, and began working where Coleman had just stopped.

"What's gotten into you?" She nearly put a hand to his ear but held off, but he acted like she had all the same. "Tell me. Now."

"Oh, well, I saw Heath here needed some help," Coleman said. "Horse got caught on the bridge; only took a kick to turn a few saddlebags over, and Mr. Dobbs had an appointment to get to. Told Heath to clean it up and return it all by sundown. I did not want him to get in trouble."

"So you'll take on the risk so that boy can get home before he meets a whipping? That's what you're telling me?"

"Not exactly, I — "

"And there is dinner to serve, but I got to run down the road searching high and low for your scrawny behind."

"I'm sorry, June."

Before starting on from there, she recognized a faint twitch upon her brother's throat, the slightest contraction, one she'd seen before when under an assault from Miss Harper, and she realized, far too late, that she was coming upon him in the same way that woman might. That she was terrifying, if not humiliating, her brother in front of this other boy.

"Come here," she said. He was already taller than her now, if only by an inch or so, grown in most ways, but she could still, as she always had, put a hand on the back of his head, pull him close to her here. "It's all alright. But come home now, okay? Heath can manage on his own. Much as you're fitting to help every soul in this world, some will just have to figure out their business without you. You hear me?"

Coleman only nodded, and soon they were back on the road, heading toward the lane to the big house. His head hung low; that spine of his protruding in a show of dourness that was rare in him. The branches upon each tree that lined the road interlaced as one, creating a vast web as far as the eye could see, so complex she could not define which limbs belonged to which. There was no birdsong and the day was growing cold.

"Tell me," June said into the silence, her voice leveled by her shame, "about that press. I ain't ever heard of something so strange in all my days."

His mood lifted then. The light reentered his face.

"Well!" he said, beginning on a speech that would last them until they reached the house, his voice filling the road and livening it once more. And only as Coleman went on, speaking mysteries she would never comprehend, did June realize that her anger moments before was born of the selfishness — the fear — she found in seeing her sibling speaking to another boy as he did with her. The threat, if one could call it that, that her brother might find connection in another. The guilt bathed her as they both carried on down the road.

And she thought now, opening her eyes to the candlelight (had she even realized they'd been closed?), seeing Isaac staring back at her, that she had now found a connection of her own. Knew that she must disabuse herself of that base fear that had ruled her life, imposed upon Coleman as well: that only the two of them might fend for the other. That no one else might be trusted.

What she would do to apologize to Coleman! But she knew, quite well, that he had forgiven her. That he would want nothing more than for her to find her own happiness. That same sense of solace she'd experienced earlier; that was present in this wagon.

Isaac was staring at her. June was staring at him. He nodded, as though realizing that both of them were now coiled by their haunted pasts that had allowed them to find one another; by fate; by this very night. The candlelight flickered new impressions against the wall. She looked upon them, and when her eyes returned to Isaac's, he'd set out the palm of one hand. Brought his index finger and thumb together and stubbed the flame.

10

Anna, in our last moments together, had gifted me with the barrette she had put upon Oliver. It was safe in the pocket of my shirt, the only memory of the Birdcage I wished to leave with.

The trunk, meanwhile, was at the rear of the wagon, bobbing like a ship in stormy seas whenever we hit a bump in the road. A soldier of Ignacio's, Hector, sat upon it, gun in hand, and he was accompanied by another, Paco, who was armed himself. Before both was their captive, Amos Turlow, still in cuffs. The man was to be consulted for directions and tell Mr. Harper, upon our arrival, that he was giving up any claim to his earned land in return for his life — and his brother's life. The trip would not be over for him at the mines. He'd be carried on to a penal colony to await sentencing, where he would spend, I gathered, more time than one might wish to (purposefully kept away from his brother, a punishment that seemed as grievous as the rest). As William put it, Amos would be swallowed up by the country whole, never settled in one place long, put to work, awaiting a trial that looked to be in the offing but would never arrive. Perhaps for this reason Amos hadn't said a word the entire journey. And he certainly looked distressed: hair oily due to the dankness of the air; sweat covering his face, soaking his shirt and swamping up his beard. The rest of us looked no better.

The mood, for all we'd been through, for all we'd risked and overcome, was somewhat dire. But still, I had Oliver. Florence had her mother's shoes, which she'd wanted so badly. With any luck, we might make it to Mr. Harper's mine in short order. A possibility that grew more tantalizingly real with every canter of the horses, every passing mile of the desert beneath us.

We'd left the Birdcage in a single wagon, the General wishing for us to travel light to avoid drawing attention to a wagon train, for Indians were common here and could attack with no notice. There was vulnerability in greater numbers. William Free, for his part, assured us we would be safe from all threats, but I knew now the man's confidence sometimes led to trouble (judging by our recent capture).

And sure enough it was William, only a few hours into the trip, who told the driver to halt, flagging us down from the pony given to him by General Chavez. Scalp poles dotted the landscape from previous expeditions that had ended in a manner we wished to avoid. Signs of abandoned campsites.

"We will turn toward the Sierra Madres," William said. "The Birdcage being north of Anáhuac, I don't think we're more than two days from Nacimiento if we keep a decent pace. I'll canvass the area. And when it's safe, we'll carry on."

Florence, at my side, was vigorously petting Oliver, so much so that the whites of his eyes would show with a spate of shock as her hand swept down from his skull to his mane. I had never seen her so jittery. Or perhaps it was merely a consequence of her own anger. I can hardly express how hurt she had felt upon finding out that her father's letter had requested my presence alone. If only I'd had the courage to tell her what it said myself, in a more palatable manner, when I'd had the chance previously... but it was all too late for that.

The dawn of the morning brought with it the silence of the barren world before us, the only sight the foreboding one of the coming mountain range of insurmountable height, one that stood in such strange contrast to the scorched-crimson tones of the desert. William told me we would go on beside the mountain, then through a valley that was well known to travelers of this land. There, we would find the mine.

"Those bushes," William said to Ignacio, pointing toward an emergence in the distance, a hedge of greenery. "I suggest we stop there. I'll scout ahead. All of you wait. If I don't return —"

"Once you return we will carry on," Ignacio said. A cigarette glowed at the tip of his lips like a tong just pulled from a fire. He ordered the driver to stall the horses. William hopped off the bed of the wagon, returned to his own mount, and quickly rode off.

A scattered bramble of mesquite cropped up before us, and Florence asked to get out to stretch her legs, which Ignacio allowed. "Just stay close," he said.

"If I may accompany her," I said. "In case anything might happen."

"If you wish. But leave the dog." He looked out over the brush. "Coyotes."

I did as he said. I followed Florence as we left out the back of the wagon, where we then met the warm embrace of the sun. The flora was belly high; a few trees were scattered across the plains. If there was any enemy here, they would see us. But there was so little movement, the slightest show of wind a startling burst in the great spans of nothingness, that it was difficult to picture any human materializing from so little.

"I do not need your protection," Florence said. "You clearly have not my best interest in mind."

"It's only by watching over one another that we stay safe," I said. "As for your interest, I will address that in a moment."

"How terribly pompous you sound, without even realizing it. Your company is more bothersome than you might know. Just leave me be."

Which I did, staying far enough away to afford her absolute privacy, close enough to gather if anything went awry. I looked upon the mountain range, those great titans towering over not just us, but the entire world. Again I was struck by the eloquence of this place; by what might be found in the wild just by putting on a pair of shoes and walking toward the unknown. Throw a blindfold on a man who believes he has seen it all, send him five hundred miles in any direction, and I can assure you he would be in awe of the mysteries, the grandeur, that falls into his line of sight in the days that follow.

When I was not imperiled, starving, or risking life and limb, I could reflect on moments like these with a feeling of great fortune, although such opportunities were rare.

I finally turned to look once more for Florence, but I could not see her. I called her name once. Twice. Only then did I begin to walk in the direction in which she'd headed, speeding up only when my calls continued to meet silence.

I was worried by the time I came upon her. She stood before a cactus, of all things — examining the plant with a judicious eye, her head tilted, her attention consumed by its particulars. Then, for reasons I could only imagine, she placed a finger upon one of its sharp paddles. A single trickle of blood patiently tracked its way down her hand.

"Florence, what are you doing—"

"I am not in the mood for conversation."

"Whatever mood you might be in, I do not want to see you harm yourself."

"Have you not harmed me already? Withholding any information that might injure my feeble mind. Planning behind my back, all while you pretend to protect me like my guardian angel. You think I am weak, Coleman. And perhaps the worst of it is that you refuse to admit as much. To afford me so small a gift after knowing one another so long."

"Your hand, Florence. Please stop that."

"A weak, weak girl you believe me to be. So weak that it did not cross your mind to consider that the second I found Turlow gone from our home back in New Orleans, I snuck into his guest room and read the letter my father had written. That I knew all along, of course, that he had not called for me or my mother."

"That can't be."

"Of course I knew, Coleman. As well as I knew it was an unspeakable embarrassment for my mother. Equally so for myself. So much so that I found it best to ignore altogether, to hope that the truth be forgotten, if only I let it be so."

At this, my voice faltered. "It is unspeakable, what your father has done, and I can't say much better for myself. Hiding the truth, even if you did not wish for it to be revealed."

"And yet it is true."

I watched as she slowly lay her entire palm upon the cactus head — let it rest upon its spiked coat, pressing, pressing, the needles bending under the weight.

Her shoulder blades unclenched. She released her hand from the cactus; inspected her palm, each line flooded with blood. She nodded with a queer tranquility, as though her hand contained something that might be read into further, some great wealth of knowledge only she was privy to.

"Do you know," she said. "Back when we were of schooling age, when you stole my books right from my bedroom, I was fully aware of your doing so. I believe you took my father's, too. Those dusty tomes from his study, ones he'd never notice might have gone missing. Snatched them right up from under him and took them up to the attic, making them your own for a time before putting them back where they belonged, swapping them out for others. I was aware of it all. And I did nothing with that information. I allowed it."

Florence stepped closer to me.

"I wonder, also, if you knew that my mother wished to get rid of all those books in your attic in New Orleans. That I told her I would not allow it. Told her they meant so much to me. The memories, in particular. Memories of my father reading them to me at bedtime, of him studying his manuals in the parlor room... that I wished to keep them. That those books lent me access to my father, even in his absence. Of course this wasn't true. But it was a *favor I paid you*. I thought if you might learn more than a book of etiquette, about the comportment of a servant, you'd grow to be more than the strange, shy fixture of a boy who occupied the basement of my home. Who might, one day, even care about the other inhabitants who lived above him. How silly I sound. But that does not make it untrue. For even if I was close to the other girls who came around for supper — those girls who gossiped with me on which color elastics they might wear for the Widows' Ball, their plans on which gentlemen they'd cozy up with at the Needle Society Gala — it was those nights alone, sneaking down to see you and June, that gave me the only bit of closeness I had with the soul of another back then. The only conversations that left me *happy*. I looked forward to them.

"But I believe, after all I have been through at your side, that it was all for naught. Call me pathetic. A charmed girl brought to nothing. But what I share with you now is my sincere belief: That your comfort in concealing the truth all these weeks — after all we've been through, after all I thought I'd done for you — is perhaps more injurious than my father's disinterest, which I've grown accustomed to by now. As sad as that sounds."

I shuddered at the note of every word she imparted upon me, and I felt the familiar sensation to withdraw from an interaction I could not stomach: one too naked, too charged, for me to bear. How to put the truth into words she might understand? That I would *never* be more than her former servant. That I had resolved to have more than an ongoing revolution of time where I, Coleman, was made to await her next request upon me. That I might offer her my condolences, my mercy, and whatever grace I might have access to in my heart, while knowing it would never go so far as to bring us any closer than we were in this very moment. The openness she sought was not mine to provide.

My thoughts were interrupted as Florence leant down to the ground. The earth was wet with her blood, the dusty sand turned ocher, and she took the mixture, applied it to her palm like a dressing, a salve, and let it set while she turned her gaze to the sky.

"If only I knew what you were thinking! But I never have. Never truly. I imagine I never will. As it was with my mother. But yes, at least I discovered my father's true intentions. However difficult they are to admit. That is something, isn't it?"

A great mass of birds appeared in a swell above us, scattering into some formation I could not make sense of. They were gone just as quickly, and by then Florence was right before me, her eyes level to my own, her face inches from mine. I could not quite understand her expression: A whispered haunting found in the sharpened point of her cheekbones, the flutter of her lips, carried the rawness of a faint tragedy. I realized then that for all her talk of how little she knew of me, perhaps I knew very little of Florence. She inhaled deeply, her exhalations hot gusts against my face. She placed her mud-soaked hand upon my shoulder; looked me up and down with a cool gaze.

"I will leave this place soon," she said. "I will return home to a life I will make my own. A life you cannot even imagine, Coleman. I ask, until that moment, that you do not lie to me again. That you treat me as your equal. I have had men lead me astray for all my years, Coleman. And when this odyssey ends, I will never leave my destiny in the hands of another again. I promise you that."

The mud oozed through the cotton of my shirt. I could feel the dampness of its mixture, of blood and dust and earth, sink into my skin. I could only stand in awe of her strange, unsettling resolve.

"Might we return to the wagon?" I asked.

But she did not need my consent. She'd begun walking back before the last word had left my mouth.

William returned and the journey continued with him leading our small band up the road toward the mountains until we were snugly amongst the thicket of bushes he'd pointed out earlier in the day. He dismounted, and soon all of us were disembarking from the wagon, Hector leading Turlow, Florence following behind. The sun was just past its highest point. Soon the weather would grow tame; Ignacio even mentioned the chance of rain.

When I ventured to the ground with Oliver in tow, Hector gave me a nudge. Made a comment I could not understand.

"Hector is going to help us set up camp," Ignacio told me. "You are to watch Turlow."

So it was that I was somehow left with the criminal, while the others had the task of preparing us for a night's rest.

Amos, standing there beside me, had his face now fastened somewhere between grimace and smile. William by then had arrived at the back of the wagon himself. He appeared weak from having done so much in a single day, all that had been accomplished to get us this far. He checked his compass once more, put it away, before surveying Amos for a moment and nodding toward a particular spot of shade beside a towering bush.

"Over there," he told me. "Set him to sit there so we can have him in sight as we work. It should not take long."

"Well, you heard him," I said to Turlow.

Turlow did not so much follow my instruction as carry on under his own directive. When we reached that stalky bush he faced up to me, his pug nose hard as a knuckle, gleaming like a polished knob under the heat of the sun. His facial hair was a momentous tangle that overwhelmed his features, his mustache so wild I thought the hairs might reach into his nostrils and stymie his breathing.

"This is what this wasteland has made of us," he said. "Two men cast aside, with nothing to show for our efforts except our own frailty. And for what?"

"You would have to ask yourself that," I said. "I am on the same path I've long wished to go on, the same one taken by my sister."

"Oh, come now. There is no reason to believe she is even still alive. It's a pity how devoted you are to someone who has in all likelihood given up hope of ever seeing you again."

"You speak as if you know a thing about us. She and I only ever had each other. To think she'd lose hope — ".

"You know," Turlow said, "I only ever had my brother. Just like you two, worked hard. Bonded over our own toil."

"It's fine for you to quit right there — "

"If only you knew what we were subjected to. And what had to be done just for us to survive. We thieved — we killed, yes — but who in this day and age, forced into such dark corners of this world, might not? I had no other option. All in the pursuit of the smallest bit of safety. All of that led me to this very moment."

"Please spare me the story, Amos. I don't wish to hear it."

"I ask you how my situation is any different from that of you and your sister. It was all I wanted to give Cyrus. A safe place. A good life..."

I wished for some water, but Hector, who was in possession of the canteen, was inspecting a wagon spoke beside Paco. I thought to look for Florence, but she must have been on the other side of the wagon, consulting with William, for she was not in sight. My thirst would have to wait.

"...When that girl's father sent that letter, asking for help, I felt it to be some message from the heavens. I would be rewarded with a slip of land that would be our refuge, and in return I need only deliver a Negro to some miner, so he might retrieve some slave woman — "

"My sister."

"Your sister. But with his promise, with a show of a bit of silver, I saw my future laid out before me. I saw my brother and myself safe. Sound.

"If only I had known," Turlow said. "That I would be made to watch him with his hands chained up, pummeled as they demanded my assistance in finding this godforsaken mine. What I would give to have never gone to New Orleans! To have never helped the captain of that ship upon my return. If only I had known..."

"Known what, exactly?" I asked, doing my best to follow along as I secretly, desperately, wished for Hector to return, so I might escape this conversation.

"Of your inexhaustible guile. The cunning of your tongue. The bare facts of your person. How you do not trust others, but only the power they wield. That you follow in the shadow of whoever might help you. Like a dog. I should have put you in a collar myself the day we left that dreadful city. Gagged you, strapped you to a board, and brought you to Mr. Harper like the slave you were. Like the servant boy you *still* are."

A great scrawl of clouds floated above us, and there was a moment of lovely shade, casting us into dark. I nearly shivered from the chill. I was praying for that rain Ignacio had alluded to, but it did not seem likely to come.

"As Florence mentioned just yesterday," I said, "it is you in chains, Turlow. You who has been made into the fool. If you were better read, you would know the ending that meets those with hearts like yours. Nothing good. Except the cuffs you now wear and the hardships that have befallen you. Lord, I wish I had the ear of another during my most difficult days, in the same way I have so graciously offered mine to you right now, but I never had such fortune. In fact it was Mr. Harper himself told me a real man must weather his hardships without complaint, and so I did, and I must say yours are not so bad, all in all. Perhaps one day I will show you my scars, Turlow. Pain of some permanence. Until then, let us end this talk. I can bear hearing of your troubles no longer. And you don't deserve to share them."

To this, Turlow had nothing more to say. That odd expression was still on his face. Finally, as though only now recalling William's orders of a moment before, he squatted to the ground in silence, his eyes straight ahead on the men repairing the wagon.

That night, everyone ate from the same kettle. It was a fine vegetable soup cobbled together with whatever General Chavez had provided or the men had foraged, which was not much. Paco had prepared the meal, and for every compliment he received for his cooking he would take a bow and smile warmly, like the proud chef he was. Oliver was beside me, in good spirits, and the food was apparently a great draw to him, as he would not take his eyes off the kettle.

I told him he had had breakfast, that he was well fed and could wait until morning to eat again. But Paco apparently had other ideas, for it was he who placed some bits of corn on the ground, which Oliver ate greedily. Hector then cackled in encouragement as Paco gave a flick of his spoon, which operated something like a trebuchet, so the dog chased after the corn that flittered across the ground some feet away before returning for more.

"You tease him!" I said, all of us laughing as Oliver raced round the fire in circles, wherever the corn might have landed.

"*Buen perro*," Hector said, before stealing the ladle from Paco and having another bite of the soup himself.

"There, right there!" William blustered, seated beside Florence and Ignacio, an object gleaming in his hand. I could see it now: It was his compass.

"What's happened?" I asked.

"The arrows have gone mad," William said to Ignacio, who looked rather unconvinced.

William shot up, walking swiftly ahead, and for reasons I can't quite explain, I felt the need to do so myself, as did Ignacio, all of us compelled on like three giddy schoolboys in league with one another.

"Allow me," I said as I caught up with him, hardly concealing how eager I was to see magic at work.

But by then William appeared disappointed, having halted beside me, slouched over in defeat.

"Well, now it's stopped. I swear it was acting strange."

I put a hand on his shoulder. Looked down at the compass, which was now acting as routine as any compass I had seen before that very day — or after, for that matter. Nonetheless I found it to be as magnificent as ever, silvered under the glow of the evening stars.

"Do you think..." I began.

William looked at the compass sheepishly, then shut it as Ignacio drew up beside us.

"What is he on about?" Ignacio asked. "Tell me."

"It's ludicrous," William said, the reluctance apparent in his voice. "But my mother gave this compass to me. And when it misbehaves — acts oddly — well, I believe her to be sending a message of sorts. She told me it would always lead me to her."

At this Ignacio stepped back, for having followed along even this far he now felt foolish when the road led to such a dubious revelation.

"It's not ludicrous," I said, my tone hushed. "Not at all. There is no reason to believe our loved ones are not with us, in some respect, even when they are physically absent. In my most trying hours I have heard the voice of my sister urging me to push on. When I am saddened, I'm reminded of her laugh, and it echoes in the distance — loud enough that I often see others turn, confused, as though they hear it too, even when it is revealed to be from another source entirely: a group of children giggling; a man whistling a tune as he makes his way down the street. But I know full well that she is there with me, embedded in my surroundings unseen, for parts of our past never disappear entirely. Ignacio, surely you've experienced something similar to what I describe."

Ignacio mulled my words thoughtfully before he offered a reply — his own testimony.

"For me, like you, it is *sound*."

He told us that he would often hear the Rio Grande in his sleep; that his home was right upon a bluff, and he would sometimes nap outside where the water flowed.

"The current was so quiet on a summer morning," he said, "and the crickets are singing their songs alongside the birds, and as I open my eyes to see it all, I wake up, for it is really a dream. It is no miracle like William describes. But it does feel real. Just as when you hear your sister. Yes. Much like that."

William's eyes had settled on Ignacio, listening so intently I thought nothing could pull his attention from this moment. He seemed captured by the man's words — as though he had never really considered Ignacio, the individual, at all until this information had been shared.

The fire crackled before us. Sparks ascended into the air, painting the darkness with a fine spread of embers. Ignacio's face was tensed in grave thought; William's eyes were set to the distance; and there I stood, fixed between a man who longed for nothing more than his long-begotten mother and a man aching for a life he could not quite claim as his own.

"Such thoughts do us no good," Ignacio finally said, once the silence got too loud. "You," he nodded at William, "take your compass back to camp, we shall take our memories, and all of us will rest."

"Yes," I said. "Rest would be useful. And do let me know if I might help in any way. I feel a bit lively. I could keep watch, perhaps."

Any show of gentleness had escaped from Ignacio's face. "Do you even know what to watch for?"

To this, I had no reply.

"Rest," he said. "It is all you need to worry over."

"Whatever you say, Ignacio. Good night. Both of you."

They only nodded. I scooped up Oliver and began to return to the fire when I heard William call my name. Before I had turned, he was at my side.

"I wanted to thank you," he said.

"For what?"

"For defending my honor at the dinner table. Before the General."

"It feels like a lifetime ago... Say no more. You were just a bit askew."

"It needed to be said. Thank you." He put his hand out, and so I shook it, and soon he was at my back once again.

My bedroll was beside Florence's, and I sat down there, curling my legs beneath me. It was late. In the near distance Turlow was snoring, an awful wheeze, Hector sitting beside him fiddling with Turlow's timepiece, which he had taken for himself. Florence slept with her feet exposed near the crackling fire, ankles swollen from travel. But she was warm, at least. Solace, always, in the little things.

"Good night, then," I said to Oliver, but he was already circled up beside my chest, a step ahead of me. When I closed my eyes, tuning out Turlow, seizing on the quiet beyond him, I could hear it for myself as a dream took hold of me: the sound of rushing water. The sound of the Rio Grande.

11

It was that hour of the morning when the cool of the previous night vanishes into the air. The heat of the day flushed through the desert as though discharged from some chasm in the earth unseen, a burst of energy that preceded even the waking of the sun. Before I'd come to, I found myself lost to another dream. I was in Mrs. Harper's garden, back in New Orleans. Mrs. Harper herself had her back to me, and the sight of her was familiar, although odd, for so rarely did she venture to inspect the flowers she had me grow. She was in a summer dress, white as snow, yet her voice was hard when she spoke.

"Get me more lye, Coleman. Just adding to my troubles again. Forcing me to do your job like so."

She was hunched over the rinsing tub, her feet covered in suds. But it was what the bin contained that caught my eye: only one article, it seemed — the yellow dress she'd worn on *The Jubilee*.

"Inside now!" she said.

But when I turned, the door of the house was locked. I looked back at Mrs. Harper, her hand now upon the washing paddle. I saw her arm, pale as the moon, lift up the dress — and it was not water upon it, but *blood*, and when the paddle landed, the blood splattered back toward me, and I could not help whimpering in shock. Mrs. Harper only struck it harder.

"Lye, Coleman. Now."

Another thud. Another. I seized in fright, and as I began to stutter — telling her that the door was closed, that I was sorry, so sorry for all I had ever done — I broke from the dream and lunged awake, gasping for air. There, again, was the thudding in my ear, quiet in the calm of the morning. I had to squint to see what was taking place in the near distance: Amos Turlow had an object in his hands, his arms violently striking what I thought to be the ground. My eyes adjusted and I finally made sense of the circumstance. In Turlow's hands was one of his boots. He brought it down with great force, slamming it upon Hector as the man lay motionless, gurgling as he made efforts to breathe.

I instinctively screamed at the sight; the camp quickly stirred, bodies rising from the dark.

"Stop him!" I bellowed. "Someone must stop him!" It was Ignacio who rose up first, grabbing for his pistol, but by the time he went to steady it, Turlow had Hector's rifle in his hand. Turlow fired one shot, so quickly I hardly had time to blink before Ignacio had fallen backward.

Paco attempted to tend to Ignacio but he protested, telling the man to get Turlow. By then it was too late: Turlow had stood up and was sprinting away, still in cuffs, slowly becoming nothing more than a dot disappearing into the distance.

William was nowhere to be seen, and it was another few moments — key moments, it felt to me — until he burst forth from the wagon where he had been sleeping.

"What's happened?" he asked, loading his own rifle as he came upon us.

"Turlow..." I said, for it seemed no other words were needed.

"He's gone," Florence said.

William seemed unfazed. He leant down to Ignacio, inspecting the man's wound, a fair bit of blood already pooling upon the ground, while

Ignacio grew immediately frenzied. He squeezed Paco's arm, pointing wildly in Turlow's direction: *"¡Vamos! ¡Dale!"*

With this Paco rushed for a horse, jumping onto it bareback, immediately giving chase.

Florence was at my side, wrapped in a blanket, surveying the situation with as much confusion as I had.

"Go wait in the wagon," William said to us. "He can't get far."

"I am going to go follow them—" William began, but with this I interrupted him myself.

"Stay," I said. "We do not need more lives being risked out there. And we must see after Hector."

"*See after Hector?*" William blustered, as though this were a joke. "Look what's been done to him."

"We should hide," Florence said, her voice at my ear, breaking my train of thought. "We will be no help to them."

Paco disappeared into the morning dark, the horse galloping so powerfully that it echoed back upon us with the deep-drawn boom of an ocean's tide striking the shore, again and again.

William was applying a piece of cloth — his own torn-off shirtsleeve — to Ignacio's arm to stanch the flow of blood. Ignacio himself was pale enough to reveal the blue of his veins beneath his skin. Blood collecting beneath him. William turned to me. Nodded to the wagon.

"Listen to her," he said. "To the wagon with you both."

I began to search about my person, but Florence already had Oliver cradled in her arms, safe there. As we retreated I could not help looking back upon William, one hand tamping the flow of blood from Ignacio's wound, the other feeling for the cartridge box at his side.

"I can help him load that gun," I said. "At the least I can assist in helping Ignacio while we wait."

"Or you can *live*," Florence said, practically tugging me at the collar. "I suggest you choose that option."

We entered the wagon and sat behind Mrs. Harper's trunk, peering over its lid as if it might grant us protection. The sky was now emblazoned by the first impressions of morning sunlight. We could see Ignacio, motionless; William still crouched at his side. I watched him remove the magazine tube from his turbine and load the weapon.

"I must help," I said. "Do not let Oliver follow."

I had ejected myself from the back of the wagon before Florence could object. Oliver yapped from my backside as I rushed forth.

"Drag him back," I said. "If there is no other option, if we are only a day away from the camps, then it's imperative we leave now. Paco will retrieve Turlow. Ignacio might still be saved."

Perhaps it was too late. His face was already pallid, his gaze fixed on someplace distant, and yet I still thought surely: *This man might live.* And only as William relented, began to lift himself to retrieve Hector, did that once-dwindling shadow reemerge in physical form from the distance: a horse barreling toward us from the void up ahead.

William halted, feet ahead of me. "No," he whispered in confusion. "That isn't Paco."

He was merely a glimmer first, a trick of the eye, then entirely real. Amos Turlow upon the very horse Paco had just ridden out on.

"How..." I wondered, stopping myself as the horse grew close.

William was on one knee, rifle perched against his shoulder. One shot? Two? What aim did this man have? The gun belched fire, the bullet striking nothing but air. Turlow bobbed up and down, encroaching ever closer, and William pulled the lever of his rifle — took aim once more.

Ignacio's hand clamped down upon my forearm. He could only look up, but it was as though he knew what William must do, knew the stakes at hand.

"He has him," I whispered. "Square in his sight."

He shot again. He missed again. The beast traveled at such speed that I do not know if either man knew what would result: that a collision was even a possibility. William had only just stood up, pulled the lever again — clearly mistiming the pace of the coming animal. It struck him with the speed of a projectile. I could hear the sharp pop of the impact,

William's cry, his body twirling, collapsing only feet from Hector himself. The horse seemingly did not notice the collision, and on it went, back into the darkness behind us.

I had gasped, frozen by the development before me, and by doing so, for the slightest distraction of that dreadful violence, I did not get to see the precise moment when Ignacio passed. It is something I would come to regret for the rest of my days.

"Ignacio," I said to him, feeling his flesh, still warm to the touch, jarringly so, and I thought it not too far-fetched that I was wrong — that he might still rise up and meet the moment. Yet it was then I registered the immense stillness that had overtaken him, its permanence, and with that, there was no question of his state. I closed his eyes before I stood up to find Turlow already circling the scene, allowing the horse to run itself to a canter, then a trot, the horse shaking at the mane; he circled me, circled the bodies he had taken the very life from — circled the wagon that housed Florence and Oliver.

"Do not even think of running," he yelled out to me. "Not that you would. You might be a coward, but you are not stupid."

Finally, he brought the horse to a halt, dismounted without a flourish, his hulking body flailing, falling, for his hands were still chained.

"The General claims he sent along his best," Turlow said. "But if those are his best then he has in his charge an army of dolts."

He had on only one boot, having used the other one as his cudgel. Heaps of blackened dirt caked his face. Leaves and thorns were caught to his trousers.

"That fellow on the horse gallops right up alongside me, telling me to halt, stop, quit, without the thought that I might just reach up myself and pull him off his horse myself while he's screaming those commands."

His smile faded; his eyes fell in my direction.

"Go to the dead one," he said, urging me toward Hector's body. "Get the key to my chains and release me. Now."

I had no option but to do his bidding. I took my time doing it, no less, as though there was some objection to his commands by my mere laziness.

Only then was I forced to cast my eyes upon the poor fellow. His teeth knocked loose at odd angles; his gums a rind of blood, his forehead dented like the blade of a shovel.

"Why have you done this?" I called out. "Think of your brother. What will the General think—"

"I don't plan on ever seeing that General again. I will go on to Mr. Harper and claim my treasure and be gone from this country altogether. The Mexicans can have that land of theirs. Lord knows I want nothing more to do with this place."

"You would abandon your brother for a bit of silver?"

The question seemed to puzzle him for a moment, but he answered it with grave sincerity.

"When my brother escapes, and it is only a matter of when, the first question he will ask me upon our reuniting is not of my health, not as to why I did not return for him, but if I successfully acquired the bounty we worked so hard, and so long, to claim. I vow not to disappoint him when that day comes. Now this is the last time I will ask for that key. I know he has it, for he did enjoy taunting me with the sight of the damned thing. Get my timepiece, too."

I had to reach into the boy's pocket. The mere touching of his person felt like a defilement, a violation so soon after his death, but I had no choice. The key was in his pocket. Right beside the timepiece.

"Well?" Turlow said.

I stood up and went to him. The man towered over me, as tall and brutish as he'd been the day we'd met in Mrs. Harper's parlor. A force I could not manage, nor cast from my life. I felt, then, that he would follow me until I had done all he wished, until I bent to my knees and obeyed him like the master of the world he wished to be. If it had been so easy to be free of him, perhaps I would have. But his aims for me were not to be found here. They were to be found in the camps — where I was to be, once again, Mr. Harper's asset. And he made as much clear.

"Get in the wagon. I care not of Indians, or bad weather, or the horses' health. We are going to those camps so I can be rid of you. So I can square things up with Mr. Harper and never, ever, lay eyes on you and that foul girl again."

The chains unclasped, freeing Turlow, and he slapped me harder than Mr. Harper had ever struck me a day in my life. His fist then landed upon my chest, and when I began to fall, he grabbed a tuft of my hair, raised me back up, and slapped me once more.

"That is enough!"

He stopped at the words. Turned to find Florence upon the tongue of the wagon.

I will never know why he might have listened to her — it seemed that, like a child hearing the words of his mother, or a gentleman dishonoring himself before a proper woman, the mere idea of her presence during such violence was enough to dissuade him from causing further harm. He pulled me up by the scruff of my neck and guided me toward the wagon.

"It's for naught, anyway," Turlow said. "He is hardened to such things. That is what years of punishment will do to a man. I believe Coleman has just the constitution Mr. Harper wished to inspire. A good, obedient nigger."

He did not ask for my help as he untied the horses, refusing to pay any mind to Florence as she upbraided him for his behavior, for all he had done.

"You are lucky," he said to me as he retrieved the very horse he had returned to camp on. "Lucky I believe her father might just give me more if I offer him his daughter with his prized little boy. Or I would treat her no better than the other girls I've brought to this country. I know a few fine brothels that would want such an ugly specimen just for the crowd she might draw."

He jumped into the wagon, and Florence stood toe to toe with him. Two imposing figures, eyes moving over one another, both, it looked, teeming with an anger about to erupt. Oliver barked wildly, his attention darting from Florence to Turlow and back again.

"What are you planning to do, girl?" Turlow put his head before Florence's, wagged it back and forth, a threat concealed in some show of mockery, for never had it been more clear than in this moment how the aggression of a man of such stature might overwhelm a woman, one doing nothing but attempting the smallest show of bravery.

"I wish... I wish you would just leave us be," she said under her breath.

His hands cupped her cheeks so hard her lips sputtered, and when she pulled back and slapped his hand away, he shoved her onto her mother's trunk, the girl crying out in pain. It was then that Oliver barked and nipped the man's leg.

"Goddamn it!" Turlow screamed. "The damn dog!"

I rushed to the wagon, but by the time I'd taken a single step, it was too late. The man put his boot to the animal's side, kicking Oliver off the wagon, the poor thing yelping, and I am not sure there is any worse noise than a pet in pain — the whimper, the sting of a human having betrayed him so. His eyes, black in the night but so large, filled with bewilderment, seemed at least happy to land right beside me in the dust. But as I went to pick him up, I heard Turlow speak up from the wagon. I had to turn to find the man scowling, arms crossed across his broad chest.

"Leave the animal," he said sternly.

"Mr. Turlow," Florence said, a finger pushed against her bloodied lip. "Do not do that to him."

He coiled his fist toward her but did not strike. His gaze burrowed into my own.

"In the wagon. Now. Do not make me come down there. Because I will. And it will not be worth the pain, alright? So come this way."

Oliver was hesitant to come near me. He lay on his stomach in the dirt, his head cocked ever so slightly, as if to ask what it was he'd done wrong. His fear was palpable. Perhaps he sensed my own.

"Oh," I said. "Well then." I turned, as cheerful as I could manage, shuddering as I embarked upon the wagon. I could not quite find any words to say to Florence, to soften the blow of what had just occurred. I could not look back down at Oliver — glimpse those eyes that took in everything, the auburn coat, those tiny paws I knew so well, one last time. I could only whisper to myself, as Turlow readied the reins for our departure.

A pity, I said under my breath. *What a pity.*

A great howl issued from Turlow. The whip fell upon the horses. The wagon rocked, pitched, and once more we were off, gaining speed each time Turlow commanded the horses to do so.

Darkness flew past us. Florence was crouched against her mother's trunk, her eyes red with tears. And the man. The man was hunched before the horses. His body shuddered as he took each breath; he wiped his forehead of sweat. It was as though he was intoxicated — fevered by his obsession to earn the fortune he presumed himself entitled to; by the mania to conquer this place, these people who called it home, all these foolish sorts beneath him. Obstacles in his path. His need to dominate was incessant.

"Go back," Florence whimpered. Then, with the clearing of her throat, she said it once again. "Go back, Turlow."

He shifted to face her, the fat upon his neck, those undulating hills, contorted by the sudden motion.

"Quiet, girl!" he said. "I am doing you a favor, bringing you to your father. You'll come to thank me."

"My father does not wish to see me. And I do not wish to see him."

He waved her off, returned his concentration to the drive, but her voice only took on more confidence.

"Everything has been taken from this man. From me. You will not abandon the dog too. You are to turn around."

To my shock, she stood up. For a moment she couldn't catch her balance, so I stood myself, took her hand, helped steady her.

"What are you doing?" I hissed.

But I saw nothing behind her eyes. It was no one I am familiar with — like her soul had been replaced by another. The soft cheeks and smile interchanged with a jagged, sunken scowl. Her lips were thin, severe. She stepped forward.

"Get back!" Turlow said.

"Turn. The wagon. Around."

Before I could say a word, she pounced upon the man. A slap first, then a grabbing for the reins.

"Get off me!" Turlow screamed. "Coleman, get her back."

He grabbed at her throat, her dress, but she parried his hand and slapped him hard across the skull. He put a hand to her thigh; he seemed on the verge of causing her to fall from the wagon altogether.

It was altogether spontaneous, what transpired. I was above Turlow. My very shadow caused him to turn and look up at the fellow who now hovered over him. Suddenly I was the bigger man. Surely it caught Turlow by surprise, what happened next.

Pulling him off Florence. The foot upon his back. With only a light kick, a tap of my boot, did the man pitch forward, screaming wildly, falling into the pounding hooves of the horses, the wagon buckling as the wheels drove over him.

The horses neighed in fright. For a moment I saw Florence under the light of the moon, her stare upon me with a mellow fixity. The wagon lurched and soon I saw her body suspended in the air, my own following hers into space. In the moments that followed, the world slowly, then suddenly, appeared to be upside down.

June:
Part Five, Amity, Mexico, 1866

That first season, June expected heartbreak. It was what she knew. Whether it was sudden or the result of a long-born term of her destiny she had not signed up for, the end was always the same. The robbing of her happiness. The stealing of her joy. And when Isaac first informed her he was setting off with the other men on one of their campaigns to protect the border, she wept in a way that caused others to come to the door of their home, certain that something terrible was amiss. Isaac had sent them off. Had placed his hands around her. Told her this was routine. All of it. The cleaning of the guns, the chants for protection over them delivered from God, the farewells, the young men bucking on their horses before they'd even left camp in anticipation of the fighting to come.

"I'll be back in a few weeks," he said. "And it will all be just as it was. Ain't you say you'd be fine with this? I thought we had this talk, June."

A talk was different from the real thing, though. And there were those specters of her past. The ones that refused to leave her be. She hardly wished to speak the man's name, but now she knew she'd have to.

"What if he comes back?" she asked.

"Who?" Isaac asked.

"Wyatt. He ain't dead. He ain't too far to find this place."

He put his hat down, grimaced at it, and sat beside her. The nightmares had been ceaseless for her first few months sleeping beside him. When Isaac reached for her she'd recoil; when he tried to calm her she only batted him away.

"Old Luther alone could keep you safe here," he reassured her. "And if Luther won't do, there's forty other men staying behind. We protect our own. If nothing else, we manage that."

The tears might keep on flowing, but already she would be laughing inside at the idea of Old Luther rousing from his rocking chair, tossing his bottle to the side, and taking a fist to Mr. Harper's face. A laugh was often all Isaac needed from her. He used humor as a trick, a manner of evasion, and when she showed a moment of lightness, he saw no reason to ameliorate her mood any further. His hat was on his head. He was already near the door.

Only when she followed him out did she see them all as one: The Indians in their breechcloth and beaded leggings, hair accented with wondrous feathers; the blacks on their own mounts, Isaac amongst them, as colorful as their counterparts, muskets and rifles across their laps.

The women of the other men prayed as they departed, invoking Jesus, the protection of their savior, *Lord keep these boys safe,* and when the dust settled, their voices dying out in the wake of the soldiers, a silence overcame the square. June did not know what to say.

Old Luther was out there in his chair, muttering on about the boys. (It was the last they'd hear from him in some time: he would hibernate like a wintered beast when the warriors were gone — rising for food, to look about, before sleeping once more in anticipation of their return.) Children huddled up to their mothers. The men who didn't ride off seemed unashamed by their roles back at home. They were necessary. For who knew what might befall their place when the warriors were gone?

Susanna, one of the few who emerged from her home to speak with

June at length on a regular basis, approached with her daughter in tow. It was these two who had helped deliver those calico dresses the day June had entered Amity. A shy woman of light complexion with an equally shy daughter who mimicked her mother, Susanna seemed impelled to engage with June. Perhaps Isaac had put her up to it. Perhaps Titus. Perhaps all of them had decided it that very first day, while June slept for twenty-four hours, that it would go this way. But the woman was beside her now. Her daughter looking on.

"Still lots to do when they head out," she said. "Ain't no holiday. Work gets done faster, really."

"Is that right?"

June looked to Susanna, but she would not look back at her. Not yet at least.

"Without the men distracting you... you'd be surprised. I'll tell you, I often look forward to it. Right now those eggs need collecting," Susanna said. "If you want to join?"

"In the heat they go bad quick," her daughter said, one hand on her mother's apron.

"Well, should we get them, then?" June asked.

"Come along," Susanna said. "We'll show you the way."

Yes, the women called themselves Sisters, and the bond they shared was an incalculable one. June was not one of them yet, but hoped to be. When the men were gone it was tradition to band together. The elders comforted the youngest, pulling them close, showing them the mountains outside, and pointing a finger that way. If ever they needed to escape, they'd say, the mountains would be their haven. No one could reach them there.

June told no one that she took reassurance from those words herself.

She got used to this life; used to the tasks required of her — the cleaning of the stable, bundling the corn into bushels to be delivered to the soldiers who stopped by once a week; she even learned to clean a musket under the tutelage of another elder, a woman who said few words — in fact could hardly hear — but had a way with her hands that spoke in a language of far more clarity than most made out with their voice.

Some of the Sisters became confidantes. Susanna, chiefly, who she soon accompanied to the chicken coop every day, a chance to learn of Titus, more of Isaac, and the role of others in the camp. There was Martha, one of the oldest women in Amity, who spent her days weaving rugs and was tasked with delivering crops to the Indians, walking back and forth between the sites each day, bringing news of their neighbors who seemed so foreign: which women were with child, if their leaders seemed angry. She would share what their medicine man had in store in preparation of a ceremony, the likes of which June could not quite understand even when Old Luther would describe them in detail, witnessed himself a lifetime ago, when they permitted him into their tents — into their lives.

Everything in Amity was open to interpretation — the pitter-patter of noise at night might be an animal, the men returning, or the sounds of an enemy they could hardly divine, ready to put torch to their homes as had happened in so many similar sites that populated the land neighboring their own. The women sometimes figured a downpour was coming by a sensation in the air that sent a shiver down their spine, one June herself never quite felt. Once they'd been right, though — warm raindrops coming down in sheets, the children playing in it, the women putting out pails — and June learned not to question such omens ever again, no matter if they were wrong more often than not.

The boredom when Isaac was gone was trying. But when he returned — a gang of horses or cattle in tow, stolen as the prize of these victors, the gleam of his turban swashing about his head, legs dangling from the sides of Starlight — it made up for the days of his absence tenfold.

There was a feral quality to his disposition upon his homecomings. She glimpsed fragments of this other Isaac, that Isaac who mercilessly hunted down his enemies, stole livestock and weapons of those men he felled; the Isaac who howled those ancient battle cries that scared animal and man alike. But he would tamp that beast in him quickly. He'd make himself delicate, soft, enough so that she'd warm to his touch. After reuniting on the porch, he'd lead her inside, guide her to the blankets upon which they slept. Slowly he'd place his hands upon her thighs, send a spate of excitement up her legs as his hands continued to explore parts of her she'd learned long ago to keep hidden. Any noise outside of the other boys' joyous whoops, still lost in celebration, was drowned out by the sounds of them both upon one another. It went like that all night, the warring and the liquor and the excitement slicking off the man like the sweat of their sex until he tired. And always he'd laugh when they finished, fishing for his pipe from his coat pocket draped over the chair beside them, desperate for a smoke.

The last campaign — assisting a group of American refugees who'd paid for the Seminoles to guard them crossing back into the States — had lasted a good week and she could have gone longer with him, but she could wait for him to have a rest. She put a hand upon his back, traced old scars, etched her name in the blade of his shoulder.

"Back in one piece," she said.

"Ain't that always the case?"

"Not always," she said, as it was fresh in her mind when she'd found a gash upon his knee prime for dressing; the lump on his head he'd told her was from just a drunken tumble off Starlight. He never gave specifics. It all felt harmless, good fun, but she knew the dangers he faced. That side of him that surfaced when he left Amity and vanished was a necessary one, an emblem of the sort of individual who didn't just weather the wild and the men who roamed there, but quelled them.

He exhaled a trail of smoke, did it again, but this time he did not lie back down beside her. Rather he turned in her direction, began to speak before catching his words with a hesitancy he did not often show. She sat up then, alert to his nervousness. Often, in times like this, the past caught up to him and mingled with the drink. He'd repeat himself, giving voice to the scared young man who had made the journey to Texas years ago, a scared boy, knowing just what was at stake.

Fifty dollars, he'd tell her time and again. *That's what those slave traders were given for each of us they caught alive. Fifty dollars.*

But this time felt different. The fretfulness wasn't the same as his sadness. She could, by now, tell the difference.

"What is it?" she asked. "You got something on your mind."

"June...have you heard of Drakesville?" he asked.

"Drakesville?" Never, she told him. But most things were new to her here. Drakesville included.

A whooping from outside caught his attention. She thought for a moment he might race to join the others, leave her where she sat, but his gaze was fastened back on her before long. His mind back on the matter at hand.

"It's a really pretty place. Right on the other side of the border. Got more deer around those parts than you can shoot, lots of land to farm, and not a soul to stop you from doing it. That's where my brother's got his land. I've seen it many times. Got all a man might need. All a woman might need, too, I suppose. I think we could be right happy in Drakesville. Want for nothing."

He was almost stammering as he spoke these words into existence. By the time he was done, waiting for her response, he was smoking again just to keep himself busy. Hardly had she ever seen him like this. Whatever he was on about, the thought concerned him deeply. Had been contemplated for some time.

"What are you saying?" she asked.

Yet already the conclusion of his entreaty was somewhat clear to her — expressed in subtle fashion as time had passed. When Old Luther shared stories fireside at night, telling of his foolhardy adventures in bringing his charges to this place, the boys and girls of the camp gathered before him. He told how the Indians once viewed him as a valued leader — welcomed him in their homes to smoke with them, to share in their decision-making — all of which had passed at some point in the past. The stories sputtered out, with those chiefs now viewed as something like cold, distant relatives, having spurned Luther due to his love of drink and his men's insistence on plundering the land in ways they found unholy.

She saw as much herself when the Indians arrived late at night, arguing over stolen goods they claimed were their own, even if they'd already been negotiated over, split before the war camps had even returned. They'd leave with what they wished and still they were not happy. No one was happy. The government and the Juaristas, not knowing the other's movements, both asked more of Isaac and the men each month: expeditions to quash the forces of raiding Apaches, guard caravans, deliver arms to soldiers who required them.

And yet little was returned that was promised. Formal land grants did not come to fruition. Demands that Isaac's people subordinate themselves to the Seminole chieftains sowed enough discord that a faction had left Amity entirely, forming their own tribe so far gone into the deep channels of the country that communication was no longer possible. The stress was visible in the eyes of the soldiers, in how they returned hunchbacked on those horses, heads bobbing with fatigue; the worry was voiced by the sisters June worked beside in the fields, who muttered the complaints they heard at night, when they were confided in: This life, as they knew it, was changing. And no one knew what might come next. So many of them had been forced from their homes, had spent so long to come so far for freedom. What did they find but more worries from all sides?

Amity, it seemed, was only a varnish that might be picked at, stripped clean, until the truth of this place was laid bare as a replica of the very steads they'd worked so hard to leave behind in the first place.

So his words did not surprise her. But Isaac was a private man; his gregariousness, his leadership, formed his own sort of façade. She hardly knew him, even if she'd slowly and surely come to see the flowerings of love between them.

"What is it you want, Isaac?" she asked. "Tell me. I can't help you with nothing if you don't share what it is you're really after. Far as I know, you *like* warring and thieving and riding that damn horse and having me here when you get back —"

"You know that isn't how it is. And there ain't no reason to put no bad words on Starlight like that."

"I'm being serious, now. Maybe I got some ideas of what you want that go beyond what goes on here day in and day out. But I need to hear it from your mouth, you understand. You want to leave here? Is that it?"

"Old Luther don't got a hold of this place like he used to. And I know the other boys trust me, they know I got their best intentions in mind, but June…" His hand fell to her stomach, tapping it as he processed his thoughts. "…I don't think I got the will to lead 'em. I don't got the will to keep riding Starlight for another man, another government. I want *peace*, is all. I want to wake up to you, and the sunrise, and think of nothing but the day I might spend doing nothing before we make our way to bed. No more guns. No more blood. That make sense?"

Of course that made sense. Nothing made *more* sense. Even six months on she jumped awake at the fear of Mr. Harper's return; at the thought of Isaac's band of men returning without him beside them, their faces stricken by the loss that she knew, roundly, would spell the end of her willingness to carry on with a life that bore with it the loss of his smile, his protection, his love.

A new home where she was not an outsider; a home that was theirs together. What could possibly be better? But she did not jump to tell him as much. Did not wish to cloud his already tortured spell of thoughts. Shadows lapped up against the cabin and fell over them both. The ember from his pipe died, and he set it down upon his lap without an attempt to revive the flame.

"I can't save everyone," Isaac said then. "But I can try and save us."

"Drakesville," she said. "Bet we could build a little home, make some calls for some real nice stone, even, build a home like the sort you'd see back where I'm from. Have a farm we don't have to share with a soul. Starlight can have her own stable. And I could have a real kitchen, fit for a man like you who needs more food than God himself."

"Mm," he said, warming to her fantasy. "I can see it."

She could feel his breath rise and fall beneath her. Reliable. How she craved for a little reliability. Knowing what might come next in a day, a year. A whole life.

"I can see it too," she said, caressing a finger from the back of his head, over to his ear, down to his neck. He shivered, looked up at her, begging with his eyes for a kiss.

"Don't tell a soul," he said. "We ain't gonna ruffle any feathers yet. It's just an idea. Seedling of a thought."

It was more than that. They both knew as much. But the truth of it could wait.

There was a moment — an hour each week — that she shared with no one else. June would wander Amity alone, then start into the pastures and even beyond, where nothing but more desert stretched out until the hills made contact with the red-lit sun. Yet in her mind she was hardly in Amity at all. She was in the past. She was with Coleman, dwelling in the memories they shared: transported back to their living quarters in Baton Rouge, her brother's face no more than a tender shadow outlined against the darkness. He never did offer her reassurance. He was not her protector. It went beyond safety, the security found in food, shelter, warmth. He was part of her. To know he was there, ready to tell her of the prank he'd pulled by repeatedly turning Mr. Harper's chair around, the man leveling the home with charges of possessing spirits; or of the squirrel he had freed from a trap set by the neighbor's children, awful boys who would have done God knows what to that poor animal. The simple joy she took in combing his hair each morning, brushing lint off his coat and placing his arms through the sleeves of it. Telling him to be brave that day. Just that one day.

"Stay clearheaded, you hear me? Don't you overthink things, or let those thoughts get you all in a row," she'd say. "You think too much sometimes. Just get through the day, with whatever they're fitting to have you do. We deal with tomorrow tomorrow."

He'd show a stiff upper lip in reply. Hard eyes. Softened, then, in a way that lent nicely to his subsequent smile, one that would always make her laugh.

What wonder there was to have a brother who could always delight her, not by anything purposeful other than just *being*. What peace she'd found with him in her life. What sadness now that he was gone.

A tangled string of memories rested atop the others with a buoyancy, a lastingness, that resisted her every effort to quash them down toward a place where they might be forgotten. When she came here, when she thought of him, they were always fresh in her mind.

Once, outside the grocer's, June had watched a whole fleet of carriages rolling down the street, packed to the brim with Negroes who looked no different from herself and Coleman, winding their way toward the road out of town — inching closer to their freedom. She recognized one man, a well-regarded chef, and a maid of the same home beside him. That man's brother had bought his own freedom years ago, and June had once overheard the chef discussing his plan to meet him when the time was right. Although she had not scoffed — the man was clearly of good reputation and esteem — it hardly seemed a possibility. Yet here he was, drawing all eyes to him and what she now realized was most likely his lover, the two of them a part of this band of hopeful souls barreling their way toward some life she could not fathom for herself. But with her shoulders tense from the weight of the grocer's food, her feet sore from a day that had already, in short order, grown so long, she wondered why she could not pack a bag of her own just like that chef and that maid.

Children, as though hatched from the clutter of these people's goods, were burrowed into the backs of the wagons. They would know a different life than this one. Experience so much that this moment, this place, would be crowded out from their memory altogether.

Shame, really, was what June felt. It was curious to her that she had heard Mr. Harper, for so long, speak of his ambitions: to expand his business, grow his fortune. Or listened to Mrs. Harper speak of her desire to be a springboard of social life in town, the center of all that might take place in this hotbox of gossip that always seemed to exclude her. And when they failed miserably to achieve their aims, the result provided her a great source of entertainment, watching their shallow lives grow only more dim.

What of these sorts before her? June was no different from that girl with her knees tight against her chest, watching from her perch on that wagon. If they could pack up, turn a blind eye to the life that had made them, and construct a new one from the necessities one stuffs into a few bags — why could June not do the same? How many lesser privileges she took pride in — ones as small as the permission to retrieve food from the grocer — while these folks had afforded themselves the privilege of the whole world entire, laid out at their feet. Just by leaving this place, they would accomplish far more than the Harpers with far less. Their lives, one day, with any luck, would be bright.

She had had to avert her gaze. Yet the sight of that man and woman, proud amongst their scant possessions, could not be forgotten. So she'd recounted it to Coleman one day, with no reply from him, only a mention that he wished them well in their future pursuits, whatever those might be.

It was a few days before her scheduled departure with Mr. Harper that she had asked him, plainly, to leave with her. That she had everything prepared. He only needed to pack. In fact, she had tallied all they would need for the prospective journey: the tins of pickled vegetables Mr. Harper had had her prepare for the journey to Mexico; biscuits she had stowed away the final few weeks from her own dinners; a bundle of potted beef that Mrs. Harper, detesting the flavor of so many kinds of meat, had had her dispose of, but which she had kept. They could be gone quickly, protected if they made it safely into the hands of the Union soldiers stationed about the city — the same ones she often saw patrolling the streets, earning the citizens' ire but always on watch.

We could go, were the exact words she'd whispered. *Start anew. Away from these people. You know that, don't you?*

When he did not answer, caught up in his own fear of the unknown, the fear of any risk at all, she was disappointed, but did not accept this as a total loss. She knew her brother better than anyone; knew that with a little time, even the passage of a mere evening, he might come around to her train of thought; might realize what their lives could amount to away from this place.

June decided to be ready. Indeed, on many nights she would sneak downstairs to the cellar with a few tins of food, perhaps a candle or two, to store away for the possible journey. She even took the risky step of pocketing one of Mrs. Harper's necklaces — one rarely worn, of course — to sell on the journey north, if need be.

One evening two days on from June's conversation with Coleman, Florence was in the parlor with her mother, making tea. Mr. Harper was in his study, and already June had finished the tasks required of her, had watched his focus become so captured by his maps that she knew they would occupy him until he fell asleep there. (She would wake him when Mrs. Harper told her to, in an hour's time, when they all took to bed.)

June found it difficult to recollect what exactly her error had been until some time later. There was one small sign — a slight falseness to Mr. Harper's abdication to the night, the sigh in which he sent her off, the whiff of performance. But still she would never know how, in that small space of time in which she went to speak with Coleman, instruct him on fetching the firewood, how Mr. Harper had abandoned his routine without her noticing. When she went downstairs, with no more in mind than a few moments on the side of her bed to sit before being called back up, it was with utter shock that she had found Mr. Harper sitting upon her bed.

She'd never seen him here, and upon first glance she thought one of the many dark souls that roamed this place, that haunted her dreams, had materialized with the knowledge, somehow, to take the shape of the very being she feared most.

Mrs. Harper's necklace — the same one she had taken — was laid out over his knee. Her clothes were scattered across the floor. In his hand was one of the tins of meat she had procured, and Mr. Harper, with a single finger, was now scooping out the flesh of the tin, slowly, deliberately having his fill.

No words, it seemed, might rescue her from the moment at hand. She could only step forward, shivering from the cold, from fright, her hands shaking under her apron, clenching the fabric as she steeled herself against what was about to befall her. What might really be death, she thought.

"You know, I purchased my wife this necklace," Mr. Harper said, pointing at it on his knee, with the same finger that was still moist from his own mouth. "A gift I believe she had valued quite highly, but I don't figure she noticed it missing. So perhaps I am wrong to think as much. What do you think, June?"

"Master Harper," she said. "What are you doing down here?"

"You're suggesting I have no right to move about my home? To safeguard my own belongings?"

With this he stood up. There was nothing to gain denying the contents of her documents box, the food she'd stowed away, the thieving of the necklace. She had no spirit to protest. Quickly he stepped toward her. She did not flinch, or even bow under the strength of the hand he put to her shoulder, squeezing so hard he would well leave a bruise. She could feel the dampness of that finger, wet from his own tongue, land beside the start of her neck.

"I saw you sneak out from the cellar yesterday. Figured, with our journey coming, you might get it into your mind to do something stupid. And sure enough I come down here to find my own food, my wife's jewelry, stolen out from under me. What you would do with it all is my question." His hand held steady. "Tell me, plainly, what you were planning. And perhaps I will show you the slightest mercy."

The moment brought to mind the powerlessness she'd felt in the few moments of her life that had been most treacherous: when a colt, let on the loose by accident, had nearly trampled her, or when Mr. Harper had put her out on the roof to sweep the shingles with Coleman, and she'd nearly tripped and fallen those three stories to the ground. There was a coolness that flowed through her, a relinquishment of all the worries, the fear, that ruled over her life. She could die — and perhaps she *would* die, and let the Lord grant her peace thereafter, for where those previous instances of her possible end felt cruel in their randomness, this was an undertaking worth any price.

"To leave this place," said June, not allowing her voice to waver, to lose its might. Not in this instance; not when the scheme had already been unearthed, when all she had left was her belief in what had once seemed possible. He could not take that from her. "To leave this place and never look back. Is that enough confession for you, Master Harper?"

Slowly he eased his hand from her shoulder, and she realized suddenly that violence would not be the punishment he'd administer this evening. That his solution to this problem must go beyond a strike, a kick, a strap brought down upon her backside; for none of that took place.

"You can do whatever you please," he said. "But really, June, you are not like those other Negroes, with their pockets somehow stuffed with coins from scrounging for pennies all these years, or those uppity fellows with some trade to take North. You have nothing but this home, this family, and that brother of yours. And I'll tell you this: If I see you try to leave me before our journey, or even set foot off this property, without my permission, it is not you who will suffer. It is Coleman. If you so much as *think* of wandering out to fetch a pail of water without my instruction, it is he I will make an example of. And I am not alone in this. Mr. King is keeping an eye out from his property down the road for any suspicious movement by the likes of yourself or his own help. Mr. Highsmith, too. Things have changed, yes, but it is only cause for us to keep a more watchful eye. To be more severe in maintaining a certain...civility in town. And if you wish to be a burden upon that civility — well, June, I will bring you along to watch your brother meet his end myself."

He had a way, this man, of burrowing toward the hidden chambers of her soul, the parts she held dearest; sanctified rooms where she harbored her love for Coleman, the memories of her mother, the dreams of another life that kept her living when the world was a cold and unwelcoming place that showed no mercy and would not give her rest. And once more, in the final days of her fealty to him, Mr. Harper had again managed to trespass there.

Coleman had always been forbidden to this man — but no more.

"That ain't right," she said. "That boy ain't done no wrong. And the law says we're free to go if we so please."

"Give it a try. See if you make it farther than the county line. No,

June…" The hand went back on her shoulder. "If you want your brother to live a long life. A happy life. You will come with me to Mexico. You will create no more silly distractions that put my aims in doubt. Believe me when I say this. He will find peace tending to my wife and daughter, tending to the home. Not following you on a death march North. He isn't fit for such things, that boy. Don't make a mistake you cannot set right."

Only later did she see that he had left the necklace there, like a gift for bearing his threats, his jealousy, his seething demands; an indictment on his lowly estimation of his wife and a promise, to June, of the rewards that might flow her way once she followed him to the end of the earth. As though any necklace might be worth the suffering she'd endured, and that which was to come.

All of this paled to the pain of when Coleman had pulled her aside on one of their final days together. How much strength it must have taken him to finally come around, she thought; it went against every fiber of his person. To look her in the eyes and mention first what went unspoken between them: that he knew, quite well, what Mr. Harper represented in her life. That he was hesitant to depart Baton Rouge, but willing to go anywhere, at any time, if it meant she would be safe from the man's grasp.

There were two Colemans she had known up to that point: the boy who once slept in her hands — a terrified small thing scared of this world but as curious of its holdings as any individual who had been born to meet it — and the young fellow who was cautious enough to survive, but too wounded inside to grow out from under her and brave walking his own path, wherever it might lead. But now there was a flash of a new Coleman. The boy growing into a man. What she would do to see what might come next for him; to see him flower into some inconceivable blossom! For with his intelligence, his soft heart, and the wherewithal to brave the world entire, Coleman could stand amongst kings. If only he had the time to do so. The freedom.

And only by leaving him behind could she purchase his freedom — and his safety. The cost of her trip to Mexico — to remove Wyatt from this place and get Coleman gone from him — was worth her own destruction.

If she trusted Coleman, both who he was and the man he would come to be, she knew he'd find his way in his own time.

So she held his hands, on that dark night they shared, and told him she would be going with Wyatt after all. He would stay, go to New Orleans with the Harper women. When the time was right, they would find one another. Knowing, in her heart, that Coleman would at the very least find himself in the end.

If only she had the chance to tell him all of this! She was unlettered. Had no means to send him correspondence. Certainly not from Mexico. But in her heart, each week, for one morning, she would note what she would regale him of if she could write. If she could share her life with him once again. Hoping, knowing, that one day when they met again, all these memories, these thoughts, could be passed along to him. It did not matter how long it took. He would know every detail of her existence he had missed, and she would learn the same of his. Nothing occupied June as much as this. To regain their bond; to mend the rift born from their separation.

June had returned from one of her wanderings, a week since Isaac had gotten back last, to find him gone. Susanna before her own lodge, a pot of sofkee simmering upon a fire — all who wished coming forward to take their fill.

"Have a bowl here if you want some?" Susanna told her. She said nothing of June's absence, but June could tell it was on her mind.

"Not too hungry," she said, her eyes still registering the goings-on of the camp — the young boy shoveling manure before the stables; Titus and their son slurping up soup on the stairs to their home. The man was usually cheerful; happy to start a day, chase his son about before work.

"Have you seen Isaac?" June asked.

Susanna looked back at the stable, and June thought he might be back there, with Starlight, but she had walked past the stables to meet here with

Susanna. She would have seen him with Starlight's brush, or a fat pail of grain, feeding his girl, singing her a tune.

"Something came up," Susanna said. "A few of the Indians riled up about some Kickapoos. An incident last night. Isaac and the boys got word this morning."

"But Titus is here," June said, eyeing Susanna's husband.

Titus, swallowing his bite, merely shook his head to distance himself from the matter.

"I ain't meeting up to fight no Kickapoos just 'cause Old Luther say we ought to. Not me."

If Isaac's cousin was sticking this one out, June feared the danger of the expedition.

"Lord," she said.

Susanna had no words for her. Only gestured at the pot of sofkee again, as if a bowl of it might tamp down whatever anxiety June had just succumbed to.

They were always leaving, she thought. *Always off somewhere.* She walked back to the house, kicking up dust along the way, considering how, in this very spot, weeks before, she'd seen a couple get married — the ritual an exuberant one, the husband chasing the wife about, her dress a splashing spoke of color in motion as she cheerfully avoided the man until he bounded up from behind her, picked her up, the whole crowd chanting, cheering them on.

June wanted that: marriage — and more. A home that was hers from the ground up. How peculiar it was that each step toward liberation had the unintended consequence of giving her the boldness to ask for more. Of looking around knowing, even with what she had, perhaps she'd bargained for less than her lot. A woman like her deserved the world. Isaac had said it himself once. But she shared his small plot of land that was slowly encroached upon by all sides. Mr. Harper and his men always a few days removed. A life of peril, even as she was settled in a cocoon of temporary safety.

She stood on the porch, facing out at the desert. A hazy coat of dust hung over the afternoon. There was fire in the distance. The brown dotting of a few horses. But perhaps it was her imagination. A desire for Isaac's return obscuring reality.

"Come back," she said under her breath. What she meant was: *Come back and start this new life with me. Come back, and let's be gone.*

It was decided in her mind. They would cross the border once more. Settle, finally, somewhere so remote, so unthreatened, that the world might finally leave them alone. When this was done, and it would take time, and more work than she could imagine...she would find Coleman, too. She would tell him of all he'd missed in the time they'd been apart. He'd marvel at this new home of theirs. She'd make a spot for them. The three of them, as one, would start a new life, and there would never, ever, be reason to leave one another's side again.

12

A sharp pain wrapped its way about my skull like a vine about a trellis. My body demanded I stay still. My mind knew better. So I tried, with all my might, to prop myself up and take note of my surroundings. A cropping of dust hovered over my head, thrown up by the crash. I had to squint, adjusting to the sun's glare, to see the upturned wagon, its contents strewn about all around us. One horse had fallen in the mess, tangled up with the harness of the wagon. It now lay unmoving. The others had managed to rise, looking over their fallen companion, wondering, rightly, how so much had gone wrong so quickly.

The wagon bed was on its side. I believe Turlow had been crushed by the front wheels. After this, when the wagon spiraled upward, Florence and I were ejected with a force strong enough that I was grateful we had even survived the crash.

She was a few feet from me, roughed up, feeling at her side, groaning in pain but alive.

"Let me help you up," I called to Florence.

"I'm fine," she said, although I knew it was not true. She could not get herself to stand, and hardly deigned to try.

"I can tell you are in pain."

"You don't look to have fared much better than I have," she said. "Where does it hurt?"

"My head," I admitted, for the pain was too much to make light of.

"It's my ribs. I believe something is broken... it is difficult to breathe..."

"We can wait for a time," I said. "We can rest."

"With this heat?" she said. "If we rest, we won't ever be gone from here. We'll die where we sit."

So she went to stand again, but with only a footstep she yelped, fell to her knees, and by then we were both bent over, crushed by the pain.

"The sun," I said. "It's like a dagger, isn't it? Like it is penetrating my skull."

"Then look elsewhere," Florence said, gasping for air.

I did not quite know what to do with myself. I thought of June, then. Thought of Oliver. Those fallen soldiers who had died protecting us. Of all that was before us, and all we'd done to come so far. Under the guise of so much contemplation, the minutes were ticking away in the exact manner Florence had urged us to avoid. But it all weighed on me so mightily, I felt paralyzed with grief, or shock, a torrent of emotions flooding my thinking. Nonetheless, I still knew well the obligations this day held in store. No different from any other. The setting of a table. The grooming of Oliver. One must rise to it. There is nothing gained by delay.

So I put my hand out to Florence. She eyed it with uncertainty. Shook her head.

"Try," I urged her. "Do that much."

And the second her palm touched my own, I raised her up without offering a note of caution, the girl howling, but rising under our collective might.

"My God."

"We've done it," I said.

"May I never sit again."

My vision was blurred. My feet seemed unsure of their own ability to take a single step.

The broken wheels of the wagon were a splintered mess flung about the ground. Everything we'd packed was now amongst the littered mess of parts.

"I must check behind the wagon," I said. I did not wish to say what — or who — I was searching for. As if to utter his name might cause him to materialize. Florence said nothing; only nodded and stood there motionless.

I walked over cautiously, avoiding the wreckage. Turlow's riding whip was snaked around a leaking bag of rice. Beside it lay all of the wagon's pots and pans, our sheet-iron stove as well. It looked as though a windstorm had swept over our expedition.

"Do you hear that?" Florence called out from a few feet away.

I thought it was the fallen mare — neighing in pain, perhaps — but then, with my full attention paid toward the noise, I could hear that it was a man. I was before the wagon now. Knowing it was unsalvageable, and knowing I could not lift it on my own, I did the only thing that seemed proper, for the noise of pain we'd heard was stemming from beneath it. I took my hand to the wagon cloth, ripped it with my hands, and stepped back; afraid, I must admit, of whatever it was I might find there.

I could only gasp at the sight. His face was slashed by the broken shard of a water jug, his bared teeth pitted with sand; his legs were stuck under, of all things, Mrs. Harper's trunk. Broken legs, I am sure, for they were not concealed by the trunk entirely, his feet poking out the back, moving not a bit.

"What has become of you, Mr. Turlow?"

I believe he was shivering; his body shocked, his spirit bludgeoned to pieces by the circumstances that had befallen him.

"Coleman," he said, teeth rattling. "Free me from here. I will forgive you for what you have done — "

"Mr. Turlow," I said. "I have not forgiven you for what *you* have done."

"I am sorry," he said, quicker than I could finish sharing my thoughts. His features suddenly softened — the lines of his forehead resolving into his brow, his eyes become those of a pleading child. "Does that make you happy? Now please…"

"It's not just the apology I seek. It is respect. And you have not shown me any since the day we've met. Do you not realize that?"

As quickly as he'd acted out some vague show of remorse, his anger grew unassailable. The man was panicked, blustering, spitting out vile words where the kind ones had failed.

"For Christ's sake! Walking scum you are," he said. "A weakling with no place in society. Not even your sister will miss you when this desert swallows you whole..."

On he went, and for the second time, in some strange fashion, I glimpsed, within that man's face, Mr. Harper himself once again — the utter rage that he would put on display in his riled-up moods. I saw others, as well. I caught sight of Mr. Harper's compatriots, those men who drank with him by the pond, outraged at my improper pouring of their whiskey, incensed when the shade of their umbrella did not properly cover the pale of their necks. I saw Mr. Highsmith, the pride of that leader of Baton Rouge, preparing Mr. Harper and all the others for their journey to this very country. So many men resembling Amos Turlow who had felt slighted by the world not bowing to their own decided destiny.

Yes, all of them were collected in this broken man before me. This sneering fellow who had kicked my dog and put us in danger at every turn, all to do the bidding of another man I disliked with even more rancor than I held for this one.

"I *tried* to do right by you," he said now. "To take you to your sister. And this is how you repay me?"

"No, Turlow. You tried to return me back to my old master. Like the slave you think I am. Yet I am no slave. I am not property to be shuttled this way and that about the world. I am a man. And, I might add, what you did to Oliver... Well, I do believe some things are unforgivable."

Turlow let out a terrible roar — his anger an outsize blast, a spewing of noise and power — and I swear on my life that the man began to *crawl*, then. Toward me. His hands clasping at the sand like it was not something that would slip through his grasp; twisting himself this way and that, the trunk moving inch by inch as his body snaked forward. I did not find it possible, and yet it was. Like a creature emerging from its cave, he was: growling, threatening, demanding blood. It is a sight I will never forget, the man gaining the leverage to break out from this entrapment, as he crept closer to my shoes, ready to pounce.

"As if I need your help at all," he said. "I need no one's help, boy. Never have. Just watch me."

I must admit that witnessing this feat caused me some amount of fear, and in shock I stepped back, letting go of the cloth of the wagon canvas. Turlow's hand was now near my ankle. Time stalled in that moment. Florence was calling out, I believe, but her voice was no more than a high-pitched note lost to the air. My heart was skipping. My head throbbed. I was, once again, fearing myself to be at the mercy of this man I could not rid the world of.

I did not know what it was, exactly, that had caused Florence to scream in shock. Nor in the cacophony did I hear the horse hooves at my back. I noticed only when the horse itself took to rest beside me. I knew from the white upon the snout whose it was: Paco's. The same one that had struck William.

And it was William who dismounted from that stallion. One eye swollen closed, a hobble to his step, but William still. And in his good hand — Oliver.

"William!" I shouted, just as Florence said the same from the other side of the fallen wagon.

He was in no mood to have a reunion of any sort. The glint of malice in his eyes was enough to stifle me.

"Take the dog," he said. "Go to the girl."

A knife was unsheathed from William's waist.

"You," Turlow bellowed. "Look at this! The Indian returns."

I took one last look at Turlow before wheeling toward William, grasping Oliver from his arms. The little fellow was no worse for wear. What resilience he had! After all he'd been through, he still had the eagerness to lick my face, to pant with glee, teeth gleaming, his eyebrows raised in delight of me.

Off we went toward Florence, still grasping her side, pained, watching me — watching beyond me, at what I myself could not bear to witness.

I thought to tell her to shield herself from whatever might come. To cover her ears, perhaps. But it was already too late for that. The guttural moans that followed from what I could only imagine was a great show of violence, of revenge. I heard the cries not with happiness, but with some relief. To know, with those last frightful howls, that Turlow had finally been taken from this earth. That I was done with him at last.

"It's over now," Florence said. "I can see him cleaning the blade — "

"Say no more," I said. "I do not wish to hear of it any further. Good riddance, I say. Good riddance indeed. We are free of him."

And I swear to it that even with all that had taken place, and with all the pain she had taken on, Florence closed her eyes and smiled at my words. Sweet as they were. Like honey on toast.

He should have killed me.

Those were the words William repeated, many times, as we meandered through the sun-baked desert. Each of us was on a horse, Florence and I on two that had survived the crash, William riding Paco's mare with the other tethered to his saddle.

"I'm quite glad he did not," I said.

"Too much bluster, that man," William said. "I drained it right out of him. I saw it flow out with the blood."

"Any more of this and I will retch," I told him.

I had, I regret to say, already done so multiple times. The crash had caused some injury, some wavering of my vision, that would not pass. I could hardly keep down water. But it was essential we go on. There was no time to stop. Half a day it had been since Turlow's death. Picture us there: all three malnourished, dried out by the heat, slumped over our mounts. We had nothing to carry any goods save William's saddlebag. I allowed Oliver to sit in the hands of William, as he was more skilled at riding — could keep him in his lap and canter on with ease. And Florence had managed to retain her mother's shoes, holding them in her own lap, sitting before her reins. To William's confusion, she had refused to leave them behind.

Allow her that much, I'd told him. One relic of her mother. A single reminder of the girl's past. It was hard enough for her just to get upon the saddle in her state. To make it this far in so much pain. For a time Florence had hardly said a word herself, the witnessing of so much death, so much destruction. After all she'd been through, she might at least bring along the shoes.

So we rode like that, expecting the mines to appear before us, plumes of smoke appearing from the distance, men toiling over deep veins in the earth, some mammoth apparatus amongst them salvaging silver from rock. But we met nothing of the sort.

"Are you sure of our path?" I asked William, trying to tamp down the desperation in my voice.

"I know as well as Turlow did," he said.

"An idea, then," I said.

But as it was so often with William, he did not provide further thought; only stopped occasionally to check his compass, assess our location.

I could hardly think straight, or stay upright for that matter, so it felt like my mind had failed my body and my body had failed my mind. It felt like a mutual betrayal. And I figured that was death. A betrayal of all one's summoned parts, coming together in league to terminate your time on this earth. The thought would not leave me, and it struck me anew each time my head pounded in pain from my injuries from the fall.

"Perk up," Florence finally said to me, after an interminable stretch of time. "Clearheaded, Coleman. Is that not right?"

I had no retort for her. Nothing. I wished for not a single thing but rest. A chance to escape from my own exhaustion.

The memory of Turlow's face was engraved upon my eyelids: that crooked, bloodied final look of torment he flashed before William had arrived. It felt as though he could still clasp onto me. Reach me from beyond the grave. Pull me down, down to him one final time...

I thought, when I saw the small town before me, over a small hillock, that my eyes had deceived me. That my headache had caused me some hallucination. But it was William who pointed up ahead, confirming the sight.

"There," he said. "This is how it goes. First nothing, and then, when you least expect it..."

"Something," Florence said. "But what? Where are we?"

William eyed the outpost before us. Some furnaces emitting smoke, but no large quarry to speak of; certainly no mine. There were a few pens of animals. More tents than one could count, and a few modest homes made of timber.

"What if they are dangerous?" Florence asked. "We should keep our wits about us."

William only shook his head. "Look," he said, a single arm extended, a finger pointed at something I could not spy at first. Then I saw. A woman. One that looked no different than the sort you might find sipping lemonade on a porch back in New Orleans. The sort I might have served right alongside Miss Harper.

"Do you think that *she* is dangerous?" William asked.

"I suppose I do not," Florence said.

"They will know of your father, perhaps. He might be right in this camp..."

William gave his mare a kick and began down the hill. I made to follow him, with what little power I had to give the same kick to my own mount, but before doing so I noticed Florence frozen still. I could see the quick pace of her breathing. The uncertainty in her eyes.

"My father," she said. "When I said I did not wish to see him...I meant it. He caused *all* of this. I could be home, now. My mother might be alive. And yet here we are, providing him more of our time. For what, Coleman?"

I understood. Even if I could offer little encouragement, something needed to be said.

"You may do as you please," I told her. "I would not judge you for paying the man no mind. But he is my only connection to my sister. Surely you know that I must go meet him..."

She produced no reply. I felt the girl defeated, scorned, but altogether still one with the goal of our expedition. Call me naive, but I believed, at this point, she wanted to find June as much as I did. If only to finish the task we'd sought to overcome.

"It's not as if there is anywhere else for me to go," she said.

"Soon," I said. "Soon this will be over. And then you may go wherever you wish."

Florence only gave her horse a kick — and I followed her down the hill toward William.

They'd uttered her name. *June.* And those people, some of them at least, were *familiar* with me. A Negro named Sandy — I'd seen that man on many occasions, a stonemason of some notoriety in Baton Rouge, the sort of individual who would not deign even to look in the direction of a man of such small stature as myself. One dissolves in the shadows of a free man of such dignity, who does as he pleases without a care in the world. No different was it in Mexico. Sandy was in high demand, apparently, poring over a list of jobs others required of him. A pipe in his mouth — freshly shaven cheeks. The fellow was thriving. But it was the woman with him we'd been directed to speak with... Celia. She was beside Sandy, standing over the man like his boss, pointing toward sites upon a map. When she saw us approach, the confusion was laid bare in her eyes.

A peculiar sight, Florence and I must have been, with William behind us, still sitting on that mare.

"*Harper*," she'd said. "*June*. Yes, yes. We knew them well."

Sandy gave us a look like we were asking for trouble; at the very least a distraction from his day.

Celia immediately stood straight up, eyeing me like I was a figment of her mind, an apparition that had somehow materialized.

"You *can't* be her brother," she said.

"Why, yes," I said. "Coleman. And this is Florence. This here is Oliver. On that horse there is William. He's led us this far because we saved him —"

"Let her speak, Coleman," Florence said politely. "Let her help us."

And Celia did. Telling us of their arrival at this place. Of Mr. Highsmith (a friend of Mr. Harper's, of course), who had led their expedition. He was off himself, breaking bread with a different band of deserters from Louisiana; eager to bring them into the fold at this very spot so as to strengthen their numbers.

"But what of Mr. Harper?" Florence asked. "What of June?"

Celia and Sandy exchanged a look of uneasiness. It was then she informed us of Mr. Harper leaving for the mines with June in tow; of the rumors bruited about their camps: that June had abandoned him and taken up with some Indians up north. And that upon doing so, Mr. Harper had lost his senses.

"The Mexicans found him not worth the trouble, after a time. Once that quarry was working at full speed, they up and claimed they didn't need his help after all. Said they ain't owe him a thing. Pulled the rug out from under him. And he was little help to Mr. Highsmith back around these parts, acting all crazy, talking 'bout June day in and day out."

"Then he got it into his head he'd found a *new* mine," Sandy interjected. "With more silver than the last! Lord, the man could not take his lickings. 'Cause there wasn't no new mine anywhere except in that addled brain of his."

Celia and Sandy told us then that Mr. Harper had often returned to the camps, begging for help in finding June and this imaginary mine, demanding that others enter his employ, only to be spurned. She was gone — *gone,* they told him. Leave it be. And when finally they forbade him from returning, lest they be made to listen to his ravings anymore, he had settled on making a home outside the encampment.

"I ain't about to say I have sympathy for such a prickly man," Celia said, shaking her head, "but he's little more than a beggar now. Still waiting to find that mine. Waiting for your sister to come back to him. It's a shame to see a man fall so low."

"But June," I said. "Is she safe?"

Celia put her hands upon the chairback where Sandy sat. Held tight to the top rail.

"If he's to be believed, they took that girl," Celia said. "Who knows what they've done with her."

"And Mr. Harper, my father," Florence said. "How might we find him?"

"Your father?" It was the only time Sandy appeared the least taken aback by the conversation.

Celia's own face dropped.

"Apologies if I offended you, speaking of him as I did."

"No, no," Florence said. "I have no qualms with you. We'd just like to lay eyes on him is all. And perhaps he can help us find this man's sister. If you could just tell us the way."

"You're sure of this?" Celia said. "Sure you wish to see him? In his current state... Last time he came around here, the man nearly — "

"He's my father," Florence said.

The woman nodded silently. There was a strange tranquility to her. Magisterial, even. Like she ran this place, at least this home, with a confidence I could not quite square. Celia reached down before Sandy, grabbed the map before him, and slid it across the table in our direction. The man began to protest, but then stayed quiet.

"Show them," Celia said. "Show this girl where she can find her father. Put it to paper. Let them get on their way."

But it was when Sandy spoke once more that my whole being felt on fire. I could not believe his words; words that were so meaningful to me but almost an afterthought for him.

"I'll do 'em one better and show them where to find those Indians, too. Save them the trouble of counting on Wyatt."

"You know?" I said.

He shrugged. "They come down here to trade every so often. I wouldn't customarily make the trip out that way — those are fighting folk. Treat us right, but we stay wary of 'em... But if it's your sister you're after, I get taking the risk. Far be it from us to stop you."

I kept my voice measured.

"Tell us everything you know. Draw it all out there. I'd be forever in your debt. Please."

Sandy smiled. Licked the tip of the pen in his hand. Soon he was drawing.

The horses had been watered, although they had little energy left. Celia had been kind enough to round up enough food for the day's journey.

"It is as far as I will take you," William said, looking at his compass anew before stashing it away. "If he has been robbed of his land, and that mine has been ceded to Captain Diaz already, there is nothing here for me. I will report back to General Chavez as I promised and carry on."

This warranted no complaint from me. He'd gone this far, was going further only as a favor, for Mr. Harper would be no help to him.

"Very well," I said.

The road was not paved, of course, but there was a path to follow, and we did so at Sandy's instructions. Florence was deflated but upright, still battling the injuries to her chest. I could spy her heavy breathing. The flush of her cheeks.

"Now that they've told us of June's whereabouts," I said, "this isn't something we must do, Florence. And you said yourself you are done with that man."

"No," she said curtly. "Now that I know he is so close. After all of this. *You were right,* I suppose I'm saying. I do have a few words to share with him after all. Let's carry on before I change my mind."

"If you insist," I said.

"Well?" William said.

"You heard her yourself," I said.

The group was silent, Florence visibly nervous — as was I. There was an insistent sense of trepidation I had with each step that brought us farther away from the camp in which we'd found Sandy and Celia. I believe I hoped, just for Florence's sake, that as the emptiness of the desert stretched on, we might simply come across nothing at all. That Mr. Harper's existence, his very person, might have vanished into this strange wilderness, another victim claimed by the wild. I prayed for little, but it crossed my mind to pray for this.

An hour passed, one which felt like an eternity. Up until now the road had been free of any sign of life save the slither of a snake or the rustling of a bush. But finally we came upon a scattering of refuse. Old clothes, torn to shreds. Shoes with no soles. Empty jars. I was looking down at the refuse when William brought us to a halt, the horses obeying the lead mare.

I did not wish to look up, really. For I was afraid what I would find. Afraid of the past I would now reckon with.

A lone tent before us signaled nothing to the naked eye but its own sheer impoverishment. More trash strewn about. The lip of the tent fluttered even without a hint of wind in the air, so threadbare it was. Nonetheless it was closed. The question of who might step forward and investigate the sight seemed to land on all of us at the same time.

"Best get on with it," William said. Already he had fished his pipe out from his pockets, readying himself for a stretch of rest he did not seem too keen on.

I looked to Florence, and she looked back. Both of us unsure.

"Will you..." Florence began.

"I'd *very* much prefer not to see that man at all. But if you can't, I will."

"I will come, in a moment. I just don't know...his condition. If he is even alive. I can't...I can't go in there and find him like that."

"Yes," I said under my breath, knowing on some level that her concern carried some merit.

"I'll go up there," William said with a note of frustration. "If it will hurry this up — "

Already I was dismounting. "No. I am willing. I know the man better than I know myself. There is nothing to fear in that tent."

But after a life shot through with fear, I did not quite trust my own words.

I slowed as I reached the entrance. It might sound perplexing, but the smell I found there was so familiar as to overwhelm me. *Engulf me.* A rankness cutting through the air, akin to sour milk. It aggravated my headache, jostled my mind. I knew immediately when I'd detected it before: back in Baton Rouge. Mr. Harper, under the attack of fever, was laid up in bed, a wet rag on his head. This same stench was palpable. June had been worried all night. Made sick myself by her inability to cure him. Not due to her care for the man, but to what might happen if he passed. June knew that Mrs. Harper did not accept her position in her home as Mr. Harper's confidante; so she believed that the family might desire to be rid of us, might be in need of money, or all along had thought of us as dispensable pests, and that his death was the sole development required to find a means to send us off: to prove once and for all that we had no value, even to them as help. What is more awful than to worry about such things! And the *smell*. The smell stuck with me. The smell had found me, again.

I opened the flap.

"Hello," I said.

But there was no need to wait for an answer. As my eyes fell upon the man, a familiar wave of anxiety fell over me. The burden of the man's very presence. Of what he might demand of me. The feeling was more recognizable than Mr. Harper himself. Gone was his stiff and forbidding frame, the manicured mustache and hair. The dandy's well-tailored clothes.

Before me was the new Wyatt Harper: a starved, goggly-eyed man clothed only in his underpants. His mustache had been replaced by a beard that nearly reached the ground. His ribs were visible, his chest deflating with every breath to such a degree that I could nearly see the outline of his organs hard at work to keep the man alive. More clutter surrounded him. The dusted-over tools he'd once used as an engineer; a dulled hunting knife; forks and spoons; so many useless articles I could not keep count of them if I tried. He was a man, it seemed, who had been made master of his own pigsty.

Mr. Harper hardly found a means to plant his hand on the ground in order to stand and meet me, and when he did, it appeared that he could hardly believe the sight before him. This individual he had once ruled over was now trespassing in his new domain. I could not help looking him in the eyes in a manner I could not recall ever doing before. A look of compassion. How far this man had fallen in the two years since he'd departed Baton Rouge! Taking my sister with him, no less. For what?

"Coleman?" his voice hardly audible, as though it had not issued words in some time. "It can't be."

His lips parted slightly in shock. His teeth were yellowed, splotched with dirt. His hair was matted into a vulgar nest.

Out of habit, out of courtesy, I was on the verge of calling this individual *sir*. But I stopped myself before that might happen. I could not find the words to address what was, to me, now a stranger.

It would turn out I did not need to. For a figure was already advancing upon the man before me, politely pushing me aside.

Florence had found her nerve to enter the tent.

She pressed a hand to her injured side. Breathed heavily. Steadied herself.

"Hello, Father."

"Florence?" His voice hardly a croak. How powerful the weight of his words had once been. Now, something light to be carried off in the wind. At the sight of his daughter, Mr. Harper made to step forward; but as Florence did so herself, he hobbled backward under her very gaze.

"You need not move one bit," Florence said. "Need not say one more word."

"My dear daughter," Mr. Harper said.

So many thoughts swirled in my mind, but there was one refrain that kept recurring, one directed at Florence: *Give him not one tear.*

"Never did I think I'd see you again," Mr. Harper said.

Florence stood over him like a giant.

"Because you did not wish to," she said. "Because you hadn't a care in the world for me. Is that not so?"

"Never—"

"I said you need not speak!"

The man's lip fluttered in what I could only take to be fright. His whole body quivered as he cowered before his own, dearest daughter. I knew that fear. Saw in his eyes the look of a man who had been beaten down by the world; a man who'd chosen to surrender to his baseness, his carnality, rather than resist. He'd allowed himself to be defeated.

Mr. Harper, I thought. *Of all people.*

"You wanted Coleman here so you might find his sister. And yet we both stand before you. And your wife would as well, had she not died on the journey to find you."

"I'm glad," Florence said then, to my great shock. "So, so delighted. For if she had discovered you like this—surrounded by your own soiled rags, with no real home to your name—the shame would have taken her from us in a way far worse than the one that fate dealt her."

"Dead?" Mr. Harper said in confusion. "What is this? Who..."

His eyes darted from side to side. From me to his daughter, then beyond us both, into some place I myself was not privy to, some place in his mind's eye.

He scratched his beard. Worked his jaw like a broken trap that could not quite close. Then he seemed back amongst us in the real world. Ready, it appeared, to plead some case to us.

"Tell me, did that man bring me your mother's jewels? I was counting on that, you know. He must have them. I'll give him his due. That I swear."

Mr. Harper craned his neck toward the entrance of the tent, his eyes flooded with worry.

"Tell me he is not here. I can't answer to that man. Not now. Dear God."

He itched a wound upon his knee until it began to bleed. Then his gaze landed on me once again.

"Coleman. Go look and tell him off if he is readying to hound me. Won't you? Yes. Give him whatever he requires to leave me be. Then fetch me some coffee. That sounds delightful right now, doesn't it? Do as I say, now."

"Coffee?" I said.

"No one is fetching you anything," Florence instructed him. "Not coffee. Not June."

"June!" His eyes bulged at the utterance of the name. "Her leaving has caused all of this. I know where she is. I have tried to make it there myself, but I had my horse stolen — my goods as well — and my health has suffered to such a degree — "

"That you can do little at all, I imagine," Florence said. "You are unwell. But you were always unwell. Eaten from the inside out by your own ambition."

"Where do you find the gall to say such a thing to me?" Mr. Harper declared, thrusting up one of his mangled hands — what was no more than a claw — to grab at Florence. "I'm your *father*."

She batted him away like a fly. "My father?"

I thought she might strike the man. Wail upon him. So I stepped forward.

"This man is not in his right mind, Florence. He is not even worth the effort. Let him be."

The cracked slit of his lips opened. And Mr. Harper, for reasons I will never know, began to giggle in delight. The coarse lines of his face expressed themselves, and before long I spied the man there that I used to know. Soon he was gone again to some pained look of confusion, scanning our faces once more for some vague sense of recognition that we could not provide him. What is one supposed to feel in such a moment? Where, for the most evil of actors, on the final turn in their journey toward their fall, might an agent of humanity catch them? Did this man deserve any pity at all?

The tent had been unbearably hot when I'd entered, but settling into the place, I was overcome by the cold between us all. A frigidity that, of all things, sowed a sadness within me. I stepped back from these two. Knowing, now, that I would allow Florence to do everything necessary to expunge this man from her heart.

"I don't wish to hurt him," she said to me. "Nothing like that. I wish only to offer him these. As a gift."

He could hardly look his daughter in the eyes as she brought forth Mrs. Harper's shoes. They had been fastened in her grip for so long that I'd altogether forgotten she was holding them. But there they were. Held out before her as an offering.

"These are Mother's shoes. We both know she loved you more than anyone on this earth, including myself. I imagine one day you will be buried here. It might be without ceremony, and perhaps no one will witness the sight, but you will die in this desert. When it happens, I wish for you to have a token of her at your side. So that part of her may rest in peace with the man she loved, and so that you might, in those final moments, take stock of the wife and mother you let die for no reason at all. Might you do that for me?"

She placed them in his hands with a startling tenderness. I do not know if he recognized their significance, even after Florence had explained as much so clearly, but he stared at them with a concentration he had yet to show at any point in our presence. And as Florence leant down, to my great wonder she kissed the man on his forehead. He made no show of her affection, merely kept staring at those shoes — as if the memories of a whole lifetime past had been channeled into some corridor of his thinking he'd long lost the capacity to access.

I had no place to be proud of Florence, for I could hardly claim to know the trait myself. But never had I seen such an act before, and never since. It was over quickly. She stood back up. Put her chin high. Then turned and left.

The tent returned to its natural silence. Surely I had no hold on Mr. Harper's attention, as his eyes were on the ground. The shoes had been cast aside. As worthless to him now as the rest of the trash that littered the place. He was so calm as to appear nearly lifeless. I looked back to make sure Florence was indeed at a distance, at which point, against my better judgment, I sat upon the ground beside him. I could smell the rankness of the man's armpits. See the vacancy in his eyes. I waited until he was forced to take account of me.

"Mr. Harper," I said. "You sent for me to find June, did you not?"

The name put a flicker in his gaze. Where his mind had been wandering elsewhere, now he seemed altogether present.

"June! Yes. I need her back. I've tried to go myself, but those *wild men* won't let me near that camp. But *you* going — yes, that would fix things..."

The man began to ramble about his mines, his treasures, his great worthiness, and I had to shush him — calmly, slowly, as though he were an infant — to get another word in.

"I want you to know, Mr. Harper, that you will never see June again. That you will never have the chance to harm her as you once did. I do not wish ill of you. I wish death on no man, certainly not one as diseased as you are. But I must use this opportunity for myself to voice my opinion. That you are no good person. The way you treated me and my sister — with such cruelty, and for so long — well, a man like yourself deserves very little, Mr. Harper. Very little indeed."

With this I eyed the tent once again. Took in the foul odor, the mess, the ants crawling upon the walls; Mr. Harper's rusted, useless tools.

"Yes. I believe this place is exactly the sort of home you deserve."

With this I stood up and dusted off my pants. Removed, as well as I could, what remnants of the place that had tainted me.

"Good luck, Mr. Harper," I said, before turning to leave myself.

13

The sky was an endless drapery of blue. I saw that Florence was adrift, still cradling her ribs with a crooked arm. William was retying the ponies together; all of them but one, in fact.

I gave a whistle so Oliver would come — which he did, obedient for a change — as I walked up to William.

"It's over, then?" he asked.

"As over as these things can be. I don't believe we'll be seeing Mr. Harper again once we leave out of here. You look to be about off yourself," I said.

"There is certainly nothing here for me." William tied the final knot of his rope firmly, securing it with a grunt, his few goods lashed to the side of the trailing horse. "As I said, I'll report all of what has happened to General Chavez."

"He'll be disappointed," I said.

"You consider that his men are now dead and he's gotten no help from Mr. Harper regarding that mine, disappointment seems like the best I can hope for."

"A man like that is used to it. He won't welcome the news, but thank you for providing it nonetheless."

"Forever the optimist, you are. Let's see if you're right."

William picked a piece of food from his teeth, wiped down his eyebrows, and patted his side to affirm the presence of his pistol. I realized then how I would miss parts of this man who had revealed almost nothing to me but managed to remain, through good and bad, a trusted companion. I did not have any friends, and he was not close to one, but I was happy to have him by my side and would miss him when he was gone.

I thought it best not to tell him as much. It did not seem the sort of thing William would care to hear. Yet it was almost as though he, too, felt something still had been left unsaid, for it was then that he cleared his throat, took me in with a sideways glance of uncertainty, and spoke.

"You know, when we first met, you asked me about my valuables. You told me I was a wealthy man. And I told you I was not."

"I remember well," I said.

"It's difficult to say, but I think I didn't *know* why I have all those things, Coleman. But now. Now, I do..."

The moment was suddenly endowed with meaning. Part of me was afraid to ask what he denoted, for he might flinch from the question. But he proceeded without my needing to say a word.

"...I know this part of the world well enough. And yet, with all I have done, I have never met up with my mother's people."

"Is that possibly true?" I asked.

"Not once."

William patted his pony, rubbed his hand along its side, his eyes landing on the long fingers of its ribs, the supple groove of its flank.

"I think I will find them," he said. "My mother spoke of their horses. Beautiful things. Treated them like prized possessions. Family, almost. Well, I can buy them a few horses. Maybe get to Bagdad, trade in what I've got for a whole stable to deliver to them. An offering, I suppose. She'd be pleased with that. I can see her now."

It was as though the woman's reflection might grow evident in the very flank of that horse — smiling back at her son.

"I am glad we both might get what we're after," I said. "You will make her proud. And I believe it will bring you joy. Really, a gift of the sort you have in mind is far more precious than any bit of gold or silver. That I know, William."

He turned to me then. Put a hand on my shoulder and smiled a rare smile.

"I hope you're right," he said, putting his hand out now to shake.

I took it in my own.

"Before you go," I said. "I'd like to thank you. For all you have done."

He rejected my gratitude quickly, scowling at the idea of it, then shaking my hand with more strength than before.

"Florence and you both paid your way and were fine companions. I should thank you two, I imagine. I would not have ever considered this path had ours not crossed. There's something special in that."

We were still shaking, rather awkwardly, a prolonged motion that required endurance to keep up with after a time.

"You are still very strange," he said, echoing the words he'd said when we'd first got to chatting, a time that felt like many centuries ago. "But you are stronger than you give yourself credit for. Try to remind yourself of as much on occasion."

"Thank you, William."

"I told you not to say that."

With this, he finally pulled back. He rifled around in his saddlebag, procuring something in hand, holding it out to me. It was, I realized after a moment of surprise, his compass of all things.

"I'd like you to have this. You'll need it more than I will."

"William!" Already he was forcing it into the palm of my hand, closing my fingers over the silver-gilt cover. "Absolutely not. I cannot accept. It is your mother's —"

"Yes, and she would want you to have it. To see you safely through."

Still I refused, stammering my objections, but he was more forceful than ever, clutching my hand over the compass still, protesting my every demurral. Once more his gaze landed on mine.

"Would you rather die out here?" he said. "You, Florence, and the dog? Is that what you want?"

"...No. I imagine not."

"Then please. Take it. I know the way back to the camp well. I will make my way from there with ease. Your journey...it will be more difficult."

"Take it," Florence said at my side. "He wants you to have it. Do not turn down a gift, Coleman."

"Okay," I said. "Okay, William." He smiled once more. There was not much sentimentality to the man, but a subdued kindness lay under his veneer of reticence.

"Thank—" I stopped myself short.

"Take that horse, too. It's yours, now. I left water in the saddlebag. Go northeast," he said, raising a finger in the air, pointing the way. "Do not go any other direction. If you feel that you will not get there, keep going onward. If you find yourself certain, without question, that you have lost your will to go on, keep going. Don't stray. Do you understand?"

I told him I did.

"Good luck to you both. You're more than capable. I've learned as much these past few days."

I thought William might smile once more. He did not.

"Hold back your horse, now."

"Until we meet again," I said.

Both of us aware, I gathered, that we never would.

I turned back to find Florence. She was as silent as I had ever witnessed her. For a moment I peered back to the tent—certain that Mr. Harper would shoot out from there, hands waving, making demands and declarations once again. But it appeared more like a mausoleum to me—the man inside already resigned to his resting place.

Florence's cheeks were still flush, banners of scarlet striping them. Her eyes left the tent and landed on my own. "Northeast, then?" she said.

I showed her the compass. It had a rusted clasp that clicked open to reveal bold, crisp red markers that displayed each of the cardinal directions.

"That is what he said."

"Then northeast we will go. As long as it is far from this tent. Far from that man. I will be happy."

"I believe I can promise that much."

"Very well, then," she said, putting her hair behind her ears, taking as deep a breath as she could manage.

"Why don't you get on the horse, now," I told her. "Give yourself a rest."

"It's you who needs the rest," she said.

"I can walk for now," I said. "That suits me just fine."

No more needed to be shared between us. I helped her mount up, watching as she attempted to conceal her pain.

The sun coated the landscape in a shimmering glisten the color of hay. A last tick of time was spent pondering the tent. Oliver, coiled up a few feet away, rose up as he shook dust from his coat.

"Please. Can we go now?" she asked.

Yes, I told her, patting my forehead dry with the collar of my shirt. I was more than happy to leave this place. Happy, indeed, to never look back.

I discovered the water William had left us, his small leather canteen, but I let it sit as long as I might before telling Florence we should have some. After we both had our fill, Oliver looked upon me with a dry tongue and sad eyes, but as always there was a limit to what I might offer him when so little was available in the first.

"I'm sorry," I said with a pat. "Hopefully we are close, now."

It had been hours with nothing appearing before us. The mountains stood unmoving at our side, and no matter how far we traveled our perspective remained fixed on that single landmark that taunted us from afar. We could not gain on it.

Wind occasionally drifted toward us with little reprieve, for it carried no cold, but a small gust was enough to nearly keep me from carrying on.

Florence was hunched over the pony. Her breathing was labored. Her eyes heavy-lidded.

"Florence," I said.

"What."

"Tell me you are okay."

"I don't know if I am."

"Let's talk. Distract ourselves."

"But I have nothing to say to you. I've said all I can."

"Tell me," I said, ignoring her. "What will you do upon your return to New Orleans?"

"Oh for God's sake, Coleman."

"Humor me."

"I don't know!" Her eyes picked up, scanning the desert, as if the answer lay upon those endless slopes of dirt and sand that stretched on before us.

"Anything," I said, stumbling forth still. "Really, any answer will do."

"I will marry Hugh. A kind man. At the very least, a man who desires me. I will live a comfortable life. I don't believe that is so much to ask after all of this."

"Absolutely not, no! At a minimum that is what you deserve."

"I want children."

Now she was getting going, her health vigorous for a moment as her imagination went to work.

"Of course."

"Many, even."

"A flock!" I said.

"All of them running about my legs day and night. I will put them to sleep early when we have guests, and in the morning I will tell them all about the party that transpired as they were dreaming. I will dress them in the finest clothes, and they will want for nothing. I will never leave their side, and they will never leave mine."

"I haven't the slightest doubt it will all come true," I said. "Every last word."

Oliver had squirmed in my hands, revealing his belly to the sun, and I rubbed it with the same pace I kept up with the pony.

"I hope so," Florence said weakly. "But what of you? I suppose I should ask what you will do when gone from here."

A silhouette of clouds unspooled before our heads. I thought for a second it might rain. But they were soon gone in another gust of wind.

"I only wish to find a quiet place," I said. "With Oliver at my feet or on my lap. My books stacked high beside my bed. Time to read. A whole day's worth of solitude would be divine. Peace for however long I wish to have it."

At this, Florence looked down at me with beleaguered eyes.

"You and those books. It is all you've ever wanted."

"It's true. I often think of my attic in New Orleans. What I might do to be back there! With one spare hour to my name. A chilly winter's morning when the heat of the fire has not risen yet, and I need only a blanket to keep warm. There might be nothing better."

"It's nice. Yes. But I do hope you have higher aspirations than that old attic. You deserve more than that, you know..."

Florence was now quiet. The pony defecated unceremoniously and I let Oliver down to do the same, but he merely ambled forth and lingered there. It was, perhaps, the only time in his life I did not see him take off when given the chance.

"I'm worried for him. He needs water."

"Give him some water, then," Florence said. "What does it matter?"

She was hardly awake. Her head drooped low. Her eyes on the verge of closing.

So I did just that, making a cup of my hand, pouring a bit of water there, letting Oliver lap up what he could, and although some fell to the ground, it felt worth it, knowing he'd had his fill.

Florence whimpered then, and I could not blame her, for the frustration of this place would tear down the fortitude of the strongest men I had ever laid eyes on. I wished to cry myself.

"Coleman," she said. "We're going to die here, aren't we?"

"Don't even think of such a thing. Consider only how close we are to our destination."

"No closer than an hour before. Or an hour before that. On and on we go…"

She trailed off, and I could feel myself panic at the thought of being alone out in this place, with no one to speak to, not a soul at my side to commiserate with, if she was to pass out — or worse.

"You must find strength," I said.

Florence only mumbled in reply. I picked up Oliver. His body was nearly limp itself. Sapped of life from this endless journey. I then took the reins from the pony and pulled them over the horse's head, for Florence was in no mind to drive herself. So I led all of us. One step at a time. Just like any stroll we had taken in the past, I thought. A leisurely jaunt. Nothing out of the ordinary.

I took to rocking Oliver like a child. I wish I had a reason for doing so. He was exhausted; dehydrated soon again. His tongue a loose appendage hanging from his mouth. When the sun returned, I attempted to shield him from it by setting him under my shirt, but it had no effect: My shirt was a tattered, soiled rag, thinned by sweat and grime. I was in no better state than a beggar.

"Without question we are nearly there, now," I said, although I did not believe the words this time.

Florence was asleep upon the pony, back bowed, her head nearly on its mane. And that mare… it was covered in sweat itself. Was yielding to the heat, poor thing.

I spoke to Oliver. I told him not to worry like Florence. I cited all we had been through together, from his days as a pup until now — from New Orleans to the coast of Mexico, all the way to the border. How many can claim to have accomplished so much in so short a life?

"We should be proud," I said, my voice emptied of all emotion now, for fatigue, coupled with my headache, had become too much to bear. "We should *rejoice*."

His eyes peeked open ever so slightly, risking the glare of the sun, gazing upon me earnestly before he dozed off again. At least that was my recollection. Who can be certain of such things whilst under the stress of so explosive a pain that felled me? The hurt of my body; the pain in my soul. The knowledge, finally settling in, that I would never see my sister again.

I hated to slip into such awful ruminations. For in entering that one domain of thought I was liable to sink back into my memories and realize once more the chief loss of my life: that of my mother. So little of her was left to me, and I dare not write of her for how it speaks to the sadness that shaped my whole existence. Yet she is who came to mind right then. Her face was sanded over by time — what little remained of it to me made coarse by the trials she had faced, the sadness of our small shared world. I recall better her dresses, yes — cotton dresses, blues and yellows and reds depending on the day, falling at her legs that I would hold in times of fright, dance about when playing with June. And my mother's hands as well, warm upon my neck as she calmed me on freezing nights when I was sick; when I was frightened or unsure that I might be able to face the day to come. Of her voice I remember only that it was rather stern but protective, that it made me believe, for short bouts, that I might be safe. Yet in being taken from her I found the loss so severe, so sudden, that I could hardly think of her at all after arriving in Baton Rouge. In fact, to think of her was to revisit the moment June and I were pried from her grasp forever. So in the past my mother remained, slowly dissolving into a shadowy wraith. And to consider that loss — to consider the prospect that June herself might join our mother as something vanquished to time — this, more than anything, would spell the end of me.

Downcast, I forced myself to look up, to keep my sights on what was before us, and what was there brought me to a standstill: an awesome flowering of trees, so stunning, the collection of them all, that it took my breath away.

"Florence!" I said, not wanting to witness the scene alone. "Wake up. Come on, now!"

I shook her limp leg, but she would hardly budge, giving me only a vague groan, a whisper really, that she needed her rest.

There was red bark on the trees, and each branch had the most beautiful yellow blossoms I had ever beheld. Something fit for a manicured garden, not a place as wild as this one. What a sublime thing it was, after nothing for so long! Oliver was again licking my hands, thirsty for water.

"There's no more," I said. "We must just go on, now."

Yet my body had other ideas. I was, I realized, surrendering to the desert. My head felt as though it had been pierced with a sickle. A blurred film descended over my vision, and what I saw after this occurrence was not of this earth. Phantasms born of a disordered mind plagued me: a whole world of individuals in line before my path, perceiving me with an indifference I could not make sense of, watching over my passage from this place to whatever might come next.

Mrs. Harper was there in her honeybee dress, just as she had appeared in the ballroom upon *The Jubilee*; Amos Turlow hovered in his vest with cigarette in hand, scowling, his expression dropped of all pretense; Paco and Hector, side by side, their hats held against their chests. There were folks from my life in Baton Rouge: Old Nelly, who baked for the Harper family and would always set aside some buns for me and June when I came by her stall (she was the only sort of mother I ever knew besides June, always generous with her advice, her words full of the same warmth and sweetness as her food); Jesse Mankins, a child who belonged to the Templetons and met an end I wish not to recall, a pleasant boy who jumped rope with me if the day allowed it, never making fun when I fell; old men and women, faces hard, whom I did not even know. Were these my people? Was that my mother, stone-faced, but in her resolve a show of love, a sign of confidence? My father beside her? Older descendants who had come to pay witness to the last of their line, floundering, tottering toward his final resting place?

I snapped back from this spell of disorientation and faced the desert before me once more. I considered taking a rest alongside Florence. A memory came to mind of Oliver and me in the garden in New Orleans, both of us in the shade of some bushes on a break from tending to the flowers — my back against the fence, the dew on the flowers making the air before me cool, Oliver lapping his tongue into the water bucket, flicks of mist landing on my face.

Keep your head, Coleman, I told myself, in a voice that felt not to be my own. *There are no ghosts here. And the past is gone.*

I looked to Florence for some injection of encouragement, but she was more gone from me than ever. Lost to her fatigue.

I was left with what was before me. Nothing but the dirtied, brown rolling hills of bushes and sand I'd grown so familiar with. The mountain now at my rear, its taunts lessened by my finally gaining ground with every hour of walking I'd braved. All of it was so familiar, a recurrence of every previous step in my journey. The only thing — truly the only thing — before me but a mere tumbleweed, an interlocked web of roots, a tangled carpet of shoots curled up at its head, scurrying across the desert, without even a hint of wind. It was something of a marvel, I thought. Floating as it was, never quite stopping, carried by nothing, off to who knew where. I paused there for some time, until it was out of range, far enough gone that I considered, understandably so, to believe that I had imagined that specter as I had those ghosts.

I wondered what would happen if I got us over one more hill. If I managed one more crest. So I did just that. Ready, finally, to fall to my knees. I swear to it I felt myself to be hardly present in the world at all by that point. I was loitering in this life, transitioning to the next. There was a peace to that process. I had resolved to embrace whatever might follow.

It was then that I spotted, right beside me, emerging from nowhere, two black men and an Indian, all three on their own horses. Animal traps were lashed to the side of their horses, large enough to hold a possum, maybe a raccoon, but empty now. They rode in a half-circle before us, brought their mounts to a stop, and surveyed me with a look of incredulity.

"What," one of them asked, "is a boy like you doing out here in the devil's wasteland?"

"With a white girl no less," the other Negro said.

"I thought my eyes might be playing tricks on me," the first said.

"Nah. I see her too." He had on a brown vest, white shirt tucked and buttoned up beneath it; a burgundy bandanna loosely festooned around the neck.

The Indian looked more circumspect than the others. He wore bay-colored leggings, a colorful shirt laced of amazing patchwork, as though from the same material as the other fellow's bandanna. The man had enough silver on his fingers to nearly blind me. He spoke to the man in the vest, made motions with his hand, and I presumed they shared some level of communication beyond fluency but nonetheless adequate for understanding one another. I wished William had been at my side. I sorely missed him.

"He wants that horse," the Negro said. "Would have killed you and taken it, but he thinks she's sick." He nodded toward Florence.

"Can't bring no sickness back to his people," the other Negro said.

"Don't blame him," the vested man said.

"She isn't sick," I said. "She is hurt, and tired. Thirsty, too. All of us are."

I rose up to strict attention, wincing for a moment from the pain in my head, the same now channeling down my back and knocking at my knees.

"Where are my manners? Allow me to introduce myself. My name is Coleman. That is Florence on the horse. And this here is Oliver. I'd say I speak for all of us when I say it's a pleasure to make your acquaintance, and that we would appreciate any show of goodwill you might have on offer."

They took my words into account. Then the man in the vest finally spoke up for his party when the others would not.

"I'll tell you how this is," he said. "We've been out here for a good two hours, looking for a horse herd we heard rumor of. But this here is the only horse we've found. Now why don't you tell me why I shouldn't cut this expedition short, make that horse our own, and leave you out here for the vultures? You have my ear, 'cause I'm right curious — but I won't be for long."

"I'd have stolen that horse already," the other Negro said. "Willy's got more patience than I do."

"Go on, then," Willy said. "Speak your truth."

The silence — whatever spark of agitation lay between us and these men — animated the air. I did not know at first what to say. The Indian was glum-faced. The other two were still waiting for me to speak, impatient for me to utter something — anything.

"June," I said, my voice no more than a croak. "My sister's name is June. I have come a long way to find her. Perhaps you know of her? If not, take whatever you wish. Do as you will. We won't last much longer out here anyway."

Willy made no acknowledgment of my plea. His mouth hung loose, his tongue rattling about in there like a flopping fish; his mind hard at work, it seemed.

"*June*," the other Negro said. "June's your sister? Isaac's gal."

He told us then his name was Otis. That everyone knew June. She'd been with their people for some time, in fact.

"I don't know Isaac," I told them.

"Oh, you will soon enough," Otis said.

Willy gave his mount a mild kick. Came by my side and put down a hand. To my surprise, this kind man was offering me a *ride*.

"Well hell, I'll show you to June," he said. "Could have saved ourselves a whole talk up in this heat if you'd just said her name from the start."

"Are —" I stammered before catching myself. "Are you playing a joke on me?"

Otis seemed offended by the mere thought and then confused, I believe, by the look upon my own face. For I had already begun to break down by then. My throat was too dry, my heart too heavy, to give this man a reply beyond a mere nod of my head. I did not mind the embarrassment of my lips trembling, my eyes watering over.

Willy told me then I wasn't fit to walk. That I was worse off than the girl. How grateful I was to take his hand in my own as he lifted me onto his horse, telling me we could ride double the rest of the way to conserve what little strength I had left.

There was a stirring in my chest as we neared this place they called *Amity*.

"Y'all nearly made it on your own," Willy informed me. "But I can't say you'd have managed these last few miles, state you two are in."

I began to tell the men of what we'd endured on our trip, but they showed little interest. The Indian, made squeamish by Florence, had left altogether with a vicious but rather impressive shrill of a call, galloping off before I could offer a farewell. The other two only smiled politely, distractedly, shaking their heads at our various mishaps while they canvassed the desert for who knew what, some unseen threat.

They'd roused Florence from her slumber with a splash of water from their canteen. Even with that she was still only halfway present, yet she was alive. I'd not been sure of that much an hour before.

"You're a sharp fella to make it this far," Willy was saying. "But you're stupid to have tried all the same."

"Hardly any water between you two."

"War parties and thieves all across this desert."

"No food for miles on end."

"Y'all must be sharp as a tack, really."

"Sharp as an arrowhead."

"Sharp as Old Luther's big toenail, and that man can spear right through his shoe when he steps wrong."

"Sharp as..."

"She will need help," I said of Florence, interrupting their game of words.

"That girl needs only some shade and some water. And we got both up ahead."

"I tried to tell him that," Florence said, still drowsy as the sun poured down upon her but coming around now. Her cheeks looked like they'd been carved out; her eyes were still nearly closed. But she was peering ahead, her head bobbing in step with the pony. "You're not to worry about me."

Oliver, in that instant, attempted to leap from my hands, squirreling about and lashing Willy's back with his paws.

"Calm that thing down," Willy said.

I held him tighter to my chest. "Easy, easy," I said, whispering now. "We are almost there. I promise this time."

And upon those very words, Amity was before us. Smoke rose from chimneys. A flock of chickens appeared to have been let loose, squawking as they pattered about. There were dilapidated cabins and huts, a few made of stone — perhaps old forts cobbled back together after having been blasted to cinder. One woman was laughing as she swept her front porch, pausing to lean over the railing, jeering at her friend, a woman in a colorful dress who looked busy mending a shoe with needle and thread under a shaded arbor. Dried vegetables hung like the limbs of heavy-burdened trees off the sides of all the homes.

There was a large barn near the middle of the place where the men had gathered, drinking and fooling around with the same insouciance the women had on display. Children who had been milling about caught wind of us having appeared and began to trail our party, as though we were an attraction that had just arrived to put on a show.

The energy, the happiness, the casual demeanor of the inhabitants of Amity transcended whatever shabbiness befell this place. For I can't imagine a soul who would rather live in luxury, suffocated by one's own station in life, than live amongst so many spirited folk.

"Willy!" a man called out from the barn. "Who's that you got there with you?"

"I don't quite see how that's any of your business," Willy said, more playfully than not. "Best you mind your own."

But it only piqued the interest of all who spotted us, and one could hear the whispered talk of my and Florence's arrival, everyone asking the same questions as to who we were and where it was we'd hailed from.

With so much transpiring around me, my mind could not settle on a single thought. The day had been an endless flurry of hardship, drawn out and with no end in sight. Now time felt accelerated. The sun was excusing itself from the sky at our backs. We were at a trot but it felt as though we were at a gallop. I figured my sister to be right around the corner at any point in time. How long had it been since I'd had a chance to freshen up? For June to see me with so many days of dust layered upon my person, my hair a tangled mess. It would not do. I told them so repeatedly.

"What I need is a mirror. Is there a mirror anywhere? I am in no state to see June."

Florence's pony was right beside me now, pent in close by the children running amok at our sides, scaring the horses.

"You look fine, Coleman," she said, her voice still weak. "Try not to worry as you do."

"She's right," Willy said. "No one's judging a man for being a little dirtied out here."

Their words helped little. I could hardly contain my unease. My heart was like a hammer pounding at the cage of my chest. I found Florence staring at me, an understated patience in her eyes.

"Remember that it's June. *Your* June. Do not worry like this over kin. This is all you have wanted."

After this, a moment more passed.

"We're here, Coleman. We've done it."

Our caravan came to an unceremonious halt. Willy swept his leg over the side of the horse and dismounted. He patted a child or two on the head, and now all of them were looking up at me, a few asking to pet Oliver, the others trying to catch a peek at Florence.

"Get," Otis said. "We gon' water these horses. Your sister's right up ahead. Some kids are putting on some show of theirs. Got a few folks polite enough to say yes to sit and watch. June…well, she always says yes. Good lady, she is. Go on, then."

All of us disembarked and the instant Oliver touched the ground—for he was as eager to play with the children as they were with him—he was lost to the crowd for a time. By now it was as though the entire camp had surrounded their newfound guests. That being me and Florence.

"Oh, come on now, Oliver," I said as I raced to track him down, keeping the children at bay as we marched forward. None of them could stop giggling, and I believe if I had not finally scooped Oliver up they would have found entertainment from his antics for the rest of the day and well into the evening.

"Do you want me to hold him?" Florence asked from my side.

"No. It's fine. I am fine."

"I will have to take you at your word."

"And you?" I asked.

"What did I tell you before? I'm perfectly healthy."

The words were uttered with a strenuous attempt to conceal her pain. She was ailed, yes, but not willing to draw attention to the fact where a younger Florence would have made a scene, demanding assistance, shrieking in pain. This was no longer that needy girl. This was a new woman. It made me happy to see as much.

Already we were walking in step with one another.

Shadows hatched off each building that we passed, an encroaching darkness slowly enveloping us in its cool, sudden grasp. The closer we got the quieter it felt about the town. It was as though word of our arrival had been passed down to each and every soul, announcing us to everyone, acknowledging the gravity of the occasion.

Past a firepit, seated before one of the last cabins in the row, a number of men and women were casually seated upon quilted blankets. There, the sun landed unimpeded and cast the scene into a near-blinding brightness. Before the onlookers, children in flamboyant costumes, dressed like warriors, readied for battle. Brooms with horsehair stitched upon them were beneath their legs, and they chased one another about as though caught in a gun battle. The men and women hooted and hollered, cheering them on. The sound pierced through the silence from just a few seconds before: a great reverberation of their whistling echoing back toward us. Words can hardly capture how nervous I was in that moment.

I paused a few feet behind the crowd, for I did not wish to interrupt the performance. The sun was so intense again as I stepped from the shadows that I could practically hear it crackle. A soft glow, the color of a ripe orange, cascaded down onto this slip of Amity. It could not have been more beautiful.

"Perhaps I should wait," I whispered to Florence. But she put a hand on my shoulder.

"June is right there," she said.

"Well," I said. "So she is."

There was no mistaking that figure, even when seeing her from the back. Her hair had been cut short, no more than a leveled puff above her head. I could sense her confusion over why the children had stopped their act — the cocking of her neck, ever slightly — surely exhibiting the same dubious glance she'd given me countless times through the years. Wondering, now, what could possibly be happening, for the children's performance had ground to a halt amidst their confusion of the gathering crowd, a new audience that had not been present a moment before. The children in the show were pointing. The crowd turned to see what it was that might be so important.

Florence stepped back then, ceding the space to me, and it was all I could do not to call her back toward me, for I felt stripped bare with all those men and women at my back, watching on.

Before I could give it another thought I found my sister, only feet ahead, staring at me. One hand covered her mouth in shock, the other at the sternum, at her heart.

She stood up so quickly I nearly shuddered. In a matter of seconds I had taken stock of her every feature: the eyes that had lit upon me each morning back in Baton Rouge; the familiar dimples just a hop away from each corner of her lips, visible whether or not she frowned or smiled (indeed, she was smiling now); those were her hands that I had always felt upon my shoulders as she now grabbed me with a cry of delight in a moment of excitement. And yes, that was her voice, calling my name, over and over, asking how, how, I had made it this far, so far, and what had gotten into me to risk my life to do such a crazy thing as this.

"Coleman, Coleman," June said over and over, as though it was a necessitated chant; as if by failing to do so she might risk my disappearance — me, Coleman: an apparition born one second and gone the next.

"Hallelujah!" an aged woman said from the back of the crowd.

There was hooting and hollering but I could not muster a single word at first, as there were tears streaming down my face, and I did not want to look a fool due to my being hysterical and whatnot, and I was so happy to see my sister, as the world — for the first time since she was taken from me — was right again.

She put a hand to my cheek to dab out the wetness.

"Sis," I said, trying not to stammer, for that was what I'd always called her, but it had been so long since the word had escaped my mouth that it felt foreign to me. I'd thought, for so long, I'd never have the pleasure of saying it again.

She put a hand over my shoulder. She led me to the steps of a small cabin, just down the road as the others watched, Florence amongst them — crying herself.

"Who is this?" she said, putting a hand on the tip of Oliver's snout before running it over his head.

"Oh! This is Oliver. He is my best friend. I've... I've waited a long time for you to meet him, June."

"I bet you've told him all about me, haven't you?"

I simply nodded in agreement, for I could not find the words. I put my head into the crook of her shoulder, hiding myself from these people. I am not ashamed to say I was much like a young boy again for a time. It is not so wrong, in my estimation, to feel like no more than a child when a miracle transpires. One loses the belief in such things as time marches on, for the world is a place filled with sorrow, and nothing is promised to you. Certainly no miracles. But one occurred that day. I could not help feeling overcome by that truth.

I let go of Oliver then, and after a turn of jumping upon us, the distraction of the children was too great. They were happy to play with him. And I was occupied with more important concerns.

For a time we just laughed, June and I, as we grew familiar with each other once again. She was older, yes, and hardened by the elements, but there was a graceful dignity to the lines on her face, the calm in her eyes. Not a hint of fear. That sense of worry — of what might come next — that had been so vested in her gaze. They were not *sad* eyes. No, whatever she'd found here had brought a joy that had never been on offer in our time together. I knew at that point, after so long apart, that my sister was alright.

I could rest.

"There's so much to tell," June said. "But you must know how much I missed you. Before anything else. That I'd have come got you but I didn't know how. I didn't have the means — "

"You don't need to explain." For a man who loves to talk, even I could recognize that in this instant we understood each other without another word needing to be said.

We might as well have been back home, when we shared the mirror as she combed my hair and readied me for the day. Such was the familiarity of that moment. That sense of calm. That feeling of love.

"I'm sorry I am in such poor condition," I said. "My hair, my clothes. You know me to be better."

"Coleman!" and with this she laughed, wiping a tear from her eye. "To think I'd care! No... I'm just glad you're here. Aren't you glad you're here?"

I held her close to me. It was the only satisfactory answer I could give.

"I always had faith," she whispered into my ear. "It was only a matter of time."

True, I thought. Faith had guided me, but fear kept me alert and my resolve kept me alive. The world, as I said, is a cruel place. Its touch so often cold. But on this day I had found warmth, happiness; community. I realized, pulling apart from June, that there was so much affection surrounding us. From Oliver panting with happiness — as curious as ever to explore his new surroundings — to those little girls with their hair in tails showing off gap-toothed smiles; the older ladies, bonnets bright, faces creased by time. I noticed it amongst those men who looked as broad and menacing as soldiers, more manly than I might ever claim to be, but kind enough to stand there without the slightest intrusion, the care evident in the way they stood at attention, hats in hand, waiting for the right time to speak a word.

"I'm sure everyone's wanting to meet you," June said.

I could not linger on the steps of that porch, I realized, for the next part of my journey was before me. Meeting these kindred souls of my sister. Her people. Now, my people.

How rude of me to keep them waiting! Where were my manners? I stood up — dusted myself off and tried to set my hair down with only the patting of my hand. I cleared my throat once, just for effect.

"If I might introduce myself," I said, my eyes still wet with happiness. "My name is Coleman. June's brother. And I have never, in my life, been so happy as you find me today."

I wished to say more, but words still eluded me. I wanted to explain my arrival. Give gratitude to the presence of every single person in this place. But the tears were upon me again.

And soon no words were necessary. The women were crowding in — hugging me close, telling me I need not say a single other thing. I was enfolded by their warmth. And in that love they shared for someone no more than a stranger, I realized I could simply stand still, at rest, and let my joy wash over me.

Silence, in that one moment, would do.

Epilogue

The flatlands of Texas went on with such immensity that June could not well decipher if it was an interminable prison she'd found herself in or a natural haven of such grandeur that the place was due reverence. The plains brimmed with pockets of violet nightshade and soapweed and all manner of cacti, but it was otherwise a naked desert of amber topsoil tinged with a yellow hue, like a cool breath of sunshine scattered by the wind.

Each morning she would wake to the silence of her home here and become attuned, once more, to the quiet life she now led two years on from leaving Amity. Her hearing had grown sensitive. The call of a coyote in the distance, the twitch of a plant outside the cabin was all it might take to cause her shoulders to tense. Often it was just the creak of the old foundations of the cabin. Always she keyed into the noise — surveyed her surroundings, ready to pick up Isaac's shotgun, take to a fast march, warn Coleman if need be.

If he had not yet left to join his brother to start the day's work, Isaac would help soothe her, telling her things were alright, that no danger was closing in on their home — that nature just spoke in many hushed tones, not all of them familiar. But when he was gone a panic would rise up in her like poison needing to be expelled. She'd get to the front door of the cabin in a fit — and when that happened it was Coleman himself who eased her worry. She could spot him within his own cabin, always, for there was routine to his day, and unless something cataclysmic had occurred, nothing untethered him from the strict habits he abided by. His calm, often enough, invoked her own.

The land was lent to Isaac's brother to work, a man named Moses who'd left Amity for better fortune and less danger in Drakesville. Moses had overseen a gang of men some years back, but most of them had gone west, south, off to other ranches God knew where — thirsty for better wages and a view of the outside world that captured young folk and drove them far from a life of mundanity herding and grazing livestock and staking fence. It had been years since Moses had sent word for Isaac to come set up a life alongside him; and another one on for Isaac to inquire with June if she had any interest in doing so. (She still remembered that fateful day, both of them lost in a tangle of blankets, Isaac smoking at her side, pained by a single question he could not quite utter until finally he did.) Long they deliberated on the idea, but when Coleman arrived in Amity there was no question that June wanted her brother somewhere safer; what better than endless acres of solitude, where nothing might disturb them? Texas, all along, held the appeal she was after.

By then, more denizens from Amity had been packing up for elsewhere. The Mexican government, which had finally defeated the French, had less need for their services at the border — and yet the battles with rival tribes never ceased. Many were set on building out a different life all their own wherever they might find it — usually fertile land nearby that the government would demand back when the time came. Others — the wiser ones, June thought — had left Mexico altogether, just as she had done alongside Coleman and Isaac. Rumor had it that over at Fort Duncan the United States government, and the Office of Indian Affairs, was recruiting their old compatriots as allies. If they were willing to resettle in the territories, under Union leadership that saw them as possible collaborators of peace, they might receive some land in return for their loyalty. Their country, against all odds, was welcoming them home again. Still, they hadn't seen any of their former townsfolk since leaving Mexico. It felt like a lifetime ago since they had.

But almost every day she could not help recalling Coleman's sudden appearance in Amity — the boy dressed in rags, face shimmering with sweat; thorns in his hair, gums blackened with dirt and grime. He'd introduced himself to the whole town before drifting back toward her and Isaac's home, collapsing there into an endless slumber she dared not rouse him from.

"You sure that's even your brother?" Isaac had said offhand, surveying Coleman from across the room. This was a joke, sure, but June registered his confusion, befuddled by the boy's peculiarity, the decorous way he moved through the world, and now made wary by how he mumbled in dreams, crying out, lost to a nightmare like a child.

"That's close to being an unkind comment," she told him. "Best you don't make the mistake of saying another one like it."

He heeded her wish that day and every one that followed.

Isaac had left early this morning after a plate of eggs and coffee, and she'd taken it upon herself to sweep a line of ants out the front door, telling them to shoo like unwanted guests. The day was young and bright and hit her with a mellow warmth that felt nice after a morning pent up inside. She held the broom to her breast, looked off down the plains, then turned to search the cabin next to her own for Coleman.

She could see him right there inside. He was already dressed. His shirt had not a wrinkle; his pants were without a crease. A shawl — one of hers, in fact — was draped over his lap as he sat at his desk. A notebook was open before him but Coleman only stared ahead, lost in thought. As was his way. The work — whatever it was — silenced him. Made him irritable on occasion. Sometimes when she and Isaac might wander outside for a midnight walk, her man grabbing her at the hips for an impromptu dance like those they'd reveled in after a celebration back in Amity, she would stymie her own happiness at the sight of her brother pacing about his cabin, speaking to no one, or perhaps to Oliver — the dog by all accounts his only friend.

June assigned some melancholy to that fact. It had once been her, of course. She was the only person he might vouchsafe a secret to. But time had changed them both. The wounds laid upon her by Mr. Harper had long ago scarred up, and no one might ever reopen them as long as she lived. She'd see to that fact, if nothing else. But Coleman's wounds were still bleeding things. His time in Mexico, the memories of what he had endured, would crop up in fits of screaming at night when the terror took over; might render him mute at the dinner table long after the plates were cleared and Isaac had gone outside for a breath of fresh air, leaving her there to ask Coleman what was wrong, urging him to tell her if only so he might return to his former self again. Yet the man of so many words wouldn't say a single one in regard to his travels. He would only tell her that Oliver would be worried over his absence back at his cabin — that he thanked her for dinner but would now take his leave.

At least Coleman had the dog. Even that had not been a sure thing. Nothing was a sure thing when it came to an individual as boisterous, as emotional, as Florence Harper. Seeing her there in Amity struck June with the same disorientation she'd had when, while cleaning a fireplace back home in Baton Rouge, a squawking bird had flown free and managed to sow chaos in the Harpers' parlor for hours on end. Florence was a tempest, more madcap than any young woman had a right to be — one June had thought herself finally rid of, but there Florence was in Amity, on ground that June considered hallowed.

When Coleman had introduced himself to the town, Florence had stepped toward June guardedly, hands at her sides, eyes cast downward. The girl who had once been large enough to block a doorway was now hardly more than skin and bones. Her face was lost to her freckles. Her lips as cracked as her father's had been when June had left that man at the mines.

"Hello, June," Florence said, and there was no mistaking that voice that had commanded her person for so many years before. June would know its tone for the rest of her life.

"Florence Harper," she said.

That was it. The declaration of her name. And in return, as though to answer for a lifetime of wrongs, all Florence had for June were tears. She stood there patiently as they flowed down the girl's face, but June's store of sympathy for that whole family had gone dry some time ago. She could only watch on silently, wondering when those doe eyes would run dry.

"Forgive me," Florence said. "I know I was not easy on you... I was a child..."

On she went. The insult, June thought, was not in the request for forgiveness but mixed into the idea that Florence had the right to cry at all. That she might feel entitled to this very conversation. Florence deserved nothing — nothing — and June would make that quite clear. Not now, though. Not when she had Coleman on the cusp of meeting Isaac, the many Sisters, Old Luther, all the rest of Amity.

"You're tired is all," June said. "How about you go rest right on over there?"

She pointed to Titus's home, thinking Florence could do no harm from there.

"That's my friends' place. I'll ask them to put you up, and I'll come back around to make sure you got what you need in time. Does that sound agreeable?"

And if that wasn't a true display of mercy, have God come down and serve a demonstration.

It was the following night at a party celebrating their new guest when Coleman told her the dog had originally belonged to Florence and her mother. That he loved it dearly, but that he would have to ask if he was ever going to keep it. June pushed her plate forward on the long banquet table they'd set up outside. The center of town was rowdy with cheer, but June had recoiled at the idea of that girl getting one more slight over on her and Coleman. She marched over to Florence, who was eating alone under the arbor enjoined to Titus's house; her mouth was open, a chicken leg in hand.

"The dog," she said. "You're going to give it to him. You understand. I'll get you home, for we don't want you here just as much as you don't want to be here, but that dog ain't going with you. He loves that thing. I see that now. So you tell me I'm heard."

"I understand your anger—"

"Not another word on it. Tell me I am heard."

The girl's face was still colored with the remnants of her tears; with whatever pain she'd brought to this place. She only shrugged and swallowed the food already in her mouth.

"Oliver is Coleman's dog," she said. "And always was. You are heard."

June let her temper ebb just enough to quiet the more violent thoughts stored away in her mind. Really, she almost felt bad for the fiery spirit she'd brought to the conversation without even letting the girl speak.

"Alright then," said June. "More food over there if you want it. You're welcome to join us."

"I am fine right where I am," Florence said.

In like fashion, Florence would keep her distance until Isaac found passage from Nacimiento. Two weeks' time, which were not bad days. The townsfolk treated Coleman like some dignitary sent from a faraway nation. Susanna took him to forage sotol, and both she and June taught him how to bury the plant beneath a pile of rocks, steam it from above, and soon uncover it again to eat, laughing all along as he adjusted to the taste with those first few bites. Isaac and the boys took him hunting, though Coleman had little interest in that pursuit beyond the thrill of riding Starlight. So they let him do just that for as long as he wished, night's shadow falling as they returned, Isaac holding the reins as Coleman sat upon the horse in the throes of happiness of the jaunt that had come to pass.

Each day, though, it was Florence he gave his attention to first. June after this, without a word on what was discussed until he'd told her and

Isaac one night at the firepit that he wished to leave as much as Florence did. It had been discussed between them. That this was June's home, yes — but not his.

Had Isaac not been already craving a new life in Texas, June did not know what she would have done — pulled in opposite directions by her brother and the man she'd one day have as a husband. Fate, to her great relief, bound their interests as one. It was a matter of packing, then, and making arrangements for those who remained here; seeing to it that Old Luther would make no fuss. Titus was no warrior, but he could manage the farming alongside Susanna and the Sisters. He'd help keep the boys in line. Isaac would visit, and they could send word if they needed him. They'd only be across the border. A world away but a day's drive on a fresh pony.

They crossed over to Eagle Pass beyond the Rio on Indian trails Isaac knew well and met no resistance on the drive. (June had worried for her brother, knowing his fear of a lake, a river, but his steadiness surprised her. He needed no reassurance at all.) From Drakesville, Isaac said Laredo might be the best bet for Florence to find a wagon train back to Louisiana.

"I can find my way if you show me the right direction toward town," she muttered. "I don't mean to be any more of an imposition than I have already. I can tell when I am not wanted."

Here she was whining, as expected, June thought. As though she would ever again pity Florence Harper. But Coleman's thoughts did not align with her own. He had hardly spoken the whole drive, yet this moment, apparently, demanded his opinion be made clear.

"We will not be abandoning Florence. I will join her if no one else will."

"Coleman," June protested. "Back home you could hardly get dressed in the morning without my helping you. Now you're saying you'll deliver this girl to Laredo and get back in one piece. After all we've been through."

It was the way he looked at her upon those words when she realized just how much he'd changed. The boy was grown now and would not entertain being cut down like she'd just done. (She hadn't meant to.

The words just came out that way, as an older sister might speak to a little brother sometimes.) But it only drove home what June had come to realize quite well: Coleman had been hardened by what he'd seen with that girl, what they'd endured as one to make it here, and against her every inward plea to resist the sheer fact of the matter, a bond had developed that June might never fully comprehend.

Isaac sensed the strain between them and stepped in before anything might escalate.

"I'll take her come sunrise," he said, indefatigable even after getting them this far. "An easy ride, no more than a day. It really ain't a problem."

"No," June said. "I don't want you driving no white girl alone out here, Isaac. It's too dangerous."

"No more dangerous than what I'm used to," Isaac told her, hat in hand, wiping the sweat from his brow. "And I figure I ain't doing it for you, June. I'm doing it for your brother."

This. This was what finally made her reckon with her own venom — the same venom that made her resent Florence with such endless ardor. It was over, she realized. That past life was just that. And this girl — this sad, broken-down person before her — might have been the same one who had made her clean up those broken plates when a tantrum overtook her; who had made her get down on all fours and lace up her boots; but it was also the same girl who had helped her brother in some fashion that was impenetrable to June but nonetheless real. She could either accept that or risk Coleman's distance from her forever. So she stepped aside. Agreed to Isaac's plan. Offered Florence whichever cabin she wished to have for her night's stay. Swallowed her own pride, her own hatred, for the sake of her kin.

Not that she believed for a second Florence had changed. The girl had been wicked, always wicked, and even on that last day she had reservations. She'd given Oliver a single scratch behind the ears as her goodbye to him. Even this small act pained Florence, for her ribs were apparently still sore, but she managed to maintain a smile, a politeness, as she stood back up. Then she drew close to Coleman, giving him not a hug but a hand upon the shoulder. The words were nearly a whisper, but they were unmistakable, said with affection.

"*Clearheaded* — right, Coleman? No matter what comes your way."

"*Clearheaded*," he said in return. "Always."

The same words June had always given Coleman before the start of a long day's work back in Baton Rouge. She wanted to say something on this, for even hearing the words brought a heat to her chest, anger rising at having this intimacy stolen from her. But June knew better than to interrupt.

With that, Florence loaded into the wagon, giving June a gracious farewell as she and Isaac started down the road. June's reservations persisted, were made only stronger by this departure. No, it wasn't until a crisp winter's morning some months on that she finally stowed her hatred for the girl entirely. That was when a different wagon altogether had come up the trail, appearing as if from nowhere. A young man in a stovepipe hat dismounted in a hurry, and June thought once again about Isaac's shotgun before calming herself with steady breaths, approaching the boy in that early flush of cold as he unloaded a series of transport crates of such shoddy construction that they nearly splintered to bits.

"You sure you're in the right place?" she asked the man. By then Oliver had shot out from Coleman's cabin, lunging at the man, and Coleman himself had appeared to collect his dog.

"I spoke to a man named Moses, who said I could find a *Coleman* here."

"That is me," Coleman said flintily.

"This is yours, then," the man said. "Sent from New Orleans."

The man said no more on the matter. Only returned to his wagon and turned himself right back down the road.

"She's done it," Coleman said. "She has kept her word."

He had not even opened the trunks. June had no idea what he was on about until they retrieved a hammer and pried the nails out of a crate. There before her was a dusty stack of leatherbound books; Coleman's books.

"Fantastic — just fantastic," said Coleman, crouching down to inspect his treasured tomes. "We can stack them for now beside my desk. When

Isaac returns, perhaps he will help me construct a bookshelf. What do you think?"

June was still stunned, but present enough to encourage the thought.

"I think he'd be more than happy to," she said. "I'll help if you need it. You know how busy he gets."

"Very well," Coleman said, still overjoyed as he lingered in the dust of his books. So this was what it took to get him as elated as he used to be! "Thank you, Sis. Oh, it will span the whole wall of the cabin. I can consult them whenever I wish. It's ideal, really."

Some time ago Florence had written Coleman, telling him she'd made it to Louisiana in one piece; that Hugh had kept watch over her mother's home, which remained in decent shape; and that she would refashion it to her own liking in time. She'd found the man who had captained the ship they'd embarked upon from Louisiana, and Florence had made it her life's mission to have him held accountable for his actions. This was spoken of at length, but in a formal style throughout, emotions held at a distance. All in all, from Coleman's reading, Florence's thoughts came off as nothing more than cordial, a missive reminiscent of those Mrs. Harper might send to a distant relative that she (regrettably) had been forced to keep in touch with by the dictates of polite society.

Nothing within it contained a hint of the generosity of this gift.

June realized, then, that perhaps Florence's cruelty was a cover for a more complex posture. It seemed possible that she could be perfectly warmhearted toward those who had earned her goodwill, and that this side of her, for a bevy of reasons, had been hidden from June almost entirely since their youth. (Yes, there were windows of time where she would ache for June's attention, come down to the basement to spend time with her out of loneliness, but these events only engendered more vitriol from Florence the next time she had the chance to dole it out, as though to conceal what joy they'd found together the previous night.)

Really, it mattered little whence this newfound charity of spirit was born. What counted was that Florence had offered it to Coleman, and more importantly, he'd returned the favor. How had it come to be, was the question.

June was left to wonder from a distance as she patiently waited for her brother to broach the subject — to open himself up to her and restore their relationship to the one they'd both cherished so fiercely only a few years before.

There she stood now, looking off at Coleman's cabin, six months on from those books being delivered. If only she knew that this was the day he'd chosen to muster the many words she'd longed for all this time...

"Would you help me with my hair?"

June blenched, nearly dropping the broom in her hand. Coleman was at the door, Oliver panting at his feet.

"You just about gave me a heart attack."

"Did you not see me wave?"

"I didn't see you at all! You are sneaky like that, you know. Always have been."

"You were just lost to your thoughts is all," Coleman said. "Like your brother in that way."

"Maybe you're onto something."

With this she leaned the broom against the kitchen counter and wiped her hands upon her apron. He was smiling, not just in that sociable manner he liked to enact at dinner when he'd been forced into a meal against his will, but with a pride she had not seen in some time. Since he'd arrived to meet her in Amity, come to think of it.

"What's gotten into you?" she said.

"What?" he laughed, pinching her shoulder as she approached the door.

"Don't you act like this is normal."

"What I have in store is far better than *normal*," Coleman said. "I think you'll be right pleased. Just wait."

All she'd been *doing* is waiting. And whether she liked it or not, she was ready to see whatever it was that Coleman had to share. Anything but silence would be a gift bestowed upon her far greater than she'd ever known.

Coleman sat on a footstool with June at his back, washing down his hair with a tin ewer while the cold water fell upon the towel across his shoulders and sent him into a shiver. She'd always known him to set a nice slick of pomade to his hair, always asking for a new mix — linseed oil or even pure lard — but nowadays he preferred it to be in the state nature intended, and so it was a great canopy of fleece that blossomed without any interference; a style he took great pride in. Still, this tradition, at least, they shared once every few days — June working through his hair with a comb, keeping it clean and untangled, checking for any manner of things she'd liked to joke about: *A beehive might be hidden in there. A whole little town of men and women in miniature. Who could really say?* Today, though, she was silent. It was Coleman who spoke first.

"We will go to my cabin after this and then to your parlor, if you don't mind."

Her *parlor* was no more than a small corner where she and Isaac stowed a few chairs and a desk beside the fireplace, but June left the comment unremarked upon.

"Really?" she asked, amused by how he'd planned this to the detail. "So, no writing for you today?"

"Actually, I was hoping I might spend the afternoon with you." Oliver panted at her feet, rolling in the ground beside some buffalo grass and making a mess of himself. "And I couldn't write more if I wished to," he added. "The work is finished."

It was difficult to withhold her shock from that statement. The writing took up his days, his nights, without end no less. She'd grown used to his solitude, the privacy of his practice. For his work to be complete gestured toward a new way he might face the world: becoming, once more, familiar with the opportunities it might hold, the joys it had on offer for a man as curious, as brilliant, as he was. Things he'd appreciated in a former life that she knew he would come to appreciate again, if only when the time was right.

"*Finished?*" she asked, struggling to fathom the idea. "Truly done?"

He stood up then, his hair still wet, grabbing the towel from his shoulder and handing it back to her.

"That's my hope, yes. Now come with me. I must collect my notebooks before we begin."

The heat of the sun swirled about them. It felt as though the parched land about the property was on the verge of being set to fire any instant. Coleman had asked to plant some trees to keep the sun at bay, and she was happy to oblige, Isaac as well, but it would take time amongst the other duties that kept them busy each day. Nonetheless, Coleman would often tell them the plans he had in store. A small plot for a garden, with some cacti of his choosing, perhaps some sage, and farther off some root vegetables, so he might contribute more to their evening meals. (Already he'd designed an irrigation system so the plants might be lush, as beautiful as the ones he tended in New Orleans.) And lining the cabins, he'd had his most specific request: mesquite trees, so come spring they might blossom with the full throes of their yellow bloom for all to see.

Little did he know those trees held such a dear place in her heart. Perhaps it was a sign. Perhaps it meant nothing at all. But they would get them planted one day, and when they were tall, and flourishing, she would tell him the story of how she had passed by them during the most trying days of her life, leaving the mines for Amity — for her freedom. All in time, she thought.

"This should take only a moment," Coleman said, ordering his notebooks in a row, shuffling them together in a noisy racket.

Even his cabin was private ground, a cell of Coleman's own making. He'd asked only for a desk, a place to sleep, some notebooks, and some fountain pens, all of which Moses had happily provided upon their arrival. With so little he had made the place his refuge.

The books rose up all about the place, organized by some means only Coleman might comprehend. A blanket-strewn corner beside his bed where Oliver slept was kept clean, but other than that the books took root everywhere. On his desk was a compass, a souvenir from his travels that had, according to what little he'd shared, been gifted to him by a friend, a man of integrity that he held dear to his heart and wished to see again in due time. Beside the compass was a red barrette that had, he'd told her, belonged to a girl of intelligence and charm beyond her age who had helped him during a difficult moment in a way he'd never truly thanked her for. Perhaps, Coleman often said, he'd see her again one day as well.

What to believe? June thought, eyeing it all one more time. By then Coleman was poised and waiting, a look of serenity on his face, more than one notebook held to his chest with both arms like a student prepared with his work.

"Ready?" he asked his sister.

"Of course," she said. "Why don't I follow you? You do seem to have the day laid out."

In the back of her mind, her various duties called. She'd told Isaac she would scrub the washbasin today, for it had built up a coat of dirt. The exterior of the cabin could also use a good cleaning. But for now, all of that could wait.

Coleman was signally unhurried, caught up again with Oliver, throwing the dog a stick that sent him flying about the property, nearly to the road. A moment passed, both of them squinting under the gaze of the sun, staring off at that shaggy ball of energy — a brown, dirty mess of a runt that loved Coleman without reservation. The dog operated on its own authority, always would, for where Coleman was disciplined and thorough, he found his balance in a pet that was his opposite in every way. In doing so, the two were bound in a strange harmony that June had grown to appreciate.

Right about now was when Coleman usually ran after Oliver. An eternal game of chase would result and June would stand there, patience worn thin as Coleman attempted to corral Oliver, lambasting the crazy beast for misbehaving so. It was, if anything, the single form of affection that pledged their relationship.

On this occasion, though, Coleman did nothing of the sort. He simply appraised the vista, staring off for some time, that grin ever-present on his face, his hair still glistening beneath the sharp gaze of the sun as it dried.

"Well," June said. "Should we go fetch him?"

"No," Coleman said. He nodded, landing on a thought that seemed to fill him with some sense of happiness, for his face now harbored a smile the likes of which she hadn't seen him show in some time. "Why don't we let him roam free? For as long as he wishes to. I like to see him so happy. Doing just as he pleases."

"I think that's a fine idea," June said, more than fine with it if he was.

In times like this before, swept up by the scenery — the numinous, desolate place they now called home — she'd speak of her own journey through Mexico, thinking that to share such details might coax him to do the same. Not now. Maybe, in this new stage of their lives together, this was all they might share: moments of no greater significance than the pleasure of the other's presence, even in silence. Both of them free in spirit, the world laid out before them. *I could live with that,* June thought. It struck her then that a place with such possibility could never be a prison. Never, truthfully, had she felt more free than in moments like this. When the world slowed. When her brother put his head upon her shoulder and provided her calm, and no one from here to the ocean might disrupt their peace.

This, here, was what she'd always wanted.

After a while, without a word, Coleman withdrew and went toward her and Isaac's home.

"Oh, you're off, ha?" she said, turning to follow. He went right up the front stairs, and without her permission, grabbed the table before the fireplace and dragged it toward the center of the cabin.

"I don't think I asked for any rearranging of my furniture," she said jokingly.

"It's only for my reading. Please," he gestured at the chair before the fireplace. "Take a seat."

"You're *reading?*"

It occurred to her then, finally, what this was — that after all this time he was going to share what had been put into those notebooks. She thought to tease him a little — explain that she wasn't no easy audience, that it best be good — but she didn't wish to end whatever spell had allowed the day to end up here. So she kept her mouth shut; took her seat as instructed.

He then placed his notebooks upon the table, sifting through them, picking one up in particular. For a time he simply stood there, as though the table were his small lectern and he was readied to make a speech.

"I realized — " his voice was a croak, and he cleared it to continue. "I realize I have spent much of my time at a remove. That I have not been the brother to you that I once was. The brother you deserve, June."

"Don't say that — "

"Please," he said, a hand in the air to halt her. "Now that I have started, allow me to finish."

Coleman collected himself. Started again.

"My journey to you was an arduous one. The likes of which I endured perhaps bravely, but without realizing how the fear of those trials might overwhelm me once they had ended. I saw things I never wished to see. Things that haunt me still…"

Now she wished to rise and hug him, for she knew exactly what he meant, had experienced her own nightmares — her own demons from the past.

"You asked me to share my story, June, but I could not find the words. How it pained me to have them consume my soul, my spirit, and rattle about my mind every day and every night. It is like nothing I might describe. And I retreated only further into myself. I spared no part of me for you, for Isaac, for anyone. It was selfish, and childish, and I make no excuses for anyone, but what it took to find you broke me in ways I could not foresee."

His voice caught. He pursed his lips and began to shift about. The words seemed so difficult to gather that they appeared to be causing him physical pain. She wanted nothing more than to comfort him, but it was more important to let him finish. To let him have his moment to say it all, every word, without interruption.

"So I wrote it down," he said, tapping the notebook in his hand. "I started from the beginning and I depicted everything that took place until I met you. I believe, if just once, I can read to you what happened, you might realize how I have become the man I have. And maybe, if I do so, and it is all expelled, I might let go of those memories. I might start afresh. Perhaps I might be the brother you deserve."

Now June was crying, but she would say nothing, make no utterance. She would let Coleman finish at all costs.

"I know you have tried to tell me parts of what you endured as well. All of it, I imagine not. Which I understand entirely. You can't write your story, I know this. But maybe, just maybe, as I tell you mine, you can ponder your own. I'd like us both to be free from the past. Maybe not today. But in time. How does that sound to you, June?"

She only nodded yes. The courage to share such a thing as his story, put down to paper, seemed to her to match that of a whole army of soldiers set out to battle. How lucky was she to call him her brother! And how blessed, she felt, that it was she who got to hear his tale.

Finally, with a moment's reprieve to gather her wits, she found the composure to talk.

"I'll listen to every word," she said. "This is all I've wanted since we got here. Please, Coleman. Share your story with me. And I promise to think of my own all along, and when the time is right, I will share it with you in any way I can. I can't write a fancy book, no, but I have it all stored away. Just like you. Waiting to be heard."

"Lovely," was all he said, in classic Coleman form. "Just lovely."

The shade found in the cabin cast a darkness over the proceeding and brought a calming influence upon the room. June settled into it. She thought, as he flipped the pages, of what the day would have in store. Sitting here, relishing his every sentence, discovering her brother's past, the blank pages of his life that had been withheld from her.

June considered once again — for the shortest moment, only by habit — what might be lost to the afternoon: the silly chores of the day she'd set out to accomplish, what sort of dinner she might put on the table without a chance to cook a meal. All of it paled against this. June had earned nothing if not the right to shirk an obligation, take a day's rest, sink into her chair and let her imagination accompany her brother's as they fell into the past. Let the washbasin rust brown all over. The cabin's walls could splinter to bits for all she cared, so long as the foundation remained strong enough for this one event to take place — until Coleman had read that final notebook to her.

So many sacrifices had been made in her short life. It was, truly, her pleasure to leave the world behind, and make a new one for the sake of her brother's words.

Coleman flipped the first page and cleared his throat once more. His tone was grave, commanding. She gripped the arms of her chair; could feel her spirit rise up within her.

Then he began:

"I had few pleasures to call my own. There was the peace found in the attic where I was made to board, the transporting comfort of the books in Mrs. Harper's library, the deliciousness of the sweet bread I purchased with my allowance from the bakery down the road each Sunday of rest..."

ACKNOWLEDGMENTS

I owe a debt of gratitude to several authors whose work was instrumental in the writing of this novel. In particular, I drew valuable insights from:

The Black Seminoles, by Kenneth W. Porter;

The Southern Exodus to Mexico: Migration across the Borderlands after the American Civil War (Borderlands and Transcultural Studies), by Todd W. Wahlstrom;

Dreaming with the Ancestors: Black Seminole Women in Texas and Mexico, by Shirley Boteler Mock;

The Texas Tonkawas, by Stanley S. McGowen; and

Life of George Bent: Written from His Letters, by George E. Hyde and Savoie Lottinville.

If my novel has, in any way, stimulated readers' interest in learning about this time in history, I encourage you to give these books a read as well.

I want to thank my entire team at Little, Brown, as well as Emily Forland and Ben George.

I also want to thank Dani and Ernesto, whose guidance during my research at the border provided me with an invaluable boots-on-the-ground education in so many areas relevant to my work.

Alejandra Cordoba, thank you for all your help with my Spanish.

And to my friends, family, and all my readers—thank you, too.

ABOUT THE AUTHOR

NATHAN HARRIS is the author of the New York Times bestseller *The Sweetness of Water*, which was an Oprah's Book Club pick, the winner of the Ernest J. Gaines Award for Literary Excellence, and longlisted for the Booker Prize, the Carnegie Medal for Excellence in Fiction, and the Center for Fiction First Novel Prize. He holds an MFA from the Michener Center at the University of Texas and lives in Chicago.

RAISING READERS
Books Build Bright Futures

Thank you for reading this book and for being a reader of books in general. As a author, I am so grateful to share being part of a community of readers with you and I hope you will join me in passing our love of books on to the next generation of readers.

Did you know that reading for enjoyment is the single biggest predictor of a child's future happiness and success?

More than family circumstances, parents' educational background, or income, reading impacts a child's future academic performance, emotional well-being, communication skills, economic security, ambition, and happiness.

Studies show that kids reading for enjoyment in the US is in rapid decline:

- In 2012, 53% of 9-year-olds read almost every day. Just 10 years later, in 2022, the number had fallen to 39%.
- In 2012, 27% of 13-year-olds read for fun daily. By 2023, that number was just 14%.

Together, we can commit to **Raising Readers** and change this trend. How?

- Read to children in your life daily.
- Model reading as a fun activity.
- Reduce screen time.
- Start a family, school, or community book club.
- Visit bookstores and libraries regularly.
- Listen to audiobooks.
- Read the book before you see the movie.
- Encourage your child to read aloud to a pet or stuffed animal.
- Give books as gifts.
- Donate books to families and communities in need.

Books build bright futures, and **Raising Readers** is our shared responsibility.

For more information, visit **JoinRaisingReaders.com**

Sources: National Endowment for the Arts, National Assessment of Educational Progress, WorldBookDay.org, Nielsen BookData's 2023 "Understanding the Children's Book Consumer"